AMERICA IS NOT THE HEART

AMERICA IS NOT THE HEART

Elaine Castillo

VIKING

VIKING
An imprint of Penguin Random House LLC
375 Hudson Street
New York, New York 10014
penguin.com

A portion of this novel appeared as "America Is Not the Heart"
in *Freeman's: The Future of New Writing.*

ISBN: 9780735222410 (hardcover)
ISBN: 9780735222434 (ebook)

Printed in the United States of America
1   3   5   7   9   10   8   6   4   2

Set in Bembo Book MT Std
Designed by Cassandra Garruzzo

I knew I could trust a gambler because I had been one of them.

Carlos Bulosan, *America Is in the Heart*

AMERICA IS NOT THE HEART

Prologue, or Gali-La!

SO YOU'RE A GIRL AND YOU'RE POOR, BUT AT LEAST you're light-skinned—that'll save you. You're the second eldest child and the second eldest daughter of a family of six children, and your parents are subsistence farmers—your mom sells vegetables at the local market and when that doesn't make enough to put food on the table, you sell fruit and beans by the side of the road. That is, until your father manages to get a job working as a clerk for the American military in Guam, where he acquires a mistress and regularly sends money back to the family, the latter gesture absolving the first. He returns every three years for a visit, which is why you and nearly all of your siblings are three, six, or nine years apart in age. On those rare visits, you treat him with rudeness out of loyalty to your mother, who neither thanks nor acknowledges your efforts or, for that matter, your existence: eczema-ridden you at eight, hungry adolescent you at twelve, all your early ragged versions. When you're old enough to know better but not old enough to actually stop talking back to him, your father will remind you, usually by throwing a chair at your head, that the only reason you're able to attend nursing school is because of his army dollars. It's your first introduction to debt, to utang na loob, the long, drawn-out torch song of filial loyalty. But when it comes to genres, you prefer a heist: take the money and run.

Growing up, everyone says you're stupid, you're clumsy, you get into at least one fight a week, and even your light skin, while universally covetable, is suspicious; your father often accuses your mother of having taken up with a Chinese merchant or Japanese soldier or tisoy businessman while he was away. Did that happen? You don't know. Is that unknown man your father? You don't know. If it happened, was it your mother's choice; was it an affair, or was it a case of—a word you won't say, can't think, a word that drifts like smog, through your life and the lives of all the women around you. You don't know. Looking at your own face doesn't tell you. There isn't anyone you can ask.

When you're hungry, sometimes you go out into the fields and stick your stumpy arm down the pockmarks in the earth where tiny dakomo crabs like to scurry away and hide, your fingers grasping for the serrated edge of the shell. Some days you collect enough to carry home for your mother to steam, using the lower half of your shirt as a basket, but sometimes you can't wait, yanking one out by the leg and dashing it on the ground to stun it, then eating the whole thing right there, live and raw, spitting out bits of calcium. Sometimes instead of a crab you pull out a wiggling frog, but most of the time you throw those away, watch them hop to safety. People warn you that those holes are also the favored hiding places of some semipoisonous snakes, but when you weigh the danger against the hunger, the hunger always wins. On the days when there are no crabs, no frogs, not even a weak snake, you go around picking dika grass, the kind that the farmers usually feed their horses. You sell makeshift bundles of them by the side of the road, alongside the mangoes and chico. On good days, the dika grass sells so well you produce a little side economy that gives you enough money to buy some ChocNut and maybe the latest issue of *Hiwaga* so you can catch up on your komiks, even though at the end of every one you have to read the most hateful words you'll ever encounter, in any language: abangan ang susunod na kabanata. Look out for the next chapter.

Around this time your mother's great love affair is with Atse Carmen, your eldest sister, who's room-silencingly beautiful in the way older sisters often are, and who gets away with everything. Atse Carmen somehow gets a gold tooth fitted in her mouth despite the fact that everyone in the family eats one meal a day, if that. So when you're eleven or ten years old, you get your brightest of bright ideas: you're going to get a gold tooth fitted, just like Atse Carmen. Not only that, but you're going to pay for it yourself. You take to pocketing even more of the money you make at the roadside—work that Atse Carmen was never asked to do, just you. But you've got three new siblings, a scrappy Rufina, Gloria the toddler, Boyet the infant, so the scant attention that might have been rationed out for you in the past gets allocated elsewhere. This time, though, it's a blessing—you can carry out your plan in peace. Well, if not peace, then: alone. It's the same thing.

You begin to save up. You go to the only dentist you know in town; not the same dentist who gave Carmen her gold tooth, but another one who apparently doesn't balk at accepting dirty and wrinkled pesos from an adolescent promdi girl. The dentist doesn't ask where your parents are; he doesn't ask if you have their permission. He doesn't ask any questions at all. He takes your money, and puts you under anesthesia, and you wake up with a gold tooth.

The pain is like nothing you've ever felt before, not like a chair leg glancing your temple, not like the non-look of someone staying in the backseat of a cool car while their driver is sent out to buy chico from your stand. Your mother isn't even angry that you used the money for the procedure; there's something bordering on pride in the look on her face when she sees you and Atse Carmen; smiling, glinting. So now you know what triumph feels like; the feeling lasts for a while. Lasts until all of your teeth, with the exception of your ungilded back molars, rot and fall out as a result of what turns out to be a poorly and cheaply executed fitting. By the time you're fourteen, you wear dentures. You'll wear dentures for the rest of your life. These early ones, which your father's American salary pays for, give you blinding headaches. You hate having to brush your teeth in your hand every night; you avoid looking at yourself in the mirror in those moments, but sometimes you slip up and catch sight of your mouth, wound-pink and hollow, a grandmother's maw in your child's face. Atse Carmen's gold tooth never falls out.

When you're sixteen, you get into Saint Louis University, a Catholic college nestled five thousand feet high in the mountainous forests of Baguio City. You'd wanted to take your aching gums to Manila, but your mother absolutely forbade it; the cost, the distance, the demonstrations. You're the second and last girl in the family to go to college. At the time your father's still in Guam; he hasn't become an American citizen yet, but it's in the process. When his citizenship comes through, your younger siblings will be able to come to America as green card holders, but you'll be over twenty-one by the time you finish nursing school, too old to be petitioned. You're going to have to become an American by yourself.

In Baguio, you brave the treacherous drive up Kennon Road, the winding road known for its landslides during the rainy season and its speeding accidents year-round. It's the only road that can take you all the way up to the city, the scent of pine trees growing stronger the higher up you get, passing the abandoned mining towns and the Ifugao souvenir huts by the side of the road selling wood carvings, like the little one of a naked man wearing only a barrel, whose titi pops out when you lower the barrel. You've seen that figurine even back home; it's a common enough little comic trinket found in any household. It's only in Baguio that you hear that the figure appeared after the Americans had built their military settlement in Baguio, the only American hill station in Asia, displacing the Ibaloi living there. You never look at that little wooden titi the same way again.

But you also don't turn your dormmates down when they all want to go to the restaurants at Camp John Hay, formerly John Hay Air Base, perched there at the topmost part of a hill in the Cordilleras, overlooking all of Baguio. You can only enter the recreation camp if you're a guest of a U.S. citizen, but one of your new girlfriends happens to be dating an American soldier and she's generous enough to invite all of you to the camp, so in the end it's like you're all dating the soldier: you get to see the golf courses, the country clubs, the rich Filipinos getting married, plucking pine needles out of taffeta. At Camp John Hay, the cost of everything is listed in dollars, not pesos—when you get back to your dorm room and start to calculate the price of a hot dog, you throw the paper away before you've even finished the math.

At SLU, most of the girls in your dorm speak Tagalog, Ilocano, or Kapampangan. One day one of the girls, Fely, says to the group: You know how they say rich people have red heels?

You have, in fact, always heard this growing up: that poor people have dusty, gray heels, and rich people have smooth, moisturized heels, red with health. You have a tendency to hide your feet, even though you've always rubbed cream into them religiously so they won't look like your mother's heels, desert-cracked. Well, I have a trick, Fely says, showing all of you her smooth, impossibly red heels. You just put merthiolate on it! Not iodine, that makes it orange. Merthiolate is the secret! After that, all of you take to staining your heels with the liquid antiseptic. From then on, you love wearing slingbacks, mules, cropped trousers. Years later, even as an adult nurse in California, sometimes you'll still put merthiolate on your heels.

There are nine of you in total, and all of you are the first inhabitants of that newly built dorm, Cardinal Cardijn Hall. You'll never really know who Cardinal Cardijn is; those are just words to you. Another new building on campus that year is the Diego Silang building, named after Diego Silang y Andaya. Now his story, you know a bit better; you remember the school lessons, punctuated with blows across the knuckles to help the kids remember. Diego Silang, the eighteenth-century revolutionary who, with the help of British forces who wanted their own piece of the Philippines, staged a revolt against Spanish colonial rule. Everyone says Diego Silang's an Ilocano, that as a revolutionary he wanted to form an Ilocano nation. Even your future Ilocano husband will remember Diego Silang as an Ilocano, will remember that the revolutionary as a young boy lived and worked in Vigan, his own hometown. But you know a different story: you know that Diego Silang was born in Pangasinan, just like you. His mother was Ilocana, but his father was Pangasinense. You feel somewhat petty for thinking that it matters, but—it matters. It matters to you.

Diego gets betrayed, of course; by the British powers that promised reinforcement, and then by a friend of his, paid by the church to kill him. Leadership of the revolt falls to Diego's wife and fellow insurgent, María Josefa Gabriela, an Ilocana with a Spanish dad and uncertain maternage—a native maid in a colonial household, maybe Igorota or Tinguian. Either way, your lessons told you that Gabriela was a beautiful bolo-wielding mestiza. The mestiza part means they'll definitely make a movie out of her life one day: people remember the mestizas. That you're light-skinned enough to pass for mestiza doesn't slip your mind; frankly, you're hanging on to it as a crucial talisman for your survival. You want to be remembered, too. Like a blow across the knuckles.

Gabriela's siege doesn't work out; Spanish forces overpower her troops, and they retreat into hiding. Eventually, the Spanish capture them and hang them all in the Plaza Salcedo, not far from the home where your future husband's family will have lived for hundreds of years before the word *Filipino* ever even existed. Abangan ang susunod na kabanata.

In Baguio, you learn how to lie to your mother. Every year when it comes to reporting your textbook expenses, you subtly up the price so that you can skim off the extra, add that to the money you save by choosing to walk instead of using the jeepneys, and use the money to go with your new girlfriends to the PX stores, buy up all the American peanuts that taste different from the fresh mani you're used to eating, worse, addictive, and check out all the exotic beauty products they have in store: soaps, powders, pomades. Most of the other girls are happy with Avon perfumes and everyone you know smells of Charisma, Elusive, Occur, or Moonwind. You, on the other hand, save up money to buy Madame Rochas, the most expensive perfume in the shop, which you've never even smelled—the lady behind the counter at the PX shop only displays the bottles behind a huge mirrored glass case, doesn't let anyone try anything on until they hand over the cash.

Occasionally, a moment of guilt interrupts your bliss; you know how stretched money is back home, and you have younger siblings who'll have to go to school eventually, too. But all the girls do it, you tell yourself, a little kupit here and there when you're living away from home, it's nothing, you could stop if you wanted to, and it wouldn't make any difference at all.

You were hoping to stay in Baguio, up there in the cool green hills, safe and perfumed, away from Pangasinan and everyone who knew you. But something goes wrong; it turns out that Atse Carmen has applied to do her nursing internship at Baguio General Hospital, too. The only thing is, because it's a government hospital, only one member of a family household at a time is allowed to apply for an internship. Everyone expected her to apply in Dagupan, closer to where she's attending nursing school; you're not quite sure why she chooses Baguio. Some part of you thinks, with a rage bordering on glee, that it's because she's somehow found a way to be jealous of you, listening to every person back home talk about what a nice city Baguio is, and how lucky little Pacita is to be going to university there, and maybe she'll get married and settle up there and the family will be able to go visit her for summer vacations.

When during one of your monthly calls back home, Atse Carmen answers the phone and preens over her acceptance, you know what it means. You're either going to have to wait a year and work somewhere else until you can apply when Atse Carmen's internship is over—or you're going to have to leave Baguio. You're starting to learn that the things you get, you don't get to keep.

Your mother at least has the sensitivity to realize that your sister's acceptance into Baguio General is pushing you out of a city you've made your own. She asks you if you want to come back to Pangasinan. She says that she knows somebody who knows somebody at the College of Nursing at the University of Pangasinan, right in Dagupan City. And maybe things will be less expensive in Dagupan than they seem to be in Baguio, she says. A stone between your ribs, you say yes. You'll come back.

When you come home, you find out the reason Carmen went to Baguio General Hospital and took your place: she went to Baguio pregnant, leaving another infant with your mother, born while you were away. You hadn't even known about the first one; no one told you she'd had a kid, and no one tells you anything about the father, or fathers. You meet the baby on your first visit back to Mangaldan since leaving Baguio, a little baby boy with his black hair in a topknot, left long in the traditional custom of not cutting a child's hair until the first birthday.

You only meet the two boys again when they're young men, after Carmen comes to live with you in California, her tourist visa having expired. Her two sons, Jejomar and Freddie, have American citizenship—they've been registered not as Carmen's children, but your mother and father's. Legally, they're your brothers. They call you Atse Paz, and not Auntie.

It'll be easy enough for Carmen to get a nursing job in California; the shortage of nurses in the state is so severe that many hospitals don't check for papers. But neither of her sons even have high school degrees, so you try to get them jobs here or there, some janitor work at one of the hospitals you work at, or sometimes you pay them to clean your house, or babysit your future daughter. You'll wonder if they themselves even know that Carmen is their mother. They look so much like her it makes your molars ache.

Once you're in Dagupan, you don't study as hard or push yourself as much as you did in Baguio. You still want to leave the country, but you're getting tired of holding up the weight of your own desires. You just want to get through the year. You get straight Cs in most everything from Anatomy and Physiology to English Speech Improvement. Your highest grade is a B, in Physical Education. Your second highest grade is a B minus, in Land Reform and Taxation.

The only person you know at the University of Pangasinan is your cousin Tato. He's two years older than you and studying either politics or law, you're not sure. He's not as light-skinned as you, but you share the inchik eyes, which is what you think about when your father comes home from Guam, gets drunk, and says, That's not my blood, pointing vaguely in your direction. You had a crush on Tato when you were kids; you used to visit their family house in the town center sometimes on your way back home from selling food or cookware with your mother at the Mangaldan Public Market. You haven't seen him since before you left for Baguio, though, so when you meet him for the first time on campus, you're surprised by how mature he looks, a man with tough meat on his bones. You know distantly about what happened at Malacañang Palace last year, the student rally, the riots, but you never talk about it with any of your friends. Once you meet Tato, you know he's involved.

He asks you, without really asking you, if you want to come to a demonstration. The look on his face says he knows you won't come. You remember that Tato went to Mangaldan National High School; every morning he walked through the massive Greek pillars of the school on the way to his classes. Back when you were kids, you and your mother were the ones to visit his house—he never came to see you or your family home in Bari. You don't really know how to put it into words, the way he looks at you, somehow kind and condescending all at once. Maybe it's just because he's older. A boy. Tato doesn't even wait for you to give the excuse that he knows is coming. He touches your shoulder and tells you it was good to see you, but he has somewhere to be.

It'll take you a long time to talk about martial law, and you'll never talk about it with anyone who lived through it with you. But for now, you don't go to the rallies, you don't join the student protests; you go silent or change the subject when someone at your table in the canteen brings it up. The fear in you predates dictatorships. No one would ever mistake you for an intellectual or an aktibista; most of the time, you don't even really understand what people are saying when they talk about the news. Reading Tagalog has always been difficult for you, even though you've gotten more or less fluent with everyday speech. But things like old kundiman from the thirties and forties where half the words for love are words you've never heard in your life; things like the complicated dialogue in some new movie where all the characters are manilenyos except for the yaya; things like newspapers—they still send you into dizzy spells. So you stay away.

But there's no staying away from this. Martial law means curfew at nine o'clock, it means streets empty except for military jeeps, it means classes where there were once fifty pupils are now classes where there are forty-eight, maybe forty-six. You and your other nursing student friends at the University of Pangasinan stay together through it all, eating all your meals together in the canteen even though some other girls have taken to eating alone in their dorm rooms, sometimes playing music if they have a record player, Bread's Make It with You crooning all the way down the dorm corridor. In the canteen, there are some girls who just start weeping into their plates, right there in front of everyone; maybe because one of their relatives has been taken, maybe just from the fear alone, stretching all of you wire-taut. No one knows if you'll even graduate, if there will even be a university left when this is all over, if it'll ever be over. Then, a year into martial law, you hear about Tato.

It's your mother who tells you that one evening, when he'd come back to Mangaldan to visit his parents for the weekend, Tato disappeared. Auntie Bobette had been outside with a basket of kangkong, plucking the leaves off the long stems, planning to make monggo for dinner once Tato was back from drinking with his barkada. By the time the food had long gone cold, by the time they were eating its leftovers for breakfast and then lunch, Tato still hadn't come back. A week later, Uncle David disappeared, too. That was how Auntie Bobette knew Tato hadn't just gone underground with the aktibista friends he'd made at school—that lesser maternal grief of the period. If her husband was gone, too, something else must have happened.

Your mother tells you that a few months later, men from the military came to Auntie Bobette's house in Mangaldan, parking their jeeps in the dika grass, startling the goats into bleating. They knocked on the door, and when she opened it, they said they were there to inform her that they were willing to pay her for the death of her husband, as befitting the surviving family of a deceased Philippine Army officer.

Auntie Bobette didn't ask what they meant, didn't ask why they were offering to compensate a death no one had even confirmed yet. She only said, And what about my son, Tato.

They didn't acknowledge her words, or even flinch at Tato's name, only repeating that they were willing to pay for the death of her husband. They spoke as if reciting a speech they had memorized. Bobette said, in Pangasinan, replying to an answer they hadn't given: So they're both dead.

She directed her words at the soldier who had been doing most of the talking, a Pangasinense commanding officer not that much older than Bobette. He'd probably known her husband well, drunk Diplomatico rum with him at the carinderia down the street, lit each other's ciga-

rettes, judged the beauty of each other's mistresses. Once again the officer said to Auntie Bobette, not in Pangasinan but in a mixture of Tagalog
and English: We are ready to compensate you, as a military widow, for
the death of your husband.

And Auntie Bobette replied, with the blazing calm of a seraph: I don't
want money. If you're saying they're dead, then you give me their bodies.

When your mother told you this story, you were terrified of the next
part—of what might have happened to Auntie Bobette, at the mercy of
four or five soldiers. You thought maybe your mother, who had never
been in the habit of calling you regularly at school and had never even
visited your dorms, was about to tell you about one more vanishing. But
instead your mother told you that the frustrated officers just turned
around, got back in their jeeps, and left. Nothing else. For years, Auntie
Bobette waited for one more knock on the door, for it to be her husband's or her son's face she finally opened to; gaunt and gulping at life, or
bloated and ragged in death, left at her front door as a final courtesy. But
it never came; it never was.

A month or so after you hear about Tato from your mother, you meet
Auntie Bobette on campus. She's just finished finally collecting Tato's
things from his former dormmates, who'd kept his belongings safe even
when the school had already given away his room to new students.

You ask how she is, sounding inane even to yourself, but you can't
find the words to speak about Tato or Uncle David. Auntie Bobette
seems to understand that, because she only shifts the weight of the bulging duffel bag she's carrying, full of some of the last things on earth that
have touched her son. She refuses when you offer to carry the bag, refuses when you offer to accompany her to the bus depot. She just touches
your arm and says, Asicasom so laman mo.

All of your classes at school are taught in English, and even though
most of your friends at UP are Pangasinense like you, most of the time
you all end up speaking to each other in some mixture of Tagalog and
English, imitating the poppy Taglish of teleseryes and radio programs.
So that means you can't remember the last time someone told you to take
care of yourself in your own language. This is probably it; the last time.

Shortly after Tato disappears, you'll meet the man who's going to become your future husband and the father of your first and only daughter,
the man whose ancestral family home stands at the center of Vigan, up
north in Ilocos Sur, one of the old colonial homes that used to belong to
Spanish officials or Chinese merchants. His family descends mostly from
the latter, but his face is all Ilocano indio, pitch-black eyes, strong flat
nose. He's an orthopedic surgeon, and he teaches and practices at Nazareth Hospital, the first place you work as a student nurse. People say that
he's only recently come back to the Philippines from having lived in
Jakarta for ten years.

It's hate at first sight. He's one of these mayaman jet-setters who've
been all over the world and speak the English of commercials and foreign movies, the English of Asian kings played by white actors. People
say that he's recently divorced, that he found his first wife, a cousin of
Marcos, in bed with another man. You see him sometimes on his rounds,
and he has a different nurse hanging on his arm every afternoon, a different girl in the passenger seat of his dark orange Fiat every evening.
He's a notorious babaero, the Don Juan of the hospital, and most of the
nurses flutter when he so much as enters the room. Yet his reputation
never veers toward the sordid. This, you discover, is less because of his
wealth or the weight of his name, and more because of the fact that every
woman who sleeps with him agrees that he's a champion at eating women
out. This is what differentiates Doctor De Vera from your run-of-the-
mill babaero, they say. The man loves to make women come. He doesn't
just rabbit-rabbit-rabbit and then tapos na, they giggle to each other,
while you jab a straw into a Coke bottle.

One day you're assigned to do your rounds with him as a supervisor.
He looks you up and down and instantly you know—your skin all
prickly, the tiniest hairs on your body alight—that if you let this happen, you'll be next.

You're not going to let it happen. You're going to get the rounds over
with and get back to the nursing station and do your paperwork without

using an English dictionary for once. In the middle of the rounds, you realize that in your haste to finish, you've advanced several steps ahead of him. You turn around. He's paused in the middle of the corridor, looking at you, amused.

You walk very fast, he says in English.

You flush. Standing there smiling, you think he looks like a darker-skinned Rogelio de la Rosa, pomaded hair and all, and before you keep on thinking up stupid things like that, you turn away from him. But it's too late. He's seen your face; he knows he's made you blush. Now you definitely have to avoid him.

But he doesn't chase you, the way you think he will, the way you expect men like him to. He's just—present. He's around with all the answers when you need advice about a patient's sepsis, he's opening the entrance door to the hospital for you in the morning when you're yawning and too unguarded to remember not to thank him, he's in the break room debating favorite desserts with other nurses when you've slipped in looking for a place to take a nap. What's your favorite, he's asking Evelyn, a young nurse. She replies, Brazo de Mercedes.

Brazo de Evelyn, he quips, and she titters, along with two other nurses nearby, hanging around the edges of the flirtation in the hopes of getting in on it themselves.

You roll your eyes and turn around to leave. Pacita, he calls. What's your favorite dessert?

You think about ignoring him, the way you should have ignored him when he opened the door for you that morning, the way you should have ignored him when he made the comment about how fast you walked. You didn't even realize at the time that he must have liked it because he'd gotten the chance to stare at your wiggling ass. Only later did you think about it, in bed, hot all over with fury and something that wasn't fury.

You should ignore him, but instead, you turn around and declare, in a voice so hard it sounds like you're delivering an insult: Tupig.

One of the other nurses, Floribeth, starts laughing. Kakanin, native cakes pala! she says. You can buy that on the side of the road anywhere.

Yes, you retort. Isn't that great?

You turn around to leave, proud that you haven't blushed at all, proud that you'll be getting the last word, proud to leave Don Juan and his admirers in your wake. But just before you turn your back, you see that Doctor De Vera has gone still, stricken.

Years later, when you're married, he'll tell you that tupig was the favorite dessert of both his older brother Melchior and his late mother. When they don't sell it at the small Filipino grocery store in the California town you'll live in together, you'll try to learn how to make it without ever telling him—and then, when all your attempts turn out disastrously, you'll give up, without ever telling him.

No matter how much you try to avoid Doctor De Vera—in your head, you address him only as the babaero, it helps to distance yourself—he's everywhere. And maybe it's just your imagination, but it feels like he's looking back at you, too. Even when he's meeting another date in front of the hospital—a young woman whom everyone whispers is the daughter of some CEO, of some company you've never heard of—it's you that he's looking back at, as he slips into the driver's seat. It annoys you, because you see through it; it annoys you, because you're meant to see through it. He's not hiding the fact that he's looking at you, and he's not hiding the fact that he sees you looking back.

The fact that he's a babaero isn't the problem. It's not just the celebrity, or that his first wife was Marcos's cousin or that he's a De Vera, of the De Veras of Vigan, or that he's a champion at, at, at cunnilingus. The problem starts with the fact that he's good at what he does; he's the best orthopedic surgeon on the island of Luzon. You've assisted him in the operating room more than once, and while he never loses the louche grace in his limbs—he and his anesthesiologist are known for singing kundiman during their procedures, so that you've become used to the sound of someone belting out Dahil Sa Iyo beneath the deafening keen of a saw juddering through a femur—there's always an expression on his face, a posture in his body, which you only ever see there, in theater. Each gesture has a calm, deliberate economy, so that even the air pressure around him seems to change, like someone descending into a mineshaft.

No, it's not calm; it's self-possession. Even in a cavern, he owns himself. So that's what it looks like.

The part that really gets to you, the part that gets to your quietest of parts, is the part about polio: you learn that his specialty is children with polio, that this was what he was doing in Indonesia, opening rehabilitation clinics in rural areas. It became less common as you were growing up, but you still remember some kids with polio around Mangaldan and Mapandan, amongst the families living even farther out into the rice fields, past the bangus farms.

Still, still, still—you're not going to let yourself be seduced by him, by the myths that cling to his shoulders: cosmopolitan Don Juan, pussy-eater extraordinaire, savior of children—it's all so ridiculous.

It *is* ridiculous, but not for reasons you know yet. You don't know yet about his brother, about his mother, about the beloved niece of his, also named after his mother, who joined the New People's Army in college and whom he long assumed was dead. You don't know that he's going to ask to name your first child together after that niece; you don't know that you're going to say yes the minute you see the wrecked look on his face when he asks; you don't know that when your daughter is around five years old he's going to learn that this niece is still alive, that she's survived two years in a prison camp, that she needs help, money, and most of all a place to live. You don't know yet that that place will be your home in California.

Most of all, you don't know yet that he'll be utterly undone by his own life, that he'll lose everything he has now, that no one who flirts with him and courts his favor in this era will remember him in twenty years, that not even the aura around his name will survive except as a source of fatigued pride, passed down to your daughter, who won't fully grasp the context or the importance of that name when she says she's proud to be a De Vera. You don't know yet that when he's an old man, marbled with lymphoma, one night while you're asleep next to him he's going to remove the oxygen mask keeping him alive, and that afterward, instead of burning his body and scattering the ashes over the rice fields in Ilocos Sur as per his final wishes, you'll put him in a box in

Northern California, ten minutes from the Veterans Hospital where you work, so at least you can visit his grave on your lunch break.

You don't know yet that you're going to love him, and that you won't be able to differentiate this love for him from your devouring hunger to be recognized. It's not that you're imagining that he'd whisk you away to his mansion in Dagupan City or Vigan or Manila and you'd live happily ever after. You've got a happily-ever-after in mind, and it doesn't have anything to do with being anybody's nobya. For that matter, it doesn't have anything to do with Dagupan City or Vigan or Manila at all, or anywhere else in this country. You already know that the first thing that makes you foreign to a place is to be born poor in it; you don't need to emigrate to America to feel what you already felt when you were ten, looking up at the rickety concrete roof above your head and knowing that one more bad typhoon would bring it down to crush your bones and the bones of all your siblings sleeping next to you; or selling fruit by the side of the road to people who made sure to never really look at you, made sure not to touch your hands when they put the money in it. You've been foreign all your life. When you finally leave, all you're hoping for is a more bearable kind of foreignness.

But while you're still here, warming yourself in the glow of someone like the babaero, you're just. Curious. You want to know what it's like to be wanted by someone like that. Most of all, you want to know what it's like to get it, and not need it. Most of the time, you need things you never get; you get things no one would ever want. But getting something you want, that you don't really need? Getting something that's just about feeding that half-sewn-up second mouth inside you, unfed and lonely, cramped somewhere between your heart and your gut? You've never had that before. You've never had it, but you want to feel worthy of it, like the woman in the hair-dye ad you've been seeing around recently. You want to feel like it's because you're worth it.

If you had a girlfriend who was telling you this story, you'd cluck your tongue, tell her to throw the guy in the trash. You'd tell her to forget his name, to practice her English and pack her bags. But it's not a girlfriend telling you this story.

As usual, you're getting ahead of yourself, but there isn't enough road in the world for how ahead of yourself you need to get. You need to get so far ahead of yourself that by the time you reach yourself, you're a different person.

You end up getting so far ahead of yourself that you land in Nashville, Tennessee. You're twenty-one years old, going on twenty-two. You have a nursing degree, a long-distance older boyfriend, and an H1-B visa. Your clothes are polyester, and most of your teeth are removable. You think you're going to lose the accent you speak English with, but you won't. Not ever.

You and a group of other Filipino nurses are hired to work at the Nashville General Hospital under the care of Meharry Medical College, which you learn is one of the preeminent historically Black medical schools in America. All your life, you've been dreaming of America, singing its lyrics and combing its style into your hair. But now the prospect of meeting actual, real-life Americans makes you apprehensive; you remember some of the crueler stories you heard back home, from the older generation who'd gone to work in the sugarcane or asparagus fields on the West Coast and returned broken-bodied and bitter, or never came back at all.

To your relief, you're treated kindly, with a kind of semipaternal, semiflirtatious warmth. Most of the doctors and managers in the hospital are from upper-middle-class Black families, and early in your visit, you and the rest of the Filipino nurses are invited to the house of one of Meharry's bigwigs, Dr. Garnett, the Director of the Division of Neurology, Chief of the the Neurology Service, and Director of the Neuro-Diagnostic Laboratory at Hubbard Hospital. The house is enormous, like something out of a Sampaguita Pictures set. You thought you'd seen the end of houses like this by leaving the Philippines. One more thing you're wrong about.

Doctor Garnett and his wife, Louise, both mestizong-itim and wearing matching pale yellow dress shirts, ply you with iced tea in blown-glass tumblers that you hold with trembling hands, terrified of breaking something so precious. They tell the nurses not to hesitate to come and seek them out should they find themselves in need, or even just home-sick. It must be hard to be so far from home, Louise soothes. Your parents must miss you terribly.

Your parents don't miss you at all, as far as you can tell, given that you haven't seen or heard from your father in two years and you only talk to your mother once a month, usually to give her a heads-up about the money you'll be wiring her. You try to think if anyone in your life has ever told you they missed you.

The only person who might miss you, though he hasn't said it that way, is Doctor De Vera. Not Doctor De Vera: Apolonio, Pol, your boy-friend, you remind yourself, the word still stiff and pinched like a shoe you haven't worn enough times to break in properly. Before you left the Philippines, you ended up lettting him take you to the movies, and then you let him take you to bed. The stories were. Accurate. You were ready for the affair to be over the minute you left for America, but he was the one who asked you, naked between your open legs and smiling, if you'd ever heard of letters. If you'd ever heard of the telephone.

So you talk on the phone once every few weeks. He's not as good on the phone as he is in his sporadic but effusive letters, most of which you don't really understand. He shifts freely between Tagalog and English, writes a lot of flowery musings on love and faith, distance and time. All of his letters are written on his personal stationery, and every silken, onion-thin page has the same header. In cursive script: APOLONIO CHUA DE VERA, M.D., F.P.O.A. Below it, in smaller, elegant capitals: FELLOW, PHILIPPINE ORTHOPEDIC ASSOCIATION. FELLOW, WESTERN PACIFIC ORTHOPEDIC ASSOCIATION. ORTHO-PEDIC SURGERY. TRAUMATOLOGY. CRIPPLED CHILDREN. PHYSICAL MEDICINE AND REHABILITATION.

He says I love you about a dozen times per letter, says he longs for you and he falls asleep dreaming of you in his arms, but he never says the words *I miss you*. You never say it, either.

It's all going well, better than you ever thought it could, until one week just after your payday you call his house in Dagupan, and a woman answers the phone.

A year earlier, you might have been shaken, but your newfound American confidence inspires you to ask for Pol in English. And it's in superior English that the woman tells you: I'm Doctor De Vera's wife. Who's calling?

This is a lie—she isn't his wife, just another girlfriend, dressing for the position that she wants. But you don't know that then. You hang up the phone, and before you know what you're doing, you drink almost an entire bottle of Chivas Regal and wait to die.

You don't die, but your roommates are shrewd enough to hide every bladed object in the apartment you share together, a fact that shames you more than having broken into the communal and as yet untouched bottle of Chivas Regal that all of you pooled your money together to buy, a gesture to treat yourselves for all the long hours. You pass out mumbling, but nobody understands you. You wake up, groggily ask for water and some food, but nobody understands you. It's only when you sober up that you remember none of your roommates speak Pangasinan.

When the babaero calls the dorm, you tell your girlfriends to hang up on him. You send him one letter to say it's over: it takes you forever to write the letter, in English, checking all of your spelling and grammar, getting the other nurses—whose English isn't much better than yours—to check all of your spelling and grammar again. You work on it so long that the letter you end up with bears no resemblance to the letter you intended to write; by taking out so much of your bad grammar, you've taken out most of your feelings, too. Now it's nothing more than a cool and polite good-bye, a last kiss from a mature woman, nobody you've ever been. There's only one mention of the other women he's been fucking, and even that is courteous: you wish him well with all of his other putas, but you're done being one of them. The letter, in the end, sounds a lot like the babaero.

A few months after the Chivas Regal episode, you'll learn about job openings at hospitals in the San Francisco Bay Area. More and more of your siblings back in Mangaldan are starting to talk about immigrating, their applications for U.S. citizenship via your father under way, so your idea is to share an apartment together somewhere out there, where you've heard there's good weather, more space, more jobs, and even more Filipinos. Eventually you get a job offer from San Jose Medical Center, in the San Francisco Bay Area. Shortly after that, you get another job offer from the Veterans Hospital in Palo Alto, also in the Bay Area. The nursing shortage that brought you to Tennessee in the first place seems to exist in California, too.

Now you have a choice. San Jose Medical is in the South Bay, where you've heard most of the Filipinos live, along with Daly City just south of San Francisco. The Veterans Hospital, on the other hand, is in Palo Alto, a moneyed white neighborhood you won't be able to afford to live in, so you'll have to commute—but it pays much better than San Jose Medical. However, if you choose the Veterans Hospital, you can't work at any other hospital; it's a government hospital, and it's illegal to work elsewhere when you're a federal employee.

You take both jobs. You prefer the Veterans Hospital, despite the commute, despite the precarity of your position there. The pay is good and the wealth of the area means the facilities are kept clean. The benefits are more than decent, and you can afford to get a new pair of dentures that fit your mouth so well that you almost, almost forget that you're wearing them. San Jose Medical Center, on the other hand, is in a rougher part of San Jose, and most of the patients are young men: Black, Mexican, Filipino, and Vietnamese, often with gunshot wounds. You learn about the fights between Mexican and Filipino gangs, young boys who could be your little brother, coming in with their faces bludgeoned, their bellies shot through. Many of the nurses have to be accompanied by hospital security guards to their cars every evening. The stress of working there takes a toll on you; after a month, you get Bell's palsy. You're not the only nurse in the hospital to be afflicted with the condition, which is usually temporary if it's treated in time. You're particularly vigilant, taking prednisone and doing the exercises so your face looks like your face again as soon as possible.

This is when Atse Carmen comes to live with you, there in your apartment in Milpitas, on a tourist visa that's about to expire. She's a messy, loud roommate, leaves her creams open in the bathroom and her panties strewn on the floor. Around this time you also find a local Catholic church attended by a mostly Filipino congregation, over on Abel Street. You and your siblings were all raised Catholic, even though your mother was a well-known bruha and faith healer in Mangaldan. In your family, Catholicism was a simple cult of personality: everything was about the Virgin. But you find you can't really attend Mass in Milpitas with Carmen at your side—Carmen, who attracts too much attention, yawns loudly during the sermon, often leaves with some tito's phone number. Anyway, you don't love attending church during the day; the Sunday morning crowd in particular tends to be a social outing for the middle-class Filipino community in the larger South Bay, Filipinos in pearls showing off their cars and bags and plaintive kids. When you start spending hours worrying about your outfit every Saturday evening, you stop the Sunday church visits. Instead, you come by every now and then late at night on your way home from work—around midnight, when no one's there, often not even the priest. Still in your stale nurse's uniform, you slip into the last pew, pray a few Hail Marys, and try not to fall asleep on your knees.

When Carmen's visa does expire and she's still there for another month, another year, you start to freeze every time you see a police car in your rearview mirror driving home. After a couple of years with you she moves out to live in San Francisco with some tisoy named Dante, a handsome kid from a wealthy family who send their son money for rent and food, which he spends on beer and driving to the casinos in Reno. Dante doesn't have a green card either. The romance only lasts for about a year; Dante gets deported shortly after beating Carmen with a two-by-four plank, sending her running barefoot out of their studio apartment into the streets of the Excelsior district in the middle of the night, ending up hiding underneath a parked car in the next neighborhood, still in her negligee. The next morning, the owner of the car crouched down to see Carmen there, fists clenched even in her sleep.

All of this you learned two days after the incident, with Dante already in police custody, and Carmen back at your door in Milpitas, half of her face and upper arm purple, one suitcase, no wheels. She opened her mouth, but before she could kill you dead with shame by having to do something as unthinkable as explain herself to her younger sister, you rushed to let her in.

You get Carmen a job as a nursing assistant at San Jose Medical, working in the emergency room, like you. Shortly after she starts working, her own Bell's palsy starts up. You tell her about all the exercises she needs to do, give her the medicine, but to your chagrin, Carmen is careless about her rehabilitation, doesn't do all the exercises. The nerves and muscles in her face never quite recover; the palsy becomes permanent. Carmen takes it all in her usual stride, turns the whole ordeal into a vivacious joke. She's still beautiful, maybe even more so than before, and the distinctive force of her beauty now makes your worship of her prior allure seem trifling and childish. Still, you'll be unmoored by the loss for years. Carmen's face was the yardstick along which you've measured so much of your life; you don't know what to do without it. Actually get to know who your sister is, maybe. But that seems unthinkable, too.

Eventually your mother, your remaining siblings, and a few remaining friends talk you into going back to the Philippines for your first visit since you left. It's a few months after martial law has been lifted, a few months after the two Filipino union leaders were gunned down in Seattle City Hall. Everyone back in the Philippines—your old friends at the University of Pangasinan, your old friends still working at Nazareth, everyone who's heard the gossip from the nurses back in Tennessee—everyone assures you that the babaero isn't around, he's still in Jakarta, you won't run into him, just come, just come home.

Your family thinks you're living in a giant house, not an apartment, and they don't know how far Milpitas is from San Francisco, the glamorous red-bridged seaside city they picture in their heads. Since arriving in California you haven't been to the beach once. Your family doesn't even know that you and Pol have broken up. Your mother never even approved of Pol, anyway; not because he was a babaero—nothing special about that—and not even because he was close to the Marcos family, but because he was so much older than you, divorced, no kids. Who could trust a man like that, your mother seemed to think. A man with baggage. You've just turned twenty-nine years old, your accent still hasn't left, and you're starting to understand what it means to have baggage. Baggage means no matter how far you go, no matter how many times you immigrate, there are countries in you you'll never leave.

So you go. It'll be your first time returning to the Philippines not as a Philippine citizen, but as an American citizen. You were naturalized just that year, so you're not even a toddler American yet, still a baby. You had to renounce your Philippine citizenship, which was easy enough, but to your surprise you found you couldn't bear to throw away the passport, its distinctive brown-black cover, the shining letters, and your young face in it, still imminently recognizable. The only thing that's different is the way the Philippine border guards treat you when you're going through customs with your new blue passport, like the look a hero gives to the kontrabida at the end of the film. Like that's exactly what you are: an enemy of life.

Atse Carmen can't go with you, of course, but she helps you pack the balikbayan box, full of children's clothes, new sandals, bedsheets, lotions, perfumes, alcohol, macadamia nuts, chocolate. On your first day back, after the long bus ride from Manila to Pangasinan, you go with your sister Rufina to the night market in Calasiao to get fresh puto, like you've always done, and it almost feels like you never left. Only when you ask the vendor if they're all out of pandan flavor, the woman behind the stand smiles at you and replies, in English, that they have a new batch, if you just wait a moment, ma'am.

No one has ever called you ma'am, certainly not in the Philippines. Startled, you continue to speak to her in Pangasinan. The woman continues to reply in English. In the tricycle on the way home, you ask Rufina what that was about.

Rufina says, They can tell you don't live here anymore.

You look down at yourself, the clothes and tsinelas that you borrowed from Rufina because everything you brought from California was too heavy for the weather. When you look up, Rufina's shaking her head, with the face that's looking more and more like your father every day, so much so that when you first saw her waiting for you in the airport in Manila, something in your chest clamped down in self-defense.

It's not the clothes, she says.

Rufina will be the last of your siblings left in the Philippines, just one year younger than you, the only exception to your parents' three-year conception rule. She's already over twenty-one, too old to be immigrated through your father's imminent citizenship. She'll never go to college, will continue working instead on the farm, bringing vegetables to market, the same as your mother. You'll have to be the one to file the petition for Rufina. Sibling to sibling petitions take more than twenty years. The rest of your siblings—Gloria, Boyet, Lerma—are under twenty-one and thus young enough to come to America as the children of a U.S. citizen, once your father's petition is approved.

Rufina always tells you that you don't have to do anything, that she has no real desire to go to America, that she likes the life she has. It's like listening to someone speak to you in another language. You brush off her words and continue filling out the paperwork.

A couple of weeks into your visit, two nurses from Nazareth General Hospital come to visit you in Mangaldan. They inform you that the director of the hospital has heard that you're back in the country and wants to see you. There's a car waiting for you. It'll be the first time you've ever been personally escorted by car anywhere.

The director of the hospital took a liking to you back when you were an intern there, liked how tough you were with the doctors and how tender you were with the patients. She's the daughter of the first woman to practice medicine in Dagupan City, and her mother delivered half of the babies in Dagupan from 1927 until World War II. In 1961, less than ten years after you were born, the current direktora took over her mother's clinic and along with her husband, turned it into Nazareth General Hospital.

Years later, when your first daughter is born in California, you contact the direktora. Over the crackling long-distance line, heart in your throat, you ask if she would do you the honor of being your daughter's ninang. The direktora, after a moment of startled silence, warmly accepts, says she'd be happy to be the godmother, and thanks you for asking. You grip this victory in your fist like pesos. You have fake teeth, you sold chico and mung beans by the side of the road, no one in your family ever had a car, your Tagalog still has Pangasinan holes in it, your fluency in English is a recurring dream that always cuts off just at the crucial moment—but. You've given your first child something like a pedigree, and no one can take it from her.

But for now, you get into the car. Waiting for you at the hospital is the direktora, whom you've always just called doktora. She greets you, kisses you on both cheeks, and then instead of asking you out to a fancy lunch like you were kind of hoping she would, knowing that it would be her treat, she says: Just talk to him. You don't know what she means, until you enter the nurse's break room and waiting for you inside is the babaero.

Skinnier than you remember, darker than you remember, more heartstopping than you remember, and he hasn't even said a word yet. He doesn't comment on your beauty, he doesn't comment on your clothes, he doesn't say anything like, It's *good* to see you again, Pacita, as plenty of the older male doctors who remembered you from your nursing days have said in the ten minutes since you've been in Nazareth, with the *good* directed somewhere around your ass.

The babaero asks how you are. You don't answer. After a long pause, he says, quietly, that he hopes you've been well. He congratulates you on living in California, says he's heard it's beautiful there and he'd like to visit one day. You feel yourself softening, which, of course, is where it all goes wrong. A lesson you should already know: the minute you let yourself go soft, it's over. In the next breath, he asks you to marry him.

You don't remember how you react in that moment. You only remember walking out. You don't stop when you think he might follow you and he doesn't. You don't stop when the nurses at reception ask you what's wrong. You ask the doktora's waiting driver, a tall moreno with puffy eyelids who looks like he could be your brother, to take you back home to Mangaldan, and to apologize to the doktora on your behalf, for leaving so abruptly and not even saying good-bye. During the journey back home, the driver tries to make conversation with you, but you barely respond.

When you get home, your mother's giving you that look. She saw the nurses, she saw the car take you away. You almost remind her that your petition to immigrate her over to the States should be finished soon, that you're working hard on moving her to California with you, putting her in a home with running hot water and a roof that won't threaten to cave in any minute, so maybe for once she could cut you some slack—but you shut that thought up immediately.

You get on the next plane to California; you don't care how many hours you'll have to work overtime to pay for the flight change fee. You should have known that you weren't ready for whatever was waiting for you, in this place that people keep telling you is home. All you want now is the cramped apartment in San Petra Court, Milpitas. Eating canned sardines and rice, safe and far away. Safe because you're far away.

But the babaero starts writing and calling. He says he got your details from the direktora. In all of his letters and calls, he asks you to marry him. Now he says he misses you: he misses you, he misses you, he's always missed you. He says he loves you, he loves you, he's always loved you. He never calls collect. He never says Marcos's name.

In your deepest of hearts, you know he needs to get out of the Philippines; that Marcos's cronies and allies are scurrying from the country as the regime falls apart. Later you'll learn that many of the babaero's friends and relatives took their wealth and moved: to Sydney, to Singapore, to Glendale, California. The doktora knew about your naturalization; she must have told him. You know what you really are—before being loved, before being missed. You're a pathway.

You might be a pathway, but so is he. You think of his first wife, her family. You think of the look his sister Ticay gave you when she first met you, like she wouldn't come close enough to buy a mango from you. You think of the parties in Malacañang the babaero must have gone to regularly, the women waiting in line to snap up a De Vera. Then, a smothered, fathom-deep part of you thinks of the look on his face when you said your favorite dessert was tupig.

Choosing to marry him will mean having to prove yourself to invisible judges, all the time, for the rest of your life. You think you know what it's going to be like, but you don't know the half of it. You don't know that the sting of amused disapproval when his siblings gaze at you will never subside, not even when the financial situation turns around and it's your nursing salary that starts making up the bulk of the money that the babaero occasionally sends back. You don't know that you'll never be able to shake the sweat-streaked terror of scarcity, or those dreams about being back in Pangasinan still clawing around in the ground for a crab. You don't know that marrying someone who's always slept with a full belly will be like being married to someone from another planet; you don't know that even just the velvety confidence of his English will sometimes send you into paroxysms of shame that you counteract with buying things you can't afford, just to prove you aren't the girl you'll always be. You don't know that you'll end up going hungry some months to buy Estée Lauder creams, Chanel perfumes, things you remember the De Vera women using freely. The person you are now won't even recognize the smell of the person you'll be in twenty years.

You tell yourself: People get married for all sorts of reasons. You say yes to him on the phone, and the warbly, frizzled echo on the long-distance call means you hear your own yes back to yourself. It isn't the voice of a woman just being practical. You say yes again, in English, and again it rings back to you, overlapping the babaero laughing and saying yes, too, yes, mahal, so you can hear for the first time what you sound like together.

When a few years later you finally, finally give birth to your dream girl, an American morena—she wasn't quite so morenang-morena in your dream—both of you nearly die during the labor. The dose of Pitocin they give you in the hospital to hasten the birth and vacate the bed ends up inducing contractions so strong that you start hemorrhaging.

The babaero, who's no longer rich, no longer a surgeon, no longer really a babaero, but now a badly paid security guard at a computer chip company just outside of Milpitas and your lawfully wedded husband, tries to make you laugh by telling you that the entire floor of the hospital room was covered in your blood, just like in *The Shining,* a film you've never seen. His green card hasn't been processed yet so doesn't live with you in Milpitas full time, spending six months in the Philippines, six months in California. And though his forlorn look of love when he leaves you at the airport seems genuine, it's not hard to see that he grows at least half an inch taller the minute he's through security, once his back is to you and he's facing the direction of home. You're the future mother of his children, but you're not home for him; not yet, maybe not ever.

But right now he's at your side, and you're still trying to give birth to the dream girl, gushing blood, moaning in Pangasinan, and to top it all off, she starts suffocating inside you, the umbilical cord wrapped around her neck. The doctors move fast; you're knocked unconscious, and she's cut out of you in minutes. Alive. You're both alive.

Throughout her childhood, you won't be able to stop yourself from constantly telling your daughter: If you were born in the Philippines, we would both be dead. She'll grow up knowing that the only reason she's alive is because she was born in America—though she doesn't seem to love America any more or less for that reason. Then again, she doesn't have to love it. She's of it.

Looking down at her in those first few moments, what you see most of all is what she doesn't have. A fate. You know what it's like to have a fate; you also know what it's like to escape one. This one won't sell chico on National Road. This one won't brush her teeth in her hand every night. As for loving America or not loving America, those aren't your problems, either. Your word for love is *survival.* Everything else is a story that isn't about you.

Ate Hero

POL DIDN'T ASK HIS OLDER BROTHER WHERE HIS
niece had been. He asked only how her injury was healing; if the surgery
had been successful; if Hamin thought his daughter would need to continue physical therapy in California, and if so, could Hamin drive to
their sister Ticay's house in Vigan, where Pol had left some of the old
equipment from his old clinics in Dagupan. Most of the drugs would be
expired or obsolete, but Pol would make do. By the time of the phone
call, Pol had had been retired in California for over five years, but everyone knew doctors and nurses rarely retired; the vocation was eternal.
Hamin had no answers to Pol's questions. He replied only, with some
composure, that according to their younger sister, Soly, Hero was physically intact.

That was the phrasing Hamin used, in English, even though they
were speaking in Ilocano. Non compos mentis? Pol asked, more to himself than to his brother. Aniá? Hamin asked, irritated. Pol reverted back
to Ilocano, said he hadn't said anything, that the line was bad. Hamin
didn't reply for a long time.

Finally, Pol said the same things he'd already said in his letter: Have
Soly send her on the tourist visa. She'll stay in the extra room. She can
help take care of Roni. Or Paz will try to find her a job in one of the
hospitals.

On the phone, neither Pol nor Hamin called her Hero. Nobody did.
Everyone still called her Nimang.

It was a few months later, in the summer of 1990, when Hero walked
through the garage door of that house in Milpitas and was met by a
young girl with raw leatherlike scars covering half of her face, her entire
neck, and down both of her forearms, that she learned you could make
more than one nickname out of the name Geronima, a name that the
De Vera family had been recycling for at least three generations.

It was this young girl who declared, rashy hand on her hip: So we have the same name, but *I* go by Roni. Spelled *R-O-N-I*. I'll call you Auntie Hero.

That was perhaps only the second or third time Hero had ever heard an American voice in real life; the first time she'd ever heard an American voice coming out of the face of someone who looked not unlike her own father. Behind Hero, Paz came through the door, carrying Hero's green suitcase, hefting its weight against her substantial hip until she could settle it on the ground next to the pile of worn-out tsinelas. She was several inches shorter than Hero, not over five feet tall, but Hero felt immediately shadowed, rebuked somehow by that tense, proud stance.

A woman Hero would later come to know as Paz's sister Gloria emerged from the living room, followed by two young men Hero would later come to know as Paz's nephews, Jejomar and Freddie. They spoke to Paz in Pangasinan; Hero didn't understand anything they said. Mangan kila, Paz was saying, pointing to plates of food covered with paper towels on the kitchen table. They were shaking their heads, smiling shyly at Hero, and heading for the garage door. Hero realized they must have been watching the girl while Paz and Pol went to the airport to meet her. Paz was picking up the suitcase again, getting ready to take it up the stairs, to show Hero her new room.

There were many things Hero should have done then. She should have said, Sorry, Tita Paz, let me take that, even though she wouldn't have been able to carry the suitcase herself. Even before that, driving through the town, she shouldn't have minutely wrinkled her nose at the smell, which she would come to know later as the famed shit smell of Milpitas, the reason why house prices were lower there. She should have made casual conversation on the drive from San Francisco International Airport to Milpitas, instead of remaining mute and clammy in the backseat. She should have mustered up the strength at least to stay awake as Pol drove in silence down the highway that Hero would later know as intimately as the vein down the inside of her own wrist, instead of creakily turning her head to its side and treading lead-limbed between buoys of sleep, only fully lucid for the last fifteen minutes of the drive. Hero saw the sign for CALAVERAS BOULEVARD MILPITAS above them, saw a large, lone Holiday Inn on her right side. Pol steered the car up the overpass, and on the way down, there waiting was the town: sun-weathered and stout, garlanded on every side by strip malls, the tarmac so uneven and rough that Hero saw Paz reach up for the grab-handle on the roof above her; not gripping it, just touching the tips of her fingers there by instinct, the reminder of the handle's presence steadying her more than the handle itself. The road remained patchy all the way to the house, down the long boulevard that cut through the town.

Upon arriving, Hero should have looked up at the house and en-thused, stretching out the creaking bones of her Tagalog: Ang ganda naman ang bahay ninyo, Tita, wow; the house was obviously newly bought and waiting for praise. Or she should have lowered her head and said Salamat, kept her head there. First impressions didn't have to be everything, but she didn't know yet that Paz was the kind of person who made judgments about people based on whether or not they treated her like she was beneath them, that she was a sensitive scanner of gaze-overs and under-words, that those judgments helped move Paz through the world, told her whom she could laugh with her mouth wide open in front of, and whom she had to wear perfume next to. There were a thou-sand ways Hero could have walked into the house in Milpitas that day to begin things, but Paz lifted the suitcase again, straightened her back, and closed off her heart.

Then she looked at her daughter and said: Manang Nimang is your cousin, not your auntie.

To which Roni said, scratching at a purplish-red plaque on her neck: Fine. *Ate* Hero then.

Pol came through the door and saw his wife on her way up the stair-case. He shook his head, gestured for her to put it down, saying he would carry it up. Paz put the suitcase back down, giving no impression that she was glad to be relieved of its weight. Then she crossed the kitchen to the rice cooker on the counter and asked, Gutom ka, Nimang? Gloria made pinakbet. Pol said it was your favorite.

By then it was too late to make a second first impression, so Hero just came farther into the house that was now her home and lied that yes, yes—she was hungry.

Pol brought the suitcase up to the small, tidy room next to the bathroom; the sheets were clean and mismatched, freshly laid. Hero followed him, and then watched as he put the suitcase down, then unzipped it for her without saying a word. She opened her mouth to tell him he didn't have to unpack everything, that much she could do herself—even if she couldn't, she would—but he was already standing up and turning around, saying,

Just tell us if you want us to help.

After more than ten years of not seeing each other, he still knew the perimeters of her dignity. You look the same, she said in Ilocano.

He laughed. This isn't the same, he said, rubbing the belly that hadn't been there when she'd last seen him.

Hero looked down at her open suitcases, the things that Soly had helped put in there, even though by then she'd had enough movement in her thumbs to handle something like packing. There was a bottle of Tabac cologne that she should have wrapped up more securely, but when she knelt down to pick it up, it was still intact and dry. She heard the warmth of Pol's laughter again, a sound she knew better and had heard more often than the sound of her own parents' laughter. She looked up and Pol said, You still wear that?

It's not the same bottle as the one you gave me, she'd said, smiling back, the feeling so foreign on her face she nearly reached up to touch her mouth.

I hope not, Pol replied. He leaned down and picked the bottle up, twisting open the brown cap and sniffing. How are they, he said, looking at her hands. If anyone else had asked, Hero wouldn't have replied. Pol seemed to know that.

She said, On a scale of one to ten?

No pain scale. You're not my patient.

It's okay. Much better since the surgery.

Pol screwed the cap back onto the bottle. We have painkillers at home. And Paz can get you codeine, whatever you need from the hospital.

Just ibuprofen or acetominaphen, Hero said. I don't want anything stronger.

Pol nodded, and put the bottle of Tabac on the nightstand next to the bed. Okay. You let us know if there's anything else you need. He turned to leave.

Hero pointed with her chin to the cologne bottle. You can have it, she said. I don't really wear it anymore.

Pol shook his head. I don't wear it anymore, either. It's hard to find here, so I stopped.

He smiled again. But it still smells the same.

She doesn't even have a driver's license, Paz argued, on Hero's second evening in California.

Hero, Paz, and Pol were sitting around the kitchen table, emptied plates in front of them. At the center of the table there was a bowl of cold white rice, a hardened crust of yellowing grains forming over the top. When she saw Hero looking, Paz tore off a square of paper towel and covered the bowl, shooing away a fly that wasn't there.

Pol was smacking the bottom of a still-sealed pack of Benson and Hedges menthol cigarettes. He said, If she can pick Roni up from school, then Roni doesn't have to be at day care or Auntie Gloria's until nighttime anymore. He pulled the cellophane off the pack, pulled out a cigarette, and lit it.

Paz frowned. And if she gets caught?

She won't get caught.

Hero felt a presence behind her and nearly jumped out of her chair, only to see that Roni had come into the kitchen, barefoot, silent as a cat. Where's your tsinelas, Paz called, rote, used to having to ask the question.

Roni shrugged and opened the cupboard, poking her head in.

Baka you'll get sick again, Paz said. The floor is dirty. And cold.

Roni pulled a can of Vienna sausages out of the cupboard and took it to the sink to open and drain. She didn't look as though she were listening.

Pol turned his head to face her, parting the cloud of smoke in front of him. What if Manang Nimang is the one to pick you up from school tomorrow?

Roni was using a paper towel to dab the excess congealed jelly from the Vienna sausages, arranging them on a plate. There's rice here, anak, Paz said, pulling the paper towel off the bowl at the center of the table. You want me to heat it up?

Nope, Roni said, bringing her plate to the table. She sat at the head of the table, bizarrely—Hero had been wondering whose seat it was, since both Pol and Paz had avoided occupying it.

Hm? Pol prompted his daughter again, using his left hand to wave the smoke away from her. It still floated over her head.

Roni was letting her mother spoon cold rice onto her plate. Early? she asked. I don't have to go to Auntie Carmen's?

Right on the dot, Pol promised. His English was less foreign to Hero's ear than his Tagalog; warped and rich, like an old record. It was the English of no country—genteel and full of idioms, which were just ways of moving the sentence forward. He said things like *right on the dot,* or *hit the nail on the head,* and whenever he ended phone calls with strangers, he would say, *Thank you, you've been very kind,* regardless of whether or not they'd actually been kind. It was more effective if they hadn't been. The words flustered and delighted the people on the other end of the line, which was generally the effect Pol liked to have on people.

Roni put her right leg up, and tucked her left leg under her. She mashed together a Vienna sausage with a small mound of rice, then brought it to her mouth. Hero didn't know yet that the girl didn't really know how to eat with a fork and knife. Perhaps naively, Hero hadn't expected an American-born girl to eat with her hands, or to lift her leg up onto the chair.

Roni chewed, then swallowed, then shrugged again. Okay, she said.

Pol gestured with his cigarette, smiling to Hero. It's settled. Nimang, you'll pick her up after school. Two o'clock. Let me show you how to get there, hold on, I'll get a pen and paper.

While he searched, Paz said nothing, just rubbed at her own arms in quiet disapproval. Seemingly just to say something, she said to Roni, You want more rice, when Roni had more than enough rice on her plate.

That was how Hero got permission to use the Toyota Corona that Pol had driven to pick her up from the airport. Paz drove her own silver Civic, a newer model than the Corona and eternally covered with a fine layer of dust and lime scale. Pol's Corona was at least ten years old and a shocking shade of blue. It had been beige when he'd bought it; he'd chosen the blue himself. He'd even changed the emblems—they'd originally been black and silver, and he'd had them replaced with gold-plated ones. The last touch was the spoiler, which lifted up from the car's back like a shark fin. Pol was clearly proud of the car; Paz had made her peace with it.

Hero liked driving the Corona, liked the reason that had put her behind the wheel in the first place. Pol had lifted an invisible burden from her shoulders by putting a concrete weight there instead, a daily responsibility. She liked the drive from the house to the school, the one long easy path in which Jacklin Road turned to Abel Street. She liked the wide, poorly paved roads, the huge sequoia telephone posts, and the smaller, desiccated trees that dotted the streets. She liked the houses, despite most of them being a familiar variation on her least favored architectural style, the Spanish colonial. She liked the loping, crooked hill she passed after North Milpitas Boulevard, a hill that brought the car closer to the thing she liked most of all: the strange new sky, low-hanging and close, deep and limpid, a body of water rather than a sky, so that she felt she was submerged in it rather than standing under it.

When Hero arrived at the school the first day, following Pol's directions, she realized she didn't know where exactly in the school she was meant to pick the girl up. She drove into the parking lot, found one of the few remaining parking spaces. Parents who had parked were standing in front of their cars, chatting with each other. Most of them were Filipino.

Just as Hero turned the ignition off, she was startled by the loud, long ring of a bell—she grabbed on to the steering wheel instinctively, arms locking, breath chopped short, the pain from her clenched hands radiating down all the way to her elbow, up into her armpits.

When she came back to herself, someone was knocking on the driver's window. Hero blinked, looked up. Roni was standing outside. There was a large scratch on her face.

Can you let me in already? she hollered.

Hero didn't know how long she'd been waiting there. She reached across to the passenger seat, pulled the lock up with some difficulty, trying not to wince. Roni rolled her eyes, crossed in front of the car, and opened the passenger door, climbed in. What happened to you, how come you were breathing like that?

What happened to your face, Hero asked instead of answering.

Roni shrugged. I got in a fight.

During school? Why didn't your teacher—

No, just now. Just after class. Roni was putting her seat belt on, shoving her backpack between her legs in front of the seat.

With who?

Can we go home? Roni demanded.

It became a regular thing, the fighting at school. Or, it had been a regular thing for a while, and Hero was only just beginning to enter into its ceremony. It went with a number of odd things she noticed about the girl.

Hero had seen cases of eczema before; she'd had it herself when she was a child, the face in her baby photos slapped-red and raw. Everyone's baby photos looked like that, in the De Vera family. It was hard for her to think of a Filipino she knew who didn't have eczema at some point. But she hadn't ever seen a case like Roni's before. At first sight, the eczema only—only—covered the left side of the girl's face, a ring around her mouth, a few patches down her neck, and two twin patches on the inside of each elbow. But daily life revealed that the mottled scarring crept down Roni's armpits (seen when she lazily stretched her bare arms, tank-topped), striped up and down her inner thighs (seen when she ate at the table while reading, tucking one leg beneath her and lifting one foot onto the chair, so that her knee was cheek-height—the way peasants eat, Hero's mother, Concepcion, would sniff), behind her knees (she ran around in shorts), between her toes (she wore thong sandals that were too big for her, probably from an older cousin, possibly male), and along the lines of both thumbs (she gestured, often wildly).

Roni made a great show of being unbothered by it. Most of the kids with eczema who Hero knew—and most of the adults, for that matter—adopted the habit of wearing long-sleeve shirts, long pants, high necks; of hiding their hands behind their backs, of looking down instead of meeting a gaze. But Roni liked oversized tank tops, liked neon shorts and jelly sandals that made her feet stink. She didn't seem to have shame.

Then there were her eating habits. At home, sometimes Roni ate in enormous quantities, at all hours of the day: canned Vienna sausages and rice, canned corned beef and rice, her mother's pork neck bone sinigang and rice, her father's baked ox tongue and rice, ramen noodles either cooked in the Styrofoam cup or crushed raw in the plastic bag and eaten like chips. But then there were days when Roni wouldn't eat at all, re-fused even to drink, was repulsed at even the idea of food. Some days would find her melancholic—days when her defiant, adultlike chatter would fade and she would withdraw into her reading or her TV watch-ing, barely looking up at the world around her. And then, sometimes, there would be days of choleric fury. Hero learned that those were the fighting days.

One afternoon, only a few weeks after she arrived in Milpitas, Hero came to the school parking lot and Roni was nowhere to be found, even when all of the parents' cars had driven away. Hero left the car and cir-cled the school grounds, which weren't large. She finally found the girl in a patch of grass behind a row of classrooms, locked in a snarling knot of children's bodies.

Hero had to drag her, gnashing and biting, while a boy at the bottom of the pile shouted, IGOROTA IGOROTA IGOROOOOOTAAAA-AAAA. The boy was as dark as Roni.

The girl squirmed in Hero's arms all the way back to the car. She was heavier than her scrawny limbs suggested. Lemme go lemme go lemme go lemme go—

When they reached the door, Roni sprung out of Hero's grasp, backed herself against the car, panting. Then she leapt forward, growling, making to run back to the scene of the fight.

Hero caught her around the ribs, locking her in the bend of her elbow. Ano ka ba?!

Roni went still, slumped against the side of the door. Exhausted suddenly, her face ashen and distant. She closed her eyes. Her bangs were sweaty, rumpled. She didn't push them out of the way. The eczema ring around her mouth had grown, was creeping down her neck and shoulders, creating a kind of hauberk. Hero felt, uneasily, that she was looking at something not altogether human; the hush of dull rage lifting from the girl's body had something creaturely in it, predatory and wounded, something that knew how to fight and not remotely how to speak.

Hero reached across Roni's body and put her key into the the passenger door lock, making Roni startle abortively at the click. Let's go home.

Roni didn't do anything for a long while. Then she opened her eyes, opened the door, and got in. When Hero was sure the girl would stay inside the car, she walked around and got in, too.

That night, Hero was watching over Roni while Paz and Pol were at work. Paz was working at the Veterans Hospital from seven in the morning to two in the afternoon, then going straight to the convalescent home from three in the afternoon to ten in the evening. Pol was pulling a double shift himself at the computer chip company, working both the afternoon and the night shift straight through. Hero hadn't yet had a chance to talk to them about the fight that afternoon, or the many fights before then; she told herself she would tell Paz when she got back home.

Hero asked Roni what she wanted for dinner. Gloria had brought over adobo and pancit that afternoon, while Roni was still at school. Gloria was the first of Paz's sisters that Hero had met, that first day in Milpitas; one of her younger ones, short, very dark-skinned and giggly. She spoke only hesitant Tagalog, and very little English. Paz said she worked in a nursing home as a cook. Pol said it was Paz who got her that job.

When Gloria came to drop off the food she prepared, her husband Tino sometimes accompanied her to help carry the containers. He didn't appear to have a job. The first thing he did when he walked through the door was to make his way to the refrigerator, asking Pol on the way if he wanted a beer. Pol rarely wanted a beer; he'd never liked drinking, even when Hero knew him back in Vigan. That didn't stop Tino from having one, or three. Sometimes it was Jejo and Freddie who came to help carry the containers. Hero assumed Jejo and Freddie were Gloria's sons, but Paz told her they weren't, without telling her whose sons they actually were.

Gloria brought food to the house at least once a week, sometimes twice. She brought things that Hero recognized but rarely ate in Vigan, afritada and adobo and pancit, which Hero associated only with festivals and holidays. She brought the foil-wrapped meat loaf Hero thought of as embutido, but which Paz called morhon. Paz would come home at midnight from a sixteen-hour shift and make sure everyone in the house had eaten, saying she'd already eaten at the hospital, before heating up a plate for herself in the microwave and eating it alone. Once, Hero ran into her on one of those nights, sleepless as usual and looking for a glass of water. She couldn't shake the feeling that she'd interrupted someone in the midst of watching pornography; there was a private sensuality in Paz's solitary eating, in the look of guarded guilt that came over her face at the sight of Hero in the entryway.

Roni was making a face at Hero's suggestion. I don't like adobo, she said. I'll make pizza. She went, barefoot as usual, to the freezer, and pulled two packages out of it.

Who doesn't like adobo? Hero joked. Pilpina ka ba?

Roni turned her head, face hard and foreign. It looked like she'd heard that question before, been teased and asked to prove herself in just this way before.

I am Filipina. I just don't like adobo. I like other things more.

Hero knew that; she'd seen the girl eat neck bones with relish, gnawing the meat down to the cartilage and then gnawing that, too. She'd even seen Roni eat dinuguan—she apparently had a taste for the sabaw, preferring just the dinuguan sauce with rice, leaving the meat and innards for everyone else. At the time, Hero had asked, delicately, if the girl knew what the sauce she was eating was made of. Roni had been amused by Hero's tone. Pig blood, she'd replied, shoveling a spoon of it into her mouth, then grinning with black-stained teeth. Oink oink.

Hero watched as Roni stood on a chair to put the frozen pies, their plastic wrappers removed, in the microwave one after the other. When the first pizza was done, Roni put a paper towel over it to keep it warm, and slipped the second one in the microwave. When the second one was done, she slipped it onto the plate and gave it to Hero.

Take this one 'cause it's still hot, Roni said, and retrieved her own pizza from the counter, removing the now-greasy paper towel and throwing it in the garbage can. Hero took two butter knives and two forks from the drawer, and handed one pair to Roni, who used it just to slice her pizza into fours. Want me to do yours? she asked. Hero wondered if Pol and Paz had told Roni to cut Hero's food for her, but Roni's face was open and impassive. Hero nodded.

When they sat at the table, Roni put her leg up and ate the pizza with her hands. Her pizza looked like the cheese atop it was already congealing, but still she ate it with gusto. Hero's pizza, on the other hand, was indeed still hot, steam rising from it.

Hero was touched by the small gesture of courtesy, at first only minutely, and then, for no reason at all, deeply and wholly. It was possible she was going to cry, here in this kitchen, for the first time since she'd arrived in America. To prevent that from happening, she stuffed her mouth with an entire quarter of the pizza, then huffed and gasped as the molten bite burned her tongue.

Haltingly, she chewed and swallowed until her tongue was numb. Then she said to Roni: I had eczema, too, when I was a kid.

Roni blinked up at Hero and, with her mouth full, just said: Mm-hmm.

The more she spoke, the more Hero became aware of her own accent, hesitant and affected. I really hated it, she continued. She pushed up one of her sweatshirt sleeves to show her own now-unblemished arm and said, I used to have it all up and down my arms, like you. It was really itchy.

She lifted her own chin slightly. I still have scarring on my neck. See?

Roni bore the tolerant look of someone enduring a swiftly waning amusement. Does yours hurt, Hero asked, somewhat desperately.

Roni didn't have to push up any sleeves to reveal her arms. She simply turned one of them over to better showcase the landscape. Yeah, it hurts.

The creams don't really help, Hero encouraged.

Roni shook her head. Nuh-uh. And I'm going to hell anyway, so.

Hero was prepared for sharing anecdotes about childhood eczema, and not nearly as prepared for the abrupt left turn into hell. Roni said it without a trace of fear or despair: she had an arm and she was going to hell. There's an engkanto who likes me, she went on.

You know about engkantos? Hero said. Then, pulling herself together: That's not—it doesn't mean you're going to hell, who told—

Grandma thinks it's a kapre, Roni went on, like Hero hadn't even spoken. There was a kapre who liked her back in the Philippines.

Hero knew what engkantos and kapres were. But she'd never known anyone in real life who claimed to be liked by one. Roni took a bite of her pizza, placid. Hero felt slightly dizzy.

After swallowing, Roni continued: They're bigger.

What? Hero said. Oh. The kapre. Yes. They're bigger. I think.

You don't know? Roni asked. You're from there. She said this without judgment, sounding genuinely surprised.

Hero didn't know how to say, My family doesn't believe in that kind of thing, we went to university. She had to remind herself: Roni is your family.

My mom and dad didn't really talk about that kind of stuff, Hero said.

The words *mom* and *dad,* the word *stuff,* felt tarry and thick in her mouth. She pressed her tongue against the back of her teeth like the words were something bitter she'd eaten.

Oh, Roni said. Papa doesn't either. But mom does. And grandma does. You know Grandma's a bruha.

That, Hero had heard about from her own father, years and years ago: Paz was a probinsyana, ragged-poor, and her mother was some kind of superstitious village healer-type bakya who didn't approve of Pol and had refused to meet his extended family, even after the marriage. After Paz's immigration petition had successfully brought her mother over, Grandma Sisang chose to live with Paz's older sister, Carmen, and her younger sister Gloria, in an apartment on the other side of Milpitas. Not with Paz.

She doesn't really like me, Roni said, still munching away on the last hand-torn fragment of her pizza. But she knows how to heal me. Kind of. Or Mom said.

Grandma even killed a chicken and sprinkled its blood around the house once, Roni added. But that didn't work. She shrugged.

So for now I'm still going to hell. Or I'm gonna die so the engkanto and I can play together.

Then she pointed at Hero's plate. Are you gonna eat the rest of your pizza?

Hero had met Paz just once, back in Vigan. Tito Pol had invited Paz to Lolo Tranquilino's funeral. Tito Pol never brought women back to the De Vera compound, and even Josefina had only come a few times throughout their marriage. That the now-divorced Pol was bringing along one of the promdi nurses he was fucking, not just to a De Vera gathering, but to his own father's funeral, was a scandal of delicious proportions. It was one of the last times Hero would step into the home on Calle Encarnacion, the place where she'd spent her childhood. At that point, only she knew that she was going to drop out of medical school.

Paz was a few years older than her; looked younger. Hero saw her alone on the veranda, in a black dress patterned with what looked like large sampaguita vines. Her center-parted hair reached just to the top of her ass; it was the most expensive-looking thing about her. She appeared to understand that beauty, at least, was also a kind of wealth. From the veranda, Paz was looking down into one of the back courtyards and watching the clutch of cooks hover over an enormous cauldron, filled with boiling oil. They were preparing to make bagnet. The slabs of pork belly were waiting next to the cauldron in a metal dish on top of several layers of cloth. The cooks had been preparing the food for days. They'd marinated the bellies, boiled them the evening before, and fried them once earlier in the day. Now they were waiting to be fried again, and then again, until the skin crisped up, popped and split.

Hero saw Paz looking around at the house, her face flickering between open wonder and blank slate, visibly impressed by what she saw and struggling not to show it. Hero tried to imagine what it might be like for somone who'd never been to the De Vera compound to experience the first sight of it: the cobblestones on Calle Encarnacion leading up to the gate, the courtyard full of mango and sampaloc trees, the now-derelict granary where nineteenth-century servants had kept the stores of maguey, tobacco, and rice from the De Vera plantations and where, family lore had it, Pol had hung a human skeleton, brought back from his time at medical school. During Hero's childhood, the legend of the skeleton had been used by all of the adults to scare their children into submission. Rather than frightened, Hero had been intrigued; sometimes she wondered if it was that early horror story that had made her want to become a doctor.

The ground floor of the house, traditionally used for carriage storage, was allocated to the servants. There were two staircases leading from the courtyard to the first-floor veranda of the house. The tiles were traditional Vigan clay tiles, and the capiz shell slats in the windows were well maintained, their iridescence kept dull and thus elegant. Inside the house, the floors and banisters were carved from molave and narra wood, gleaming from regular hand polishing, and the sawali ceilings were intact, with the woven, aged bamboo mats above preventing both sound and light from bouncing around too harshly. Pol and the rest of his brothers preferred to be out on the veranda or at least in the atrium, where the air was less stale. The women stayed inside, out of the sun.

Hero saw Escolastica approach Paz, stepping out onto veranda from inside the house. Tita Ticay kept her distance but looked Paz up and down, the white skin of her face making her raised plucked eyebrow look even more dour. Did your family's driver bring you here, Pacing? she asked. Hero hadn't ever heard anyone call Paz anything other than Paz or Pacita.

Paz smiled, and answered the way Hero would learn she always answered: rather than lying, or even dodging the question, she preferred to speak the supposedly shameful truth as if it were something to be proud of. Of course not, she said, her voice sweet and direct. We're too poor to have anything like a car.

She made it sound like it was desirable not to have a car, ridiculous to even want one. Hero had been impressed, not least of all because even she'd gotten in the habit of slipping out of a room whenever Tita Ticay entered it, terrified of her venomous tongue, her keen eyes, the ease with which she spotted weakness, and the pleasure with which she toyed with it.

Hero watched Paz watch Escolastica leave. Paz turned stiffly back around, to see the cooks slip the bellies once again into the cauldron.

When Paz came home from work, Roni was already asleep. She seemed surprised to see Hero waiting for her, used to Hero already being holed up in her room, not sleeping but listening for the newly comforting sound of the garage door opening late at night.

Can't sleep? Paz asked without waiting for the answer. Did you eat already? I brought some daing na bangus from work. My coworker made it. It's real Pangasinan bangus.

Hero shook her head. I already ate.

Paz took out the large container holding the bangus and put it on the table anyway, opening it so the smell of vinegar-marinated fried fish wafted up. Me, too, she said, nevertheless reaching for a small piece of crispy flesh and popping it into her mouth.

Hero opened her mouth, still unsure of whether or not to use English or Tagalog when talking to Paz. Paz had a habit of speaking to Roni in a mixture of English, Tagalog, and Pangasinan. It felt like Roni didn't really know the difference between Tagalog and Pangasinan, and moved between the two interchangeably as if they were one language. Nobody had told her otherwise, Hero supposed. But for Hero, listening to the mixture was like listening to a radio whose transmission would occasionally short out; she'd get half a sentence, then nothing—eventually the intelligible parts would start back up, but she'd already lost her place in the conversation. But when Pol would come in, they'd switch to English, and like adjusting a dial to get a sharper signal, Hero would be able to tune in again.

When Pol initiated conversations, he initiated them only in Tagalog or English. He spoke Ilocano only to Hero, but even then, half the time they spoke to each other in English. Pol had told her that Paz knew Ilocano, but Hero had never heard the two of them speak it to each other. Hero had the sense that Pol's Ilocano was stuck in time, that he only wanted to speak it with the people he'd always spoken it to, but even when Hero and Pol spoke in Ilocano with each other in California, there was a playacting stiffness in their voices that hadn't been there back in Vigan, when Hero used to hang on his every word.

Finally Hero said to Paz: May nangyari sa Roni.

Paz tensed, but kept picking at the fish. She had taken off her shoes, so Hero could see her feet, covered in the light beige nude compression stockings that she wore, like many nurses.

What happened, Paz asked. English, then.

She's getting into fights at school, Hero said. I don't know if her teachers know, but it's happened more than once.

Again—Paz cried, then stopped herself, looked at Hero and flattened her mouth, as if realizing she'd let something show that she didn't want Hero to witness. Paz squeezed her eyes shut, emphasizing the puffy, purpled circles beneath them. She covered the container of bangus again, then went to the sink to wash her hands. Okay, she said over the sound of the water running, so Hero had to strain to her hear. Her voice was stiff and clipped. Thank you. I'll talk to her.

When she finished washing her hands, she passed Hero and nodded to the container of bangus. You can eat that, she said.

Paz sounded angry, not just generally, or not even just at Roni, but specifically at Hero. She wondered what she'd said wrong, but once she was back in her own bed she realized that of course she'd struck at Paz's pride, the boundaries of which she should have already been well aware of; she should have known that it wounded Paz for Hero to report on Roni's behavior. Was there any other way to say it, Hero asked herself. But she already knew the only other way was to not say anything at all.

Hero had already understood that Paz was the breadwinner of the family. If she worked at the Veterans Hospital in Palo Alto alone that would already have been a decently paid job; but she also worked at San Jose Medical Center, and then sometimes at a nursing home in Mountain View. It explained, to some extent, how they had been able to afford what to Hero seemed like a moderately large house, four bedrooms and two stories, but soon Hero learned that Paz's salary paid for more than just the house. It quickly became apparent that Paz was also helping Gloria and Carmen pay their rent, that she was putting relatives still in the Philippines through school and helping to rebuild her family home back in Mangaldan, that she was paying for a lawyer to help Carmen obtain her green card, along with seemingly a hundred other obligations that meant that Paz's not insubstantial salaries were spread wide, far, and thin.

Paz was putting nearly everything but the house on credit, paying off only the minimum amount of debt each month. And when she bought groceries, she categorically refused to budget; if Roni was hungry and wanted frozen pizzas, then there would be ten frozen pizzas of that brand in the freezer. When it came time to buy cleaning supplies or toilet paper, it was brand-name items, never the generic supermarket brand. Only when she went to a Filipino or Asian grocery store did Paz permit herself to pursue bargains.

Pol, on the other hand, kept very little of his money in the bank, preferring to pay for everything with cash, cash that he kept hidden somewhere in the master bedroom, cash that made his wallet bulge. He'd
always been like that, even back in the Philippines; most of the De Vera
men were. There was a uniquely masculine pride in pulling out a leather
wallet and letting everyone around see it thickened with bills. But here,
it seemed more a matter of comfort than pride; Pol wanted to see the
money he had in front of him. He never used a credit card. I don't trust
them, he said to Hero.

Once, Hero accompanied Paz and Roni grocery shopping at Magat,
the only Filipino store in Milpitas, looking for soft-shelled crabs to make
for dinner. Next to Magat was an LBC Express branch advertising good
rates for balikbayan boxes and money wiring, and next to the LBC Express was a Vietnamese restaurant, a video rental store, and a large Walgreens drugstore, so overlit that the white glare from behind its windows
hurt Hero's eyes.

Can we go rent videos and then eat Vietnamese soup after Magat?
Roni was asking her mother.

And what about the crabs?

Roni, undeterred, offered: Then what about tomorrow?

Paz shook her head. May duty ako bukas, anak.

I can take her, Hero said. Paz startled, as if she'd forgotten Hero was
there at all.

Cool! Roni said, and rushed through Magat's entrance, victorious.

Paz hesitated in front of the door. She likes the soup with tendon, she
said finally. The number one.

Hero nodded, then followed Paz into the store, all the way down the
center aisle toward the back, where propped on a milk carton was a large
balikbayan box full of small gray crabs, their claws a gradient blue, then
red at the tips. They jostled each other lazily, sometimes took a swipe.

Roni was already there, reaching her hand into the box. Hi, softy, she
was saying. Hi, softy.

Softy? Hero asked.

That's what I call them, Roni said.

A young woman wearing a checkered panyo over her hair came up to them from the back room. Kumusta ka na, Tita, she said to Paz. Mabuti, Paz replied, and returned the question.

Okay lang, the woman said, reaching out to tug at Roni's ponytail. Kumusta ka na, ading? You're getting so tall.

I'm the second shortest in my class, Roni said, then tugged her ponytail out of the woman's grasp and ran off toward the candy aisle.

The woman laughed, then looked up at Hero. Hi—?

Paz turned to Hero and said: This is Bebot. It's her family's store. Then she turned to Bebot. Ito si Geronima. Pamangkin ni Pol.

Oh! the woman said. Geronima? Tocaya ni Roni, pala!

What? Roni asked from the next aisle, without turning her head or even meeting their gaze. She was holding a bag of something called White Rabbit and a clear box of yema balls wrapped in yellow and red cellophane.

She's your tocaya, Bebot called. You have the same name.

Oh. Yeah. But I call her Hero.

Hero? Bebot repeated, laughing. Then she turned to Hero. So you're Tito Pol's niece! Are you just visiting from back home?

Hero nodded, then shook her head. No, I'm—I'm staying with them. Here.

Oh, good! How do you like it? Are you gonna work as a nurse like Auntie Pacita?

Paz interrupted to ask then, sorry, before she forgot, if they could have ten soft-shell crabs—and if they had any king crab legs, by any chance?

Bebot touched her hand to her face, said, Ay, hindi ko alam, we haven't had any lately. Let me check in the back with Dadong. Teka muna, Auntie, ha?

She quickly moved around them to the storage room in the back. Hero didn't know if she could thank Paz for her interruption, if she should even acknowledge that it had been an interruption, or if Paz had meant it to be one at all.

While they waited, Hero glanced toward the row of VHS and

cassette tapes of films and albums, most of them Filipino, some of them from Taiwan or Hong Kong, arranged on a shelf behind her. Someone was a fan of Nora Aunor—several of her films took prime place in the display: *Impossible Dream, And God Smiled at Me, Tatlong Taong Walang Diyos, 'Merika, Himala.* Hero stared at the cover of the last tape. Aunor with her hands clasped to her chest, staring upward.

Himala was the first film Hero saw after she'd gotten out of the camp, weighing less than ninety pounds, couldn't stand to be touched. Tita Soly had moved to Manila from Vigan with her two daughters around the same time that Hero had started college, and had told Hero to come over whenever she wanted, her door was always open. More than ten years had passed between that offer and the day that Hero showed up at her door in Caloocan, sure that she had the wrong address, that after this much time there'd be no way her mind would have remembered something as specific as Soly's address, not with everything that had been poured out of it since.

Tita Soly was the only one of the aunts Hero trusted. Maybe she wouldn't want to see her, Hero thought at the door, maybe she wouldn't even recognize her, considering they hadn't seen each other in more than a decade, considering the state she was in, but Tita Soly opened the door that day and cried out *NIMANG,* so loud it hurt her ears. Though it was possible Soly's voice hadn't been all that loud after all—at the time, all of Hero's skin had felt like an ear, any vibration that passed over it at a high enough frequency could have pierced it.

Soly had to tell Hero what year it was. The first day, Soly's boyfriend had given her arroz caldo and she'd thrown it all up, and they did that a few more times until she could finally keep it down. It was the beginning of a beginning. One of the first next lives. Hero stayed for two years. One of those hazy early non-days, she'd been on the sofa, wrapped in two old blankets dusted with Johnson's Baby Powder and the Gotas de Oro cologne that Soly must have been dousing her two daughters in, along with a ghost of Arpège, which Soly had worn even when Hero was still a child. It was a wordless comfort, to know that Soly still wore the perfume, and Hero lost whole weeks of her life to burying her face in those humid blankets, falling in and out of consciousness, letting that fleeting, furry wisp of sandalwood wrap her up in its arms. Soly didn't have maids or cooks or even a yaya for the kids, which was rare for anyone even moderately middle-class, and definitely rare for someone from a family like theirs. Just a labandera who came by once a week, an older woman from Ilocos Norte named Amalia who put a VHS tape in the machine one afternoon and told Hero, It's the new Nora Aunor, it came out—then cut herself off, didn't want to tell Hero when the film had come out in case it reminded Hero that she hadn't been around to go to the movies.

For two years, Hero slept in the living room alone—Soly had avoided making Hero stay in any room with a lockable door. Soly hid away in her own room, probably to call Hamin again and see if he or Concepcion would come get her, or visit, or at least talk to her. They never did. In those days it was difficult for Hero to differentiate between waking and sleep, so she wasn't sure how much of *Himala* she dreamt up, and how much of it was really in the film. There aren't any miracles, Elsa said to the crowd. Walang himala. Sometimes in Hero's dream she was Elsa; sometimes she was the friend; sometimes she was just another person in the crowd, waiting her turn.

Mas gusto ko si Sharon Cuneta, Paz said, and yanked Hero back into the world.

Hero turned her head dumbly in the direction of Paz's voice—still in Caloocan, still wrapped in powdered blankets, the new metal plates cold inside her hands, Tita Soly shouting on the phone in another room, alternating Ilocano with English when one language couldn't contain her anger, JUST *TALK* TO HER, HAMIN—

And then Paz was standing in front of her, in Milpitas, lifting a bag of live crabs.

I prefer Sharon Cuneta, she repeated, pointing with her lips to the cover of *Sharon*. The young woman on it was smiling, light-skinned, and rosy-cheeked. Then she moved in front of Hero's body, blocking her view, and opened her wallet to pay.

Those early months in California, the person Hero felt most comfortable around was, of course, Pol. She'd always adored him, even when she was a kid in Vigan. He was the one who first showed her American and European movies, the one who let her borrow from the collection of Harvard Classics he'd amassed in the De Vera home. When she was ten years old, she'd asked Pol if she could borrow some of his cologne. When asked what she wanted to use it for, she replied, I want to wear it. To which Pol replied, smiling, Do you want to learn how to play pusoy, too? Hero shrugged and said, If you'll teach me. Pol had liked that answer.

A few weeks later, he gave her a brand-new bottle of the Tabac, with which she later liberally anointed herself and all of her possessions. She carried that small white ceramic amphora-shaped bottle with her until it ran out, and then she bought another one with her pocket money. It didn't quite smell on her skin the way it smelled on Pol's; what it became on her was hers alone. She even liked the stinging burn it lifted up from her skin on first contact; it felt like the liquid was doing something to her—something that rearranged her cells, down to the very atoms, making the whole of her different, and in making her different, making her more herself.

Not long after she began wearing Tabac, Concepcion complained to Pol about the smell; not only that she smelled like a man, but a particular type of man, a babaero. An adolescent girl, smelling like a playboy, it was unthinkable.

Pol replied, still smiling: Babaer*a*.

Concepcion pressed her lips together. Manong. Please don't even joke about that.

When Hero decided to go to University of Santo Tomas to become a surgeon like Tito Pol, he'd been the first person she'd told, and the only one who was openly pleased by the news. Her parents, on the other hand, had mixed feelings. Concepcion was unequivocally against the idea, found the profession unbecoming of a woman, not least of all a

De Vera woman. A pediatrician, perhaps; an ob-gyn, better, or at least a general practitioner. A dermatologist or a dentist would have also been acceptable. But choosing the punishing hours of the surgeon's life, entering into its traditionally, and appropriately, masculine world—absurd. Most of the De Veras of their generation were coercing at least one of their children to take up law, if only to prepare to fight the future of land reform, the inevitable battle all the older families would eventually have to wage to keep the land they told each other was their birthright.

It was the way Pol so easily said *babaera* that told Hero that Pol knew something about her, something Hero herself was only just starting to sense the shape of. It was just a feeling. Just the way he knew what to ask, what not to ask, how to skirt around a tender spot, which pronouns to avoid when he was speaking in English about some hypothetical lover of hers, and how to switch languages at the right point in a sentence in order to take advantage of the lack of pronouns in Tagalog or Ilocano.

Soon after Hero entered high school, Pol got married and moved to Indonesia to open up a rehabilitation clinic for children with polio, under the auspices of the World Health Organization, and in all likelihood the good graces of the current president, who was the cousin of Pol's new wife, a mestiza beauty from Ilocos Norte, sosyal in all the ways Pol had never been. Pol's departure only heightened Hero's desire to become a surgeon herself.

Hero had heard the story: Tito Pol decided to become an orthopedic surgeon after the death of his mother from spinal tuberculosis. The kind of knowledge he'd acquired through his job was precisely the kind of knowledge that would have saved her. Hero's famously beautiful tsinay grandmother, her namesake, the original Geronima De Vera, née Chua, was the descendant of upper-middle-class sangley mestizos, their ancestors Hokkien-speaking merchants who'd made their wealth in the Philippines during the colonial period. They'd remained, intermarried, became that curious new thing: the Filipino. Famously beautiful meant she was white-white-white, practically lavender, or at least she appeared so in the retrato of her that hung in the De Vera home.

Once Hero got into UST, she only intermittently saw Tito Pol,

finding reasons to skip the Christmases and Piesta dagiti Natay celebra-
tions, avoiding her parents, with whom she spoke less and less. In the
Philippines, she'd see him once, just once, after dropping out of UST.
She'd needed a place to hide outside of Manila, before she went into the
mountains for good. The first person who came to mind was Pol.
The only person.

In the middle of the night, Ka Eddie brought her to Tito Pol's large
house in Caranglaan, Dagupan City, close to Nazareth Hospital where
he had begun working. A large house, but nowhere near as large or as
imposing as the De Vera house in Vigan, or even the bungalow Tito Pol
had bought in Quezon City, along Sampaloc Avenue, though by Hero's
time the street was called Tomás Morató Avenue. Hero didn't know Dagupan or Pangasinan at all; she'd gone straight from Vigan to Manila for
college, no real stops along the way. She wasn't even sure if the address
was right, and the narrow street offered no clues. But the minute they
pulled up, Tito Pol opened the steel grating in front of his door, like he'd
been watching from the window. Didn't hesitate, didn't even look at
them closely, didn't look around to see if they'd been followed, if he was
in the sight lines of anyone. Just said, waving his hand like they were late
for dinner: Come in, come in.

When only Hero got out of the car, Eddie keeping his hands on the
wheel, Tito Pol left the doorway to approach them, making to help Hero
with her bags. There weren't any bags. She put her hands in her pockets.
Eddie had a look of visible shock on his face at the sight of Pol coming
out to help, and not a maid or houseboy.

By that point she'd only known Eddie for a year; he'd been the one to
regularly accompany Teresa on her recruitment trips to the universities
in Manila, her second-in-command. Hero had taken a liking to him
right away. Eddie had been just a teenager when he'd joined the New
People's Army in Isabela. He'd grown up on a small island just off the
coast of Palanan town, an area that the Agta people had designated as
sacred and used for marriage rituals. When Eddie turned fourteen, the
family of an important Isabela province politician purchased the island
by pushing through legislation with the Bureau of Lands of the Regional

Department of Environment and Natural Resources that declared the island *alienable and disposable*. Eddie and his family, along with nearly all of his neighbors, had paid taxes on their land for years, but they possessed no documents showing proof of ownership of the land there; Eddie's parents hadn't been able to read or write. The island was subsequently vacated, then renamed in honor of the politician's family, who built private holiday cottages all along its coastline.

Early on Hero had remarked that she and Eddie shared a similarly brutal and deflating sense of humor, which expressed itself in contrary yet complementary ways: whereas Hero would speak gruffly, unadorned, Eddie had a deliberate, flamboyant way about him, rakish and bitchy, pointing randomly at students sitting cross-legged on the floor of a common room in Hero's UST dorm and picking on them to SPEAK UP, BATCHOY, I can't hear you! Years later, Eddie told her that he didn't believe in student recruitment; he doubted the sincerity of the kids who'd been inspired by the First Quarter Storm, by martial law. Most of the people in Isabela were people who'd been part of the resistance long before Marcos ever happened on the scene. Eddie let Hero know, grinning, that she was by no means an exception to his suspicion.

Of all the people she'd lived with in her time in Isabela, it was Eddie who made her feel what it might have been like to have an older brother. Eddie, singing Trio Los Panchos songs, understanding only the lyrics, not the language. The band had visited Manila in the late fifties and early sixties, performing in Araneta Coliseum; Hero had asked Eddie if he'd been there himself, and he'd only laughed at her. Nobody dared to confront Eddie for singing in Spanish, but even if they did, Hero knew what Eddie would have said: the trio were from New York, from Puerto Rico, from Mexico. That meant they were practically Filipino. For so many nights, it was Eddie's voice that lit the way home for her, climbing up a cut of the mountain with burning thighs and hearing him sing Filipinas by Trio Los Panchos, the high ironic flourishes of his warble never quite masking the low filial murmur of his hum.

Tito Pol leaned over the half-rolled-down driver's side window. Salamat, pare, he said.

Eddie swallowed, shook his head. He said in Tagalog that Hero knew was usually so polished, so full of flourishes, self-taught just like his near-perfect literary English, but which now was staccato-shaky and nervous—that he had to go.

Pol intimated, also in Tagalog, You don't need a place to—?

Eddie shook his head. He didn't move his hands from the wheel, as if he thought that looking too long at Pol, or even talking to him, might be contaminating.

I have a place to stay for tonight. It's better if we're not together. We'll pick her up at dawn, Eddie said.

Once inside the house, Hero recognized Pol's taste everywhere: the paintings of cockfighters and pastoral mothers holding children, a print of an Amorsolo and probably an original Paco Gorospe, heavy molave chairs, a burnay jar from Vigan, abel table runners, a wall packed with books. A screen door creaked open; it was one of the maids, entering the house from the outdoor dirty-kitchen where all the food for the household was cooked.

Good evening, sir, good evening, ma'am, she greeted in English. Good evening, Hero murmured.

The maid's face asked silent a question of Pol. Are you hungry? Pol asked Hero.

Hero shook her head. The maid approached, searching for the bags she would help carry. Pol told the maid in Ilocano that Hero didn't have any bags.

It was almost completely dark in the house; Hero could barely see Pol's face, standing in the doorway. She couldn't tell if he'd aged or not. He smelled the same.

Do you want me to call your parents, Pol asked, in Ilocano.

Hero shook her head. They won't want to talk to me.

All her life she knew her Ilocano had an odd accent; it was the side effect of her mother having never really made the effort to speak or even learn her husband's language. Hamin and Concepcion had met at a party in Manila, and she'd charmed him by insulting Ilocanos with a cliché— her very first words to him were: You're Ilocano, so that means you're stingy. She'd dared to use the word that followed Ilocanos around wherever they went: kuripot. It rattled and stung the austere pride of the rest of the De Veras when they heard the story later, but apparently it'd worked for Hamin.

Hamin was by far the most taciturn of the three brothers, the least capable of living up to the De Vera name, lacking entirely the aura of charm that Melchior and later Pol built up around their family. Hamin was the sibling least suited to his family's grandeur and thus became most zealous about upholding its reputation. But perhaps only in his choice of spouse had Hamin been honest with himself: He'd have preferred to be a manileño. He'd have preferred to be born to other people. It was inevitable, then, that Hamin and Pol would be alien to each other: the idea of wanting to be from Manila, the idea of wanting to be anything but what they were, was anathema to Pol, who stood outside his family but never stood apart from it.

The De Veras descended from a tangle of Spanish landowners, Hokkien merchants, and, most thickly and undeniably, native Ilocanos. Prospective brides always weighed the appealing wealth of De Vera men against their less appealing darkness. Despite all the Tabac and three-piece suits, they couldn't shake or spend away that unmistakable, mutinous look of the indio. It was a look that reproduced itself defiantly throughout the generations, no matter how many button-nosed and auburn-haired mestizas were ushered into the family. The order of the De Vera siblings went: Aurora, Melchior, Benjamin, Escolastica, Remedios, Rosalina, Apolonio, Soledad. Or rather: Orang, Mel, Hamin, Ticay, Reme, Rosa, Pol, Soly. After Rosalina, there had been another daughter, Apolonia, but she'd died not long after birth. They'd lost the girl, but saved her name.

Pol was the family's youngest and therefore most indulged boy. Yet, contrary to his position, he often became more, not less, commanding in Hamin's presence, playing the older brother to his older brother. It was another reason they'd never really gotten along. Pol liked to cultivate his image as a debonair, intellectual Don Juan de Ilocos, pomaded and rakish in surgeon-white, slipping into a Fiat with the top down. Yet around his brother, the mildest discussion of money or religion would make Pol lose the slink of his hip, and suddenly he was shrewd and unsubtle, rejecting some catechism of Hamin's and quoting Bertrand Russell.

We'll make them talk to you, Pol was saying.

Hero shook her head again.

Pol paused, considering his words. Nimang. Are you sure?

Hero knew that he wasn't talking about whether or not she was sure that she didn't want to speak to her parents. She looked down at the floor, the cold lacquered tiles she could feel but not see, the gleam a temperature more than a look. They weren't in Vigan, so the tiles weren't Vigan terra-cotta tiles, not exactly; but they were close enough. She knew their kind. The feet that tread on them, the world they held up. Pol was in all likelihood still going to parties at Malacañang Palace.

I'm sure.

Tito Pol didn't say anything for a long time, and then: You always have a home with me.

Hero wiped a hand over her face, just to do something with her hands, with her face.

That was answer enough for Pol. Get some sleep, he said. I'll wake you up when they arrive.

In the morning, Teresa and Eddie came to the house, just as scheduled. Tito Pol gave Hero a leather wallet, lightly used. She didn't have to open it to know there were several thousand pesos in it. It was too big to put in her pocket, so she held it behind her back, awkwardly.

Eddie was watching the conversation, or the wallet. Teresa was smoking, flicking ash out of the window, gaze averted. Wanted to look like she wasn't watching or listening, but the feline direction of Teresa's ear gave it away.

Pol put a hand on Hero's face, drew her into his arms. Tabac, faded. He hadn't reapplied any cologne in the morning. His hair was still neatly parted, but looser, a strand falling over his forehead; he hadn't reapplied his pomade, either. He'd stayed up, maybe waited by the window. He'd smoked, more than once.

Apo Dios ti kumuyog kenka, he intoned.

It was an ancient thing to say, rare, formal, embarrassing. She opened her mouth to joke her way out of it, but Pol pulled back and held her face in his hands. Then, with the gravity of a prayer as uttered by one who knew that a prayer could also be an important kind of lie, he said to her, in English: You're a De Vera. You always will be.

Milpitas

WHEN IT CAME TO RONI'S ECZEMA, PAZ AND HER
mother had given up on doing the healing themselves. Roni's case was too
advanced for a bruha of Grandma Sisang's modest caliber, chicken blood or
not. Paz's mother started calling in all of her contacts and all of her favors,
all the faith healers and bruhas she knew, or knew of, in the Bay Area.

The first faith healer who called back lived in Hayward. She was only
available at two-thirty in the afternoon on a Thursday, just after Roni's
school day. Pol would still be sleeping at that time, and Paz didn't get off
her first shift at the Veterans Hospital until four, and she then went
straight to the nursing home, which left Hero to take her.

The day of the appointment, Hero was afraid she would find Roni
fighting again. But the girl filed out of the classroom with the rest of her
peers, speaking to two girls, one of whom looked Filipina, the other of
whom looked maybe Mexican; Hero still wasn't entirely sure how to tell
where all the people she saw in Milpitas came from.

Roni waved good-bye to her friends, then watched them join their
parents. She waited in place for a few minutes; the girl cut a glance in
Hero's direction, just for a moment, before returning her gaze to her
friends' backs. Hero stayed put.

The parking lot gradually emptied, as most of the children had been
picked up. Only then did Roni relax her shoulders and begin walking
toward the car.

Hero understood finally that Roni's aim was to avoid her classmates seeing her in the Corona. Once, when they were in the parking lot of the other
large Asian grocery store in town, Lion's, Roni even threw herself down
into the footwell of the front passenger seat. What are you—Hero said, and
Roni interrupted with an impatient, Just wait a minute, just wait a minute!

Hero paused, hands still on the steering wheel, and watched a woman
and a young girl exit the supermarket and put away their metal shopping
cart. Hero vaguely recognized the girl from Roni's school. They made

their way into the parking lot, disappearing eventually among the cars. Roni slowly lifted her head, so only her bangs and eyes were visible above the window. Okay, she said finally. Let's go.

Hero found it all somewhat ridiculous—didn't everyone know by now that the Corona belonged to her family? But maybe Roni wasn't used to the Corona picking her up directly at school; after all, before Hero arrived in Milpitas, Roni was used to being picked up from school by aunts or cousins, or Pol only after he woke up, long after the rest of her classmates had left.

It was strange to have respect for a child, and stranger still to lose respect for one. With all her toothsome pride, Hero would have expected Roni to be above that kind of embarrassment. That she wasn't somehow irritated Hero.

When Roni was folded into the footwell, she asked Hero, What's up with your thumbs?

Hero stiffened, looked down at her thumbs on the steering wheel, their positioning. From where Roni was seated, the angle of her gaze meant she could see the knobbled bones in the base of Hero's thumbs.

Roni continued: I saw them before. Are you double-jointed or something?

Yes, Hero said, trying to sound easy, casual.

Roni considered that for a moment, then extended her own small hand. Wiggled her thumb around, making the base joint pop freely. Me, too.

Hero looked down at the child's thumb, articulate and flexible. She couldn't think of anything easy or casual to say about it.

Your friend and her mom are gone now. As expected, Roni forgot all about Hero's thumbs as she climbed out of the footwell and started chatting again.

In Hayward, the woman who opened the mosquito-screen door to them was about Paz's age, somewhere in her midthirties. Behind her, a small dog was shrieking. Elvis, quiet! Elvis, quiet! Then the woman smiled apologetically at Hero, then at Roni. Sorry, come in, come in.

The furniture in the small home was covered with plastic. Figurines of elephants, all of them with their trunks raised, were placed all over the house; they came in different sizes. There was a large one next to the door, and a series of smaller ones, in gradually increasing sizes, perched atop the television. Some of them were made of wood or ceramic; one small one on a fireplace mantel looked like it was made of low-quality jade. On the walls there were portraits of the Virgin Mary everywhere: full-body, reaching out a hand to the viewer; on a cloud, hands folded, looking upward pleadingly; just her preternaturally youthful face, white and beloved. There was also one standard portrait of Jesus: long hair flowing over his shoulders, his red heart open, encircled with thorns and topped with a tongue of flame.

I'm Melba, the woman said, holding her hand over her heart. Are you Paz?

Hero shook her head. No, no, I'm Geronima, Paz's niece. Roni is my cousin.

Ah, okay, I see, Melba said. Now she turned her attention to Roni. And you must be Roni.

Roni was looking at one of the elephant figurines with interest. The small dog was sniffing at her feet; she paid it no mind. She turned back to Melba, then nodded.

Gutom ka ba, Roni? You want something to eat? We have cookies—

Roni brightened. Cookies?

Melba laughed and led the way to the kitchen. Hero hesitated, then followed them. In the kitchen, there was a large portrait of the Last Supper hung above the dining table, which was covered with a plastic tablecloth patterned with grapevines and bunches of grapes.

Anong gusto mo? You like chocolate chip? Or peanut butter?

Both!

Hero turned to her, fast, embarrassed. Roni—

Melba opened two packages without blinking an eye; a blue Chips Ahoy! package, and a transparent package of peanut butter sandwich cookies, off-brand. There you go, Melba said.

Thank you, Roni chirped, stuffing her face with a sandwich cookie.

Melba turned to Hero and began speaking to her in Pangasinan, a long sentence that sounded inviting, conspiratorial.

Hero held up a hand and said, Sorry po, sorry, I don't understand.

Melba stopped and held up her hands in apology. Oh, sorry! Were you born here, too?

Hero shook her head. No, I—I'm Roni's cousin on her dad's side.

Oh! It's because you said you were Paz's niece, kasi. Sorry. Then Melba pushed the package of Chips Ahoy! across the table to Hero. Ikaw mo, have some.

Hero had never really liked sweets, and had especially never liked American sweets. But Melba was smiling encouragingly, so Hero dutifully took one of the cookies from the package, along with the paper towel Melba handed her, to put it on. Salamat po, she forced herself to say, and ate.

Hero wasn't sure how the whole process worked, and she had been too self-conscious to ask Paz for details beforehand. She had the feeling her ignorance would come off as superiority to Paz, and she wanted to avoid the obvious: that she had no exposure to these types of things because she was from a different class, that she remembered friends of hers in college making jokes about probinsyanas and their hexes. Hero's own childhood eczema had gone away when she was in college; she never knew why, and she'd never questioned it. Most people she knew outgrew it. Her father had had severe eczema in the webbing of his hands and feet. Pol gave him various creams, which sometimes worked. None of them worked as well as mashed coconut flesh and petroleum jelly, used as a kind of poultice, which Hero's yaya Lulay had prescribed, until Concepcion put a stop to it; the smell of fatty coconut on her husband's hands nauseated her.

The people Hero grew up around generally ridiculed faith healing, loathed the camphoraceous smell of Efficascent oil, used by all the worst quacks, that would remain on a yaya's hands whenever she came back from a visit to her country family. Hero remembered even Pol speaking as a physician, frustrated at the prospect of the people, mostly poor, being preyed on and deluded. But even Americans and Europeans came in droves to visit faith healers. The ones with the most international fame tended to be the men who called themselves psychic surgeons, who claimed to remove imaginary toxins and parasites from the bodies of their patients. White people always thought they were full of toxins, so you could make a lot of money just by claiming to be able to remove them.

There were stories Teresa told the cadres, about the early days of American health in the Philippines. Paul Freer, the first dean of the Philippine Medical School, met with W. Cameron Forbes, the governor-general of the Philippines in 1913, to show Forbes one of the newer medical schools in the colony. Freer showed Forbes what the governor-general later described in his journals as *a rather gruesome dissection,* then declared to Forbes that the first hundred autopsies on Filipino bodies—oh, just the first hundred! Eddie always interrupted—had proven beyond a shadow of a doubt that the natives were inherently unhealthy, prone to all manner of plagues, cankers, and skin disorders. This frailty meant they were constitutionally underequipped for physical labor. Worse, there was a danger they would spread their infirmity to whites. Emily Bronson Conger, a nurse from Ohio who'd spent time in the Philippines, Hawaii, and Japan, wrote woefully that she wanted to *dip them into some cleaning cauldron.* Edith Moses, the wife of Bernard Moses, then-secretary of public instruction and member of President Taft's Second Philippine Commission, used to hose off her servants with disinfectants, during the cholera wave of 1902. *The trained baboons and monkeylike coolies needed to be house-trained,* she said of the young boys who polished with burlap the narra wood floors of her home on the shores of Manila Bay, facing Corregidor.

American guards told Moses to be wary, too, of the fiestas the natives loved to throw, especially in the streets: the contact with the crowd, the distracting lights, the pungent smells—and most of all, the risk that such parties carried within them the potential for revolt. *I think our guard was rather disappointed that the fiesta went off without any trouble; one of the boys told me he was "aching for a scrap," but another said he didn't want "to kill no niggers, they hadn't done nothing to him." It is a miserable life—that of a soldier in peace— and I don't wonder these boys would like to see a little active service,* Moses wrote in a letter, which Teresa read aloud to the cadres from a tattered hardback book, the cover of which was missing.

One thing was clear: the locals had to be cleansed before anything could be done with them. Inspections, experiments, education, regulation; medical schools and rigorous training. Perhaps that obsession with cleanliness was part of why Americans invented the water cure in the Philippines, Teresa suggested. She used to point out Tanauan on maps of Luzon, her finger encircling the whole province of Batangas. She would tell the cadres:

They put the men on their backs. There would be one American soldier to stand on each limb, to keep the man down. They put a stick in his mouth to keep it open, and poured a pail of water directly into the mouth and nostrils. If the men didn't start talking by then, then another pail, then another. Then another.

Victor G. Heiser, a Pennsylvania doctor who'd survived the Johnstown Flood of 1889 and became the Philippine Director of Health in 1902, declared that his project was to *wash up the Orient*. It was Heiser who came up with the condition called philippinitis. According to him, symptoms included *mental and physical torpor, forgetfulness, irritability, lack of ambition, aversion to any form of exercise*. Heiser had a mental and physical breakdown in 1908, and placed the blame on his dealings with Filipinos, the Herculean effort of converting them into people.

After Teresa finished those lectures, cadres who didn't want to do their share of clean-up duty or night patrol would joke: Kumander, may philippinitis ako kasi eh—

Teresa would grin. Mabuti walang gamot. Good thing there's no cure.

From what Hero observed, Roni was smeared generously with something that smelled minty-sweet and burnt, like plastic; a mixture of holy water, Efficascent oil, and Vaseline. Melba didn't ask Roni any questions but kept her eyes closed, listening for a voice that Roni gave no sign of being able to hear. Sometimes Roni opened one greasy eye and caught Hero's gaze. She stuck her tongue out. Hero tried to school her face into a scold and failed. Melba didn't notice.

Afterward, Melba said it was difficult to tell what was wrong with the girl, but she would find some creams and waters they could take home, if they would just wait in the living room. When they were alone, Roni got up from the love seat she'd been sharing with Melba, and joined Hero on the bigger couch, the plastic cover squeaking beneath them.

Hero nudged her. Oi. Kumusta?

Roni shrugged, looking down.

Hero tilted her head in mock-appraisal, bent down to take a closer look. So what, all-healed ka na?

Roni burst into laughter, relaxing for the first time since Hero had picked her up from school.

Yeah, it's aaaaalllll better now, she replied, the greased scars around her mouth stretching wide.

It turned out Melba couldn't really heal Roni, or even begin to try; she wasn't strong enough of a bruha. What Roni needed someone whose powers had wider radius, someone who could speak and listen and hurt across distances. The source of Roni's illness was too distant, too clever. If it was a curse you were dealing with, the radius was necessary. Melba was pretty sure it was a curse; her theory was that someone had been jealous of Paz, perhaps someone who had known her growing up, some-one still in the Philippines, reaching out to take revenge through Roni's body. That meant it was trickier than dealing with a kapre or even an engkanto. Human cause was always more dangerous. Engkantos, at least, could be negotiated with. They had ethics.

Melba gave them the number of a woman in San Jose who might be able to help. I don't know how much she still does this; matanda siya kasi, she's old now. She might be retired already. But call her. If you can't see her within a month, come back to me. We'll try again. Ingat kayo, ha? Roni, take some cookies with you, here, here.

In the car on the way home, Hero noticed Roni staring at her. What, Hero said, trying to keep her eyes on the wide California roads, having already learned that most of them were potholed, uneven, not all that different from roads in the Philippines.

Roni asked, How come you always forget to put on your seat belt?

They were on 880 North, going seventy miles an hour. Hero looked down at herself quickly, even though she knew what she would see. I forgot, she said.

Papa's the same, Roni said, already leaning over.

No, no, stay there, I'll do it, Hero said. She held on to the steering wheel with one hand, then shrugged on the seat belt so it hung loosely over her left arm, like a suspender or gun holster. She tried to pull it across her body, but the car jerked, and began to drift toward the lane divider. So she left it, lodged in her armpit.

Roni didn't look amused. Papa leaves it like that, too, she said.

She leaned forward again, stretching her own belt taut. She grabbed onto Hero's seat belt, yanked it down hard, so that the stiff, smooth belt cut uncomfortably into Hero's neck. She tilted her head back, put her hands back on the wheel to steady the car's path. Then a click; fastened.

Thank you, Hero said, craning her neck to get away from the tight fit.

Roni leaned up, tugged on the belt to give it some slack. Hero relaxed.

Thank you, she said again, meaning it this time.

They teach you this kinda stuff in school, Roni said, leaning back into the seat, her cursed face smug.

It's good that you eat a lot, Hero said to Roni one day, after she'd cooked her own corned beef properly, sitting down to join the girl, who was eating her own corned beef straight out of the can so it was still viscera-red and cold. When I wasn't much older than you, I knew girls who dieted.

'Cause you diet, huh, Roni said.

Hero blinked. No, she said.

Yeah-huh. Roni was eating with her hands again, her left leg tucked under her, her right leg propped up so her right arm rested on her right knee. She scooped a mound of rice and pink beef into her mouth. Chewed, then swallowed and said, I used to not eat.

Hero paused, her fingers curled around a ready mouthful of food. What do you mean?

Roni replied while eating, so Hero could see the pinkish-brown meat being chewed by her back teeth. *A year ago, I only ate Nestlé baby milk.*

Formula, she meant. For the first four or five years of her life, not all that long before Hero arrived in California, Roni had been given nothing to eat but canned baby formula, usually Nestlé brand. At the time, she was being raised by Paz alone; Pol hadn't come over to live with them in California permanently but shuttled between the Philippines and Milpitas, six months here, six months there, still in denial about the new chapter of his life. Paz and Roni were living in the apartment on San Petra Court where Gloria, Carmen, and Paz's mother now lived, just off Junipero Drive. It was on the side of the town closest to the county penitentiary and the run-down shopping plaza, Serra Center, with its movie theater, dollar store, and Vietnamese restaurant. Paz's petition for Grandma Sisang had come through, and she had only recently arrived. Her father Vicente's long years of service as a clerk for the American army in Guam were about to come to fruition: he was finally going to get citizenship, and most of her younger siblings would arrive shortly after. Paz had been naturalized a few years before Roni's birth.

But in those early, early California years, it was just the four of them—Paz, Carmen, Grandma Sisang, and Roni—living in the small apartment for half of the year. When Pol was around for the other half, they gave the bedroom to him and Paz, with Roni sleeping sometimes in the bed with them, and, later, in a secondhand crib. When Pol left for the Philippines again, Grandma Sisang and Carmen took back the bedroom, and Paz and Roni slept in the living room; Roni on the couch, Paz on the floor. The floor was carpeted with shag, at least. When Vicente's citizenship came through, Gloria and Boyet were the next to arrive in California, taking up residence on the living-room floor. Lerma was just waiting to finish nursing school, and then she'd be on her way, too. They were running out of space on the floor. Carmen joked that Lerma could sleep on the kitchen table, like a rack of lechon.

When Paz and Pol heard about the house lottery in the new neighborhood being built in Milpitas, just off of the 680 interstate, the whole thing sounded like a dream. By that time, Pol was inching closer and closer to staying permanently in California. Paz knew a real house would help matters along.

The night before the lottery, Paz and Pol slept in the car outside the plot of land where the new neighborhood was going up, just so they would be there first thing in the morning for the draw. They were parked in a line with other cars, full of young Mexican and Filipino families doing the exact same thing. They left Roni, then just a toddler, with Carmen, who dropped her; just once, lightly. She never told anyone. Grandma Sisang saw it happen, but didn't tell anyone, either. By the time Paz and Pol came home, they had a down payment on a house and Roni had a fading bruise on her hip, indistinct against the eczema that was already there. Her parents, in their euphoria, never noticed. By the time they moved into the new house, Roni had been living on Nestlé formula for four years.

Hero remembered the Nestlé campaign. She'd never intended to become an ob-gyn, so perhaps she'd avoided the worst of the push, but she distinctly remembered fellow students being encouraged to discredit breast-feeding. They were taught the science of Nestlé formula, and interns and residents were used to the spiel, how to get new mothers hooked on the formula with a decent amount of intimidation and a free trial. Just mix with water. Easy enough. Easy enough, despite the fact that many of the poorer women they'd recommended the formula to lacked access to clean water. The campaign must have been in full swing during the last of Paz's years in the Philippines, so she would have missed the boycotts organized much later: the poor directions, the contaminated water, the children who died. All Paz would have known when she got pregnant in California was that she had to make sure she could get her hands on some Nestlé.

It was a miracle Roni's teeth were growing in normally, if somewhat crooked and slow. In an attempt to wean her daughter off the formula— busy as she was, it took her awhile to realize that she was going to have to start feeding the child solid foods—Paz started to hide the formula cans, replacing them with other kinds of food, the kinds of food Roni should have been eating for years. Mashed peas, mashed carrots, mashed apples.

Roni stopped eating entirely. One day, after days of only feigning to eat, the girl fainted, gaunt as a cricket and ice-cold to the touch. Paz and

Pol—the collapse must have occurred during the Californian part of his year—rushed her to the hospital, where she was fed intravenously. It was the first non-formula meal of her life.

Hero said, What do you mean, you only ate baby milk?

Roni just shrugged.

It tasted pretty good, she just said, which wasn't an explanation. But she didn't mean to give one, and Hero didn't know how to ask for one.

During the day, when Roni was at school, Paz was at work, and Pol was asleep, Hero cleaned the house.

Paz had never asked her to, though Hero had seen her lose her temper a few times about the state of the house, especially when Roni ran through it without her tsinelas, the bottoms of her bare feet nearly black with greasy dust.

Paz's temper was at its worst in the evenings, and especially on her rare days off. She didn't know what to do with herself on days off, and spent them looking around the house, being alternately shamed and irritated by the mess, starting to clean, and then stopping halfway through, usually by starting a fight with Roni, or Pol, or sometimes her sister Gloria if she was dropping off food or asking to borrow some money for her husband. The bones of the house, pretty enough but built hastily for the town's rapidly expanding population, didn't hold up well to neglect. It wasn't like the De Vera mansion, the antique bones of which meant that even a mess came off as eclectic—not that the De Veras' servants ever let the house get messy. The house in Milpitas needed constant tidying in order to look decent. Hero offered to clean. Paz refused, at first, but Pol talked her into it.

You'll be less stressed, he said. Gloria doesn't live here anymore, and she works now. Nimang has the time.

Paz's mouth firmed at that. It looked like another thing she didn't want Hero to know; that Gloria cleaned the house for Paz, that Gloria had lived in the house. But Hero knew that she wasn't the first relative— the first relative of Paz's, at least—to stay with them; sometimes, when they mentioned a sister or cousin of Paz's, they said things like, When they were here, or She left it in that room, or She used to. Chronically messy though it might be, the house had enough space to house any relative who needed a refuge, temporary or permanent.

Pol offered to give Hero pocket money to clean the house. You can go to the movies more, he reasoned. She hadn't gone to the movies once since arriving in Milpitas, and it hadn't occurred to her that she should start. Hero hadn't even considered that they might pay her for the work; it was the least she could do in return for everything they'd already done for her.

So during the day, she cleaned. She thought that after one week she'd run out of things to clean, never having cleaned a house before, but she found out how wrong she was after three days. There was never any end to cleaning, especially in the kitchen, where the family spent most of their time. Even with Paz and Pol only cooking from time to time, and Gloria only occasionally using the kitchen herself—most of the time Gloria brought already cooked food to the house—the floor needed constant mopping to prevent it from looking dingy and greasy.

During one of those cleaning sessions, Hero entered Paz and Pol's bedroom for the first time, where in fact, Roni also slept. Even though one of the bedrooms in the house was ostensibly for Roni, Hero had soon noticed that Roni never slept in it, never even went inside. On rare occasions, she did her homework in that room, especially late at night when it was too cold in the kitchen or the living room, or she was in one of her moods and wanted to be alone; but when it came time to sleep, she always gathered herself together and slinked off to the master bedroom.

Hero had wanted her own room when she was even younger than Roni, a space of her own to retreat to. There had always been more than enough space, both in the De Vera home and in the nearby villa Hamin moved them to later, just before she entered high school, just as he was beginning his political career. A councilman should have his own home, he thought, even if he laid claim to the De Vera name. The minute Hero asked for her own room, she got it. She'd never considered the possibility of sleeping in the same room as her parents. She couldn't imagine not having enough space, like in Paz and Pol's first apartment; equally, she couldn't imagine having the space and not being able to get used to it.

Not being able to stand the distance. She couldn't imagine even wanting that kind of intimacy, what having it might feel like.

Now Hero saw that the master bedroom, though larger than the bedroom Paz and Pol had given to her, wasn't all that deserving of its name. Though the reason why the room seemed so small was also because there were actually two beds in the room, pressed up against each other to form, essentially, one large super-bed. One of the beds was queen-sized; Pol and Paz's, Hero guessed. The other bed, closest to the window, was smaller, double-sized perhaps. When Hero pulled the fitted sheets back so she could wash them, she saw little reddish-brown pinpricks, which at first she thought was dirt, but when dusting it off did nothing, she leaned in closer and realized that they were traces of blood, there on the bed where in the middle of the night Roni might have unconsciously scratched an arm, or the back of a knee, or a neck.

Hero stripped the dirty sheets from the bed, carried them down to the garage, put them in the washing machine. When they were finished washing, she put them in the dryer. She moved like an automaton, staring at the machines as they rumbled and chimed. When the sheets were done, she went back upstairs to redo the two beds. Hero worked quickly, so that the bed was still body-warm when she was done. The tiny blood stains wouldn't wash out of the sheets; they must have been there for years already.

Every day when Hero finished cleaning, the joints in her hands sore, she would think that she'd have a minute to herself, get to catch another look at one of the American soap operas she'd unwittingly gotten caught up in after starting a tradition of turning on the television while she vacuumed—then she'd look at the clock on the microwave in the kitchen and realize it was time to pick Roni up from school.

She'd never known days as short as the ones in California; in Vigan, she remembered days that would never end, boredom while waiting for the next meal, lonely hours ticked away reading magazines. Pol noticed that she didn't want to read books anymore, and without asking about it, he said she was welcome to the issues of *Time* and *Newsweek* and *U.S. News and World Report* scattered around the house. Like a good subscriber, he read each week's news promptly, but kept the old issues around, especially for

Roni, who liked to look through them. Sometimes there would be an American gossip magazine that Hero would flip through, recognizing nobody; those were bought by Paz and read, Hero suspected, in the middle of the night.

Her own room was easy to keep clean because there was so little in it. The things Hero brought to Milpitas: A pack of Dunhill cigarettes, the foil still on it. Clothes Tita Soly gave her; some of them borrowed, some of them new, most of them oversized. A bottle of Tabac cologne. A bootleg cassette tape of Talk Talk's The Party's Over, bought on Recto Avenue after she'd been living with Tita Soly in Manila for a year, the first time she'd left the house on her own. Bought for the cover and the title, then listened to over and over and over. A cassette tape of songs recorded on the radio in Soly's kitchen: New Order, Ultravox, Go West, Fiction Factory, Friends Again. WXB 102.7 FM, *The Station That Dares to Be Different*. A packet of papers about thumb exercises.

No pictures, no letters, no keepsakes or heirlooms. Nothing from her parents. A few weeks after arriving in Milpitas, when there was nothing left to unpack, nothing left to busy her hurt hands with, nothing left to do but start trying to feel at home, Hero put everything but the clothes back in the suitcase under the bed and left them there.

Melba called the house one afternoon, when Hero had just brought Roni back from school. Hi, is this Pacita?

No, sorry, this is her niece. May I take a message?

It's Melba, you remember? You brought Roni to my house in Hayward— Oh—yes, yes. Kumusta po kayo?

Mabuti, mabuti. I'm just calling because I think I gave you the wrong number, last time. You know the old lady I told you about, in San Jose? I was wrong, they live in Milpitas.

Milpitas? Hero repeated. We live in Milpitas.

That's what I thought! Melba crowed. So it'll be really convenient for you guys. I'm gonna give you the phone number, okay? And you give it to Atse Pacita. Do you have a pen and paper?

Uh—yes—no, hold on, I'll get something. Roni? Roni? Can I borrow a pen and paper?

Roni looked up from the kitchen table where she was doing her homework. She tore a page out of her notebook and gave it to Hero, along with the pencil in her hands.

Hello? Yes? I have a pencil now.

Okay. The number is 408—

Hero wrote the number down, repeating each digit after Melba. Then the name of the older woman. Adela Cabugao.

When Paz called the number, Adela's daughter answered, and when Paz said who she was and what she was calling for, the daughter said, loud enough so that it echoed in the kitchen where Paz was sitting,

Pacita? Pacita Edades? Si Rhea 'to—

Rhea! Paz cried out.

It turned out Adela Cabugao was the mother of a former coworker of Paz's, back at San Jose Medical, and then at the nursing home. They'd lost touch after Rhea had started working at Kaiser.

It was Melba De La Cruz who gave us your number, Paz said.

Rhea made a sound that was like her voice, shrugging. She said Melba was nice, but didn't really know what she was doing, and she had the bad habit of thinking every illness was the result of a jealousy-fueled hex. She means well, she allowed. So anong nangyari sa Roni? She's sick?

Very sick, Paz said, her voice somber. Can Lola Adela help?

Bring her in, Rhea said. She gave Paz the address of the restaurant, which was where Adela and her husband usually spent their days. Just come in any afternoon, it's fine, you don't need to make an appointment or anything. She's usually available from two o'clock onward. Paz wrote the address down, saying thank you a few times in the process.

My daughter works at the Vietnamese salon next door to the restaurant, Rhea said. You remember Rosalyn?

Rosalyn! Paz exclaimed. I only met her once, when she was, oh, a kid. How old is Rosalyn now?

Twenty-six. Can you believe that? Still no boyfriend.

Twenty-six, wow, dalaga na.

But still no boyfriend. She broke up with Jaime. You remember Jaime?

Ah—mm—

I thought they were gonna get married. And you know JR? He's in high school already.

No kidding, wow. Lalaki siya.

He's so moody, Rhea laughed. Alam mo. Teenagers. Teka, how old is Roni now?

Seven years old, Paz said, hesitating.

I still remember when she was a baby, diyos ko. Did you do the fiesta for the seventh?

Paz went silent. Her face shuttered. Hero didn't know that the fiesta was something Paz had avoided thinking about: the lucky seventh birthday of any Filipino child, and the traditional big party that had to commemorate it. Paz wasn't thinking about it; she wasn't thinking about it. And when Roni's seventh birthday came and went and it was all too late, she wasn't thinking about it. They hadn't saved enough money to throw a big party by her seventh, anyway, so it was over, she wasn't thinking about it. Roni's eighth birthday was coming up in mid-February, not that many months away, and even though Paz wasn't thinking about it, she had come up with an idea, which was that she could throw Roni a double birthday, for both her seventh and eighth. Eight was a lucky number, too, she'd already reasoned to Pol.

So Paz kept on saving up for it, this party that should have already happened, without admitting to herself that it was what she was saving up for. There were enough things she had to save up for, so it was easy to say, This is for Carmen's lawyer, or This is for my mother, or This is for Rufina's petition, or This is for buying a used car for Nimang. If there was a soft, sirenalike voice in her that hummed, And this is for Roni's seventh-eighth birthday—she made sure to shut that voice up for its insolence, afraid that even thinking the thought would be punishable. Roni was alive past seven years old, that had to be enough; why tempt fate? But Paz couldn't put the idea of the party away.

On the phone to Rhea, she was half honest. Oh, she didn't want one

for her seventh, kasi eh. We're thinking of throwing her a big fiesta for
her eighth, na lang.

Rhea laughed. You need someone to cater?

Hero heard Paz and Pol fight for the first time, over the faith healers. Pol
had long declared them a waste of time that would only continue to drain
Roni's already erratic energy. It was cruel to drag her up and down every
Filipino house in the Bay Area, subjecting her to gossips and charlatans. All
for your superstitions, he said, the English word pointed and unsparing.

Paz didn't have a counterargument. On the way to work, she slammed
every door she met. She worked her normal sixteen hour days, occasionally even worked a twenty-four-hour shift, and when she came back
home at night, she slept on the couch.

For the next week, Paz didn't speak to Pol, though several times Hero
saw Pol lingering in the doorway of the bathroom or the entrance of the
kitchen, any room Paz was in, waiting for his wife to acknowledge his
presence. Pol didn't seem fazed; her recalcitrance, that tigas ng ulo spirit,
seemed to be one of the qualities that had attracted him to Paz in the first
place. Paz only faltered when she and Hero were alone; she didn't seem
sure whether or not she should include Hero in her freeze-out.

During those tight-lipped days Hero began to notice a peculiar slack-
ening of the entire left side of Paz's face, subtle at first and then more
serious as the week went on, until Hero came home with Roni in tow,
just after school was over, to find Pol and Paz in the kitchen. Paz was sitting still at the kitchen table as Pol hovered over her, gently squeezing
eyedrops into her left eye.

When he was done, Paz turned to face Hero and Roni, coming in
from the garage. Hero nearly ran into Roni, who'd frozen in place at the
sight of her mother. The left side of Paz's face was paralyzed, the weight
of her drooping cheek pulling down the raw pink socket of her left eye,
leaving it dry and bloodshot.

Huwag kang matakot, anak, Paz hurried to say to Roni through the pliant side of her mouth. Don't be scared. It's the same as before. It'll go away in a few days.

Pol didn't say anything, just replaced the cap on the bottle and took up a pack of tablets.

Roni stared at her mother, her entire body still. Hero moved around her, stepping fully into the kitchen, and took stock of the bottle of artificial tears, the pack of prednisone tablets.

Bell's palsy, Pol said, quiet.

Hero nodded. She was distantly familiar with it as a common side effect of the job, more common in nurses, nursing assistants, and ambulance workers than in doctors. Paz had a hand lifted to her chin, catching and wiping at a stream of drool from the left side of her mouth with her right hand. Her left arm was slack on her lap. Pol took up a paper towel and wiped at her chin.

That night, before Paz could make her bed on the couch, Hero saw Pol intercept her, taking up the extra pillow and blanket Paz had left there into his arms.

Even in her state, Paz managed to look stubborn. She sat down on the couch, prim, and stared up at Pol. Her sagging eye rebuked him.

Mahal, Pol tried. Still no movement.

Finally, Pol relented: If Roni says it's okay, then—okay. Let her go to the faith healers again next week. If she says it's okay.

Paz stood without breaking their gaze. Pol was reaching for her hand, knowing he'd said the magic words. On their way up the stairs, he kept a steadying hand on her left elbow, though it seemed as though feeling had already come back into her arm, that she'd been better for hours.

On the day Hero was supposed to take Roni to see Adela Cabugao, she didn't show up with the rest of her class after school. Hero's shoulders sank.

Hero got out of the car, bracing herself to drag the girl out of yet another fight. As she began to walk toward the yard where the fights usually took place, however, a white woman in a blue blouse with a Peter

Pan collar approached her, shielding her eyes from the sun. Excuse me? Are you Ms. De Vera? Roni's cousin? You're here to pick her up?

Hero froze. Uh, yes? I'm Hero—nima?

I'm Mrs. Waverley, Roni's teacher. Roni's in detention right now. She'll be out in an hour. She may be suspended for the rest of the week. Will Roni's parents be home this evening? I'll need to speak with them personally.

Hero found English words slow to come, prickly and heavy on her tongue. She tried her best. Detention? For an hour? What did she do?

Mrs. Waverly crossed her arms. I think it's best if I speak with her parents directly. Will they be available this evening?

Yes, Hero said, knowing at least Pol would be around before his shift. Yes, her father will be available.

Good, Mrs. Waverly said. She had brown hair she'd blow-dried then hairsprayed into a wavy bob, falling just at her chin. It made her look like one of the soap opera stars Hero sometimes saw in the afternoon, but much less successfully. She smelled strongly of perfume, something not all that dissimilar to something Hero remembered the De Vera women wearing, like No. 5 but with the volume turned up to a screech, creating a three-foot radius around the woman's body, a force field of scent. Hero took a step back in self-defense.

Roni will be out in an hour, the woman repeated more slowly, as if she thought Hero might not have understood the first time.

When Roni finally appeared in the parking lot, at the end of the hour, there were extra-wide Band-Aids on both of her knees. Hero was leaning against the hood of the car, which had long gone cool. Roni's hair had been taken out of its ponytail; she was in the middle of scraping it back into the elastic. When her hands were free, she waved. She looked perfectly at ease, even cheerful.

When the girl was close enough, Hero pushed herself off the car, bent down to take a look at Roni's knees. On the way there, she checked the rest of her; her face didn't have any new scratches on it, her arms didn't either. The same eczema scars, weeping a bit but that was normal.

What happened to your knees?

Roni grinned. That was when Hero saw it: one of her front teeth, a baby tooth next to the left canine, had been knocked clean out.

What—anía—what the hell happened to your teeth! Hero was too shocked to make it sound like a question.

Roni opened her mouth to explain, but then started laughing, and couldn't stop. She laughed and laughed, head tilted back, gappy teeth exposed, leathery lips on the verge of splitting with the strain of it.

I—huhhuhhuh—I—huhhuh—

Hero started to smile helplessly, just as a reflex, like yawning after seeing someone else yawn.

Uhhhhhhh, Roni began, still laughing, her eyes filmy-wet with tears. I started a war!

Hero blinked at her. A war? What—

Then she stopped. Shook her head.

Get in the car. I'm taking you to your appointment. Explain on the way.

Roni was practically dancing to the passenger door. Mrs. Waverly's gonna call home about it aaaaaanyway. I'm not coming to school tomorrow—!

Get. Hero exhaled, tired all of a sudden. Get in the car.

Okay, so what happened was—huhhuhhuhhuh—that was Roni, manic in her triumph—what happened was, a week ago, Vincent said girls aren't as strong as boys, right? He said it during morning recess. He said, girls aren't as strong as boys, and so, I said, yeah, they were—

What Roni actually said, according to the same boy, and which Mrs. Waverly relayed to Pol later that evening on the phone, cordially leaving out some of the nuance in her retelling, was: GIRLS ARE TOO AS STRONG AS BOYS!!! I'LL FUCKING CUT YOU UP!!! I'LL FUCK-ING CUT YOUR TITI OFF!!!

This alone would have been enough for detention, but that wasn't the end of it.

—and so I said, The girls challenge you to a fight then! At lunchtime! Vincent and some of the boys said uh-huh uh-huh yeah, you and who else? So I got Christine and Ria and Jocelyn to agree and even Charmaine joined in and then some of the other girls overheard and they don't like Vincent or Mikey, either, so they joined in—

Mrs. Waverly told Pol that the fighters consisted of around seven boys, and around ten girls. All in all, the participants included more than half the class. Two other boys had lost baby teeth, one of the girls had smashed the glasses of another boy, one girl had lightly sprained her wrist. All of the children were covered in minor scrapes and bruises. They'd been fighting in a part of the yard farthest away from the recess monitors, behind a row of trees, but they would have still been visible to any adult paying close attention. Mrs. Waverley said that from what she could glean from the kids, the fighting had been going on for most of that week.

When Pol demanded why the fighting had missed the notice of so many adults for so long, Mrs. Waverly didn't have an answer, only a tepid apology. Pol's way of not accepting the apology was to refrain from saying *Thank you, you've been very kind* at the end of the conversation. Yes, all of the kids fighting were Pinoy, Roni confirmed, when Pol asked her.

Roni said that during detention, a new friend of hers, a girl named Charmaine Navarrete, had been let out early, after claiming that she hadn't been involved in the fighting at all, and had only been trying to stop her fellow classmates.

Roni wasn't part of it, either, Charmaine explained to their teacher. She'd just gotten caught up in it, because the boys were teasing her. Charmaine was a light-skinned, church-going Filipina, top of the class, whose parents regularly donated to the school, and who often helped the teachers clap the chalkboard erasers after class. In short, Charmaine was one of Mrs. Waverley's more civilized wards—but Roni told Hero later that Charmaine had in fact been one of the most savage fighters, and when one of the shortest boys in the class had his jaw locked around Roni's hand, teeth starting to break the flesh, the taller Charmaine had come up from behind to pick him up by his torso and toss him to the ground like a rag doll. Roni probably wouldn't have been friends with Charmaine at all but for that suppressed capacity for violence beneath her polite, behaved veneer. Mrs Waverley believed Charmaine's story, and because she'd vouched for Roni, was prepared to allow Roni to leave with her.

Come on, Roni, Charmaine singsonged from the doorway to the classroom. Let's go home.

Roni said she remained in her chair. She was staring straight ahead at the whiteboard, where I WILL NOT FIGHT DURING RECESS was written in capital letters.

I was too part of it, Roni declared, ensuring her suspension. I started it.

They were parked in front of the restaurant, part of a large, multi-building strip mall that included Lion's Supermarket. Hero had been there a few times, but she'd never noticed a Filipino restaurant in the complex. She looked up. BOY'S BBQ & GRILL in neon, the specials written on the window hand-painted in Gothic letters. The name alone should have given it away.

Hero turned the engine off, but kept her seat belt on. Putting it on was a habit now; Roni made sure of that. She turned her head and looked at the girl. Okay ka ba talaga?

Roni was still smiling. Yeah. Her head was lolling against the seat. After telling the story, she'd been quiet for the rest of the short drive, dazed and sensual from her battle.

Hero looked up at the restaurant, then back at Roni's face. Are you really sure you still want to go to the appointment today? Your mom said they're more flexible with their time than Auntie Melba.

Roni shook her head. No. I'm okay. Let's go. The excitement had faded, leaving her unusually amenable, full of goodwill toward the world at large.

The restaurant was empty when they walked in, save for one young light-skinned man in his mid-twenties, who didn't look Filipino, at least not at first glance. He was eating a plate of what looked like beef tapa with rice, using his hands. There was a television propped up on top of a VCR, both on a table in the corner of the restaurant. It was playing a cartoon Hero had never seen before. The young man was watching it as he ate.

Hero and Roni went up to the cash register, next to the counter display of different Filipino dishes, left in heated metal trays, illuminated from above with fluorescent lights. Nobody was working.

Hello? she called, toward the open door that seemed to lead to the kitchen. No answer. Roni's attention had been caught by the cartoon; she drifted toward it.

Hello? Hero called again.

Who're you looking for, the young man said, just as a very short moreno grandpa in a green Oakland A's baseball cap came out from the back door that led to the kitchen.

Uh—Hero was stuck between answering the young man and re-addressing the older one. Adela Cabugao?

The young man pulled a paper napkin out of the metal napkin dispenser and began wiping his hands. She's next door at the hair salon. I'm about to go over, I'll show you.

Uh—Hero turned back to the older man, who was smiling politely and retreating back into the kitchen. She could hear the sounds of a radio, narrating what sounded like a baseball game.

The young man stood, took his plate, and brought it past the counter, through the open door. There was a brief pause; it sounded like he was rinsing the dish himself. Then he reappeared, brushing his wet hands on the front of his trousers. Okay, let's go.

Oh—you don't have to go all the way—if you just tell us where it is—

It's cool, I'm heading over there anyway.

Roni was still watching the television. She was laughing absently to herself; someone onscreen was falling down a cliff.

What show is this? she asked the young man.

It's not a show. It's a movie. *The Castle of Cagliostro.*

It's funny.

Ask Rosalyn to borrow it, the young man said, opening the door to the restaurant and waiting for Hero and Roni to pass through it.

Thank you, Hero murmured, still feeling nervous. He was handsome in the way she sometimes liked, in men, soft and tough. And—mestizo, she admitted to herself after a long minute, her throat tight and uncomfortable. His eyes were down-turned at the corners, giving his entire face a sleepy look, with eyelid creases sheening softly with day-old sweat and lashes that were thicker and darker at the base than at the tips. He smelled profoundly of fried garlic.

Who's Rosalyn? Roni was asking.

I'm taking you to her.

They walked down the strip mall, six or seven parking spaces away. The young man walked slightly ahead of them, in black uniform slacks and a white T-shirt that looked like it might have been the undershirt to something more formal. A security guard's lanyard hung from his front pocket, gently hitting the side of his knee as he walked. There was a tattoo on his upper arm that was faintly visible through the white shirt.

They arrived at a glass door that said, in cursive script adorned with roses, MAI'S HAIR AND BEAUTY. The young man pushed open the door.

Hero was struck immediately by the heavy smell of shampoo and perming chemicals, the glaring, peach-white lights of the salon. Loud music was playing, not in English or Tagalog. She didn't recognize it. There were other women cutting hair, but they didn't exactly look Filipino either—Hero remembered what Paz had mentioned, that the salon was a Vietnamese hair salon.

Rosalyn! the young man boomed. People here to see your grandma.

A young woman at the far end of the salon, wearing a San Jose State University sweatshirt, turned around. Hero went still. The woman was standing in the hair-washing station, amidst a row of sinks. Her hands were covered in thick clouds of foam, knuckle deep in the black mane of a customer, who was covered in a nylon cape, head tilted back, eyes closed in bliss.

The young woman didn't stop massaging the scalp in front of her, but smiled and nodded at the door where Hero and Roni stood, lifting her chin in greeting.

Hey. Take a seat. Be right with you.

Not waiting for Hero, Roni sat down in the waiting area, pushing aside some of the weathered beauty magazines that were piled there.

The young man was still at the door, his hand propping it open so it chimed, over and over.

I'm gonna go pick up Gani and Ruben, the young man yelled. We'll be back tonight.

Okay, Rosalyn yelled back.

They both had to speak at that register to be heard over the music. They had the same type of American accent; Hero hadn't heard enough accents to know if it was Californian or not, but it must have been. She looked down at Roni, who was absorbed in a fashion spread. She sat down, tried to breathe through her mouth. The scent of ammonia was making her dizzy.

Ten minutes later, a shadow fell over the magazine that Hero was pretending to read. She looked up. Rosalyn was standing there, smiling.

Hero took a startled breath through her nose. Rosalyn smelled heavily of shampoo, resinous and balsamic, like forest sap. Hero recognized the smell only because it was the same one Paz and Pol kept at home, which she'd had to start using herself, since it was the only brand they ever bought. Revlon Flex, some part of Hero's distracted mind remembered. The smell of it was all over Rosalyn's hands, her arms, wafting a wave of scent into Hero's nose when she reached out first to shake Roni's hand, then Hero's. The gesture was oddly formal.

Are you Roni? the young woman asked.

Roni nodded silently.

Okay, I'm Rosalyn. That's my grandma over there. Rosalyn pointed to a woman whose deep-black hair, curly either by nature or by perm, was in the process of being shaped and sheared by one of the Vietnamese women who worked at the salon. The two were chatting, like they knew each other well. Hero felt her own body gradually loosening in relief at the shift in attention.

She's getting a haircut right now. But if you wait a bit she'll be with you. Is that okay?

That's okay, Roni said.

Whoa! Rosalyn saw the gap in Roni's mouth for the first time. Cool, d'you lose a tooth?

Roni lit up, happy to be reminded of what had just occurred that day. She started grinning again. Yep! I got in a fight today.

Cool, cool. Rosalyn turned her gaze back to Hero, who stiffened again. Sorry, what's your name—

Uh—Geronima. Roni's cousin.

Hero, Roni interjected, pedantic.

She—ah, calls me Hero. People also call me Nimang. Tita Paz calls me Nimang—

Hero was fumbling her words, but there was no helping it. She added, Tita Paz is Roni's mom—

I know Auntie Pacita, Rosalyn interrupted. What do you prefer?

What?

To be called.

No one had ever asked Hero that before. She didn't know what to say; she didn't even really know what the answer was. Uh—whatever's fine.

Okay, Uh-whatever's-fine. Rosalyn smirked, then looked down at Roni. Hey Roni, d'you want your hair washed?

Roni tilted her head, then cast a skeptical glance at the sinks. My hair? Right now?

Yep. I'll do it for free while you're waiting for my grandma.

The girl hesitated, then shook her head. No, that's okay.

Are you sure? I said it's free, right—

Roni's face took on that telltale stubborn cast. No. I'm okay.

Okay, Rosalyn said, holding her hands up. She pointed to Hero. What about you?

The whole column of Hero's neck, up until the skin under her eyes, was glowing with heat. No, I'm okay.

What? Come on.

Hero hadn't gone to the hairdresser in—she couldn't remember how many years. Washing her hair under the shower had become a brisk, perfunctory task. The toll it took on her hands to really massage her own scalp wasn't worth it, she'd told herself to make do with a mild soaping of Flex. Most of her effort went into tying all of the hair up into a ponytail at the beginning of the day, which she only took out just before bed. When she'd been at Tita Soly's house, Tita Soly cut her hair for her, just trimming bluntly at the ends to keep it manageable. She'd cut Hero's fingernails and toenails, too, washed her face and underarms, even helped her kaw-kaw, a brisk hand pulling back her vaginal folds, pouring warm water from a tabo over the tender skin.

Rosalyn saw the opening and took it. Yeah, okay. Let's go, Uh-whatever's-fine.

She turned around, walking toward the sinks, not looking back to make sure Hero was following.

Hero wasn't following. She hesitated, still sitting next to Roni, who went back to flipping through the same magazine. You don't want to go? she asked, not looking up. It's free.

It's not that.

It's free! Roni repeated. It's FUH-REE.

You said that already, Hero muttered, and got up.

She made her way over to Rosalyn, who was theatrically tapping the seat in front of one of the sinks. Hero sat down in the chair. Rosalyn whipped out one of the black nylon capes Hero had seen earlier.

So your clothes don't get wet, she explained, even though Hero could have guessed the reason. The cape held together with Velcro at the back of Hero's neck; she tried not to shiver as Rosalyn fastened it.

Lean back, Rosalyn said.

Hero complied. She heard a snort from behind her.

I'm not gonna wash your hair in midair. Lean all the way back, like you're lying down.

Hero did so, slowly, feeling dizzy as she did. There was a hand at the back of her skull; Rosalyn was easing her head down into the basin of the sink. Hero's breath was coming out shaky. She inhaled, then exhaled. That didn't help.

The jet of water hit her head suddenly, the pressure direct and warm, the sound of it loud enough to distract her from her thoughts. The growing heaviness of her wet hair was drugging-good, heavy, liquefying. Hero tried to let go into it, couldn't. The tendons of her neck were strained as she tried to keep her head lifted in the sink, uncertain of how far back she could really lean on it, if the neck rest would really support her skull's dead weight. She tried to close her eyes, but found they wouldn't remain shut; they kept fluttering open, twitching and blinking.

Rosalyn's face appeared above her. She was threading one hand through Hero's sopping hair, feeling along the scalp. The other hand was controlling the spray. Hero's breath stuttered.

Relax, ate, Rosalyn said, almost too soft to be heard over the water. I'll be gentle.

Hero had never been a romantic. She'd never been someone who fantasized about dream lovers, marriage, dramatic heartbreak. Often, people—men, mostly—interpreted her diffidence for coquetry, told themselves there was a smoldering sexuality beneath all that silence. They were mistaken. She neither smoldered nor was coy; she wanted to fuck and be fucked, that was it. She liked silence, it wasn't a pose; she was never good at small talk. Sex, she understood; that hunger had been in her from the beginning, from the very first self-administered orgasm. It was part of the feeling she always had, of standing outside of everything. But that wasn't all that bad, either; the way sex exacerbated how she already felt was grounding. It hooked her in place, let her know where she was, chased away all the muddled, murky feelings she had— about her desires, about whether or not she could really become a surgeon, about the life that Teresa was offering her in the NPA, about being a De Vera.

Hero had sex for the first time at fifteen, with a boy in her class; she'd sucked him off and he'd stuck his fingers into her, dry, without ceremony, nails too long. He came, she didn't. That didn't deter her. The next time she had sex, also with a boy, she discovered she couldn't come just with his dick inside her, despite liking the way it made her feel. She showed him where her clit was, after he came. This second boy reacted like it was both a source of personal dishonor, then amusement, and then finally, his unbelievable good fortune, the way she was so straightforward about her desires and how to answer them. They kept having sex for over two years; people thought of him as her high school sweetheart. Francisco. It was the longest she'd ever been with one person.

She stopped having relationships entirely after Francisco, and stuck to sex. She had sex with a girl for the first time at college, in the UST dorms, a law student who had a fiancé. But he was studying abroad in America, and the girl was having doubts. It wasn't cheating if it was a girl, went the law student's logic. Hero liked eating the girl's pussy—and would have liked having hers eaten in return, but the girl never offered—but that alone wasn't the answer she'd been looking for. If anything, it made her realize that she wasn't looking for an answer; that sex hadn't been a question at all, but a sentence, lone and complete.

They'd broken both her thumbs, in the camp, right at the base, near the joints. That was where it was hardest to heal—thumb function made up around half of the entire function of the hand. It was a Rolando fracture, not a Bennett's fracture; graver, the base of the metatarsal fractured in two places. Nerves fucked, only salvageable with surgery, which wasn't going to happen anytime soon. Maybe the guards had medical training and did it on purpose. She'd known the minute it happened. It helped, to know what kind of fracture it was, to think about the morning she'd learned about the term, what the lecture hall looked like, how attentively she'd written down the definitions in her notepad, how diligently she'd studied the pages later.

When she was younger, Pol said that hand trauma posed the most difficulty for an orthopedic surgeon; to return a hand to what it had been pre-injury was nearly impossible, considering the complexity of the hand, the network of tendons, nerves, bones, muscles, veins, soft tissues, the fine tiny movements and the intricate mechanics that made them possible. Hands were more complicated than the people attached to them. A broken heart, that's easy to fix, Pol used to remark. Hearts heal. They even improve. Hands are never the same.

After it had been confirmed that the prisoner who spoke Ilocano and said she was only a country doctor was, indeed, a De Vera daughter, and therefore closely related to a family friend and relative through marriage of Marcos, she'd been immediately released from the camp, two years after she'd been taken. Amends were made to the De Vera family for the oversight. The year Hero left for California, Hamin won a landslide election as mayor of Bantay, close enough to Vigan that he and Concepcion wouldn't even have to move—though of course they did. New beginnings. Hero had never seen the new house in Bantay; Soly said it wasn't that much larger than the De Vera house, but more modern. Tita Soly never said who'd paid for the surgery, plus the hefty bonus for the doctor's discretion on the side, but in Soly's silence Hero thought she could sniff out the trace of her parents.

When she'd first decided to become a surgeon, Pol gave her a book that he'd read when he was in medical school, written by some French philosopher she'd never heard of. *The Phenomenology of Perception*. It wasn't from the De Vera library. She asked what it was about. Pol said, You have to read it to find out. But it's a good book for orthopedic surgeons. Read the part about phantom limbs.

It had been too difficult to understand when he gave it to her, but by the time she got to college, she was ready for it. She read it again and again, until its spine broke and she had to tape it together. She lost it around the time she dropped out of medical school, joined up with Teresa and Eddie and everyone. It didn't matter anymore, anyway. She wasn't going to be a surgeon, after all—at least not one that needed French philosophy.

That was what she told herself, but there were lines she still thought about years later, in the room she shared with Teresa and the others, lying on a buri mat on the floor, still smelling faintly of the sampalok leaves used to bleach the straw. The part about phantom limbs. The part about sexuality. The part about no one being saved; the part about no one being totally lost.

Hero clenched her fists as Rosalyn poured a generous handful of conditioner into her hair and massaged it in, from the roots all the way to the ends and back again. The pain in Hero's fists helped. Grounded her, let her know where she was, chased away the muddled, murky feelings. Most of all, it helped to keep at bay Rosalyn's promised gentleness—which hurt, just as Hero had known it would. But you couldn't tell a person you just met: Please don't be gentle. Anything but that.

The First Picture of You, 1990

WHEN HERO RETURNED TO RONI, HAIR WASHED AND
blown dry, the girl had torn through a dozen fashion magazines, sample
perfume flaps thrown open and savagely rubbed at, producing a hazy
veil of mingled scents around Roni's body so strong that Hero stopped
just short of sitting back down next to her. Oh, you're back, Roni said,
sensing the shadow above her. She was still peering down at her outer
right forearm, where there was no eczema, just a fine layer of black hair.
She sniffed at it, considering. *ex'cla-ma'tion.*

Then she looked up, took Hero in. Balked. Said, You look, uh. Different.

Hero knew that, hair cascading down her back, free from its usual
ponytail. Something soft touched at her shoulder. She looked down to
see Rosalyn's fingers pulling back.

Hey Roni, Rosalyn said. My grandma's gonna be ready for you just a
little bit. You wanna eat something? You want some barbecue?

Roni slapped her hands atop the magazine in her lap. Barbecue? Yeah!

Tell my grandpa that I sent you, and that grandma's on her way.

Then Rosalyn flicked at Hero's shoulder. Don't drop your thing, she
said, before walking away from them, back toward the sinks.

Hero reached up to touch her own shoulder. The hair elastic she'd
been wearing earlier was precariously balanced there.

Roni was halfway out the door. There wasn't anything Hero could
think of to say back that didn't sound stupid; she had to quit while she
was ahead. Rosalyn was out of earshot anyway. So when Roni said,
Hurry up, let's *go*—Hero hurried up. Went.

There were a few more people in the restaurant when Hero and Roni returned. At one table, what looked like a family: a mom, a dad, and two
toddlers, one of whom was beating on the other mercilessly. The one

being beaten was sucking a thumb, oblivious. At another table, two middle-aged men wearing uniforms that resembled Pol's security guard uniform: gray slacks, itchy-looking blazer, cheap badges. In front of all of them, Styrofoam plates, filled with sticky white rice and barbecued pork.

The grandpa was out of the kitchen now, perched on a chair behind the display counter. He'd brought the radio out with him; it was still broadcasting the baseball game. Hero saw Roni shoot a glance that way, disappointed.

Kumusta po kayo, ako si Geronima, ito si Roni, we're here waiting to see Lola Adela. Rosalyn told us to come here.

Lolo Boy smiled vaguely, adjusting his baseball cap. Okay—sit down, anywhere.

Salamat po, Hero murmured and pointed Roni toward a table at the back of the restaurant, in the far corner, away from the other customers. Go sit down.

Gutom kayo? Lolo Boy called. It was odd; he was speaking Tagalog, but his accent in Tagalog was more American than anything else, as if he'd come to America as a youth and had spoken both languages simultaneously so that they were one. It reminded Hero of the way Roni would sometimes switch between English, Pangasinan, and Tagalog, seamlessly, oblivious to the differences between them.

Hero forgot that Rosalyn had mentioned barbecue. She looked down to ask Roni, but Roni had understood the question.

Yeah, I'm hungry! she replied, climbing into a chair so she was kneeling on it, rather than sitting on it, her hands slapping at the table.

Lolo Boy's smile turned genuine. What do you want to eat?

Barbecue! Roni cheered.

Barbecue! Lolo Boy cheered back. Roger. He turned around and began busying himself with the plates, filling one with a heaping mound of rice and three sticks of barbecue. When he took a second plate, he stopped and glanced back at Hero, only just remembering she existed. Ah—ikaw rin, you want barbecue?

Hero nodded. Oo po, barbecue na lang, thank you.

We have a lot of other dishes, Lolo Boy said, gesturing at the metal

warming dishes. Meron kami, ahh, afritada, adobo, pinakbet, pinapai-
tan, laing, kaldereta, daing na bangus, tortang talong, lechon kawali—
take your pick.

Barbecue's fine, po, Hero said, though her heart had skipped at the
mention of pinakbet.

Lolo Boy looked skeptical; why, Hero couldn't quite figure out. He
made no move to fill the plate. Waiting.

Okay, sige po, pinakbet, Hero said, flustered, more to shuffle his ex-
pectation off of her.

Pakbet! Coming up.

Hero turned to Roni. Sit down properly in your chair.

Roni flopped down, losing energy abruptly. I'm hungry. How come
they turned the TV off? I wanted to watch that show. Ah! We forgot to
ask Rosalyn.

It's not a show, it's a movie, Hero said, wondering why she even remembered.

Lolo Boy appeared in front of them, holding their plates. One barbecue, he announced, sliding the plate in front of Roni. At isang pinakbet.
He lifted his chin at the utensils gathered in an empty can of Chaokoh
coconut milk, washed and repurposed. There's forks and spoons there.

Roni was picking up a stick of barbecue with her hands, not even
looking at the forks and spoons.

Hero reached across her for a spoon. The first bite was sitaw and kala-
basa, sweet, but the sabaw was just too bitter and too salty; they'd been
overgenerous with the bagoong, and there was too much okra, not
enough ampalaya. Maybe American-born Filipinos didn't like ampalaya,
she thought. It was fine; this version wasn't her favorite, but it was fine.
She had another spoonful, then another—then another, getting hungrier
as she was eating. It often happened to her like that; she wouldn't realize
how hungry she was until she started eating. But by the time that happened, the food had an inverse relationship to her hunger: eating, she got
hungrier, but the food wasn't enough, ran out too fast, even if it wasn't
even that good. She and Roni ate in silence.

The door opened with a chime. Adela walked in, her hand raised to greet the customers. She stopped at the family for a moment, chatting with the woman then reaching out to firmly pull back the chubby fist of the toddler who hadn't yet stopped beating on its sibling.

Del, Lolo Boy called.

Adela turned around, the toddler's fist still in her hand.

Boy gestured toward Hero and Roni.

Adela glanced over at Hero and Roni without moving her head. Hero straightened in her chair.

Then Adela let go of the child's fist, turned, and waved. Hi guys, she said brightly, in English. I'll be with you in a minute.

Her accent, when she spoke English, was stronger than Boy's, but only just. They both sounded more American than Paz or Pol. Her demeanor reminded Hero of Rosalyn; that tone in her voice when she'd told Hero to relax.

Hero became aware of someone's small hand reaching over to pick up her spoon. She looked down; Roni was stealing a large bite of pinakbet.

Don't take people's food when they're not looking—

You can steal some of mine.

Then it's not stealing. Still, Hero leaned over, picked up a stick of barbecue and bit a chunk of it off. She was startled; it was surprisingly good, flavorful, juicy, overcharred in the best way, so that the sugar in the marinade became smoky and caramelized. She took another bite.

Adela walked over and sat down across from Roni. Hello, hello, she said, leaning forward to put her elbows on the table. Adela left her mouth wide open when she smiled; Hero saw she had two gold teeth in the upper row.

Roni hesitated, looking down at Adela's hand. She seemed to be calculating as to whether or not she should give Adela the mano. Amused, Adela let her. Roni touched her forehead to the tops of Adela's knuckles and mumbled, Mano po.

Lolo Boy was approaching the table with a plate of sticky black sampalok candy, wrapped in red cellophane. He placed the plate down onto the table while Adela patted her pockets, pulling out a packet of Lucky Strikes. She turned to her husband and made a face at him. Lolo Boy went back to the counter, then returned with a lighter. Adela had the cigarette in her mouth, leaning forward without skipping a beat into the space that Boy lit up.

Thanks, handsome, she said. Don't overdo it, Boy replied, but left the lighter on the table.

Adela leaned forward again, plucking one of the sampalok candies off the plate, pulling off the cellophane and chewing at it, then spitting out the shiny maroon seed and licking the salty-syrupy residue on her fingers. Then she took a drag of her cigarette and brought her gaze over to look at Roni, again without moving her head. Just the skating over of those mobile, precise eyes, so open they were unreadable. It was the look of a person confident enough that she didn't have to bother with defenses, the look of someone whose feet were planted firmly but flexibly in the ground, muscles loose and warm.

In Hero's makeshift clinic, the small kitchen in an abandoned nipa hut, stitching up Teresa's forehead after she'd gotten into a fight with a young man from the village who'd taken a new female cadre into an alley and tried to shove his tongue down her throat. Her first time treating Teresa, hands trembling and voice brusque, ordering her not to laugh or she would make a mistake, Maybe you'll think before you act now that you've seen how much a head wound bleeds, and Teresa chuckling through gritted teeth, Donya, people think scars are sexy in their leaders, and do you really think this is my first head wound? What Hero had thought to herself back then was what Hero thought to herself now: There isn't anything, anything in the world scarier than a strong person.

So. I hear you're kinda sick, Adela began, smiling like it was an inside joke, waving the smoke away.

Hero was sent to a faith healer, just once in her life. Neither Hamin nor Concepcion knew about it. As far as Hero knew, it wasn't their idea. It was all Lulay's doing.

Lulay, a woman so scrawny she looked like she'd either die within the day or never succumb to death at all, like one of those fasting saints Hamin used to talk about. It had been Concepcion's firm policy not to have young, beautiful yayas or maids in the house, even if Hamin had never really been the babaero type, nowhere in the league of Melchior or even Pol. Lulay had worked for the De Vera family all her life, as the personal maid of Hamin and Pol's mother, the original Geronima De Vera, and then, after her early death, as Escolastica's yaya. Escolastica had never taken to her, and so when Hero was born, Lulay came to live with them.

Lulay only spoke Tagalog to Hero, but neither Tagalog nor Ilocano had been her first languages—what language was her first, Hero never knew. Lulay didn't talk about it. Lulay had age-washed tattoos on her upper arms and chest that Hero only vaguely remembered seeing when she was a child, when they would be in the bath together. Lulay was from the north of Luzon, that much Hero knew, which meant she was practically a local, and thus an artifact from a rapidly disappearing era of De Vera servitude; the newer generation had begun looking farther afield when it came to their help. Hero's younger cousins were raised and driven around by people from Negros, Samar, Davao, Sulu. Hiring servants from farther-flung provinces made it more difficult for a rebellious or disgruntled or newly-in-love maid or driver to run away, back to the safety of their friends and family. As far away as possible from a comfort zone: that was the best state for a servant. The younger De Veras enjoyed their modernity.

The night before she was taken to the faith healer, Hero had swum home through the blissful fug of Francisco's father's rum and half a crushed Valium, sneaking in through the servant's entrance on the ground floor. She'd done it a hundred, a thousand times before; she was sure her parents and all the servants knew, but she hadn't yet been punished for it. She'd been with Francisco, as usual. She was sixteen, had just finished high school, was a couple of months shy of moving to the UST dorms. Francisco's parents were sending their son to study in the States, somewhere on the East Coast; Hero could never keep the names of the towns or schools straight. Francisco's family was far richer than Hero's, as the regional distributers of Coca-Cola, but theirs was newer money, which allowed Hamin and Concepcion to keep Francisco and his parents at a patronizing arm's length, while simultaneously dropping hints that the two should marry.

Hero was on the verge of breaking up with Francisco; she just hadn't gotten around to it yet. She had the feeling he was in the same place. But it seemed neither of them could bear to give up the halfhearted but still somehow addictive fucking, using each other up and flopping over like rags when they were done, then starting up again as soon as one or the other felt the itch creep up again. While it was going on, it was good. Sex was always good. What made Hero feel like climbing out of her skin with revulsion was the rest of it: the way girls at school she didn't even know came up to her eagerly and said, You and Francisco make such a good-looking couple; the way older strangers smiled on the street when they walked arm in arm after the movies, his sweater tied around his waist to hide the cum stain; the way flower sellers on the street came up to them, gave Francisco a free rosal; the way Francisco had to give it to her under the seller's approving eye, and Hero had to hold it in her hands or tuck it behind her ear, and smile.

Around the time Lulay took her to the faith healer, Hero had been forgetting to eat more and more often, and then, when she finally remembered—it was her body remembering for her, the sudden gnawing raring up from the depths of her like a recurring nightmare—she'd eat until she was sick, and then eat some more. But no matter how much she ate, the food had lost its taste. It wasn't just food. She'd stopped wearing Tabac, she'd stopped reading. Tito Pol was in Indonesia and she hadn't seen him for nearly a year, but she knew that even if he were in town, she would avoid him. She didn't want him to know about this part of her, this limp shred of a girl she'd discovered herself capable of being. She wanted to protect the person she was when she was with him, the curious, smart niece she'd been all her life. She didn't want him to meet this version of her: banal, hungerless. Someone's nobya.

When Hero arrived home, Lulay was sitting cross-legged on the tiled floor in front of Hero's bedroom, her thin, gristly arms crossed. Nodding off into the liver spots on her chest. She woke up when Hero's footsteps approached.

Walang hiya, she said blandly. No shame. The insult was a greeting. Hero opened her mouth to reply, and threw up instead.

Lulay stood up, gripped Hero by the upper arm, hard. Took her to the servants' bathroom. Grabbed a blue plastic bucket that was next to the drain, dumped the waiting water out of it. Kicked it in front of Hero so it rattled like a top, before settling. She stuck a finger down Hero's throat, made her throw up in the bucket, which stank of watery piss, like someone had missed the drain or hadn't cared. Stuck the finger deeper when Hero's throat closed up, then pulled it out with a fresh stream of vomit, until Hero's eyes were streaming with reflexive tears, snot coating her lips.

Lulay took the small tabo next to the sink, filled it up with water, grabbed Hero by the hair. Stuck her head over the bucket again, then poured the water over Hero's head. Hero choked, spluttered, then finally relaxed. Lulay did it two more times, the water only a fraction warmer the third time.

Walang hiya, Lulay spat out again. She brought Hero to her bedroom, a dry towel draped over her arm. At the sight of the mess she'd made when she'd thrown up the first time, Hero dumbly made movements to kneel down, meaning to clean up the vomit, but Lulay pushed her out of the way, making a tsk-ing sound.

Get in your room, she said, wiping at the watery chunks with the towel. Hero hesitated, holding on to the door to steady her. Lulay didn't look at her. Sige, she snapped.

Hero was in bed, one hand pressed on her own forehead, one foot on the floor to stop the spinning of the room, when Lulay came back inside. Go to sleep now. Tomorrow we're going to see my friend.

Hero barely heard her, grunted in response. The hand she was keeping on her forehead felt important, like it was keeping her brains, or something worse and more precious, from pouring out.

Tsh, Lulay muttered, and closed the door.

The next day, Lulay took her to a woman's house. They went on foot, avoiding Concepcion's driver, avoiding the kalesas in the road. Lulay didn't explain who they were going to see, or how she knew her; she didn't explain what they were doing, or why. She'd never been the warmest of yayas, but Hero hadn't ever seen her quite this irate. Still, when they walked on the road, Lulay took the side closest to the cars. If half the sidewalk was shaded and the other half was in sunlight, she made Hero take the shaded side even if it meant Lulay was walking on the cobblestone road, dodging passing tricycles.

The woman they were visiting lived in an old house in the center of town, and was about as old as Lulay. She worked as the cook for a small, no longer very rich family, at least judging by the state of the bahay na bato: several of the capiz shell window slats were cracked or missing altogether, one of the balconies looking like it had been ripped clean off, maybe in an earthquake. The fabric store on the ground floor appeared to be theirs.

Lulay brought Hero to the kitchen, had her sit on a stool while the woman finished chopping onions. Lulay stood. They talked to each other like old friends, not in Ilocano or Tagalog. Hero still thought it was Kalinga, or Bontoc, but those were all wild guesses, she had no idea really. She couldn't understand a word.

She doesn't even know why she's here? asked the woman, in Tagalog. Hero was meant to overhear it, then—though the woman hadn't been addressing or even looking at her.

She doesn't care, Lulay replied. Never mind.

It didn't last for long. Hero didn't know if it was because her condition was minor, or if it was already beyond help. The woman's name was Angelica; that much Hero remembered.

By and large it consisted of holding Hero by the arm and finding out if she was possessed, if there was anyone around her who wished her ill, if there was anyone in her parents' life who wanted revenge and was taking it through her child. The woman listened and listened, but nothing answered back.

Hero let it all happen to her like it was happening to someone else, like she was an animal in the forest, playing dead. Sitting on a stool in the kitchen, smelling the raw onions, the sweaty film of her own residual drunkenness passing out of her body, leaving behind a migraine. A stranger's tobacco-sweet breath in her face, making it worse. Searching for demons, finding a person.

There's nothing, Angelica said, again in Tagalog, again for Hero's benefit. Wala.

Meron, Lulay insisted. There's something.

Hero thought of saying: I'm not sick, manang. I just have a boyfriend.

Angelica had to get back to work, favors to friends notwithstanding. She apologized to Lulay, who accepted the apology grudgingly, which was her way of being kind. For Lulay, it was a kindness to hold grudges, to be stingy with forgiveness; it made things matter.

She and Hero departed back into the damp and heavy afternoon heat. They cut through Plaza Burgos on their way back home. On a hot day, it felt like the whole of Vigan was there, selling something, eating something, the kids playing, the stands hocking empanada, Vigan longanisa, ukoy, big melting scoops of buko ice cream, sandwiched in a sun-warm pan de sal. Hero didn't feel drunk or even nauseated anymore; the hangover had officially begun, skin dry and parched, stomach hollow. She needed to eat. She was going to pass out and die if she didn't eat. She stopped just to the side of the plaza, and said she wanted an empanada. Lulay huffed, but didn't protest.

Hero paid for two, gave one to Lulay, who accepted it but didn't make any moves to eat it. Hero never liked to eat while someone else was watching without eating, but she was hungry; no helping it. She ate, fast, the just-fried empanada crackling under her teeth, burning her tongue, staining her fingers orange. She didn't even bother with vinegar. It was the grease she wanted; she didn't want anything to cut through its weight or interfere with the longed-for weight in her belly. Being this hungover made her feel like a balloon, tied to a long and fragile string, battered about by wind and sun, too high, apt to snap off at any moment. The food yanked her back, shoved her in the shade.

There's something wrong, Lulay said.

Hero's chewing slowed. She had papaya in her teeth, she could feel it.

There's nothing. Your friend said.

Lulay was staring out into the square, watching the people. There's something wrong, she said again.

Hero was nearly finished with her empanada. She licked at her fingers. Looked around at the plaza, at the statue of José Burgos, and the rolled-up piece of paper he held in his hand, only its title visible. PRO-TESTA.

She put the rest of the empanada in her mouth and averted her eyes from the square. She'd never been sentimental about Vigan before. It was too pathetic to start now.

How much did you have to pay her? Hero finally asked. You'll be reimbursed.

Lulay looked back at her with more disgust than she'd ever looked at Hero before. Hero relished the disgust; it told the truth, at least. Walang hiya talaga, Lulay said again, looking disgusted even with the words themselves, with having to say them, having to mean them, a girl in front of her who deserved them. Then she held the uneaten empanada out in front of her, like she'd known all along that Hero would still be hungry.

The only person Hero ever told about the faith healer was Teresa. Late at night, staying overnight at a farmer's home at the foot of the Sierra Madre before they would make their way back up the mountain, seven hours on foot up to the cluster of nipa huts where the cadres had made their tempo-rary base, past the fields that had once been full of native red and white corn, increasingly replaced by the yellow hybrid corn crops that were spreading in both the provinces of Cagayan and Isabela.

By the time Hero arrived in Isabela province, the cadres had already witnessed several of the upland settlements in Cagayay Valley gradually being converted into cornfields, from rolling banana plantations to old colonial ranches left to ruin. For years, commercial representatives and government employees from the Department of Agriculture had been visiting farmers in the region, offering what was called advertising deals, in which farmers were given free hybrid corn seeds and agrochemicals. They needed only to purchase their own fertilizers, and of course to sell whatever harvest they reaped back to the original seed company. Such corporate-government teams had already successfully convinced farm-ers to plant hybrid rice years before, and they expected the same success with hybrid corn. The difference between rice and corn, however, was that a fraction of the hybrid rice harvest could be kept to feed a farmer's household, in addition to being sold for an income. The hybrid yellow corn, on the other hand, was used only as stock feed: a pure cash crop, unsuitable for human consumption. The hybrid corn was also more prone to rot than rice, which made it difficult to store, and few farmers were able to pay for the kinds of equipment and warehouses that would protect their harvest. In fact, what Teresa was increasingly hearing, which she relayed to the cadres in Isabela, was that the majority of any income earned by the farmers off the hybrid corn was often spent paying back the exorbitant loans they'd taken out to cover the other investments required to grow the new crops in the first place, like expensive tractors.

They were at the home of one of those farmers, Chito, a man who'd once been a logger and who'd gone into debt after a harvest failure. He'd had to give up some of his land as collateral—It's called land-grabbing, Eddie corrected, acerbic. Chito's son had a wet cough, which Teresa had heard during a village meeting she'd held, one she and Eddie held to help organize an upcoming picket outside the seed company's regional head-quarters. The boy had been coughing at his father's side, sick enough that he should have been in bed, but old enough, ten or eleven, to be told that it was time to start becoming a man. When he coughed, he looked mor-tified, covering nearly his entire face as if hiding from view would make the sound less distracting.

At the end of the meeting, Teresa pointed with her lips at the boy and said, I know a doctor.

It was Hero's first year in Isabela and her bedside manner, though never warm, was at its least personable. Hero's forbidding gaze, her huge assessing silences, menaced the boy, made him refuse to be touched or to even open his mouth. Teresa diffused the situation by pointing at a gecko scurrying up the wall of the farmer's nipa hut, its tiny tail sweeping over the bamboo stalks.

These are good for coughs, did you know that? Teresa said to the boy. You want to try it? The boy shook his hand, but his shoulders relaxed. Teresa took the gecko by the tail and dangled it over her mouth. The boy burst out laughing, then coughed again. From that point on, Hero told Teresa what she needed the boy to do, and Teresa translated.

Eventually Hero would learn that a cadre doctor had to be someone people could trust. Over the years, she was surprised to find that people did, actually, trust her. She'd never thought of herself as a trustworthy person before. But it had to do with how awkward she was, how blunt, how poorly educated in Marxism. Something about it rang true to people, at least the people in Isabela. That was what Teresa said, anyway.

People don't want their doctors to be charming, donya. They just want them to know what they're doing. You don't have to be Rogelio de la Rosa to splint a leg.

Teresa had a host of nicknames for her. There was Nimang, which everyone used, and doktora, and then sometimes there was donya, or la biguenya, or donya biguenya, or donya doktora, or some other combination that included all the epithets. They weren't as formal with their kasama names in Isabela; someone would introduce himself as Ka Jerusalem, then a week later admit that you could call him Jay. Teresa introduced herself to the cadres as Ka Teresa—along with Eddie, she was one of the few who made no differentiation between her kasama name and her real name, and Hero followed their example. Eddie, insouciant, sometimes even called Teresa Tessie. What Hero loved most wasn't the cadre names people chose, but the word *kasama* itself: kasama, pakikisama. In Ilocano, the closest word was *kadwa*. Kadwa, makikadwa. *Companion,* but that English word didn't quite capture its force. *Kasama* was more like the glowing, capacious form of the word *with*: with as verb, noun, adjective, and adverb, with as a way of life. A world of with-ing. In Isabela, Hero was with.

Teresa reacted to the fact that Hero had come from Vigan differently from most people in Manila, something that had taken Hero some getting used to, those first few months at UST. There, when she said she was from Vigan, a hush of fear would come over people's faces. The braver ones would ask things like, Is it true that you'll get shot for looking someone in the eyes for too long? Is it true that the warlords kill people in the street and no one says anything? Hero was at a loss for how to answer any of those questions; it was the first time she'd caught onto the fact that this was the impression outsiders had of Vigan. Not that it was an old colonial town, Ilocano, full of austere traditionalists and especially pretty at night when the lamplight glimmered off the cobblestones.

She brought those qualities up sometimes, when people asked, and received blank stares in return. No one knew all that much about Vigan except that it was a no-go zone, a kingdom of terror, along with the rest of Ilocos Sur and Ilocos Norte. At the time, Hero tried hard to think back on her childhood, on her adolescence, her teenage years, running around the Calle Crisologo, fucking her brains out, coming home drunk, losing days to a hangover and a book, keeping silent at dinner. When she figured it out, she felt stupid. Of course she'd never had cause to feel afraid. The warlords people were talking about were her neighbors and godparents, the longtime friends and business partners and sometimes spouses of the De Veras. It was the first time she'd really had to think about where she'd come from, what it meant.

But Teresa never mentioned it, never mentioned the Quiambaos or the Ibarras, never even said if she recognized the De Vera name, which she probably didn't; it wasn't like they were the richest or most prominent family—just another one of the old guard. When Teresa talked to Hero about Vigan, it was with a childlike, teasing kind of affection, referencing only Vigan's most stereotypical, postcard-worthy qualities. She said things like, So did you go to school in a kalesa? Did you have a silk fan? Was your house made of damili tile? Did men still do harana? Were you ever serenaded outside your window? Bashful, Hero admitted, to the sound of Teresa's ensuing laughter, that she had in fact been serenaded.

Hero wondered about it, about why Teresa never talked about Vigan the way other people did. There were some cadres among them who made disparaging remarks about Hero being a biguenya, making hints about her real loyalties, but Teresa cast a cold eye on those remarks until they died down. Hero's increasingly indispensable skills as a doctor didn't hurt.

That night, after sending the boy to bed with promises to return the next day with a guaifenesin-based expectorant for the mucus, they'd given Chito and his wife two American-made M-14s to defend themselves against landlords or rustlers. Or if anyone from the military comes to threaten you about the demonstration, or any of those debtors try to take more of your land, Eddie added. As usual, there wasn't enough ammunition to last them if a real fight broke out; Teresa and Eddie said, as they always did, that they'd try to get more, but it was usually months before they were able to keep their word to villagers. Even the cadres themselves were limited to firing four or five rounds a day, assassination missions included. It was the gesture that counted. The mother boiled monggo for everybody, and the father put the guns in front of the altar, where a brown-skinned Santo Niño watched over them all, his face illuminated by two red candles burning to stubs on either side of him.

By dinner it was just Hero and Teresa in the hut, Eddie having left to meet up with two of the newer recruits, Amihan and Jon-Jon. Chito told them to sleep overnight, it was too dark to make their way through the mountain. Teresa was a night owl; she often ended up in some long conversation with one of the cadres late at night. Sometimes it was Hero; more often than not it wasn't. Either way she would stay awake in their nipa hut, surrounded by warm bodies, listening to Teresa and her interlocutor debate faith, or distribution of wealth, or maternal love. Hero knew she wasn't the only one staying up one more hour just to be able to fall asleep to Teresa's voice.

Hero mentioned Lulay's faith healer friend to Teresa that night. They'd been talking about faith healers because the boy's mother had previously resorted to them for the family's illnesses, too poor for any other remedies. Teresa rolled over on the mat to face her, intrigued. And what was it like?

Anticlimactic, Hero replied in English.

Teresa rolled back onto the mat, looking up at the roof. And why did your yaya take you there in the first place?

Hero shrugged, said she didn't know. She described what the time had been like, how she'd been acting out. She never had any shame when talking to Teresa, not even about her sexual past, which she'd never talked about before, not even when it was her sexual present. Teresa didn't care about that kind of thing. She tolerated the ribald jokes made by some of the cadres, was aware of the minor or major sexual affairs that were going on, but kept some crucial part of herself out of the fray. It wasn't possible to involve Teresa, not in that way. Teresa let details like that flow over her, like she was standing at the wettest part of a shore, warm water lapping at her feet. Just enough to be part of it, but never enough to be dragged in by the tide.

Hero paused in the middle of her story, closed her eyes. She called me walang hiya.

She probably hated my guts, she went on, interrupting herself. Of course. Most yayas hate the kids they have to take care of.

Teresa picked absently at her nose with her thumb. Oh, definitely, donya. I always take the people I hate to faith healers.

Then she flicked the hardened snot away and started laughing to herself, the sound of which Hero was getting used to: Teresa laughing to herself, at Hero's expense. She'd grown to like it, even, the way Teresa's fond ridicule made her feel pliant and real, like being suspended by the scruff of her neck in someone else's teeth.

Reimburse, Teresa repeated. Tangengot. You didn't even know that faith healers can't accept money, otherwise they lose their powers?

How was I supposed to know that? Hero snapped, growing crabby. It was my first time.

A long silence. Then she said:

I don't even know what was wrong with me then.

Teresa didn't say anything; Hero thought she'd fallen asleep and turned her head slightly, just to check, but Teresa's eyes were still open.

Tanga, she said again, quiet. A lover's bower voice, without the lover or the bower. Then she said: Depression yan, 'diba?

Hero stopped. The word had never occurred to her before.

Walang hiya, Teresa mused to herself. Well. Kahit ano. Whatever. There are worse things.

Teresa closed her eyes, sleepy at last or pretending to be. That's one of the things I like about you, anyway, donya. That you have no shame.

No. Teresa had never wanted anything like that from anyone. The things Teresa wanted from people were easy to know, easy to give: a working knowledge in Ilocano and any of the indigenous languages in the north, but especially Ibanag, considering where they were; a quick study in the use of old Armalite and AK-47 rifles, American-made M-16s or M-14s, sometimes the rare Russian-made one, sometimes even a pilfered Garand circa World War II; the ability to put a knife in the chest of a mayor or landlord on a regional bus and walk away with no injuries, minimal witnesses; a personal archive of good jokes, creation myths, local folklore from your particular town or village, or at least your parents' local town or village, since sometimes there would be a cadre from suburban Manila who barely even knew the basic myths of Apolaki and Mayari; a commitment to being, not brave, not even honest—Teresa was neither naive or cruel enough to expect bravery or honesty from people, not all the time, not even some of the time—then, accountable. Responsible.

Hero had never known that such a thing could be attractive, even desirable; she'd long had the feeling that she had to hide that quality of hers when she was with other people her age, especially when she was with people she hoped would like her. At UST that was the case, drinking and fucking around, chary of being thought of as a stick-in-the-mud, as people often said, in exaggerated American English. Growing up, it had been one of the reasons she'd never gotten along well with her cousins.

But Teresa liked sticks-in-the-mud; liked people who thought twice, considered the consequences, worried at a years-long knot of fear deep in their chests, and still acted. Hero began to learn that there were all kinds of responsible people, not just stick-in-the-mud types like her. There were people who told lewd jokes from morning to night and gave the impression of being utterly unreliable in every aspect and yet threw their free arm over your body at an abrupt stop on an unlit road, seeing a Scout Ranger's jeep passing, reaching for an M-16, telling you to unlock your door and get ready to run. There were people who, even completely drunk after a successful raid, everyone high and horny from the victory, still jumped back when their calloused hand brushed yours, eyes blurry and unseeing, mumbling, Sorry naman ha, I didn't mean to, are you— and even when you pushed for it, more than willing, lonely between your legs, said things like, I'm too drunk, you're drunk, it's not, not—right.

Teresa's father was a journalist; disappeared first. Her mother was a lawyer representing a farmer's union in the Sierra Madre; gone a few months later. By that time, Teresa had graduated from college, had been working in Manila as a journalist herself. When she understood that she wasn't ever going to recover her parents' bodies, she stopped writing and resumed contact with a group of ex-Huk rebels who'd known her mother, two of whom had been her godparents. It was out of the anti-Japanese Hukbahalap rebellion that many peasants, not necessarily Huks them-selves, but sympathizers, informally began the process of land reform. They'd toiled on the same land for generations without any hope of own-ing it, but the rebellion empowered them. In the tumult of war, many were able to seize property and depose tyrannical landlords, beginning one of the first distributions of wealth in the nation's history. Some of the landowners had already run away to Manila long before the Huks and peasants arrived on the scene, collaborating with Japanese occupiers in exchange for safety and lifestyle upkeep—when the war was over, there would be time enough to return and wrest back their birthrights.

It was the U.S. Armed Forces in the Far East, together with the Southwest Pacific command of General MacArthur, who saw in the Huks not an ally in the fight against an Axis power, but a significant Communist threat in itself. After the war, the Huks were ordered by the American military to relinquish their weapons and cease contact with each other altogether. One of the first stories Teresa ever told the cadres was a kind of NPA origin story, about the massacre of over a hundred former Huk fighters in Bulacan; intercepted on their way home to Pam-panga, they'd been detained and then summarily executed by Filipino and American forces. U.S. intelligence helped draw up further lists of prominent Huks around the country, who were eventually murdered or imprisoned. Those who weren't captured fled into hiding: in Zambales, in the Cordilleras, in the Sierra Madre. In Isabela. Two such ex-Huk leaders who'd fled were a married couple. Teresa's godparents.

They were the ones who reached out to her first; they'd heard about her parents' murders in the newspapers. Teresa never told Hero about the early days of her own recruitment into what would later become the NPA, but she did say that she'd been around Hero's age. Those godparents, Renata and Efren, were no longer alive. Hero had never asked, but it wasn't difficult to infer that Teresa's predecessors had been killed; that she'd been forced to inherit her position as kumander upon their deaths.

By the time Hero arrived in Isabela, the New People's Army had its operating principles, the rules by which Hero would eventually come to live ten years of her life, embedded inside them like the tang of a blade within a hilt. No gambling and no drinking were two of the early rules, though Teresa was especially lenient on those two when she saw how good Hero was at cards, and how much it bonded everyone else to try to beat her.

The other rules were straightforward enough. To speak politely. To pay fairly for all purchases and to offer fair prices for all things sold, from the most gnarled kamote to the least-rusty semiautomatic. No brawls or physical abuse; woman-beating in particular would merit immediate expulsion from the ranks. Anything damaged had to be either repaired or paid for by the person who'd done the damaging. Avoid destruction of crops, even during skirmishes. Humane treatment of prisoners, even if they'd harmed a comrade. All sexual relations had to be undertaken between consenting adults.

There were three capital offenses for which the punishment would either be execution or expulsion—the latter simply a prolonged form of the former, for many cadres. The first offense was informing on the movement to state forces; self-explanatory. The second offense was rape—abuse of women is class exploitation, Amihan would spit out, her voice diamond-hard. The third offense was recidivism: if you kept stealing from other cadres or local farmers, if you kept harassing female comrades; if you proved you couldn't, or wouldn't, learn.

There were sometimes tensions between cadres and locals—often when a local had been beaten or tortured by AFP officers in an attempt to smoke out an NPA camp or cadre, or when one of the local militant groups that had been armed by the government to act as a counterinsurgency would kill off some other rival group out of personal or political bad blood, blaming the murder on the NPA. The latter happened more often than anything else. Whenever a local businessman would hire men to raid a rival's warehouses, or a local politican would kill an election opponent, or some regional oligarch's mansion was looted by false friends or disgruntled former employees, the easiest way to write off the crimes was to blame the New People's Army.

Beyond the small, daily work they did as local enforcers, especially in villages where people had already been bitterly taught to mistrust the police, Teresa and Eddie made a point of putting larger regional grievances front and center in their resistance strategies, which served the group's political beliefs, while also pragmatically helping to avoid civil conflicts by proving their loyalty to the people. Chief among them was corporate logging, which by the time of Hero's arrival was slowly reaching the peak of its boom in Isabela. Logging roads had been cut throughout the Northern Sierra Madre, all through Cagayan Valley. Marcos declared all public lands in a forty-five mile radius around Palanan as the Palanan Wilderness Area, supposedly to protect the forest's resources, as well as give the government a strategic advantage in the fight against the mountain's most dangerous inhabitants—us, Teresa said, when she explained it to Hero the first time, smiling.

When Amihan and Jon-Jon arrived in Isabela, one of Jon-Jon's major projects was confronting the corruption between the logging industry and the government, both local and national. Government forestors regularly turned a blind eye to regulation violations in exchange for bribes and personal favors, and the rapacious, unchecked logging such corruption permitted would only lead to more devastating consequences, Jon-Jon insisted. The scale of deforestation was so dramatic that post-typhoon floods would almost certainly be able to flow unimpeded, where the trees might have once provided a barricade. Instead, Jon-Jon said the unimaginable would eventually become the inevitable: whole villages would be buried in mud, worlds swallowed up in minutes. The loss of life would be catastrophic. The year before Hero had been captured, the principal project of the group had centered on plans to wage a large-scale attack on one of the largest forest concessions in the Northern Sierra Madre, near Maconacon, with the intention of burning a major industrial sawmill to the ground. Hero didn't know if the operation had ever taken place.

In Isabela, they'd moved around from sympathetic village to sympathetic village, rarely staying in one place for longer than a year, just to be safe; permanent camps made for convenient targets. NPA didn't stand for New People's Army, some cadres joked, but No Permanent Address. Or sometimes: Nice People Around. Teresa particularly liked that one. If AFP officers came to a village where they'd set up camp, locals could be relied upon to protect the cadres who'd been in their midst. After enough time, they'd determined that cadres were preferable to soldiers, those chicken thieves and brutos, who stomped into people's homes, drank too much beer, groped the women, looked down on mountain people, and protected the interests of wealthy lowlanders and foreigners.

From what Hero could remember, their encounters with AFP officers, typically at the borders of their chosen village, were minimal and perfunctory, the soldiers bored young men lounging with machine guns behind bulwarks of green sandbags. They rarely recognized an NPA cadre in civilian clothes, even if they were standing next to each other in the palengke, pointing at the same malaga. AFP officers left villages suspected to be NPA-occupied alone if there were enough armed cadres and supportive villagers to make an outright raid more trouble than it was worth. It was only when they thought that there was a valuable piece of information to be had, or if a person particularly valuable to the overall NPA and CPP infrastructure could be captured, that an attack became likely. But they weren't particularly valuable, in Isabela.

Hero had heard stories of more hardline Maoist groups, either deeper in the mountains or farther down south toward Manila, out of which often came rumors of purifications and purges, defections and coups. There were more powerful groups with clearly delineated hierarchies, whose leaders were often bigwigs in the main leadership of the Communist Party of the Philippines itself. Sometimes they were rumors that those groups practiced the same tactics as the government—that they planted bombs in civilian spaces and planned attacks on public gatherings, framing the military as responsible, in an effort to incite the people over to the revolutionary cause. Teresa was firmly opposed to such tactics—Amihan was more ambivalent—but she also never confronted her fellow commanders about it during the leadership convocations she attended every year. The week before those meetings was the only time Hero ever saw Teresa openly grouchy, which, she later realized, was how Teresa looked when she was nervous.

For years there was a rumor that Teresa had been asked to step up as the secretary general of the CPP, but that she'd turned the position down. Hero asked her outright if it was true and Teresa laughed it off by saying, Donya, would I turn down the spotlight? But Hero knew that Teresa would have done exactly that. For all her ebullience, Teresa liked being a big fish in a small pond. Liked small ponds, generally.

What interested Teresa wasn't power, or wasn't only power. It was change. Not change in the grand or demonstrably transformative sense, but change in the tectonic sense; change in the tectonic duration. Teresa accepted the title of kumander but kept the parameters of the role loose, so that people had the sense not that they belonged to something that already existed and would exist without them, greater than their individual lives—but rather, that they belonged to something that depended on them every day to survive; something that they were also in the process of making, slowly and clumsily, on a small, small, practically imperceptible scale. A few pieces of cracked earth, side by side: rubbing, shivering against each other. An eternity or two later, you had a volcano.

Lola Adela didn't keep them long. She asked to see Roni's arms, asked where else on Roni's body she had the eczema, if it itched more at night or in the morning, if it itched more after she ate certain foods or drank certain drinks. Roni said she'd never thought about it before.

Adela had only half finished her plate of sampalok and smoked two Lucky Strikes by the time her questions were up. Her demeanor was lazy, easy, like the answers were important but not particular weighty, like nothing Roni could say would faze or disturb her, like she wasn't even particularly interested in Roni or her disease beyond this conversation.

During most of the conversation, Hero didn't know what to do with herself, though Adela never made her feel as though she were intruding, and Roni didn't seem to care whether or not Hero overheard the conversation. Still, she turned away to pay attention to the other customers, to the radio broadcasting the baseball game, and Lolo Boy listening intently to it. Only when she watched him listening did she realize it wasn't a live radio broadcasting at all; he was listening to a taped recording. It was of a previous radio, or even television, broadcast. On the tape there were other ambient sounds: plates moving, people speaking in Tagalog, like he'd held a recorder up to the TV itself.

Oakland A's vs. Boston Red Sox, Adela said.

It took Hero a minute to realize Adela was addressing her, and not Roni.

It's the Oakland A's vs Boston Red Sox game last month, Adela repeated. Ninth inning. You like baseball?

Not. Really, Hero replied.

We made it to the World Series this year, Adela lamented. But. You know.

Hero didn't know, but Lolo Boy overheard his wife, and shouted back in English, Next year!

Adela smiled tolerantly. Then she turned her attention back to Roni, sipping at her half-smoked cigarette, eyes trained on the girl. I'm gonna get some more sampalok. You want some to take home? Maybe your parents want some? You like tamarind?

Roni nodded. I like it. It's sour.

Adela smiled. Okay, you wait here. She got up, passing Lolo Boy, brushing her hand on his shoulder in greeting, then disappeared into the kitchen.

Hero looked down at Roni. They were silent for a few minutes, then she finally asked: Okay ka ba?

Roni nodded. I like her.

Before Hero could ask why, Adela came back out, carrying a Tupperware of tamarind candy. So you come again next week, ha? Same time? What day is today?

Thursday, Lolo Boy called, though he was behind the counter. Hero wondered if he'd been listening this whole time.

Thursday, Adela repeated. Come Thursday afternoons. Okay?

Okay, Roni said. The door chimed again.

Hero turned to see Rosalyn walk in, already looking at them. You're still here! she gasped in mock horror. It must be serious then. Roni bounced up in her seat and waved.

We're almost done, Adela said.

Hero blinked. As far as she had seen, they hadn't done anything.

You guys should stay for karaoke tonight. It's fun.

Roni stopped bouncing. I don't like karaoke, she said, slumping back in her chair. I hate karaoke.

Sorry, I must have heard you wrong, I thought you said you don't like karaoke.

I hate karaoke!

Rosalyn turned beseeching eyes to her grandmother. Hold up, you're not finished, this kid needs serious help—

Okay, okay, Adela said, gesturing for Rosalyn to calm down. Then, to Hero: You guys, stay for karaoke. Call your mom, tell her to come after work.

Rosalyn chimed in: It's really fun. Lots of people come. Everyone. You don't have to sing if you don't want to. We'll have a lot of food—

Sorry, Hero interjected, sensing that talk of food was going to work not just on Roni, but on herself. We have to go home. She pointed at Roni. She got into a fight at school today. She needs to talk to her parents.

Adela looked intrigued. Fight?

Roni opened her mouth, pointed to the gap. Ah, Adela said.

Hero got up from the table. Thank you for the food.

She went to the cash register to pay. Behind her, she could hear Rosalyn saying to Roni, That gap you got now, why don't you get a gold tooth put in like my grandma? That would be cool. And Roni replying, Don't wanna. My mom had gold teeth when she was a kid and they all fell out. Oh, for real, Rosalyn murmured.

After Hero paid Lolo Boy for the food, she turned around and said, Come on, Roni, let's go.

Yeah, go face the music, Rosalyn snickered. Your parents are gonna belt your ass—

They don't do that, Roni said, making her way over to Hero. Then stopped, turned around. Hey! The TV show.

Rosalyn blinked. What TV show?

It was a movie, Hero said. Her face felt hot again, the skin there too tight. *Castle of* something.

Castle of Cagliostro? Jaime was watching *Castle of Cagliostro* in here again? Rosalyn made a wet sound in the back of her throat, mocking.

He said to ask you to borrow it.

Oh—yeah, sure. Rosalyn stood up, went to the TV and VCR. She ejected the tape, looked down at the label to make sure it was the right one. *The Castle of Cagliostro*. There you go. You gotta rewind it though.

Cool, Roni said.

Say thank you, Hero prompted.

Thank you, Roni said, without looking up, still peering at the tape, the image of a man in a green suit on the label.

We'll return it to you when we come back next week, Hero said.

Don't worry about it. Actually, don't even wait 'til next week. Come back tomorrow—we do karaoke on Friday nights, too. Thursday, Friday, and Saturday nights, we're always doing karaoke in here. Sometimes on Saturdays they push the tables to the wall and do cha-cha, line dancing, whatever. It's fun. Come by.

Hero looked down at Roni. She's, uh. She's suspended for the rest of the week, so we'll see. If her parents let her.

Rosalyn looked at Hero, opened her mouth to say something, but then stopped herself. Okay. Sure. See you, then. Uh-whatever's-fine.

Hero smiled stiffly. Rosalyn winced.

Joke got old, right? Okay. Yeah. Later.

Hero turned to Adela and Boy. Salamat, ha, Lola Adela. Lolo Boy. See you next week.

Bye, Roni said vaguely, cradling her treasure, half out the door.

Hero started the car, made sure Roni put on her seat belt, put on her own. Checked the dashboard, the front seats, the transmission, the gas meter. She didn't know why she was checking all of those things until she lifted her eyes and saw that Rosalyn and Adela were standing in the entryway of the restaurant.

Adela was waving. Rosalyn was just looking. Hero lifted a heavy hand, found it took her a long time to put it back down. She looked in the rearview mirror, then behind her twice, just to make sure she wasn't backing up into anybody. It felt like she needed to be extra careful. She drove away before she could look back, or wave a second time.

Pol was awake when they got home; they knew because the garage door was open. When Hero pulled the car up the driveway, he came into sight, sitting on his chair next to the card table, smoking. Hero parked outside, turned off the engine, unbuckled her seat belt, opened her car door, climbed out.

Roni hadn't yet moved. Roni, she prompted, before looking at the girl's face, and stopping short. Roni had on a full-blown Our Lady of Sorrows look, seven daggers in the heart. Surprise, then sympathy, thickened in Hero's throat, fast, as it always did when Roni looked her age. But there wasn't anything she could do. They were already here.

Let's go, Hero said, quieter.

Roni took off her seat belt, opened the car door. Took her backpack out, and held it in one hand, just by the left strap. It was as if she'd only just been made aware of this possibility—that Pol might be angry with her. Hero realized, then, that this might be the first time she was going to ever see Pol angry at Roni; the first time she was ever going to see him angry, period.

Geronima, Pol said, face obscured behind the smoke. Halika dito.

At first Hero thought Pol was talking to her, and was startled when Roni began shuffling forward, face lowered, toward her father. Another first: she'd never heard anyone call Roni by their shared full name before.

Nimang, Pol said. Can you make me a coffee, please?

Hero nodded jerkily, neck stiff. Of course.

She made her way into the garage, then realized that she hadn't even closed the car door yet. Roni hadn't, either. She jogged back awkwardly, saw that Roni had left the videotape and the Tupperware of sampalok. Hero retrieved the lot, then closed the doors. The sound they made was too loud in the dense silence of the driveway. When Hero passed, on the way into the kitchen, Roni hadn't lifted her face yet. Small, wretched sounds were coming from her body; she was crying, but softly and to herself, trying to bury it in her chest, so the tears wouldn't be misconstrued as an attempt to garner sympathy. She had her honor.

Hero heard Pol say: Look at me, Geronima.

Hero put the Tupperware in the refrigerator, unsure of its proper storage. The video she put on the table, then started on the coffee. When Hero was finished, she didn't know what to do with it; whether she should bring it out, whether Pol had actually wanted coffee, or whether it was just a way of telling her to leave. She hovered near the kitchen door to the garage, trying to overhear. All she heard was Roni sniffling. It wasn't a good time to interrupt. She went back to the coffee. It would be cold by the time Pol was finished. She considered going upstairs, but found she didn't want to be far away, even though it was none of her business, not really. She started making another coffee, drinking the one she'd just made herself. It was far too sweet, full of vanilla-flavored creamer, the way everyone knew Pol liked his coffee. Hero drank it anyway.

The second coffee was finished. Hero had drunk half of the first coffee. She stared down at both cups. The idea of making a third one was absurd, and yet. Just as Hero was about to pull a third cup from the cabinet, she heard shuffling. Pol's tsinelas. They were coming back inside.

Pol came through the door first, holding his large glass of Coke and ice. Behind him, Roni was hiccuping, eyes swollen, nose red and moist with snot.

Hero brought the coffee cup over to Pol.

Thank you, Pol said. Roni sat down in her customary seat, limp with misery, her backpack slumped between her legs.

Do your homework, Pol said. Added a final blow: Mom's on her way home right now.

At that, Roni's face looked on the verge of crumpling again, her eyes squeezing shut. But then, she steeled herself. Opened her backpack. Searched for her workbook, pulled it out, rummaged around for a pencil. Both of her hands were shaking. Suddenly, her eyes caught sight of the videotape, and stuttered there for a minute, the most animal part of her brain remembering recent pleasure, some dumb feeler within her grasping blindly at it.

Pol was holding one of the black plastic combs he usually kept nearby; he had one in the pocket of his work uniform, one in the pocket of his bathrobe, and one on the table somewhere, next to his cigarettes. In one hand was the comb, in the other hand was a white panyo. He was threading the thin white fabric of the panyo between the individual teeth of the comb, back and forth, back and forth, so it gradually dislodged the gray dirt that had accumulated there—skin cells, old pomade, dust. It was a ritual he performed regularly; he was a fastidious person about things like that. He'd been like that in Vigan, too.

It wasn't anything out of the ordinary, seeing him do it, but that seemed to be what hit Roni the hardest; the deliberate economy of movement, his absorption in the mundane task, while she hung from a wire, waiting to be forgiven. Roni looked at the comb in his hands and promptly burst into tears. Loudly this time, no holding back. The sounds echoed in the room; rose in great woeful waves, then died down to wet, choking gasps, then a brief silence, while Roni gathered strength—then lost it, and the wails rose up again.

Pol sighed with his chest more than his mouth, and said nothing. Let it happen, waited for Roni to lose energy. Hero thought Roni would apologize, even beg—but she didn't, or couldn't, say a word.

Pol's face had been impassive since their arrival, but for just a moment, Hero saw it flicker. He looked, briefly, like he might say something, reach out. But he pulled back and repeated, somehow to himself as much as to Roni: Do your homework now.

Most afternoons Hero offered to help Roni with her homework. Today she knew she couldn't. She had to leave her there.

Hero took the videotape, not meeting Roni's gaze, knowing she was unlikely to attract it anyway. Roni hadn't looked at her since they arrived home, had forgotten anyone else existed; the world had narrowed down to encompass just the people who were angry with her. She hoped the girl would know that she meant to keep it safe, not to confiscate it. Went to her room. As usual, she'd only slept three or four hours the previous night; maybe she would take a nap.

It felt, as soon as she hit the mattress, as though she'd lived two days in one, her body sack-heavy and numb. For the first time she was aware of the hair on her head, its weight and its texture, how foreign and new it now felt. It was different, getting your hair washed at a salon. She wondered why. Where had Rosalyn put her elastic while she was washing Hero's hair, she wondered. She thought about whether or not Rosalyn had slid it onto her own wrist. Then tried to stop thinking about that.

Drifing between sleeping and waking, Hero tried to remember the last time she'd gotten in trouble at school, but couldn't think of a single time; for all the fucking around she and Francisco had done, both of them had been good students, well behaved. She remembered getting into trouble once or twice, perhaps, for speaking Ilocano to a friend when only English was allowed on the school campus, but even then she'd always gotten off leniently, with a warning. There were other students, often young men from less wealthy families, for whom speaking Ilocano would merit a nasty beating and daylong exile in front of the school's altar.

She had no idea what Roni was learning in school, whether she got good grades, what subjects she enjoyed. As far as she could tell, school was a place for Roni to fight. But probably whatever Roni was learning in class, Hero had learned, too, even down to the history—in Vigan they'd learned about things like the capitals of all the American states, Colorado mountain ranges. It was Teresa, not a schoolteacher, who told Hero about the genocides that had expunged a sixth of the population from Luzon alone, six hundred thousand souls. The total number killed in the archipelago, including the genocides on Samar, was generally accepted to be around one and a half million.

I want no prisoners, Teresa said to the cadres, quoting General Jacob Smith, who'd presided over the genocides in Samar. *I want you to kill and burn; the more you kill and burn the better you will please me.* Smith, nick-named Hell Roaring, introduced a system called reconcentration, segregating the common population from so-called revolutionaries by containing the former in what was called a reconcentrated zone. The point was to sever the guerrilla fighters from the rest of the civilian population, Teresa explained, depriving them of access to food, shelter, sympathy. The reconcentrated zone was placed under strict military surveillance, and everything outside of the zone was treated as a no-man's-land. Anyone unlucky enough to be outside of its perimeter— maybe a parent or ex-lover was a revolutionary, maybe a sick relative lived on the other side—was shot on sight. Their bodies were left next to the homes that had already been razed, cattle that had been massacred, crops that had been left to decay. Let no livelihood be salvaged from the earth; that was the official policy. Smith's fellow general, J. Franklin Bell, carried out a similar campaign in Batangas; according to his own calculations, over six hundred thousand Filipinos were killed within three years. Hero didn't know of any official Filipino calculations.

Another word for what the Americans were doing, coined by a Republican congressman, was *pacification.* Bell bragged that he'd found the secret of pacification: *They never rebel in Luzon, because there isn't anybody there to rebel.* President McKinley was more succinct; he called it extermination. Hero didn't learn any of those words at school.

What she did remember from her time in school was a painting by El Greco, the Greek Spaniard who produced portraits of saints and

messiahs and royals. The teachers in Hero's Catholic school mostly practiced the kind of two-faced, Padre Dámaso–style authoritarianism that
had passed for pedagogy in the archipelago for over three hundred years,
abstemious piety with a touch of fondling, but they would occasionally
extend their lessons to art when the artwork's subject was religion. El
Greco's work passed educational muster in Vigan, and so when Hero was
around ten years old, she saw the first and only painting she ever loved.

Her teacher showed the class a portrait of Jesus that Hero hadn't ever
seen before, nothing like the blandly virile one Hamin hung next to the
more traditional De Vera pastorals, Jesus dewy and muscular like a
Hollywood idol, shining hair flowing over his shoulders. The El Greco
had been painted around the time Magalat was organizing his revolt in
Cagayan—that wasn't how the teacher framed it, but years later, Hero
drew the two things together, looking for a familiar face in the foreign
frame. In the painting, Jesus was raising two long anemic fingers in
greeting or postponement, and he had strabismus, a quality Lulay used
to spout about as a feature shared by mystics, geniuses, thieves, imagina-
tive children, and those possessed by kapres. One eye looked the world
in the face. The other eye needed a break, and wandered off.

The teacher said the name of the painting was El Salvador del Mundo.
But in no painting had Hero ever seen anyone look less like a savior of
the world. The expression of Jesus in the painting was one of grievous
humility and reticence. His face was hollow-cheeked and wan, and in his
gaze was the inconsolable calm of someone who had long ago reconciled
himself to the knowledge that the world was totally unsavable.

For years, Hero thought that the title was meant to be ironic. But
only in California did Hero remember the painting again and finally
realize what she hadn't been able to know, back then; what the face in the
El Greco painting actually looked like. It just looked like an adult. Someone who'd once been a kid, and wasn't one anymore.

It was evening when Hero woke up. Paz was home, and yelling. Loud
enough to echo all the way upstairs, through Hero's door. She got out of

bed, crept near the door. Paz's voice was muffled, but it sounded like, AND WHAT THANKS DO I GET—FOR WORKING EVERY DAY AND NIGHT LIKE A DOG—WHY DO I HAVE TO PAY FOR THAT KID'S GLASSES—HUH—YOU KNOW WHAT THEY CALLED YOU—YOU KNOW WHAT HIS MOM CALLED US—HUH—HUH—

Hero thought about opening the door, to more distinctly hear not Paz's words, but Roni's or even Pol's response. But she worried about the sound the door would make, the attention it might draw. Maybe drawing attention was just what she needed to do, to distract Paz from her tirade. She put her hand on the doorknob—then heard them, the stomping footsteps, getting closer, hammering on each stair like a blow. The loud, frustrated hissing and a fist slamming against the wall, then the door to a bedroom slamming closed.

Hero waited. Listened. She couldn't hear Pol or Roni at all—then she heard the papery shuffle of tsinelas. Pol, walking around, still in the kitchen. Hero strained to make out voices, but either they weren't saying anything, or they were saying it low, only for each other.

She heard the other door open again. Stomping down the stairs, again. Paz's voice, still hard, but not as loud. Tired and barbed, directed at Pol. I have to go back to work. I'll get in trouble. Then a final hiss: Bahala na kayo!

Hero couldn't hear Pol's response. The sound of the garage door opening, a car engine starting up. A car driving away. The garage door closing. There were still noises coming from downstairs; the television. Hero's mouth was dry and woolly from sleep. She badly needed a drink of water.

Roni and Pol were sitting on the couch together, watching television in the living room, all the lights still on. Roni was slurping noodles out of a Styrofoam cup; Maruchan instant noodles. Pol had the same noodles, but he'd put them into a separate bowl, added a raw egg to it, which he was stirring, his eyes on the screen.

A handsome older bald man was onscreen, looking like he was dying of a head injury. He was talking to a much younger man, with a soft, pretty face. They were both wearing red and black uniforms, covered with dust, gold insignias on the chest. Teresa also had a uniform, though she wore it only on the days when journalists or party bigwigs were coming to visit. Khaki green with patches on both sides of her chest, just above the nipples: NEW PEOPLE'S ARMY on the right side. And on the left side, TERESA MACALINTAL. Teresa often joked that it should be the other way around; that she should be wearing NEW PEOPLE'S ARMY over her heart.

Once, in the early days, both of the patches fell off, and it was Hero who sewed them back on, the sutures tight, the uniform still warm from Teresa's body, which was sitting across the room in Hero's clinic in a tank top, chain-smoking and making fun of one of her counterparts, a commander from Bataan who'd mistaken Teresa for one of the commander's wives. Later, the newer uniforms came updated with patches that stuck on with Velcro, but Teresa never switched over, saying the uniform was good luck, she'd stayed alive this long and wasn't about to test it. Hero had never believed in things like bertud, or anting-anting, amulets that would protect someone the way rumors abounded that Marcos himself had once paid someone to embed a piece of holy wood into his back for protection. But whenever Hero saw her handiwork, the white stitches holding up Teresa's name, a splinter of her believed.

You guys are still awake? Hero asked.

I took off work, Pol said, turning around on the couch to face her. Roni didn't turn around. Pol picked up the remote and paused the show; a recording then, not a live broadcast.

Nangánkan? You want cup noodles?

No, I'm. I'm not hungry. I already ate.

Pol didn't try to hide his disbelief. When? You've been in your room.

Hero opened her mouth to argue, but her stomach answered for her, in a low rumble. The corner of Pol's mouth lifted. See.

He stood. I'll make another one for both of us, I'm still hungry. You want raw or boiled egg?

Hero stepped forward, hands stretched out, but in refusal. Boiled, but—no, no—I don't—I'm not that hungry—

Pol had already gone back into the kitchen, rummaging through the cabinet for another Styrofoam cup.

Hero stood behind Roni awkwardly, hands behind her back. The girl still hadn't turned around.

Hoy. Roni. Okay ka ba?

Small shoulders shrugged. Hero swallowed, then walked around the couch to face Roni. The girl's eyes and nose were swollen and red, like she'd been crying for hours with no respite, and had only just stopped. The eczema around her eyes was inflamed, cracked open and still wet with pus. The tears must have stung the sores. Roni's eyes were unfocused as she sucked another mouthful of noodles, sabaw splashing onto her cheeks. She wiped at them with the back of her hand, messily.

Someone had replaced the extra-wide Band-Aids that Hero assumed a teacher or school nurse had applied to Roni's knees. Now there were large squares of gauze on both knees, stained with iodine and blood, neatly taped down. Hero had forgotten about Roni's other injuries, besides the missing tooth. The gauze protected the scrapes completely while making them look much worse than they were—someone had overdone it, but someone had done it well. The work had been done by a practiced nurse, used to changing dressings daily. Hero thought of Paz, screaming and slamming doors, then kneeling in front of Roni to carefully change her bandages before she left for work.

Your mom won't be mad at you forever, Hero said. She'd never sounded so stupid in her life. She forged on. She loves you. Really. A lot.

Roni's gaze went glassy and vacant. Could you move? I can't see.

Hero shuffled clumsily to the side, then remembered the show wasn't even running. There wasn't anything to watch; the only view she was blocking was of the bald man's dying smile, garbled with gray pause scratches.

Nimang, Pol called from the kitchen. Come here, tell me how much egg you want in yours.

Hero stood up. Roni had curled up even more into herself on the couch, knees drawn up, hand clutching the cup to her chest, still chewing on noodles. Her eyes were fixed on the screen.

When Hero approached Pol, he was in the process of peeling a boiled egg.

Paz is working night shift tonight, he said.

Paz rarely worked night shift; she said herself she couldn't handle it, was more suited to working from six in the morning until midnight than the other way around, even if the shift was shorter and paid more.

Hero didn't ask about it. She held her hand out. I'll peel the egg.

Pol didn't hand it over to her, continuing to thumb the shell off the white egg flesh, slowly, deliberately, in one single strip. Then he took a knife, cut the the egg in half. It was boiled perfectly, no gray around the edges. The yolk was smaller and paler than the ones she ate in Vigan, but then, they'd often used duck eggs. He cut the halves into quarters. The Styrofoam cup of noodles was waiting, its paper lid sealed over, no steam escaping.

She reminds me so much of you when you were younger, Pol said.

Hero went very still. Pol picked up another boiled egg, cracked it on the counter, fatter side down, so the small air pocket there shattered easily. Started peeling it.

Hero dared to glance back in the living room. Roni still hadn't moved.

I think she's much stronger than I was at her age, she said.

Pol smiled down into his chest. The sulfurous, bodily stink of too many peeled boiled eggs was starting to fill the air. No. You were like that, too. Both of you. Tangken tabungáw.

Hero hadn't eaten a tabungáw since leaving Vigan as a teenager. Manileños called it upo, she remembered. When she was a kid, there were still people who hollowed the gourd out, dried it, used it as a hat from the rain, made musical instruments out of it. Some political ally had given Hamin a gift of it once, a decorative bowl made from dried tabungáw rind, handpainted, beautiful. Concepcion scoffed at it, said the gift was an insult to good taste, and gave it to her driver for Christmas. Bottle gourd, hard as wood on the outside, even when it was ripe. And on the inside: melting, mushy-sweet. When someone said, You're hard as a tabungáw, it was a gentle rebuke, a way of turning a hardass over to expose her underbelly, remind her of her thin-furred and woundable parts.

The last person to call her that was Amihan. Amihan, crossing her arms while they stood together at the entrance of a sinanglawan they'd stopped off to eat at on their way back from buying supplies at the botica in Ilagan City. Waiting for the heavy rain to pass before they could drive safely back up the mountain, the first time they'd ever been alone together, only a few months after her arrival in Isabela.

Amihan had been adopted by an ex-Huk farming commune over in Tarlac. Her own parents had been tenant farmers; first they'd witnessed the arrival of the Japanese, whose attempts to liberate Filipinos from the colonial Western stranglehold that had deformed their true Asian culture mostly consisted of taking the lightest-skinned women away to abandoned shacks and repeatedly raping them. Amihan still remembered her mother rubbing both of their faces with charcoal and dirt, praying for Our Fickle Lady of Ugliness to have pity on them, not knowing that there was no such goddess, no such safety. Then they'd been liberated yet again by the Philippine army, who behaved more or less the same as their predecessors, but now in a language they could understand. By the time Amihan was born, an older sister had already died of pneumonia, leaving just Amihan and two younger brothers, twins. Keeping all three children wasn't an option, so like most farmers in the area who couldn't afford their own families, they put one child up for adoption.

Amihan was almost a teenager when her parents gave her—later she would finally say, sold—to the landlord of a sugar plantation on the other side of the province, where first she'd worked as a housemaid. When she turned fourteen, ropy and broad-shouldered with hair she'd shorn herself, she started working as a day laborer on the plantation, cutting cane and learning how to curse. Less than a year later she would incite a small mutiny over wage increases and working conditions, burning a quarter hectare of cane to the ground in protest. The other farmers called her kuya even though they were older, which was acceptance enough. A group of ex-Huk laborers took note of her influence and daring; they invited her to their stronghold in the mountains of Zambales. By that point Amihan hadn't seen her family for over five years, and knew that if she left, she would likely never see them again. She accepted. Sometimes in the streets she saw a pair of smiling twins and her heart would skip, but that was the extent of her homesickness.

The ex-Huks maintained a formal Maoist training school in Zambales, which was why Amihan knew so much about Maoist and Marxist ideology even though she, like Hero, was skeptical and detached about the orthodoxy; more concerned with its effects, the structure it made visible. By the time she was twenty-one, the people who'd raised her in Zambales had evolved into little more than a sophisticated gang network, posing no substantial threat to the local government troops, with whom they lived in tense but mutually beneficial peace. They were led by Kumander Virgil, who established their urban base in Angeles City, near the Clark Air Base. The local economy was exploding with the increase in American forces stationed there on their way to or from Vietnam, and somebody had to cater to the twangy-voiced boys and their simple appetites—open up jueteng dens, open up undeveloped land, open up girls. Some of the American government forces even regularly hired bodyguards from the private security company operated by Virgil's right-hand man, Tonio, the bespectacled chinito who'd introduced Amihan to the concept of mass base, taught her at fourteen to break the wrist of any man who touched her without permission.

If Tonio had been like Amihan's gruff older brother, then Virgil had been her adoptive father. Virgil, gold on his neck and fingers, a younger and younger sweetheart at his side, had been convicted of rape and financial opportunism by a party court-martial and stripped, for a few months, of his command. Not long after his conviction, however, he managed to get himself reinstated, largely because the party members who opposed him started turning up dead. Amihan saw stronger, battle-scarred men tremble in Virgil's presence, and yet with her he'd always been patient and tender, never forgetting to remove his tinted sunglasses in her presence so that she could see the sun-spotted wrinkles around his eyes when she made him laugh. Later Tonio told her that Virgil had lost a daughter early on to meningitis. Amihan would have been the daughter's age, if she'd lived. You don't keep anyone, and everybody can be replaced: that was all Amihan knew about family.

Amihan had become a district commander by the time she was twenty-four, had gathered her own gang of intimates and loyalists, along with a small, but not negligible, amount of turf. As the years passed she became something between a treasured daughter and a thorn in her adoptive family's side; she'd never been good at hiding her displeasure with some of the practices that had become routine under Virgil's jurisdiction. What protected her for the time being was that she was a woman—more important, a daughter—but she knew in her bones that it was possible that she, too, might turn up in a dumpster behind one of the American bars, shot cleanly in the head, body untouched, a sign of paternal love. One day Virgil instructed Amihan to stop supporting a group of farmers being evicted from their lands to make way for a Voice of America transmitter. She refused. Not more than a week later, her second-in-command was beaten to death in a jueteng den, right in the heart of Amihan's turf. His face was unrecognizable, the silver ring on his pinky finger and the childhood bolo knife scar on his arm the only identifying marks. That was Jon-Jon's older brother.

What happened between her departure from Angeles City and her encounter with Teresa, Amihan never divulged, but Jon-Jon was the only one left of her gang still with them in Isabela. She didn't say what happened to everyone else, or if she did say it, she didn't say it to Hero.

Amihan was often mistaken for the real kumander of the group, but she always corrected new recruits, and denied it when people said she would make a good kumander one day. Hero always had the feeling it was because she was afraid she might one day turn into Virgil—that more power would trigger some heretofore untapped potential for greed, planted in her early education and waiting for water.

The only person Amihan really respected in the group was Teresa, and that was because the first time she'd met Teresa, Amihan had been in police custody, getting her breasts felt up, and Teresa had approached the constabulary, panyo covering her hair, pretending that she was lost, before elbowing him in the trachea then shooting him in the gut. That was the kind of thing you had to do to win Amihan's loyalty.

Hero still had no idea what it was in her that had first drawn

Amihan's surly, lingering gaze, but after a couple of years they were groping at each other in the back of Jon-Jon's jeep when Hero was supposed to be stocking up on supplies at the larger botica in Ilagan, hands shoved down each other's pants, Amihan scowling even in orgasm. Afterward, Amihan stalked off like they'd just had a fight, like she didn't want to ever see Hero's face again, and that lasted until the next time they saw fit to feel each other up.

Amihan, who cut through people's naiveté with the rusted-over elegance of a bolo. Amihan, who had a particular way of laughing that Hero still remembered in her dreams: one high-pitched bark, then a machine-gun firing of tinier ones, each increasing in force. Hero didn't know what it said about her that she'd found that laugh sexy.

Amihan, who said to Hero, right before muttering Tangken tabungáw under her breath at the entrance of that sinaglawan, weeks before they'd started sleeping with each other, without looking Hero in the eye as if she were impatient with herself for even caring, as if it had never occurred to her that the words could also apply to herself: Teresa says you're not as hard as you look.

Roni's suspension was unremarkable. She moped around the house while Paz and Pol were at work, opening cabinets in the kitchen to look for food, then closing them without retrieving anything, no hunger in her, just a listless need to do something with her hands. Hero still had the videotape of *The Castle of Cagliostro,* but neither of them were mentioning it; perhaps Roni knew what Hero was thinking, which was that she wasn't sure if it was all right to let Roni watch the movie if technically she was being punished. Hero busied herself with cleaning, sweeping the floor in the kitchen and wiping at the countertops and the greasy stove, doing the dishes, drying plates individually instead of letting them air-dry in the broken dishwasher as usual, working until her hands had to tell her to stop. Then she moved to the living room to watch the bad daytime television she was slowly starting to enjoy, letting it pass through one ear and out the other. All the while Roni moved between the kitchen and the living room and the bathroom like a restless ghost, rattling at random doorknobs along the way, never meeting Hero's eye, passing her on a parallel but never-intersecting track.

When the phone rang late in the afternoon, they both jumped at it, grateful for the interruption.

Hero got to it first. Hello?

Hello? Pacita?

No, this is—her niece. Geronima—

Nn, nn. Geronima, it's Adela. From the other day.

Hero could hear the sounds of a busy restaurant over the phone, plates, a strain of music. Yes, I remember.

I'm calling to talk to Roni, see how she's doing. Nandyan ba siya?

She's here. You want to talk to her?

Please.

Hero turned to Roni. It's Lola Adela. From yesterday. She wants to talk to you.

Roni, who was looking in the kitchen cabinet for the hundredth time that day, poked her head out. Okay.

When on the phone, she stood up straighter, as though Lola Adela was watching. Hi.

Hero listened to Roni's side of the conversation: Um. Okay. Um, I don't think so. I have to ask my parents. They're at work. No. Well. I can ask Ate Hero. Okay.

Roni looked up, moving her mouth away from the receiver. Lola Adela wants to know if we can come to karaoke tonight.

Hero was one hundred percent sure that they could not, in fact, come to karaoke tonight. I don't think that's a good idea, Roni.

Roni relayed the verdict, said: Okay. Uh-huh. See you next week. Yeah. I'll give it to her. She handed the phone back to Hero. Wants to talk to you.

Hero picked up the phone. Hello?

You can't come tonight? Adela asked without preamble.

It's not a good day. Roni's in trouble. She's grounded.

Adela didn't respond right away; she sounded like she was listening to someone talk, someone in the room with her, whose voices Hero couldn't make out.

Tell her yourself, Adela said, but she wasn't speaking to Hero.

Uh, Hero ventured. Hello?

Someone in the restaurant cried out, Just—

Adela sighed on the phone. Hello? Geronima? You're there?

Yeah, I'm—

You can come alone, you know, Adela said. Even if Roni can't. Everyone's welcome. You're not the one grounded, right?

The possibility had never occurred to Hero. Ah, she said, trying to find a way to refuse without sounding like a, a—Teresa's voice, warm, *stick-in-the-mud*—she flattened her lips, breathed out. Sorry. That's very kind of you to offer. But I don't think I can come tonight. Sorry. Next time.

Next time, Adela repeated loudly, also not for Hero's benefit. Okay. We'll see you next week, ha? Okay.

Adela had an abrupt, borderline rude manner on the phone, like the medium itself displeased her. Hero stumbled, I—sure, okay. Salamat, po—

Okay, okay, bye, Adela said, and hung up, but not before Hero could hear her tsk-ing, exasperated, to someone in the room, Ikaw naman—

By the time they went back to Lola Adela's next Thursday, things had returned to normal. Only Paz had become a little more withdrawn, more brittle than usual. Hero saw Paz change Roni's bandages once more, inspect the wounds. They were healing, they must have been; they hadn't been that deep to begin with.

When Hero picked Roni up from school, she showed up on time, with the rest of her class. If she stayed a little longer, it was in the parking lot, where Hero could see her from behind the steering wheel; and it wasn't to fight, but to talk with other kids in her class, not just the two girls Hero had seen with Roni before, but a gaggle of other kids Hero didn't recognize, a couple boys, one of whom might have been the one who'd called Roni an Igorota. The fight—or maybe the suspension—had eased some of the strange tension around Roni, or earned her some form of respect. Not because she'd fought, but because she'd gotten in trouble; because they'd seen her injured. For that reason, she was starting to be liked.

At the restaurant, Adela was waiting for them in the back, smoking a Lucky Strike and picking at a plate of jeprox. Boy was chatting to a group of men in the front of the restaurant, but tipped the bill of his baseball cap at Roni, then Hero.

Kumusta ka na, kiddo, Adela greeted. You guys hungry?

Roni nodded. You want barbecue again? Adela asked. Roni nodded more vigorously. Adela looked over at Hero, asked the question with her eyes. Hero nodded once. Okay, sure.

Adela stood up, went over to the corner. Placed the cigarette in her mouth so it hung loosely over her bottom lip while she filled two plates with white rice and barbecued pork. Hero watched the cherry of the cigarette grow longer and longer, waited for the ash to fall into their food, but it never did. When she returned, she didn't sit down, but put the plates in front of them, then reached forward and flicked the cigarette's long cherry into the ashtray on the counter.

For a long time, Adela watched them eat—mostly Roni—while smoking and sipping at calamansi juice. Roni, unlike Hero, didn't care if people watched her while she ate; Paz often made a habit of it. Sometimes, that was the only way Hero ever saw Roni and Paz spending time together; Paz would come home from work, late at night, bearing a large aluminum tray of food she'd either gotten from some of the nurses at work or picked up from Gloria on the way home. Roni would eat a bit of it, as her midnight snack. Paz wouldn't eat at all, just leaning on her chin, looking at her daughter with tired, half-closed eyes. Murmuring: Ang sarap naman. It makes me happy, watching you eat like that.

Hero put her spoon down, full. Roni was still going strong. Adela smiled at Hero.

You want a cigarette?

Hero blinked at the carton stretched out toward her. Uh. No, that's okay. I—quit a while ago.

Adela made a longing sound. Good for you. I wish I could quit. But you know.

Hero did know. She'd been smoking since she was twelve or thirteen, like everyone else she'd grown up with. Hamin said he'd started smoking before he was ten; that he'd tasted his first cigarette before he ever tasted his first empanada, that he could more easily tell the difference between types of Virginia tobacco than he could tell the difference between cooked papaya and cooked tsayote. Purong Ilocano, Concepcion muttered, with her customary mixture of disdain and grudging sexual interest.

It wasn't really true that Hero had quit smoking, not exactly. In the camp, she'd only felt two cigarettes against her lips, both of them incitements to get her to talk, to give someone up. She hadn't talked; she hadn't finished either cigarette. When the guard put the first one out on her stomach, it was a surprise. The second one, she'd been expecting, so she knew to inhale deeply so there was more ash than ember on the cigarette once it touched down on her belly. That was long before they'd gotten to her thumbs. By the time she got to Soly, she couldn't keep a cigarette between her fingers for more than a few seconds without crying out and dropping it, and in any case it took months for the look of the red cherry at the end to stop sending her heart racing. Some part of her missed smoking, though. The part that never learned.

Are you Ilocana? Hero found herself asking.

Adela smiled. A little bit, she said.

Hero didn't know what that meant, but knew she wasn't going to ask. I don't speak it, Adela explained. Boy can speak a little bit, he used to work with a lot of Ilocanos when he was younger. But we always spoke to each other in Tagalog and English. From the beginning.

Hero believed her, though privately she'd thought that both Boy and Adela had choppy accents even in Tagalog, and they often made what Hero knew were grammatical mistakes—their handle on tenses was especially irregular. But in their speech the errors occurred so frequently as to appear less like mistakes and more like natural vernacular texture, like they'd been living outside the country for long enough to have transformed the language into an intimate dialect, the rules of which were known only to them. In English, on the other hand, they were much more relaxed, even fluid. Boy's accent was especially American, which had surprised Hero the first time she heard it. Boy was usually so quiet, she'd just assumed that he was like Paz's siblings, unshy people who'd been locked into themselves by their stumbling English.

You're Ilocana, Adela said. Hero nodded.

Full, right? Where were you born?

Hero nodded again. Vigan. Ilocos Sur.

So you speak Ilocano?

Hero nodded, then tilted her head mid-nod. I'm losing it, she said.

Adela picked up the jeprox tail and crunched down at it with her molars. Happens to everybody.

I'm half Ilocana, half Pangasinense, Roni announced, after swallowing. She said it, as always, like it had been taught to her.

Yep, that's right, Adela said. Your mom's Pangasinense. Very difficult language.

Roni shrugged. Dunno.

Dunno, Adela mimicked. Do you know if you like sotanghon? Noodles?

Roni looked doubtful. I've never had that. Like Cup O' Noodles?

Adela glanced over at Hero, still smiling. It's kind of like Cup O' Noodles. It's a very Ilocano dish. Hero didn't know what to do with the warmth that passed through her body at the thin thread of conspiracy—camaraderie—that Adela had thrown out to her, so easily, just with the word Ilocano.

Roni looked up at Hero for confirmation. It's good, Hero said, giving it.

Adela put her hands on the tabletop. Okay. I'm gonna make it in the back, now. You'll take it home?

If it's good, Roni said petulantly.

Adela laughed. Can you guys wait, or you want me to bring it to your house? I can get Rosalyn to bring it over. But if you wait, you can stay for karaoke.

Roni was still resistant to the prospect of karaoke, but now she was looking at the TV and VCR in the corner, both of which were turned out. She was thinking, Hero remembered, about the videotape that was in her backpack, waiting to be returned to Rosalyn, even though she'd never gotten the chance to watch it.

Could I do my homework here? Roni asked, directing her question not at Hero and Adela, but more at the TV itself.

Hero sighed. Let's call Tito Pol and ask if it's okay.

When Roni came back from her phone call home with Pol's permission to stay, she was bouncing with newfound motivation for finishing her homework. Adela stood up. Okay. I'll start making the sotanghon.

Roni stopped. Wait. Is that it?

Is what it.

Our. You know. Thing. Roni looked away, then gestured vaguely at her own skin. The healing stuff.

Adela had an unlit cigarette between her fingers, was tapping it on the counter.

You're right. Okay, halika dito. Come here, she said, gesturing for Roni to approach. Lift your face to me.

Roni took two small steps toward Adela, raised her chin. Adela passed the hand holding the cigarette over Roni's face, just covering above it. She hummed, in appraisal or approval, it wasn't immediately clear.

Put out your arms, she said, and Roni complied, then closed her eyes for good measure, even though Adela hadn't ordered her to.

Adela passed the hand over the arms there, lingering on the parts with eczema, making slow circles in the air.

Abracadabra, she intoned somberly.

Roni opened one sore eye, indignant. Is this a joke?

Adela grinned, gold teeth glinting. Then pinched Roni's nose, the cigarette filter brushing against the girl's skin.

Huwag kang matakot, she said, so softly that Hero wouldn't have heard it, if she wasn't straining to. Ligtas ka dito. So you just let me worry about the healing, okay?

When Roni was finished with her homework—done sloppily, even though Hero told her again and again to write the letters neatly; her handwriting was terrible, even for a child—she practically thrust the videotape into Hero's face.

Can we watch it now, can we can we can we can we—

Hero took the video out of Roni's hands. We should ask Lolo Boy and Lola Adela if it's okay. They didn't say. The TV's not even on.

Roni slumped back in her seat. Okay.

Hero stood. Boy and Adela were nowhere to be found; in the kitchen, she surmised. Hesitating, she made her way to the door, unwilling to poke her head in. Ah—excuse me—

Just come in already, Adela barked.

Boy and Adela were standing by the large stove, Boy in the middle of knifing a whole chicken into parts, its guts collected in a metal bowl, Adela watching over a large pot of boiling stock filled with older, frozen bones and wings.

Uh—can Roni watch a video on the TV? Rosalyn lent it to her last week.

Oh, Adela said. I don't know how to work that thing. Can you ask Rosalyn to set it up? She's in the salon.

Hero opened her mouth, but words came out slower than she intended them to. Sure. Of course. Okay. Thanks.

She went back out into the restaurant to relay the plan to Roni. The girl bounced up. Okay, let's go!

It was early evening when they walked out of the restaurant, leaving Roni's backpack and scattered homework papers at their table. A chill in the air, the sky that strange shade of violet it turned here, pale but deep at the same time, late enough there was no orange in it. Hero put her arms around herself, shivered in her long-sleeve shirt, no sweater. Looked at Roni, who was wearing something similar. Malamig, 'di ba? she said.

Roni's arms were swinging all the way to the salon. Not really.

They pushed open the salon doors, the cold picking up in a heavy, sudden gust that slid just past them. Hero looked at the sinks, but Rosalyn wasn't standing there; there was another young woman, talking to a young man, both of them probably Vietnamese.

Hey, Roni! came a voice from the other side of the salon.

Hero turned her head as if she'd been the one called. Rosalyn was sitting down on a stool just in front of a young woman who was seated in one of the hairdressing chairs. The young woman's face was angled toward a large mirror lit bright with vanity lights. Rosalyn's back was to the mirror, focused on the young woman, so the mirror reflected the woman's face and Rosalyn's long, sweatshirt-covered back. The young woman's face was cupped in one of Rosalyn's hands, her eyes closed, hair pulled back from her face with a cloth headband, towel around her neck and shoulders. Rosalyn's other hand was holding a slender brush. She was smiling at Roni.

So you get into any more fights?

Roni grinned, raising herself up on her toes. Not yet.

Rosalyn flicked her gaze up to Hero, then looked away, back to the upturned face in front of her. She leaned forward, applied something to the young woman's eye, then pulled back.

Whatcha doing, Roni asked.

Makeup, Rosalyn replied. Wanna see? She looked at the young woman, who'd opened her eyes. Is that okay? she asked, low.

The young woman nodded, turned her face slightly, careful not to disrupt Rosalyn's work. Hey. What's up.

What's up, Roni repeated. She looked impressed. You look cool.

The young woman laughed. Thanks. It's all her, she said, pointing her lips at Rosalyn.

Rosalyn gestured with a hand. Janelle, Roni. Roni, Janelle.

Your eyes look cool, Roni said.

You're so cute. Ask Rosalyn to do it for you, too.

Roni didn't, though, content to look at Janelle, whose eyes had been enlarged and shaded with what looked like a complicated mixture of shadows.

Rosalyn met Hero's eyes for the second time, lingering at last. Hey, what's up.

What's. up, Hero repeated, sounding stiff even to herself. That relaxed Rosalyn, somehow. It was only in that moment that Hero realized that Rosalyn hadn't been relaxed.

Can you help with the VCR? Roni asked. Your grandma said. I wanna watch *Castle of Cagli. Cagli. Cagliostro.*

Rosalyn leaned back on her stool, hands between her legs, balancing. She laughed. What, you didn't watch it yet?

I got in trouble. I forgot. So can you? Or. Roni glanced at Janelle. Are you busy—

Rosalyn tilted her head to Janelle. I'm kinda busy, yeah. Can you give me like five minutes, let me just finish up her eyes? Then I'll come do it for you quick. But then I gotta finish working on her. She's got homecoming tonight.

What's homecoming, Roni asked, still hugging the video. Hero was glad that Roni asked, so she didn't have to.

It's a dance, Janelle said. Her face in the mirror, lit and glowing, looked less real than the face gazing at Roni and Hero; its contours hazier, skin poreless, brighter.

She's got a daa-aaa-aaaate, Rosalyn teased.

You'll go to homecoming, too, when you're older, Janelle informed Roni. This year's my last one, now that I'm a senior in college. Wait, how old are you?

Almost eight.

Oh, really? You kinda seem older.

Like how old?

Like a hundred, Rosalyn interrupted. You guys wanna take a seat? She indicated to the two empty hairdressing chairs next to Janelle. You can sit here if you wanna watch. We don't have any more appointments tonight, so no one's gonna come in.

Roni climbed into the chair closest to Janelle, eyes hungry. It looks cool, she said again.

Hero hovered awkwardly next to Roni, hands wringing, then finally sat down in the free chair next to her, farthest from the action. She looked at Rosalyn, who wasn't looking back at her, but scrutinizing Janelle's face. Hero looked at Rosalyn's hand instead, the brush held capably in it, then at the long line of her back in the mirror, then at Janelle's eye, a denser black line cutting through the cloudy shadow and extending just past her lashline, slightly lifting the corner of her eye.

She does the best makeup in the whole South Bay, Janelle said, sounding sincere but stilted, trying not to move her face too much. I have to use tape when I do this at home.

Shut. up, Rosalyn muttered.

Probably the whole Bay Area, Janelle amended.

Cool, Roni said, leaning forward so she was practically crouching on the chair on all fours, her hands balanced on the arm closest to the two young women. Rosalyn was blending something on Janelle's eyelid with her middle finger, then using a different, shorter brush to blend something out beneath her lower lashline. When Janelle opened her eyes, there was a more defined halo of bronze diffused around the crisper black line, making her eyes recede, the expression in them faraway, secretive, ancient. It did look cool; Hero had to agree.

Okay, Rosalyn said, brisk. You need to curl them?

Janelle lifted up one corner of her mouth. What do you think?

Rosalyn made a tsk sound, but turned to the assortment of tools and brushes that had been laid on the counter in front of the mirror. Janelle rolled her eyes, defensive. Just 'cause *you* hate curled lashes—

What's curled lashes, Roni asked, practically hanging off the chair.

Janelle held up a hand. Nah, nah. Don't get her started on curled lashes, overplucking your brows, uh, why you should use lip liner as lipstick, why you should use *eyeliner* as lipstick, why you should use mascara as eyeliner—

Would you. just. chill, Rosalyn muttered.

Janelle made an ooh-ing sound. It was true her brows were very thin, like they'd been plucked and redrawn in a skinny, perpetually haughty line.

You don't want to show her your lip trick? Janelle leaned forward, pointed at her own lips, which were painted a very dark brownish red. You put brown or black eyeliner on the bottom lip, red lipliner on the top lip, then smudge them together and the color you get afterward stays forever, you need cooking oil to take it off—

Then she glanced back furtively at Rosalyn and her face turned serious, like she regretted making fun of the process.

She's the best. Go look at the album of all the girls she's done. Go ask Mai for it, it's behind the counter—

Just chill already, damn, Rosalyn snapped, louder. Hero knew all of a sudden that she was embarrassed; this was what Rosalyn looked like when she was embarrassed.

Janelle was laughing. How're you gonna be shy in front of an eight-year-old—

Rosalyn was holding a silver contraption Hero didn't recognize in one hand, a blow-dryer in another. Inexplicably, she started blow-drying the contraption, loud, purposely drowning out Janelle's voice, who sat back and rolled her eyes at the tactic. Roni, for her part, was mesmerized, staring hard at the contraption, the blow-dryer, then Janelle, like she was trying to figure out a puzzle.

Rosalyn tested the temperature of the contraption on the back of her hand, gently at first, then holding it there against her own skin for just a second or two longer. She held it up to Janelle's eye. Don't move, dumbass.

Hero watched as Rosalyn slowly clamped and then curled Janelle's lashes, focusing on the outermost corner. She took a tube of mascara, deftly wiped off the excess on the rim, applied the inky black to the base of the lashes with with a kind of stamping motion, then, drawing the lashes outward, followed the line she'd drawn on Janelle's eyelid. She repeated the whole procedure on the other eye.

Roni looked like she'd just watched someone perform a magic trick. Wha-at, she whispered.

Janelle opened her eyes, looked at herself in the mirror. She smiled at the face she saw there: someone who wasn't quite herself, but wasn't anything like a stranger, either; someone she recognized, and enjoyed living in, every now and then. She looked at Rosalyn, who was studying her own work with a critical eye. She moved to stand behind Janelle, so she could look at it in the mirror, too, edges blown-out with light.

In the mirror, Rosalyn's gaze eased over to find Hero, who'd been looking and looking at the reflection of Rosalyn, forgetting that the reflection belonged to a person who could look back.

Rosalyn looked away first. She turned to stare directly at Janelle, looking at her face close up, in the real world.

Don't act like you don't know it looks hella good. Janelle preened.

Rosalyn rolled her eyes. Then turned away from the mirror, toward Roni and Hero. The direct gaze felt less intimate to Hero than the brief glance they'd shared in the mirror.

You guys want me to set up the VCR now?

Uh, Roni said. She looked like she'd forgotten all about the VCR, the tape, the movie, her desire to watch it.

Look at her, she wants to watch you, Janelle said. Let her stay, it's cute.

Rosalyn ignored her. Let's go, I'll help you set it up.

She turned to Janelle. Just gimme five minutes.

I'm good. Janelle shrugged. She was smiling at Roni. Nice meeting you, Roni.

Nice meeting you, Roni returned, polite. Then, honest: You look so cool.

Janelle's smiled widened, lit up by the flattery, by her own beauty, the feeling of being admired by another girl. Thanks, ading.

Then she glanced over at Hero. Hey, nice to meet you, she said, not quite as heartfelt. She didn't even know Hero's name; Rosalyn hadn't introduced her and Hero hadn't introduced herself. See you around.

See you, Hero said, though she wasn't sure she would. She followed Rosalyn and Roni out of the salon.

A woman called after them—Mai, Hero remembered—Rosalyn, you finished?

I'm just gonna go to the restaurant for a few minutes. Janelle's not done yet.

Can you close up tonight?

Yeah, sure, Rosalyn said. Mai tossed a set of keys toward her and Rosalyn plucked it out of the air mid-flight, with one hand. She jerked her head at Hero and Roni. Let's go.

Rosalyn led the way, back into the cold air. She made a big show of shivering, of tucking her arms into her sweatshirt, so the fabric arms flopped about, limp and empty.

It's hella cold already, she breathed.

Puffs of air were forming in front of her mouth with every word. The fluorescent lights that lit the pathways between the strip mall's various restaurants and stores diffused an unreal bright blue-gray light over them, washing out their features. The light made it feel colder outside than it was.

I'm not that cold, Roni said.

That's 'cause you're a kid, Rosalyn explained. Kids have higher body temperatures.

There was a pointy bulge around Rosalyn's upper chest, where Hero assumed she was hugging herself. She turned to Hero. Look at your Ate Hero. She's cold.

That's different. She's new here. She's not used to winter.

Rosalyn turned to Hero. When'd you come over?

Few months ago.

Rosalyn let out a whistle, a larger cloud of steamy breath blooming in front of her. Wow, I thought you were just from, like, Hawaii or the East Coast or something. Your accent isn't that strong.

It's super strong! Roni interjected.

Your accent's super strong, Rosalyn said, turning fast to one side so a fabric arm slapped weakly at Roni's shoulder. You're more of a fob than your ate.

Roni pushed it away, sulking. Is not. Am not.

You'll lose it the longer you're in school. I was like you when I first came over.

I was born HERE, Roni groused.

Okay, okay—

You weren't born here? Hero asked.

Nah, Rosalyn said. Came over when I was four. Here we are, she said, pushing the door to the restaurant open, and hurrying into its warmth.

Boy was back behind the counter, but Adela was still in the kitchen. Rosalyn pushed her arms back out into her sleeves, lifted a hand in greeting; Boy saluted back. Then Rosalyn made her way over to the TV, started hooking up cables to plugs.

Hero wanted to ask her more questions, about when she'd come over, where she'd been from, what she'd thought of it, if she ever went back. If she still spoke Tagalog. Her grandmother was Ilocana—probably, Adela had said—but did Rosalyn speak Ilocano herself, how did she become a makeup artist, why was she working in a hair salon. Hero didn't know why she wanted to ask all those things, or how to stop herself from wanting to know them, how to stop newer questions from forming in her head.

Tape, Rosalyn said, holding her hand out while still facing the VCR. Hero had a vivid memory of herself, watching a surgeon in one of the teaching theaters at UST, holding his hand out for an instrument, a white-stockinged nurse placing it in his hands. Roni put the videotape on Rosalyn's palm. Hero watched Rosalyn's fingers close around it. She inserted the tape into the VCR, and all three of them watched the scratchy blue screen shudder to life.

There you go, Rosalyn said. Call me if you need anything else.

We're staying for karaoke, Roni said, still a trace of reluctance in her voice.

Rosalyn stopped. Looked at Roni, then up at Hero. Yeah?

'Cause we have to wait for Lola Adela to finish the sotanghon, Roni explained.

Rosalyn's eyes darted to Hero, then away again. You're sticking around?

Yes, Hero said, finding she wanted to be the one to say it.

Okay. I'll see you guys later then. Hero watched Rosalyn exit the restaurant. She shivered to herself, tucked her arms back into her sweatshirt, and started jogging back to the salon. Hero made herself turn away before she could watch Rosalyn disappear from view.

They'd reached the scene where Lupin started scaling the castle toward the imprisoned princess Clarisse, at first rangy and determined, then panicky and shrieking as one slip from a sloping rooftop forced him into a running leap toward safety, grasshopper legs straining, green blazer flapping—when Rosalyn walked back into the restaurant, which had been steadily filling up with people. As Hero and Roni watched the movie, the restaurant had slowly filled to capacity around them, families and groups of friends at every table, everyone ordering plates of barbecue, lumpia, kaldereta, jeprox, drinking bottle after bottle of beer, they'd run out of the Filipino beers early, the San Miguels and the Red Horses. Most people were now drinking Budweiser, or switched to Pepsi or Coke spiked with bottles of rum or bourbon pulled out of backpacks and duffel bags, neither Adela nor Boy blinking an eye.

Rosalyn spotted Hero and Roni, raised a hand to them, then went over to her grandma. To whatever Rosalyn said, Adela shook her head, waved her away, toward a table full of men and women, all of whom looked about Rosalyn's age. Rosalyn didn't sit down with them, but hovered, making conversation, one of her hands resting on the back of someone's chair; a young, possibly teenage morena wearing large hoop earrings, who looked up at her adoringly. One of the men at the table popped the cap off a Budweiser bottle and handed it to Rosalyn. Hero watched her mouth something, Thanks, then take a long, long pull from it, throat straining.

When she'd finished swallowing, she turned her chin slightly, so that it looked like she was listening to someone at the table, but the angle brought Hero into her line of sight, and their eyes met. Rosalyn didn't wave this time, but lifted her beer in greeting, then pointed to the beer itself. Mouthing, You want one?

Before Hero could decide whether or not she did, Rosalyn had turned to the man who'd given her the beer, appearing to ask for another one. He didn't have one to give her, so Rosalyn turned back to Hero, put up a finger to say, One sec, then made her way back to the counter, ducking below it, to open the door of a small refrigerator solely for drinks.

Rosalyn surfaced with a Red Horse, came over to Hero and Roni, standing aside to make sure she didn't block Roni's view of the television. Last one, she said to Hero. Usually it's my grandpa's. Don't let 'em see you drinking it, it's hard to get Red Horse around here.

Hero didn't know who 'em were; she could have meant the room at large, not just Boy, who was already drinking a Budweiser and distributing playing cards to a table of men.

Thanks, she said, accepting it, the bottle cold and wet on her fingers. There was a print of Rosalyn's fingers on the condensation on the glass surface. Hero's hand smeared the trace. She began, Do you have a bottle op—but Rosalyn took back the bottle, held it to the edge of the table, and wrenched the cap off in one quick movement. She handed it back to Hero, then lifted the butt of her Budweiser. Cheers.

Cheers, Hero said, slightly abashed.

Rosalyn looked over at Roni. Hi, Roni, like the movie?

Roni hadn't looked at either of them, transfixed by what she was watching, giggling to herself at Lupin hamming it up for the princess, asking her to believe in him. She nodded without looking at Rosalyn. Hi—yeah—

Rosalyn took another long pull from her beer. You guys wanna come sit with us over there? Pointing to the group she'd just left, who were engrossed in conversation with each other, or what looked like merciless teasing, the girl with hoop earrings shoving at the shoulders of two laughing men.

Hero studied Roni's face. I don't think she's moving anywhere.

Rosalyn laughed, then shifted her weight from foot to foot. Right. Yeah, okay. I, uh. She took a step backward, like she was going to go back to her friends, then stopped, pointed at the empty seat next to Hero.

Can I, and Hero nodded, gesturing, awkwardly standing half up to make room, even though Rosalyn had plenty of space to move. Sure.

There was a plate of puto and kutsinta on the table in front of the chair Rosalyn had just slid into. Half an hour earlier, Adela had come by with it, On the house, she'd said, for them to snack on while watching the movie. Roni had absently gnawed her way through four kutsinta and one puto, never taking her eyes off the screen. Rosalyn was looking at the plate now, but didn't make a move for them.

Have some, Hero said. We already ate.

Yeah? Rosalyn brightened, took a puto and shoved it whole in her mouth. Cool, I haven't eaten since breakfast.

Working hard, Hero said, sounding idiotic even to herself.

It's starting to be that time of the year, Rosalyn said, her words muffled by the sticky rice. Homecoming. Thanksgiving. Early Christmas dances. Early Christmas parties. Work parties. Whatever. Everyone wants their makeup done.

And you're the best in the South Bay, Hero added.

Rosalyn stared at her for a too-long moment, long enough that Hero thought she might have to apologize. Then instead, to Hero's alarm, Rosalyn slammed her own face down onto the table, cheek to the surface, the impact rattling the plate. Even Roni looked over briefly, before deciding the commotion wasn't more important than the movie.

Rosalyn was groaning, her eyes shut. She talks a lot of shit, Janelle, jeeez—

A deep breath, then: Anyway. Sorry you guys had to stick around, for.

It's fine, Hero interrupted, sensing Rosalyn would go on in this manner if she didn't. It was cool. Like Roni said. Really.

Rosalyn didn't lift her head from the table, but opened her eyes, peering up at Hero from there, her face smushed into the red-plastic-topped surface. The position made Hero feel nervous, like she was an intern being asked to hold a seizing patient down, keep them still so the first incision could be made safely.

She pushed past it. You're really—good. You, you do both hair and makeup?

No, Rosalyn said, sitting back up, calming down, reaching for her beer again. Not hair, not really. I just wash hair and sweep up at the end of the day. I don't know how to cut hair, not like Mai and them do; there's a whole way of cutting Asian hair 'cause it's thick, I don't know, something to do with the hair shaft. Like you gotta layer it? There's all kinds of techniques, I don't know. I just do the makeup.

Hero nodded by instinct, then found she didn't actually understand. So why. A hair salon.

Rosalyn started peeling the label off her bottle with a short thumbnail. I just started working over there 'cause my mom and Mai were friends, you know, we're neighbors, the restaurant's nearby, Mai's been cutting my mom's hair for years, doing my grandma's perms and stuff. And then she found out I did makeup sometimes, at girls' homes and stuff. For parties, you know. Cotillions and prom and dances and things. I made okay money off it. Mai used to have a girl over there who did makeup, but not that well, it was more, like, eyebrow waxing and stuff. So they weren't making that much. Now she's got me, and because they're a salon they can afford better stuff. Like theatrical makeup. Professional grade. Wholesale. So I can use that stuff and drugstore stuff and. Mix.

Rosalyn tore off the upper corner of the label with more force than was necessary, balled it up and flicked it away. Anyway. This is probably hella boring to you, sorry.

It's not, Hero said.

Rosalyn let the bottle go and started rubbing at the tops of her thighs. And you? What do you do? You've been here for a couple months, you said—

Hero opened her mouth and was about to say, I'm a doctor.

She closed her mouth again, took a breath; gathered. I mostly help out Tita Paz and Tito Pol. Roni's dad. Around the house, I mean. Cleaning and—taking Roni to school, picking her up. Things like that.

Rosalyn looked at her, then slightly past her, worrying at a thought like one might pick at a scab, obviously wanting to say something but holding it back. Hero liked that; how obvious it was. Okay, Rosalyn decided on saying. And you like it?

What.

Shrugging, I don't know. Living here. Started picking at the rest of the beer label. California, I guess.

This was—small talk, Hero thought to herself. Though why people called it small, she didn't know. The effort it scraped out of her felt immense, exhausting, like she should have studied for days beforehand just to be ready for it, like she'd need to sleep a dreamless sleep all night just to recover from it. Before she could answer, she felt the presence of someone standing beside her.

Rosalyn looked up at the presence, rolled her eyes. How late are you?

Hero followed the line of Rosalyn's sight. It was the sleepy-looking tisoy she and Roni had met the first day. He had a plastic cup of what looked like Coke in his hands.

The dude that was supposed to relieve me showed up two hours late, what was I gonna do. I didn't even get overtime for it.

Then the young man lifted his chin at Hero. What's up.

What's up, Hero returned woodenly.

Rosalyn gestured with her beer. Jaime, Ate Hero. Ate Hero, Jaime.

You guys were here last week, Jaime said. He jerked his head at the TV. Who's watching *Cagliostro*?

She is, Rosalyn said, pointing at Roni. You made a fan.

Jaime waved a hand in front of Roni's face, saying Hello-oo, but she barely reacted, moving instinctively so she could see the television, making a vague shooing motion at him, like she was swatting a fly.

Are we staying here or are Ruben and them gonna set up at your house?

Rosalyn shrugged. Ask my grandma, she's in the kitchen. I could stay.

Lemme get some kare-kare first.

Oh, what, you don't have diarrhea anymore? Rosalyn asked, smiling. Hero coughed.

Jaime's eyes closed to slits. Why are you like this.

It's brave to eat kare-kare, I don't think I'd wanna eat peanut sauce after being on the toilet for two days.

It's 'cause you're new, Jaime said to Hero, unfazed. He leaned in to the table to pick a kutsinta off the plate. Around a full mouth, he went on: She bullies people when she's nervous.

Rosalyn said, Good choice. Kutsinta. Something sticky—

Jaime pushed at the side of her head, but made it so the movement was more his hand ricocheting off her skull, no real pressure. I'm gonna get something to eat.

Remember, sticky things, plug up—

Rosalyn was starting to seem more like the woman Hero had met that first day, jocular, winking. She was still grinning, but she visibly became more awkward again, the farther away Jaime got from the table. Rosalyn didn't have to sit down with Hero and Roni in the first place; she'd done her job as the granddaughter of the establishment, she'd shown two newcomers ritual-perfect hospitality, she could rejoin her friends. Hero was usually good at letting things like that go, knowing when to call time on something.

Instead she said: You don't have to call me Ate Hero.

Rosalyn blinked over at her. Oh—yeah, no, it's just. A habit—

I'm—technically it would be manang, for me, anyway. Hero gestured imprecisely at herself. Ilocana.

Right, Rosalyn said, nodding. Okay. Man—

But just Hero's fine, Hero cut in. Or. Whatever. Geronima.

Or Nimang, she added out of habit, but something in her chest—night-blind and near-atrophied, dying out for sure but not dead yet—clenched down hard. She didn't want Rosalyn to call her Nimang. Like Pol with his reluctance to speak Ilocano, she didn't want anyone in the world to call her Nimang, not if they hadn't spent years calling her Nimang, not if they hadn't met her as Nimang, a world or two ago. A name had a lifespan, like anything else.

It was funny to discover this about herself only now: it was possible to have such deep, immovable desires without ever even knowing it; apparently there were desires that could live at the core of a person for years and years. It was funny, how little she could know of herself, how much there was still to witness, to be stumped by. It was funny, in that way of things being funny right before they dug deep, wrenched, and tore. Hero had once been the kind of person who started laughing when she was in pain—that was her body's natural reaction to shock, which they all discovered when she took a wrong step coming down a mountain slope and badly twisted her ankle, had to be carried back to their nipa hut slung like a sack of rice over Jon-Jon's shoulders, a fireman's carry, hands free to reach for his gun, and Teresa behind them making a big fuss the whole time just to keep her distracted, declaring, We need a doctor to treat our doctor! Amihan muttering from the front: Of course the first time Nimang would get hurt it'd be falling down a mountain.

Hero, Rosalyn was saying, and Hero forced herself up, out, back into the restaurant. Forced herself to tune in and hear it: her name, being called.

That's—Rosalyn's still unfamiliar face, smiling faintly, shoulders relaxing—kinda cool, I guess.

They didn't stay for karaoke. Adela gave them a stainless steel pot of so-tanghon, with an extra bag of dried mung bean noodles even though Hero said they had plenty at home. A woman Adela's age had begun badly singing *Endless Love* to the room at large, which as far as Roni was concerned, was their cue to leave. See you next Thursday, Adela said, and Rosalyn echoed it, saying if Roni liked *The Castle of Cagliostro,* she'd lend her some other movies she'd like even better.

They went to the restaurant every Thursday after school, met Adela, who had a chat with Roni, sometimes about her eczema, sometimes about other things entirely, like school or food or other kids at school. They even spent most of Thanksgiving's Thursday there at the restau-rant, since both Paz and Pol were working, taking advantage of the hol-iday overtime as usual.

Sometimes Adela didn't give them anything, sometimes she gave them leftovers from whatever hadn't sold that day at the restaurant, and sometimes, rarely, she gave them things that Hero finally recognized as ingredients for herbal medicine: pinya and ampalaya leaves crushed to powder, dried herbs that Adela said they grew themselves in their own backyard, Filipino medicinal plants that Hero hadn't seen since living in the mountains.

Roni started finding excuses to stay in the restaurant—she wanted to watch a video, she wanted to finish her homework, could Adela make sotanghon with more ginger in it, she could wait—until Hero got the hint and they made it a ritual, Roni doing her homework silently beside Hero, or watching the TV that was now set up for Roni's benefit, some new videotape that Rosalyn had recommended propped up, waiting. There was *Laputa: Castle in the Sky,* and *Nausicaa in the Valley of the Wind,* and Rosalyn said there were other cartoons, not movies but actual shows, that she could lend Roni, too, all of which Roni accepted gleefully, greedily.

Hero tried to remember if she'd watched as much television when she was younger; but then, they hadn't had television, not like this. The De Vera house was one of the first in their neighborhood to own a Betamax, but it was a status possession, rarely used; in general, the De Veras were bewildered by the televisual. Rosalyn got most of her videos, both the cartoons and the action movies, from the Taiwanese shop on the other side of the strip mall, which operated mostly as a video rental, but also sold books, tapes, and Hello Kitty paraphernelia.

What's that, Roni had asked once when she came upon Rosalyn reading one of the books she'd bought at the Taiwanese shop. *Cat's Eye,* Rosalyn replied. Is it good? Roni asked. Uh, can you even read? Rosalyn had retorted, which was a challenge as good as any Roni had ever gotten.

So Rosalyn also started lending Roni the comic books, along with loose sheets of paper with what she said were translations on it. Ruby, the daughter of the Taiwanese rental place's owner, usually did the translations for Rosalyn herself: sometimes paid, sometimes in exchange for makeovers. The store often got in the Chinese translations of Japanese comic books—the word was *manga,* Rosalyn insisted—before they were licensed for any other languages, so there was a whole informal network of fans who distributed translations.

Hero's only knowledge of things resembling manga were Filipino komiks, things like *Darna,* but she'd only watched the films; the one with Vilma Santos, or the older one, with Rosa del Rosario. She mentioned something once about thinking komiks were just for kids, but Rosalyn flashed a searchlight-look of hurt and betrayal onto Hero so harrowing that she fumbled the words back immediately, like almost dropping something and catching it just in time.

The cue to leave every Thursday night was still karaoke. Roni's demeanor changed, turned tetchy and anxious. Even Rosalyn started to notice, giving them a heads-up before the singing would begin, saying, Sorry, it's about to get real ugly, Roni—as she carried in the machine with Jaime's help.

Hero began to look forward to Thursdays, to the moments when Rosalyn's shift ended, usually around four if she didn't have to close up or have a makeup job, and she came in to see her grandmother, have a beer, make comments on the film she'd recommended to Roni. She was being gradually introduced to Rosalyn's friends, who were getting used to seeing her and Roni in the restaurant. There was, of course, Jaime, Rosalyn's best friend and neighbor since they were seven, who had intimate and encyclopedic knowledge about all the animated films Rosalyn was recommending, yet would only admit to that fact if Rosalyn said something he disagreed with, like when she said Fujiko Mine was the best character in *Castle of Cagliostro,* and he said she was so much better in the shows.

Rosalyn called him Lowme most of the time, once saying to Roni, half drunk: You get it, Roni, *Jaime, High-me,* Low-me, you get it?

Jaime looked over at Hero and deadpanned: She though that up in the eighth grade and hasn't come up with anything new since.

There was Ruben, a shorter, heavyset moreno with a shaved head who DJ-ed—mostly in people's garages—and Isagani, or Gani, a tall, wiry kid with glasses who DJ-ed along with Ruben, and was even darker than Ruben, what Concepcion would have called negrito. There were other men who sometimes came to the restaurant and hung out, and whose names Hero had trouble remembering, but these first two were Jaime's boys, or so Rosalyn called them. Though to Hero, it was obvious that the person who was really Jaime's boy was Rosalyn.

Then there were more girls than Hero could keep track of: Janelle, who was in her last year at San Jose State as a theater major—she hinted that Rosalyn had been a theater major herself; Lea, the morena with the hoop earrings, a nurse and apparently Ruben's younger sister; Rochelle, also morena but with chinita eyes, also a nurse, and Isagani's much shorter girlfriend; Maricris, a Visayan-born mestiza and singer of some kind, member of a girl group that Rosalyn described with hyperbolic praise. They were the ones Hero could remember, the ones who came to the restaurant most regularly, mostly because they all lived in Milpitas, or at least Berryessa or Fremont or, the farthest, Maricris, in San Jose. There were other friends they mentioned to each other, who were apparently to be found at the parties that Janelle and Rochelle started inviting Hero to. The parties took place in Rosalyn's garage or in Ruben's— although sometimes they went to attend Ruben and Isagani's gigs in Union City, Daly City, or even all the way up in San Francisco.

Rosalyn invited Hero to those parties, but her invitations were intermittent and palpably lackluster. Which was why Hero never went, at least not in those first few weeks. Later she realized that Rosalyn's lack of enthusiasm wasn't because she didn't want Hero to come to the parties, but because sometimes she herself didn't want to go—despite being, to any half-observant eye, the magnetic center of her gang. Do I need to see another dude spinning Planet Rock with his dick? Rosalyn retorted. I got work.

It was—friendship, some part of Hero's brain registered, distantly, dully, like hearing a song she hadn't heard for years, trying to place it, trying to remember who it was by. It was friendship; she was making friends. Rosalyn had figured out that Hero was new, that she didn't know many people—any people—in the Bay, and was doing the thing Rosalyn thought she did best: bringing people in, connecting them to each other, making of herself a rope that people could swing across, to get somewhere else.

And it worked. Even when Rosalyn wasn't in the room, people would come into the restaurant and recognize Hero or Roni. Jaime would grab two beers out of the refrigerator after his floater shift, hand one to Hero without even saying hi. Rochelle would come by with a bottle of her perfume because the week before Hero had stopped in her tracks, sniffing at the air, said, Who, who's wearing Avon's Sweet Honesty? and

Rochelle's face had broken open, delighted. Hero said she hadn't smelled it since leaving the Philippines, that every girl she knew back then had worn it, along with other Avon perfumes like Charisma Elusive, Occur. She didn't mention that the one of the first girls she'd ever fucked had worn Sweet Honesty.

It was possibly Hero's first time making friends with no shared cause, whose lives and deaths weren't on Hero's head or under her scalpel. Which meant that often she had the feeling of not knowing what the hell she was doing; where the boundaries and codes were in these friendships, in how people acted, what people said, or gave, or kept back. Before she met Teresa and Eddie, she'd had family members, and people she was fucking. Teresa and Eddie were neither of those things.

Hero didn't know what friends were supposed to want from each other, what was normal to want from a friend. More specifically, she didn't know what Rosalyn wanted from her, what was normal to want from Rosalyn. Most of the time, Rosalyn looked like all she wanted was to gather people in the restaurant and keep them there, talking, drinking, full of food, quick to clown on each other, while she drifted easily, aimlessly, from its center back out to its periphery, vigilant and smiling, a sentinel. But sometimes Hero would see a look of remoteness pass over Rosalyn's face, so distinct it was frightening, and then it would feel as though Rosalyn was one step away from walking out of the restaurant and never coming back, like she'd brought all these people to one place with the sole purpose of distracting them, sleight of hand, while she slipped out the back door, into a waiting car. It was this look on Rosalyn's face that Hero recognized the most—feeling it like the look was on her own face, just under the skin, at that tissue-thin border where the look settled, became soul. It was the look that made Hero feel like she was getting to know her.

One evening, Rosalyn asked if Hero would come with her, just outside the restaurant. Hero spared a glance over at Roni, who was watching *Fist of the North Star,* Jaime and Ruben's joint selection of the evening.

Hero followed, thinking maybe Rosalyn wanted to smoke and

wanted to do it with company, but once outside Rosalyn didn't pull out a pack of cigarettes. Come to think of it, she'd never seen Rosalyn smoke, at least not in the restaurant, like everyone else did. Jaime was a chain-smoker as bad as Adela, the two of them spotting each other cigarettes when one or the other's pack would inevitably run out.

Rosalyn began: Can I ask you something, and sorry if it's weird.

Something deep in Hero's muscles tightened. What?

Rosalyn stared at her. Then she said: Roni's parents. They treat you—do they treat you okay?

Hero stopped. The tightening in her body was stuck now, confused. Uh. Yes?

I'm serious, Rosalyn said. She wasn't holding a beer bottle, no cigarette to keep her hands occupied. You can be honest.

They treat me okay, Hero said, still confused. They treat me well. Really.

Rosalyn didn't look satisfied with that, so Hero had to keep talking: They're good to me. They're—Tito Pol's always taken care of me. Better than my own parents, she said, surprising herself by telling the truth.

Rosalyn studied her. She started to relax in slow, suspicious fractions, then deflated like a balloon. She rubbed a hand over her face. Okay.

What, Hero started, then shook her head. Her body felt bruised all over from the tension, still unsure if she could let it out. What's this about?

Ugh, Rosalyn closed her eyes. I'm a dumbass. Okay. Sorry.

What is this about.

Rosalyn made a frustrated sound then started talking in a long, rushed stream: Look, it's just—my mom has a cousin, she came over from the Philippines a couple years ago, she didn't have papers either, and she started working as like a maid for some family down in Glendale and—they—they don't let her go out anywhere, they don't even let her go out of the house, she's only ever called us twice, and, it's not like she can do anything or they'll get her deported and—look. I just, you—you—you never come out except for with Roni and only then to see my grandma, you never come to the parties, you never go out on the week-ends, it's like you're on house arrest or something—I don't know, I thought maybe something like that was going on.

Hero blinked.

Rosalyn didn't meet her eyes. Is. anything like that going on?

No.

But you don't have papers, right.

No, Hero said after a moment, drawing herself up rigidly.

But they're good to you?

Hero felt herself softening at the hard, faithless look on Rosalyn's face. They're good to me.

You—Rosalyn took a breath. Listen. If you want a job, or. Some-thing. I could hook you up. At the salon or at the restaurant. It's getting hard for Grandpa to be up all day, serving people, plus cooking the food the night before. It's not like we would pay you a lot. I'm just saying, if you. If you wanted to get out of the house or something. Or, you could help with the catering. We need people to help out with that. For events and stuff. It's a pain.

Hero had to say it. I can't hold a knife, she said finally.

The look on Rosalyn's face told Hero that Rosalyn had already no-ticed her thumbs. Hero didn't know how she felt about that, then de-cided she hated it completely. She didn't want to imagine the moment Rosalyn must have noticed, what she might have thought, how long she'd been carrying that knowledge around with her, what she'd made of it since. And now every moment of passing humor, affection, comfort that had furrowed between them since Hero and Roni walked through the doors of the salon that first day was—That's fine, Rosalyn said, too fast, like she was ready for it.

I can't wash dishes if it's for too long, Hero said, looking away. But I can load a dishwasher. Work the register.

Rosalyn nodded, encouraging: Yeah, sure. It's mostly just, yeah. Like you said. Working the register. It's mostly just so someone's there at the counter during the day when Grandma and Grandpa are in the back.

Hero crossed her arms, so her hands were hidden underneath her armpits. I'll ask Tito Pol and Tita Paz. Then, at the renewed look of suspicion on Rosalyn's face, revised her words: I'll think about it.

Rosalyn cast a look back into the windows of the restaurant, into the blue, red, and yellow words written by hand across the glass, the Gothic script of the letters so traditional and familiar Hero could have been looking at any restaurant in Vigan, BBQ—ADOBO—LECHON KAWALI—HALO HALO, then through the letters, at the people inside watching the television and eating.

Okay, Rosalyn said without meeting Hero's eyes. Think about it.

She rubbed her hands up and down her own arms. Let's go back inside, I'm freezing.

Hero obeyed and turned around. She was closest to the door, and was about to open it, but then she turned back to Rosalyn. Your aunt. In Glendale.

Yeah.

The family, Hero said. What are they?

Rosalyn looked at her, waiting. Hero clarified. Are they American? Puti?

There was a look in Rosalyn's eyes that Hero recognized, not because she knew it on her own face, but for much simpler reasons—it had been turned on her enough times in her life for her to be familiar with the feel of it, the gripping weight in her stomach, throat dry, when she received it. A Lulay-worthy look of irritation and disappointment. It was a relief to witness; Hero knew where she was in the world again when someone was disappointed with her. They're Filipino, Rosalyn said, already sounding tired of the whole conversation. Then she walked through the door that Hero hadn't realized she was holding open.

Hero mentioned it to Pol one afternoon, that Rosalyn had offered her a job. He said it was fine with him, as long as she could still pick Roni up from school—he'd talk to Paz about it.

Then he said, You know, Nimang, if you want to go out sometimes—late at night, I mean, when Paz is home and I'm at work. You could.

If you had someone pick you up, he added, apologetic. We're saving up to get you a used car, but—

You don't have to do that, Hero interrupted. But. If I worked for Adela. I could save up myself. And help out.

You help out enough, Pol said. He smiled. Roni likes going to the restaurant. She's always talking about Lola Adela this, Lola Adela that. Ate Rosalyn, Kuya Jaime.

It hadn't occurred to Hero that Roni might be talking to Pol about their Thursday nights. She opened her mouth but Pol beat her to it, said: I'm glad you're making friends. It's good for you.

So, he continued. You should feel free. You're not a child.

Hero didn't know how to explain it to Pol; she hadn't known how to explain it to Rosalyn. It hadn't ever crossed her mind that she wasn't going out as much as a woman her age should, or would want to; it hadn't crossed her mind that someone would think she was being treated badly, held captive. She knew what it was like to be treated badly, held captive. She didn't know what her life looked like to other people.

She didn't know what to do with the look on Pol's face, his relief at the prospect of Hero making friends. She didn't know how to tell Pol, or even Rosalyn, that she liked going out only once a week, that it gave her something to look forward to and something to miss when it was over; limitations were a comfort. She'd never had the sense that anything she'd been asked to do since arriving in Milpitas was a chore. Rather than feeling as though she were Roni's chaperone or babysitter, she was convinced that it was the other way around; that Roni's presence was protecting her, shepherding her. The responsibility of being Roni's caretaker was a pivot joint, a saddle joint, something that allowed the bones of Hero to rotate and flex, knowing its axis was fixed, though fragile. Her anatomy professor, second year, pontificating to the class in fake British-sounding English, famous for his long digressions: *Every traumatic injury is different, because every body is different: every fracture, every strained muscle. One patient will be able to walk on a leg that another patient will die with. These instances are not miracles, but the order of the day. The diagnosis is not a life sentence but an* aphorme: *a starting position, a jumping-off point. Once we accept that, the rest is elementary, dear Watsons—the rest is just our job.* She'd nearly failed that class.

Hero had always thrived on being useful. For the first time since dropping out of UST and getting into the car with Teresa and Eddie, saying, I have some medical knowledge, for the first time in nearly ten years, Hero knew what she wanted from the things she had. That was enough. That was more than enough.

Hero told Rosalyn she could work during the day a few times a week, between the time she dropped Roni off at school and before she picked her up. She didn't want to work every weekday; still wanted to be able to clean the house, which felt like one of the central labors that earned her place at home. She wasn't ready to give that up yet, even if it tired her hands out more and more lately, especially with the cold. Rosalyn told Hero to just bring Roni straight to the restaurant after school.

She does her homework here fine on Thursdays, Rosalyn reasoned. What's the difference? You guys could be alone at home like nerds or hanging out here. Hero said she'd bring it up to Roni. Roni, unsurprisingly, chose the restaurant.

Hero also told Rosalyn about what Pol had said, about going out, about needing someone to pick her up. Yeah, we got you, Rosalyn said, waving her hand, like Hero had told her this ages ago and she'd long ago agreed to it. Me or Jaime'll pick you up whenever. Just beep me when Paz gets home, we'll come and get you. I'll get you my number.

Beep, Hero repeated, which was how Rosalyn found out that Hero didn't have a pager. Which was in turn how it became Jaime's job to scrounge up a pager for her. They didn't let Hero pay for it.

Because he stole it, Rosalyn explained. Jaime held up a hand. I didn't steal it.

Rosalyn clarified: Someone else stole it and his friend who resells them gave him one for free.

Jaime didn't say anything to that, busying himself with writing down Hero's new pager number on a napkin. Then below it, his and Rosalyn's. Below that, an abbreviated key of pager codes.

People started to recognize Hero; she started to recognize people. The morning customers, usually security guards just off their night shift, ordering coffee and tapsilog, didn't say much, especially to Hero, and when they did, they spoke to her in English. They came awake when Boy reemerged from the kitchen, switching to Tagalog, usually chatting about baseball, or about paying back money someone owed to someone else. Then there were the lunch customers, nurses, more security guards, a couple of DMV workers. Hero got used to the words, *Kumusta ka na, mare?* started to look forward to saying back, Mabuti, mabuti, and meaning it.

Though Adela and Boy faithfully cooked a variety of other dishes— the adobo, the menudo, the kaldereta, the afritada, the pinakbet—the best sellers by far were the pork barbecue or the pancit. Once again, Hero thought to herself that the Filipinos in the Bay ate on a daily basis the things Hero remembered eating only during fiestas and special occasions: pancit, lechon kawali, bibingka. In the restaurant she never saw anybody eat any of the things that she'd been used to growing up: the lomo-lomo with intestines, lungs, liver, and heart; the sinanglao with kamias fruit instead of tamarind; the pipian with pasotes, the Vigan longanisa that was smaller and crispier than the fat, sweet Kapampangan-style ones they served in the restaurant. And nobody in the Bay seemed to eat goat. Paz and Pol didn't even eat goat at home. It was odd.

But the work itself was easy, just as Rosalyn had said. In the afternoon there was a long empty lull in the restaurant, punctuated for Hero by having to pick Roni up from school. When they returned, Jaime would be there, alone, the way he was the first day, eating something with his hands. Rosalyn came into the restaurant every couple of hours, saying she was on her break, stealing a guava juice out of the refrigerator, making fun of the unmoving way Hero sat on the chair behind the register, listening to Boy's radio.

Don't you get bored? Rosalyn asked once. You want me to get you some comic books?

Without thinking about it, Hero replied: What about, a schoolgirl and her demon servant who save the world with the power of love?

Rosalyn froze, which made Hero freeze in turn. She used to make fun of people all the time, in her own way—Teresa and Eddie got a kick out of it, how blank-faced she usually was, what a contrast it made to her sometimes macabre, often unwittingly mean retorts, delivered as if she were commenting on the weather.

Rosalyn put her guava juice down. Hero was about to apologize, then Rosalyn said: Ohhh. I get it now. You're an asshole. See, now I know that about you.

She left. Hero wasn't sure if they were mad at each other, if she should go after her, until Rosalyn came back less than fifteen minutes later with a stack of comic books—manga, Hero could hear her insisting again—all of them stuffed with weathered sheets of paper. Ruby's translations.

Okay, smartass, some schoolgirls and demons to keep you busy.

The Glass Mask, Please Save My Earth, Rose of Versailles. Few of the books were finished; Rosalyn only had the first few volumes, so even if there was some storyline that piqued Hero's interest, even vaguely, she'd end up frustrated when Rosalyn said, Oh yeah, sorry, Ruby doesn't have the next volume yet—maybe next month.

Hero didn't pretend to understand all of them, and most of them she stopped reading halfway, until Rosalyn explained that she had to read from right to left, not from left to right. Also, don't let my grandpa catch you reading this stuff too much, she said. He's got a thing about— Japanese stuff. You know. He used to work on the American navy base in Cavite.

All in all, Hero didn't love the comic books, at least not as much as Rosalyn wanted her to, and not as much as Roni was starting to. Maybe Hero was just too old to be moved by stories of pure-hearted maidens, usually blond, aristocrats or girls-next-door, chasing their dreams, fighting to build careers, on the cusp of getting raped but being saved in the nick of time, long resisting and then finally falling into what was always, eventually, requited love. What Hero did like was the way Rosalyn came into the restaurant, checked out what Hero was reading, and asked if she'd reached a certain part in that particular volume yet—and when she found out Hero hadn't, the way she complained, God, you read so slow, and hurried her along, along, along. Hero liked the pull of Rosalyn's push, knowing something in her hands was waiting, and if she just kept going, she'd get to it.

Since both Paz and Pol were working on Christmas Eve, Rosalyn invited Hero and Roni to spend Noche Buena at their house.

We're making lechon, Rosalyn said. Grandpa is. A bunch of people are coming. You can finally meet my brother. Don't bring any gifts. I'm broke, so don't expect any from me, either.

Rosalyn picked them up from the house in the afternoon, pulled up to the driveway in a beat-up-looking four-door Honda Civic. Roni had insisted on waiting in the garage, perched on Pol's regular seat, with the garage door open.

Nice house, Rosalyn said, the engine still running, as Roni and Hero approached the car.

It looks bigger from the outside, Roni said.

Usually people say thanks, Rosalyn laughed.

The car looked like it had recently been an unsalvageable mess but someone, Rosalyn, had tried to tidy it up in a hurry. It smelled, still, of cigarettes, two crushed Marlboro packs on the floor in the back, Jaime's, and a trace of food, something garlicky and sweet, like some barbecue sauce had spilled not that long ago. There were cassette tapes scattered across the front passenger footwell, like they'd been hastily swept there from the seat. You can sit in the front, Rosalyn said to Hero.

I wanna sit in the front, Roni protested. Kids ride in the back where it's safe, Rosalyn said, pointing.

Hero picked up some of the cassette tapes off the floor, not wanting to crush them with her feet. Sorry, Rosalyn said, stretching down to push a few of them to the side, making room.

Hero looked down at the tape cases, many of them cracked from someone sitting or stepping on them. The Cover Girls, Cynthia, Queen

Latifah, Jaya. You really take care of your things, she said, toeing an empty one.

Yeah, yeah, Rosalyn said, beckoning with her hand. Gimme those, I'll put 'em over here. It's always a mess, don't worry about it. Hero got in, shut the door, which shuddered at the impact.

Everyone good? Arms, legs, tails, everything in? Rosalyn called out loudly, as if there were more people in the car than just the three of them. Ye-e-es, Roni chirped. Good, Rosalyn said.

She put the car in reverse, then did the thing that Hero had always found oddly sexy whenever she was in the front passenger seat and the driver she was riding with did it: put her hand on the headrest just behind Hero to steady herself, craned her neck around, then backed out with one hand on the steering wheel, a single easy, fluid, slightly too fast motion.

On the stereo, a girl was singing in a voice that had been electronically altered, so it staggered, hiccupped, like a voice shaking its head, rethinking, persuading itself one way, then persuading itself another way.

Hero didn't know what the expression on her face was, but Rosalyn saw enough there to choke out a derisive laugh and say, Oh, shit, you don't have to judge the song that hard!

Hero blinked, shaking her head. No, I wasn't—

Okay, so you don't like freestyle. Okay. The fuck music do you like, then?

I didn't say I didn't like it. I don't, I don't know it.

Okay, so what do you know. What do you listen to?

Hero thought about it. I don't know. New Wave. British bands. Friends Again. Fiction Factory. China Crisis. Aztec Camera. Talk Talk. Lotus Eaters.

Rosalyn glared at Hero out of the corner of her eyes. Talk Talk, okay. It's My Life. Fine. Everything else? You're full of shit, you made up all those names.

I'm not, Hero cried out, not sure if she was angry or if she was about to start laughing, teetering between both. I have a tape full of songs from most of the bands I just mentioned. I recorded them off the radio in Manila.

Where? You have a tape at home?

In my room—

Rosalyn sped up to a stoplight, which was turning yellow, and made an illegal U-turn on Dixon Landing, steering them back toward North Milpitas Boulevard.

You're getting those tapes, I wanna hear fuckin'—Lotus Eaters, or whatever.

When they got back to the house, Hero rushed out of the car with Rosalyn's voice calling behind her, Hurry up, I wanna get some China Crisis in before we get to my house, too.

Hero went straight to her bedroom, onto her knees, digging underneath the bed for the things she'd stored there. She took the two tapes, shoved the rest back underneath the bed, clambered back outside. When she approached the car, she caught a reflection of herself in the window, out of breath, low ponytail loosened, flushed, vital with purpose. Rosalyn was making grabby hands, saying, Hand it over.

Hero found she was—nervous, waiting to play the tape. She hadn't listened to it in a while, not since Soly's place, though she'd listened to it nearly every day, then. She was afraid Rosalyn wouldn't like it, which wasn't fair, she knew, considering she'd made fun of Rosalyn's music within a second of hearing it. There was always something nerve-wracking about letting someone listen to a piece of music one liked, but it was more than that. Hero was afraid she herself wouldn't like it anymore, afraid that the music would have flattened with time, afraid that she would listen to the song and have to confront an older part of herself—afraid that she wouldn't like, or worse, wouldn't recognize, what she encountered there, who.

The strains of that first song burst into the car, loud, too loud, the volume still at the level Rosalyn had left it at, so even Hero was taken aback, heard Roni in the back going, Whoa, but then Hero sank, sank into it, the succor of recognition, that song, that sound, that first long, echoing shout. Hey! It was still—she was still. She hadn't lost any of it. It was all still here, waiting for her. Her head on Soly's kitchen table, the radio blaring, her hands just starting to forget themselves for parts of the day, everything else in her remembering—and the music, opening up a crevice, just small enough, where the remembering could happen safely, where she could close herself up in it without then having to worry about having accidentally sealed off the exit behind her. Knowing she'd have to get up and rewind the tape to feel again whatever it'd helped her to feel. Knowing she'd brought herself into this feeling, and she could bring herself out.

Rosalyn was quiet, long enough for Hero to realize that she herself hadn't said anything, that she'd closed her eyes, leaned her head back against the headrest, clenched her fists, not enough to hurt, just enough to anchor her in the car. Then, with too much dry warmth in her voice for Hero to not be able to tell that she was covering up one feeling with another—she was starting to be able to predict, just a little bit, the times when Rosalyn might cover up a feeling with another—Rosalyn said,

Okay. But any lyrics sound hella deep when you can't make out a word they're saying, you know that, right?

Rosalyn's house was full of people, smoking, drinking in the garage, setting up card tables and stacking mah-jongg cases onto them, a boom box blasting something Hero didn't recognize, kids everywhere, chasing each other, in the kitchen, seated around the table, women placing meat filling into lumpia wrappers and rolling them tightly into short, squat sigarilyos to make lumpiang shanghai, stacking them on a large plate; in the living room, someone setting up the karaoke machine, testing it, One two, one two, and out past the sliding door, the mosquito screen, into the backyard, a group of men plus Adela were standing around a roasting baby pig, turning it on a spit over a bed of charcoal.

Rosalyn led them out into the backyard, said: Grandma. Roni and Hero're here.

Maligayang Pasko, Adela said, waving her cigarette at them. Get something to eat. There's some barbecue inside.

Merry Christmas, Hero and Roni greeted, polite.

Roni was glancing over at a group of kids her age, taking turns playing an Atari game set up on a desk in the corner of the living room. Rosalyn beckoned with her hand. Roni, come here, I'm gonna introduce you to my cousins. Roni bounded over to join Rosalyn, who took her to the group of kids, none of whom looked particularly interested in Roni. Still, Hero watched Roni sit down on the floor next to them.

Don't worry so much, Ate Hero, Rosalyn said, startling her; Hero hadn't even seen her come back to her side. Let your girl socialize, it's good for her.

I wasn't worried, Hero said. You looked hella worried, Rosalyn said. I'm gonna get us some food. You want lumpia? Hero nodded.

Rosalyn's house was about as big as Paz and Pol's, though older, built sometime in the seventies, the shag carpet oily to the touch, the musky scent of several generations of people, most of them cooks, buried deep in its fibers. Someone, a distant relation of Rosalyn's, was wandering around the party with a huge black video recorder propped up on his shoulder, taping people, asking people to say Merry Christmas. There were pictures everywhere, in frames on the wall, in frames on the fireplace mantel, propped up on the altar just at the entrance of the house. On the mantel there was a photo of someone who was probably Rosalyn, maybe three years old, held in the arms of someone who was definitely Adela. It looked like the picture had been taken in the Philippines, judging from the foliage behind them, the concrete block of the house, the iron fence Adela was holding on to.

Hero stepped closer to look at it. Next to it, a more recent photo of Rosalyn and an adolescent boy who looked just like her, whom Hero hadn't met in person yet, hadn't even seen at the party, the younger boy dressed in graduation robes. Behind it, a larger framed photo of Rosalyn and someone who was almost certainly Jaime, Rosalyn in what looked like a Communion dress, Jaime in a child-sized tuxedo, chubby-faced. They were holding hands, both looking sullen. In front of it, a smaller photo of Rosalyn and Jaime, twelve or thirteen years old, on what looked like a school gymnasium turned dance floor, arms around each other. Hero couldn't see Rosalyn's face, only Jaime's, the shock of blush across his nose and cheeks.

Don't creep on people's baby photos, came a voice behind her.

Hero turned and saw Jaime. He was holding out a plastic cup for Hero, another one in his left hand. Merry Christmas.

Hero took the cup, brushed it against Jaime's half-empty cup. Merry Christmas. Cheers.

They're setting up the karaoke, tell Roni to hide, Jaime said.

Hero saw her in the living room, sitting on the floor, playing with two other girls; it looked like Roni was pretending to be some kind of animal, and the girls were feeding her something that looked like crumbled-up puto.

Another young man approached, not Ruben or Isagani, someone Hero didn't recognize. Pusoy, pare. You in?

Jaime nodded. Okay, the young man said, lemme go find a fourth. Ruben's out, he wants to set up the decks. It's just Gani and me and you so far. Arnel says he's only coming at ten.

Jaime turned to Hero. You play?

Pusoy? Hero asked. She nodded, hesitant.

Fourth, Jaime pronounced. Let's go.

The young man looked immediately wary. Uh—we could play with three—

Nah, it's better with four, Jaime said, downing his cup, making his way to the garage.

The young man was still looking at Hero. I'm Dante, what's up, he said, not sounding like he particularly wanted to tell her, or know.

What's up, replied Hero, who didn't want to know, either.

At the far end of the garage, closer to the washing machine and dryer, Ruben had finished setting up: two turntables, two speakers, a sub-woofer, an amplifier. He was pulling vinyl records out of their sleeves, piling them methodically beside the turntables: Incredible Bongo Band, ESG, Africa Bambaataa, Roxanne Shanté, The Four Tops, Exposé, Bill Withers, Los Angeles Negros, Shannon, Coke Escovedo, Lonnie Liston Smith, Soho, Too Short. There was a folding table already set up near the speakers. Isagani was sitting there, shuffling the cards and waiting.

Playing pusoy again for the first time in years, what Hero hadn't counted on was how hard it really was to hold a set of cards: the fine movements it took, to grip them between her thumb and the other four fingers. By the fourth game, her hands were screaming, but she'd won three times, Jaime was cackling, Dante was silently growing more and more livid, and she had no intention of stopping. Rosalyn had found her during the second game, a plate of food in her hands, but had pulled back at the grim look on Hero's face, said she'd keep it warm for her, and when Hero gave no indication of wanting or even noticing the food, ended up finishing the plate herself by the sixth game.

By the eighth game or so, Roni entered the garage and bounded over to Hero's side of the table, eyes glued to the money. Did you win allll that?

Fold them for me, put them in your pocket, Hero said, taking a sip from her cup. We'll rent videos at Ruby's place while you're still on Christmas break.

Look how sweet Hero can be when she's not full of shit, Rosalyn said, dealing the cards that Dante had left behind in a huff, saying he was going to look for Lea.

Let's play pusoy dos instead of pusoy, she told Jaime, who nodded.

Ruben started playing a record, and Rosalyn yelled back, without looking at him, Watch out, Ben, Hero hates freestyle—

Hero huffed. I didn't say—

Wait, what? Jaime said, picking up his cards.

Hero hates freestyle, Rosalyn said. She made me listen to her music in the car when I picked her up. She only listens to music about white people having feelings.

Are we going clockwise or counterclockwise? Hero asked loudly, pointing around the table.

Counterclockwise, Jaime said. You're next.

Hero put down a four of spades.

Rosalyn was undeterred. She demanded of the table in general: You ever heard of Lotus Eaters? Fiction Factory?

Without waiting for an answer, she put down the king of clubs, and both Jaime and Isagani groaned.

Why do you always have to jump to the face cards when we're just getting started? Jaime demanded. You play like a fuckin' kid. Then he looked at Roni: My bad.

Roni shrugged again, started slowly moving sideward, away from Hero, toward Jaime, taking a peek at his cards. Sit down here, he said, yanking over another folding chair, its metal legs screeching on the concrete floor. She climbed into it, folding her legs beneath her as usual. Jaime switched his ashtray to the other side of the table, waving the smoke away from Roni.

Do you know how to play pusoy dos? he asked. Roni shook her head. Okay, just watch me, I'm gonna beat all these suckers and take their money.

Lowme, quit flirting with a kindergartener, Rosalyn said, examining her cards.

I'm in the third grade, Roni corrected.

Oh, okay, never mind then. Rosalyn rolled her eyes, then pointed down at the king of clubs. Anybody? Everyone begged off, and she preened, put down a pair of tens; hearts and spades.

I hate your ass, Jaime muttered. Pass.

Hero looked down at her cards. She had three aces she was saving for a future play, but—fuck it. She put two of them down, spades and diamonds. Her hands didn't hurt anymore, or she didn't feel them. It might have been the rum and Coke; she knew it wasn't. Now Rosalyn was crowing, Look who came to play—

A few games later, Boy came into the garage from the kitchen, asking Rosalyn and Jaime to move their table down, so the older relatives could play mah-jongg next to them. A woman who looked a lot like Rosalyn approached Jaime and Rosalyn, put a hand on Jaime's shoulder. Did JR come out of his room yet? she asked.

Rosalyn said, I knocked just like an hour ago. He already got some food, he's eating it in his room.

The woman tsk-ed, then her eyes fell onto Hero and Roni. Are you Roni?

Roni, in the middle of balancing two cards against each other in an improvised teepee, nodded.

I'm your Auntie Rhea! I used to work with your mom! I'm the one who told your mom about Lola Adela. How's your eczema, ha? Is it getting better?

Roni withdrew from Rhea's bombast, face shuttering. She nodded into her own chest. I think so.

You think so? Rhea repeated, stepping closer, smiling. That's good! Let me see. You're— She reached a hand out to take hold of Roni's arm, but Roni jerked back so quickly she nearly fell sideward out of her folding chair. Hero shot out both arms instinctively to catch her, but Rosalyn was already there, pushing Roni back onto the chair with one brusque shove, then letting go just as swiftly.

Mom. You're embarrassing her.

How, I'm embarrassing her? Then Rhea turned to Jaime. Am I embarrassing her? Jaime held up his hands, staying out of it.

Rhea lost interest in Roni, and turned stern.

Jaime. You go up and talk to JR. Get him to come down.

Mom, Rosalyn said.

JR listens to Jaime, Rhea argued. Tell him you're playing cards. He likes cards.

We're taking a break right now, Jaime said. I'll go up and ask him again if he wants to eat down here.

See, Rhea said to Rosalyn, pointing to Jaime, who was already leaving. See how easy that is? She followed Jaime into the house. Rosalyn didn't move, face stony.

Hero stood there, awkward, along with Roni, Rochelle, and Isagani. Gani broke through the silence first, said, I'm hungry, too.

On their way back into the house, Rosalyn leading the way, Rochelle untangled herself from Gani's arms, turned around. Held out a paper gift bag to Hero.

Hey, hold on. Here. Christmas gift for you.

Hero blinked down at it, then felt horror creep up from her feet into her stomach, her chest. Sorry, I—don't have a present for—

No, no, no, Rochelle said, waving her hand. Don't sweat it, I didn't even buy it myself. It's just some Avon perfumes my mom had around the house. We had some Sweet Honesty, I remember from when we were talking about it. I threw in some other stuff, too. We don't even use it, it's just in storage. I saw it and thought of you.

Hero's hands felt like they were made of old clay, dried out and crumbly. She took the bag, didn't know what to say. Thank—thanks, I mean.

She stood up straight, met Rochelle's eyes, her warm, questionless face. Amihan, the third or fourth year in, handing Hero a plastic bag full of elastic bandages, saying: Maligayang Pasko, doktora.

It's really nice of you, Hero said, making sure the words were said clearly. Thank you.

No big, Rochelle said, while Isagani hugged her from behind, kissing at her ear. Hero felt, more than saw, someone watching her. When she looked, Rosalyn's back was obscuring Roni's, stepping into the kitchen, her cheerful voice saying, You wanna eat the best lechon in the Bay?

In the backyard, the pig had long been pieced apart on the patio, most of its left flank missing, head still intact, apple in its mouth. The wooden pole it had been spitted on was lying in the grass, glistening. Several bottles of Mang Tomas were scattered around. Jaime, Rosalyn, and Roni were hovering near an old plastic slide, Roni perched at the top, Rosalyn leaning with one knee on the steps, Jaime at the bottom, unlit cigarette hanging out of his mouth, telling Roni she needed to put more sauce on her lechon. Isagani and Rochelle were sitting on the ground, sharing one plate between them. Hero had a plate of food, given to her by Adela, too much meat. She wasn't really hungry, but she knew better than to say that out loud.

She made herself another rum and Coke, approached the slide. There was hardly any light in the backyard. The whole space itself, including the yard and garden, was surprisingly expansive, much bigger than the one at Paz and Pol's house. There were rows and rows of something that looked like vegetables or herbs, and here or there, trees that might have been lime. Hero pointed to one. Is that calamansi?

Rosalyn looked up. Yeah. Grandpa and Grandma planted all those. All the vegetables, too, over there. Kamote and everything.

Hero squinted toward where Rosalyn was pointing. Rosalyn hopped up, put her plate down on the step. I'll show you, come on.

Hero looked back at Roni, who was glowing with laughter, dipping lechon in Mang Tomas, the scars on her face looking faded in the dim light. She's fine, ate, chill, Rosalyn said, wiping her hands on her jeans, setting off toward the far end of the backyard.

Hero left her plastic cup on the step next to Rosalyn's food, and followed. Rosalyn started pointing out things in the ground, shrouded in darkness. In the summer there's tomatoes there, and eggplant, and green beans, and kangkong. We still have some sweet potatoes. And Grandpa grows all kind of herbs for Grandma's work. They had friends and stuff bring them seeds from the Philippines. Some of it doesn't grow so well, but most of the time they find a way to make it work. Depending on the time of the year we have akapulko, and lagundi, and sambong, and tsaang gubat and niyog-niyogan, komprey, abang, buyo-buyo, tanglad, gumamela, luya, malunggay.

Rosalyn listed them all off by heart, like it was nothing to know them all, like they were the first words she'd ever spoken. You know a lot, Hero said.

Rosalyn shrugged, looked away. Grandma taught me all that. Since I was a kid she said I inherited some of the power, so. But really it's my mom who should be knowing all that shit. Grandma says my mom's power's even stronger than hers. But she doesn't want to. You know. She likes being a nurse.

Kind of the same thing, Hero said. Rosalyn bent down, stroking at a plant leaf, maybe a kamote top, then tearing off a piece and chewing at it.

Kind of, she said doubtfully.

Lola Adela isn't really so much a bruha, anyway, right, Hero said. She's more like an—albularya.

Nah, nah, nah, Rosalyn said. She just works on like a case-by-case basis, whatever people need. Herbs, prayers, whatever. She's a bruha for sure, though. You know, when I was a kid, before we left the Philippines? I was like four. I started having seizures. No reason, I didn't have epilepsy or anything. Just in the run-up to us about to leave, I'd go into these fits, like, foaming at the mouth, speaking in tongues and shit. Grandma treated me. I don't even remember what happened, but even my mom said that it was like hella scary, Grandma started talking in a voice that wasn't hers, like, outta *The Exorcist*. People said it was a bunch of things that were causing the fits. There was someone in our neighborhood who was jealous that we were going to the States, so maybe they put a hex on us. Plus there was a kapre nearby who didn't want me to leave either. So it was like, a double whammy. It was wild.

Hero waited for more, and when more didn't appear forthcoming, said, Then what?

Rosalyn shrugged. I don't know. I guess we just left. I think Grandma might've sacrificed something, like a rooster or a kambing. No one really explained it. I'm just saying, she's a legit bruha. I'm more like an apprentice.

Hero smiled, couldn't help it, let the words hang in the air for a beat before speaking again. Makeup artist and apprentice bruha.

Rosalyn laughed, standing up, dusting her hands off on her thighs. I'll put that on a business card. Rosalyn Cabugao, Makeup Artist and Apprentice Bruha. Bruha-in-Training.

I'd hire you, Hero said.

Rosalyn's laugh faded as she started wandering along the edge of the backyard, even farther out, close to the fence that separated them from the next house, pointing out more vegetation like she was introducing Hero to family members.

Grandpa planted these trees here when I was a kid, when we first moved in. Another calamansi, and then there's a couple persimmon trees around here, too. We have the persimmon trees you can eat right off the tree like apples, not the ones you have to let get mushy before they taste good. Look, there's still some fruit. You should've come by in October, we were giving bags of them away. Now just the ones that stayed green or ripened all weird are left. Look, this one's—too hard. Probably still green, I can't see. Wait. This one's good.

Rosalyn yanked a persimmon off of a tree, wiped it on her shirt, tossed it to Hero, who couldn't grasp it, dropped it on the ground.

Even in the shadow, Hero saw Rosalyn's face go pale. Sorry, she stammered.

It's fine, Hero said. It was fine. She picked the persimmon up from the ground, wiped it on her own shirt. Bit into it; sweet and overripe, icy cold to the teeth.

A long silence. Then: Your hands, Rosalyn said.

Hero didn't stop chewing; she'd known this was coming, ever since Rosalyn had rushed to say, That's fine, about Hero not being able to handle a knife.

It looks worse than it is, Hero preempted, knowing that wouldn't be the end of it.

It was darkest here, in the farthest reach of the backyard, outside the grasp of the patio light, outside even the gradually darkening halo it cast onto the soil. Jaime and Roni and the others were in another world entirely, too far away to hear their voices. Hero couldn't see the expression that was on Rosalyn's face when she said,

Can I ask how that happened.

Hero looked down at the persimmon. If she thumbed along the place she'd bitten, she'd feel her own teeth marks; see them, if she held it up close.

I was part of the New People's Army for around ten years. I got captured. I was in a prison camp for two years. It happened there.

That was something else to discover, then—another of the funny, dug-deep, wrenched-open, torn things: it was possible to say it, just like that, in four sentences, easy, short, in a backyard with someone she'd known for only a couple of months. Bones shivering, clenched up, still not used to the new weather, hurt thumb inside the flesh of something sticky.

She wasn't finished; there was more, the hardest part. I was a doctor, Hero said.

Her voice sounded steady, at least to her own ear, but she could feel the shaking, gripping her from neck to ankle, elbows, in her knees, in all of the badly mended joints of her hands. She brought the persimmon back up to her mouth, bit into it, just to do something, to stop the shaking. She tried to bite, but couldn't. Her teeth wouldn't sink in. She didn't have the strength to bite down.

Rosalyn was still watching her, though Hero couldn't see her face. She had another one of those bolo-sharp thoughts, absolute: if Rosalyn tried to hug her, she might vomit.

Rosalyn didn't try to hug her. Gimme that, she said, holding a dim hand out to the persimmon Hero was trying to bite into. Hero gave it to her, glad to have a hand free again. She heard, rather than saw, Rosalyn biting into the persimmon herself.

Put out your hand.

Hero put out a hand, dumb. Rosalyn placed a small fragment of persimmon—invisible, saliva-wet, juice-sticky—into the center of Hero's open palm. Hero looked down at it absurdly; then just as absurdly, put it in her mouth. Tried to chew, found she could.

She heard Rosalyn take another bite, heard the wet, crunching sounds. Hero held her hand out without having to be told. The second piece of persimmon was even softer, like Rosalyn might have chewed it a little bit before putting it in Hero's palm.

This is—hella gross, Hero said, copying Rosalyn's way of speaking, knowing Rosalyn would notice, because it was the kind of thing Rosalyn would say, the kind of thing Hero found herself sometimes wanting to say, because she was hanging around Rosalyn so much. She put the second piece in her mouth. Her face was hot, the only place in her cold-stiffened body where blood was starting to churn again, thawing out. Something in her was shaking, and she thought that was all it was, until she heard the words Are you—laughing? come from Rosalyn's shadow, her voice still low.

Hero didn't, couldn't, answer, but held her hand out for the third piece of persimmon she knew was coming. Rosalyn put it in her palm. It tasted yeasty, like Budweiser and pig fat, and then chalky, glacial; one side of the persimmon was unripe. Hero knew then, with a wry, bleak, doubtless humor, that life was long, that this third or fourth life she was on was long, long, long, not even all the way started up yet, not even close. She'd fallen down another slope; now she was being carried back up the mountain. Listening to Rosalyn's chewing noises start up again in the dark, Hero's throat ached, all the way down the arteries, down to where the throat met the heart. She held her hand out for the next bite.

The music had picked up considerably since they'd decamped to the backyard; now the garage was full of people Hero had never seen before, men, a few girls clustered to one side, listening as Isagani spun a Jungle Brothers record, the bass of it thudding up from the floor into Hero's chest. Jaime was behind the decks, sitting on the ground and chatting to Ruben, smoking. Roni was on her second wind, drinking hot chocolate out of a mug that said World's Best Grandpa.

I don't wanna go home, she said when Hero told her it was time to go. I wanna stay here.

Your mom's waiting for us.

So? Roni said, licking her lips.

Rosalyn came up to Hero. I'll drive you, she said. Then she turned around to call to Jaime. Lowme, move your car out the way, I'm gonna drive them home.

Jaime pushed himself up, parking the cigarette in his mouth and jogging over to his car, a dark brown Supra that looked more beat up than Rosalyn's Civic, with a large spoiler on the back, larger even than the one on Pol's Corona. Without bothering to close his driver's side door, he backed his car into the street, to make room for Rosalyn to back out herself.

Merry Christmas, he yelled when he was done, hanging out of his car, words warbled by the cigarette, voice echoing all the way down the long street. Yo, Hero, we're going up to the city for New Year's Eve, you doing anything?

No, Hero said. Jaime sounded drunk. Okay, come up with us, then! I'm driving. Rosalyn, you tell her. Roni! Roni! Night, Roni! Next time we'll watch some *Dragon Ball,* okay?

Roni was still holding the cup of hot chocolate, half empty, so Hero took it out of her hands. I'll just put this back in the kitchen, she told Rosalyn, then jogged back.

Adela and Boy were there with a group of other older aunties and uncles, picking at the food, talking. They'd cleared some of the food away and set up the mah-jongg pieces, but looked like they hadn't been playing for a while. Adela turned wide-awake-looking eyes to Hero, who brandished the cup.

Roni still had this. I can wash it.

Don't worry about that, Adela said, shaking her head, standing to take the cup and put it in the sink. Take some food with you.

No, it's fine.

Come on, Adela said. She pointed at the table in the corner, at the other women who were filling paper plates with mounds of pancit. Just take some.

Boy stood and started putting pancit in plates himself, wrapping it with foil and handing it to Hero silently, brooking no argument. She accepted it, said, Thank you.

Then she turned to Adela, who was still rinsing the cup. Thank you, Lola Adela, ha? Hero said. For inviting us. Roni had a lot of fun.

And you? Adela squirted soap onto a sponge, back still to Hero. You had fun?

I had fun, Hero said, surprised again that she was telling the truth.

Adela turned around, studying her, then drew her into a one-armed hug. Her hands were still covered in foam. Okay. Good night. Drive safe. Merry Christmas, ha? Boy, she called to her husband. Aalis na sila.

Boy glanced over, saluted them, military-perfect.

Salamat po, Hero said. Merry Christmas.

See you next week, Adela said, and Hero warmed at the words, used to them, liking that she was used to them.

Outside, Rosalyn and Roni were in the car, Roni in the front seat. When they saw Hero coming, they pointed and laughed. Early bird gets the worm, Rosalyn said, gesturing to Roni. Hero opened the back door and got into the seat behind her. The car was steamy-warm, a cocoon. Rosalyn put her hand on the headrest behind Roni, started reversing the car.

Hero looked up at Rosalyn's house as they backed away from it, saw the lit-up parol that someone had hung from the rooftop. Tiny blinking lights in different colors, lighting up different parts of the star, long paper and tinsel streamers flowing down over a window on the second floor, frail strips fluttering in the wind.

Was that there when we arrived? Hero asked, pointing.

Rosalyn stopped the car, looked up. Yeah? Maybe you couldn't see it because it was still daylight out.

Hero gazed up at it. Said, softer than she meant to:

I didn't think I would see a parol this year.

Rosalyn paused, then continued backing down the drive, narrowly missing the other parked cars, face giving no clue of having seen how closely she'd come to scraping them. Go to Magat next year, she said. They always sell them.

The drive was short through the mostly carless streets, everyone in the town at home, neon lights illuminating the signs of strip mall stores that were all closed. The Talk Talk album was still playing, Rosalyn having left it in the stereo, but she'd turned the volume down, glancing over at Roni, whose head was lolling against the window, eyes shut.

It was the latest Hero had been out, since coming to Milpitas. There was something different about seeing the streets she'd gotten to know so well during the day at night: vacant, yet not empty, life still warming the air here and there. It was in the spectral glow of the orange streetlamps, the coordinated performance of the stoplights, block after block, so the light was green for them all down the long, long street, even into the distance where Hero knew they wouldn't turn, an unending string of green lights, beckoning them, letting them know there was still more street to be sure of. They barely talked, hollowed out by the luscious fatigue that only fun could arouse, the heavy silence kneading time down like a muscle, relaxing its tendons, loosening its tethers. When Rosalyn turned into the neighborhood streets the road darkened and narrowed again, but the houses were lit up, not only from without, but from within, parties like the one they'd just left, with garage doors open everywhere, and as they passed Hero could see, hear, people playing pusoy, mah-jongg, music, their Noche Buena still going strong.

In the driveway of Paz and Pol's house, the lights were off. Hero didn't know if Paz was home yet. She got out first, remembering the foil-covered pancit, circling around the car to open the front passenger door. Roni was already asleep. Hero put the plate on the roof.

Come on, Roni, she whispered, kneeling down to the girl's level, unbuckling her seat belt for her. Let's go.

Roni moaned in protest, squirreling deeper into the seat, hair covering her face. Hero took her by the shoulder, shook her gently. Roni.

You want me to carry her—Rosalyn offered, but Roni was blinking awake.

Huh? We're home?

Hero rocked back onto her heels, knees cracking at the squat, then stood back up. Time to get up now.

Roni wiped at her eyes, then clambered bonelessly out of the car, bumping into Hero's body. Hero steadied her with one arm around her shoulders. Roni leaned into the touch.

Hey. About New Year's, Rosalyn whispered, not wanting to completely wake Roni up, which gave each word a sense of portent.

So we're just going up to the city to somebody's house in the Excelsior, she continued.

I thought it was in San Francisco.

Excelsior's in—Rosalyn stopped. Have you ever been up to the city? Just the airport.

Rosalyn let that sink in. Okay. Well. Come with us, then. Jaime's sister lives up there, too. I'll pick you up.

Roni was faceplanting into Hero's stomach, drooling, starting to—chew?—on her sweater. Okay, Hero said. She picked the pancit up off the roof, the loud sound of the crackling foil making Roni's brows knit together mid-dream.

Okay. Get her to bed, Rosalyn said. Wait, hold on. Your tapes. I still have 'em. Just let me eject—

It's fine, Hero said. You can borrow them. If you want.

Oh. Okay.

Good night. Merry Christmas. And. Put a seat belt on, Hero added, wishing she'd said it, noticed it, earlier.

Rosalyn looked down, at the seat belt that was still hanging off of her left arm like a suspender. She buckled it, then gave Hero a thumbs-up.

Okay. Merry Christmas, she said. Good night. Actually—wait, actually, wait, wait, hold up—

Rosalyn was holding a hand out, just as Hero was about to step backward and close the front passenger door.

Rosalyn leaned over the seat, propping herself up on one hand, stretching the belt taut so it cut into her neck, looked painful.

Okay, so what song's good on this thing? The Talk Talk. Like your favorite, I mean. What should I listen to?

Hero paused, one palm holding up the pancit, the other hand still on Roni's sleep-heavy shoulders.

I like Hate, she said.

Rosalyn stared up at her, unblinking, like she'd heard a punchline she didn't get the meaning of yet. Then her face split into a grin, eyes half closed, gleeful. Hate. Okay. Fuck. Merry Christmas.

Hero and Roni came in through the front door, which was rare for them; they were used to coming in through the garage door, using the electronic door opener that was permanently clipped to the Corona's driver's side visor. It was one of the first times Hero was using the house keys that Pol and Paz had given her the very first week.

Roni was about to walk onto the living room carpet, shoes still on, her eyes half closed. Oi, oi, teka muna, Hero whispered, kneeling down to put the plate on the floor and untie the girl's sneakers. Your shoes—

Roni let Hero take the shoes off. Hero slipped off her own sneakers, picked up the plate again, then took Roni's hand, and tiptoed toward the kitchen. The house looked bigger in the dark. There was a noise from the kitchen—Hero jumped. Someone was inside.

When she looked closer, a dim shaft of light cast onto the border where the kitchen met the living room. She pushed Roni back toward the front door with more force than necessary and put the plate back on the floor.

Hero waited in the living room, obscured by the wall. She'd go for the balls if he was taller than her, the eyes if they were the same height. She wished she had a bottle with her, the Red Horse bottles they had at the party would've been good, bigger than average, the glass thicker. It'd been a long time since she'd had to fight, and she'd never done it all that often in the first place, just field training against Eddie or Amihan. It was her job to patch people up, not bust them open. Her hands were sore, and if she had to fight they would be inoperable for days, maybe weeks, but the adrenaline would take care of it for now. Then Hero smelled perfume.

Paz was sitting at the kitchen table in the dark, sleeping, her arms folded under her head, still in her nurse's uniform. Only the light above the stove was turned on; maybe she'd turned the kitchen lights on and thought they were too bright, or didn't want to waste energy. Hero turned the kitchen light on herself, momentarily going blind at the shock of it. Paz didn't wake. There was half of a white-frosted cake was on a plate in front of her, *rry stmas* in red and green letters still visible. Next to it, a large aluminum tray full of pancit. Just in front of her hands, a small package, its wrapping torn into, a red ribbon, still tied in a bow but slipped off in haste, tossed to the side. A perfume. Ysatis. An envelope upon which was written, in Pol's surgeon's scribble, *Mahal*.

Paz stirred, finally, at the sensed presence of someone near her. Roni? Hero's breath started to slow. Sorry—we're late—

Paz sat up, rubbing her eyes. She saw Roni, now solemnly waiting at the entry to the kitchen, holding the plate of pancit.

Merry Christmas, anak.

She didn't wait for Roni's reply, continuing, voice gaining strength: Gutom ka? I brought cake from work—

Paz stood, like she was going to get a plate, then stumbled, her legs still asleep. Hero reached out to steady her, but she was too far away, so Paz ended up bracing herself against the table instead. There's pancit—

We already ate, Roni said. She lifted the plate as proof.

Paz stopped. Hero looked at the badge hanging from a lanyard around her neck. PAZ DE VERA, RN. VETERANS HOSPITAL, MENLO PARK.

Okay. Matulog na tayo then. Let's go to bed.

Paz turned to Hero. Salamat, ha, Nimang? For bringing her to the party. Did you guys have fun?

Hero nodded.

Paz looked around the kitchen like she'd forgotten something, like she didn't know what to do with herself now that she was awake again. Okay. Help yourself if you want to eat. Roni. Let's go up.

She picked up the opened gift, ribbon and all, then went to her daughter, pushed some hair away from her face; Roni let it happen, too sleepy to resist.

Paz lifted her chin to Hero, who watched the two of them retreat from the kitchen. Listened to their socked and stocking steps, climbing the stairs out of sync. Hero put the foil-covered plate down next to the cake and the tray of pancit. She still wasn't hungry. She went to the stove, turned the light off, then felt herself start to shiver uncontrollably, the joints in her groin tightening and convulsing. She reminded herself, matter-of-factly, that it was just the adrenaline passing out of her body. Finally she made her way up the stairs in the dark, feeling along the walls, relying on sense memory to take her back up to her room.

Rosalyn said she'd pick Hero up around six on New Year's Eve. She'd take Hero over to her house, where everyone would be getting ready. And guess who's doing everyone's makeup for free, Rosalyn grumbled.

You don't have to do mine, Hero said.

Don't think you're getting out of it that easy.

Roni had become increasingly moody with the approach of New Year's Eve, annoyed at the idea of Hero going out without her, and worst of all, with people she knew.

How come I can't come? What time is Ate Rosalyn picking you up? Where are you going?

Pol and Paz had Hero's pager number, but they gave her a roll of quarters, told her to find a pay phone and call them at any hour of the night if she needed to be picked up, for whatever reason. You know I don't sleep at night anyway, Pol said. So don't hesitate, ha, Nimang?

Rosalyn was playing New Order's Leave Me Alone in her car when Hero climbed in; it took Hero a minute for the sureality of that to sink in. This song, in Rosalyn's car, in California.

So this is some real heavy shit you left me with, Rosalyn said. I'm, like, a depressed person now.

All the girls were already at Rosalyn's house, even Rochelle, who had told them earlier that she would go up with Isagani, and meet them in the city. They were going to somebody's house, a friend Ruben used to DJ with; Lea said the friend was kind of like Ruben's mentor and hero. Rosalyn was coralling the girls into place in her bedroom like a sheepdog, telling them to stay on the bed while they waited. She got to work on Lea first.

Hero hovered at the edges of the chat; they were talking about people she didn't know, or had only met once or twice in the restaurant or at Christmas. It was the first time Hero had ever been in a girl's private bedroom; in college she'd fucked girls in dorm rooms, and then in Isabela no one had a private space. On the nightstand beside the bed there was a

stack of comic books, two videotapes, various picture frames: Rosalyn's
Holy Communion, Rosalyn's confirmation, Rosalyn and Jaime, Rosalyn
and the younger boy Hero was guessing was her brother, Rosalyn and
every girl in the room except for Hero. On top of a chest of cabinets,
there was a row of different types of lotion, large pump bottles of hospital-
grade moisturizing hand cream, a bottle of Palmer's Cocoa Butter and
several packets of A&D ointment pilfered from a hospital.

Facing the bed was a desk covered by a blue towel, over which an
array of makeup brushes and tools had been neatly arranged, all of them
newly clean, their handles polished. Even the toolboxes full of makeup
on the floor in front of the desk and at Rosalyn's feet were neat and organized. Nothing in the room was even a fraction as tidy as the makeup.

Rosalyn made up all the girls, only explaining what she was doing
when she was asked, which turned out to be the whole time. Throughout her ongoing stop-and-start lecture, Rosalyn made a big show of
being put-upon and annoyed, saying she'd told everyone these tips about
a billion and one times, before going on to explain it all again, for the
billion and second time.

There was something infinitely comforting about being in the room
of someone in her element, confident in her skills but ready to improvise.
It reminded Hero of shadowing surgeons in the teaching theater at UST.
Then she thought of a scene in *The Castle of Cagliostro,* Lupin cooing at
Fujiko that she looked her loveliest when she was absorbed in work.

Someone was nudging Hero from behind. It was Janelle, with a photo
album. Her eyes had been shadowed in a satiny maroon color, the center
of the lids dotted with gloss, giving her a vengeful Virgin Mary look,
which had apparently been her goal. Hero had watched Rosalyn use
multiple lipsticks and eyeshadows, crushed into a plastic palette case, to
capture the right gradation of red.

Check this out, she whispered, so Rosalyn wouldn't hear.

It was full of pictures of girls, most of them Filipinas, most of them
taken at school dances, some of them by professional photographers,
some of them amateur photos. In nearly all of the photos, the color of the
girls' faces was completely different from the color of their bodies, the

faces ghostly and pinked, like someone had put calamine lotion all over their cheeks, foreheads, chins, while the skin on their neck, arms, decolletage was usually some shade of warm, sheeny brown. The faces looked like they'd been pasted onto the bodies, like the heads belonged to other people entirely.

This is before Rosalyn started doing people's makeup, Janelle confided.

She took out another album, flipped it open. And this is after. In these newer photos the heads looked like they belonged to the bodies they were on. She's hella good, right, Janelle whispered. Hero stared down at the pictures. Yeah, she said. She's good.

Finally it was Hero's turn. You don't need to put any makeup on me, Hero said again. Rosalyn rolled her eyes. Yeah, yeah, you're a natural beauty. It's some lip liner. Just chill.

Then she caught herself, put her brush down. I mean, if you don't want to, that's fine, of course, just. Hero slid into the chair, mostly to erase the strained, unnatural look of deference on Rosalyn's face.

Rosalyn's hands were warm, bony, the pads of her fingers soft. She was putting something all over Hero's face, focusing on her cheeks and the area around her nose and mouth. Hero closed her eyes; it was soothing, like being massaged. She understood why so many girls gave their faces up so easily to Rosalyn's knowing touch.

Rosalyn left Hero's forehead and chin bare. You don't put it all over? Hero asked, eyes still closed.

She could feel Rosalyn's breath on her face when she answered: I don't like it like that, it ends up looking like a mask. Which is fine, that's what some people are into, I can do that sometimes, too. But usually I like it like this, thinned out. That's why I mix it with face cream. And then you just put heavier coverage if you want it. For zits and scars and moles and stuff. If you want to cover that stuff, I mean. You don't have to. For Maricris, when she's performing, I won't use as much face cream and I'll powder her down so everything'll last even when she's moving around and sweating. But for just a night out, I think this feels more comfortable. It doesn't look that bad when it's faded, sometimes it even looks better, when your sweat and oils make it, like, real.

Rosalyn went quiet again, concentrating on putting something that felt like pencil, then a soft paintbrush, on Hero's eyes. In the distance, she heard Maricris ask, So Hero, do you have a boyfriend?

Hero went still. No.

Did you have one back in the Philippines?

Hero thought about what she should say. Kind of, she answered.

Open your eyes for me, Rosalyn said quietly, and when Hero complied, started blending shadow into the crease, comparing both eyes as she went.

But what, you broke up 'cause you left?

Y-es.

But do you guys still keep in touch, or?

Stop making her talk, it's messing me up, Rosalyn hissed, breath puffing out over Hero's cheeks. It smelled minty; she'd probably chewed some gum before she started working, knowing she was going to be in people's faces.

Hero heard the bounce of a mattress, someone flopping backward. I want kids.

That was Rochelle speaking. Maricris muttered, This again. Rochelle continued: Gani still says he's not ready yet, though. But my mom had me by the time she was twenty-three. That's three years younger than me.

Rosalyn had finished working on Hero's eyes, was now applying something that felt dry but pliant along the outline of her lips, then filling in the flesh of the lip itself. Hero shivered; it tickled.

Just be grateful you got a good dude. I'd rather have no kids with someone like Gani than have five kids with—

Dante! That was Maricris, giggling. Then, a tense silence. Maricris went on, Oh, come on, Lea.

What? I didn't say anything.

Just—

What, I don't even give a shit about him anymore. Hey Hero, Lea said, shifting the angle of the conversation unsubtly. Do you want kids?

Could you guys shut. up. for two. seconds, Rosalyn bit out. You're distracting me and she's gonna come out lookin' like the fuckin' Bride of Frankenstein.

She turned back to Hero, and gently swept a stick of waxy lip balm across the center of Hero's mouth. Press your lips together for me, she said.

Hero obliged. Rosalyn went back in with a cotton swab, cleaning up the edges. Hero stared at her ear, the long grown-out side bangs tucked behind them.

Hero didn't end up looking like the Bride of Frankenstein—though if she had, she wouldn't have minded, if the movie she had in her head was the one Rosalyn was thinking about, too. She looked the way Janelle had looked, the first time Hero and Roni saw Rosalyn doing makeup: ancient and remote, possibly even beautiful. Her eyelids and lips were a similar shade of nut brown, the lips sharp, the eyes diffused around the edges. Rosalyn leaned back, examining her work.

You have that little fold, she said obscurely.

What, Hero opened her mouth to ask, knowing her voice would be hoarse, but Janelle was already coming over.

What little fold, she asked. Lemme see. Ooh, it looks good!

That little fold, look, the one above the lashline. You know hella people get surgery for that little fold?

Do I have it? Janelle leaned into the mirror.

You don't have it. I kind of have it. Lea has it, look. And Hero has it.

Hero had never even thought of her eyelids as having—qualities, really. They were eyelids. But some part of her was warmed by Rosalyn's comment; she looked in the mirror, at the line that Rosalyn had pointed out, so new to Hero's eye that Rosalyn may as well have drawn it on herself.

Jaime came to pick them up, not in the Supra he'd been driving the night of the Christmas party, but in a minivan that belonged to his mom, which all of the girls teased him about, from Milpitas to San Francisco, all up along 237 and 101. Rosalyn sat in the front passenger seat, and Hero sat all the way in the back, next to Janelle and Rochelle. Before starting the long drive, Jaime had called out to the van: Arms, legs, tails, everything in?

Hero found herself, absurdly, giving relationship advice to Rochelle. She'd never given relationship advice to anyone before, but now she was saying something about being firm and open about her needs. Rochelle nodded, face serious, like she was taking Hero seriously, like she genuinely thought Hero's opinion was meaningful, and not blatant improvising from one half-baked truism to another. Hero felt like someone else was talking with her voice; like she was being possessed and she just had to stand aside and let this particularly helpful dwende have its playtime.

She couldn't hear what Jaime and Rosalyn were saying, only that every now and then, Rosalyn would smack Jaime across the upper arm, laughing. When they passed San Bruno, South San Francisco, Brisbane, Hero turned her head and saw, to her surprise, the ocean.

Is that the Pacific? she asked, her voice cracking more than she'd expected. A wild thought occurred to her, terror-struck and tender—if that was the ocean, then the Philippines was just on the other side. If she jumped in and swam, if she could swim that far, she'd reach it, clamber onto shore and everyone, everyone would still. be there.

Janelle looked out the window. Nah. That's the Bay.

The party was boring. New Year's Eve parties were boring, Hero thought—all that anticipation, for nothing. The house in the Excelsior was small, and yet there were more people stuffed in its garage, spilling out into the streets, hanging out of the windows smoking, than had been at Rosalyn's Christmas party. The minute they arrived, Rosalyn turned to Hero with murder in her eyes, saying, See what I mean about spinning Planet Rock with their dicks? Hero didn't, in fact, see what she meant; she didn't know what Planet Rock was.

Rosalyn handed Jaime and Hero each a Coors Light. The girls had dispersed, Lea and Rochelle to find Ruben and Isagani, Maricris to find the other members of her girl group, Janelle tagging along. Young men kept coming up to both Jaime and Rosalyn, bumping fists, asking how were things, what was good. Sometimes people took note of Hero, said hello, but most of the time, they didn't. When Hero told people her name, they asked, looking confused, like they must have heard her wrong: What? Like superhero?

Rosalyn started pointing out people to Hero, with Jaime adding commentary where he saw fit: DJs who were getting famous but still stuck around to play at parties and stuff, DJs whose friends had gotten famous and left the Bay for L.A. or New York, a couple of dudes who did graffiti—Rosalyn pointed at Jaime and said, He used to do dumbass shit like that, to which Jaime said, Watch it—and a group of dudes who were in their own singing group, one of whom was dating someone from Maricris's singing group.

Hero had the feeling that Rosalyn was talking not because she wanted Hero to really know who the people were, but because she found it reassuring to catalogue the people she saw, to make sure she remembered who everyone was and where they were from and how she knew them. Some people Rosalyn didn't know, and she said so, pointing without even trying to be subtle about it. Hero met the eye of one of the men who'd noticed himself being pointed out. He pointed at himself, confused, as if to ask, Me? and Hero shook her head, looked away.

Someone flopped down next to Hero; two someones, no, three. Janelle, Rochelle, and Isagani. They were holding plastic cups. Isagani smelled heavily of marijuana. Where'd you get the cups, Jaime asked. Rochelle pointed inside the house. They got a whole bunch of liquor. Good stuff.

A'right. I'm gonna get something, Jaime said, standing up, leaving his beer behind, putting out the cigarette he'd been smoking. He pointed to Hero and Rosalyn. What you guys want.

Rosalyn stood. I'll come. I wanna see what they got myself.

Jaime was still looking at Hero. Rum and Coke?

Hero shrugged, Sure.

Janelle, who looked half drunk, brought her knees up to her chest, and lay her cheek on her knees, taking care to keep her made-up eyes from smudging. She watched Jaime and Rosalyn leave.

Those two should just get married already, she said. They're so good together. They were so in love. It's hella obvious they still want each other.

Hero didn't blink. She took a long swig from her beer; watery, saliva-stale. When did they break up?

Few years ago, Janelle said. They went out all through high school. I only met them then, but I think they were together even before that. Right?

Since fifth grade, Isagani supplied, stroking at Rochelle's hair. Like since they were ten or so.

And then they broke up like dumbasses in college, Janelle muttered. And now look at them. Look at Jaime. Just fuckin' around with hos from all over the place.

Fucking chill, damn, Isagani said.

I'm just saying. You only have one life. What if, I don't know, what if one of them got hit by lightning or got in a bad car accident or some-thing. I don't know why they're playing like they're not meant for each other.

Maybe they're not ready, Rochelle said, sipping from her cup. She turned to Isagani. Smokes? Isagani handed her his pack of Marlboros.

You're not DJ-ing tonight? Hero asked him, not even realizing she was changing the subject until she was doing it.

Nah, Isagani said. They got bigger DJs than me here tonight. I'm just ringing in the New Year with my baby. He tugged at Rochelle's hair as she lit her cigarette and looked away.

Janelle waved a clumsy arm. See. Look at you guys. How come Jaime and Rosalyn can't get their shit together like you guys, huh. And have a bunch of cute-ass babies.

Not everyone wants babies, Rochelle said.

Girls do.

Hero said she doesn't want kids.

Janelle shook her head. Everyone says that at first, but when you meet the right guy, it's different.

Rochelle's face hardened. She put the cigarette to her lips, took a drag from it without looking at anyone. Isagani's hand around her knee tightened. Hero took another long pull from her beer, finishing it in one go.

She stood up. I'm gonna find the bathroom.

Hero wasn't stupid. She knew, not deep down, but skin-shallow, shimmering at the surface of her body like a damaged nerve, that Rosalyn probably had some kind of a crush on her. An older woman, a shady background, a slight remove: Hero had spent her teen years and even college years nursing crushes, sometimes platonic, sometimes romantic, on older people, especially older women like that. Teresa was a case in point. Though what she'd felt for Teresa was something much less and much more than a crush—what Hero felt for Teresa was something she didn't have a name for. Not then, not now, not ever. She preferred it that way. A feeling with Teresa's face on it, and no words.

Rosalyn had probably never even slept with a woman before. She liked stories where girls—thieves, vampires, witches, aristocratic revolutionaries—fell in love at fourteen and stayed with that person, that boy, forever, after overcoming countless obstacles. She probably didn't realize she was flirting with Hero, that her behavior might be misconstrued, that someone more serious and less scrupulous might actually take her up on the signals she was unwittingly putting out.

What Rosalyn aimed at Hero, the teasing, puppylike interest, excited at the appearance of a strange knight, was something that had only formed after seeing Hero's thumbs, after knowing Hero didn't have any other friends, after hearing words like New People's Army. Hero didn't need to know the details of what was really between Rosalyn and Jaime to understand that whatever history was there was real, and heavy, and long. Long was the crucial part. Hero didn't know anything about long, heavy, real loves, but she knew what they had in common with a crush. Absolutely fucking nothing.

Hero didn't really have to pee, but she joined the line of girls for the bathroom anyway, just to have something to do. There must have been another DJ inside the house, because the music was even louder inside than it was in the garage, the beat so loud, so penetrating, she had the feeling her own heartbeat was altering to keep time with it. She looked around the party for Jaime or Rosalyn, but didn't see them. Someone passed her, then stopped, looked down. It was the man from earlier, the one who'd pointed at himself when Rosalyn had waved a dismissive hand in his direction.

He leaned forward and shouted into her ear, You were talking about me. Earlier, with your friends. What'd you say?

Hero leaned back, shook her head, then leaned forward. My friend was pointing out people she knew. She didn't know who you were.

Okay, the guy shouted. I'm Peter. What's your name?

Hero, she shouted back.

Hero, he repeated, brow cut together in the center. Hero, like—

Superhero, she finished, getting it over with. He started laughing. Okay, that's cool. You have a cute accent, too. Perplexed, Hero said, Thank you.

Peter gestured at the line. You're gonna be waiting here forever, you want a drink? Hero lifted her empty bottle of Coors Light, showing him.

Peter laughed. Okay, you want a real drink? He handed her the cup he'd been sipping from, which looked like it was full of Coke. What is it, she asked. Coke and Jim Beam, he shouted in her ear, the dense lavender cloud of his cologne flooding her nostrils.

She didn't pull away. Took the cup and drank from it it. She and Francisco used to make Coke and bourbons before they fucked, and then again right after. It's good, she said.

Hero found out that Peter was in San Francisco for law school, that he'd lived in Glen Park first but just moved to the Excelsior. He was originally from Los Angeles, and he missed it, the Bay didn't compare, sorry. He'd been to a couple parties in the Bay by way of his roommates and liked them, but wasn't all that into the music. Hero told Peter—very little, really: that she'd just come to the Bay so there was no need to apologize (though something had twitched in her, defensively, at his critique); that she worked in a restaurant; that she didn't have any particular feelings, positive or negative, about the music.

By the time Jaime found them, they'd wandered away from the bathroom line and had tucked themselves into a couch near the back of the house. Hero didn't know how long he'd been standing there before she registered his presence, looking down at Hero in disbelief, cigarette tucked behind his ear.

The hell? Rosalyn and Rochelle have been looking all over for you. Rochelle said you went to the bathroom like over an hour ago, Jaime said. We're outside in the driveway.

Okay, Hero said. She was halfway into her third Coke and bourbon, still not feeling even remotely drunk. The time she got drunk and Lulay was waiting outside of her bedroom, she must have had something more like ten, possibly along with a Valium that Francisco had gotten from a friend. Three of these watered-down drinks, more Coke than bourbon, was nothing. She wasn't like Janelle, two-shots soppy, all over the place.

Jaime waited. Then turned and walked away. Then he stopped, spun around, came back, knelt down next to Hero, shouted into her ear: If you go home with him but want a pickup, page me. 911. You got my number, right?

Hero pulled back. Jaime didn't wear any cologne; smelled of detergent, cigarette smoke, rum, metallic-y sweat. He repeated, You got it, right?

Hero nodded. Jaime got back up. Okay. We're in the driveway, he said again.

I heard you.

That's not your boyfriend, right, Peter said-shouted when he left. I don't wanna get jumped by any boyfriends or dads or brothers tonight—

No boyfriend. No brother, Hero said-shouted.

Hero opened her mouth to start another conversational thread, but found abruptly that she was at the end of the line, no more talk in her, big or small, no more interest in knowing anything else about him. There was nothing left in her but the gnawing, swollen, thought-obliterating need to fuck. She leaned in and shouted into his ear, You want to take me to your place?

Peter, stopped, startled, jostling his just refilled cup of Coke and bourbon so it spilled over his fingers. Hero stared back at him, expect-ant. He made a shape with his mouth, a whistle Hero couldn't hear. Okay. Yeah. Let's go.

He stood, and Hero followed him, something edgeless and frantic in her finally settling. They went out the front door, which led them down a winding path, bypassing the driveway, partially hidden by a hedge. Over the top of it, Hero could see Rosalyn and Jaime sitting on the ground, talking to Rochelle and Isagani. Hero didn't even know if it was close to midnight yet. She knew if she stayed looking at them, Rosalyn would turn around, notice.

Hero didn't stay, didn't look. Peter said-shouted, You coming, and she didn't have to shout back; she didn't even have to answer. She was.

Ang Dalagang Pilipina

THE NEXT MORNING, HERO THOUGHT ABOUT CALL-
ing the house in Milpitas, asking Paz or Pol to pick her up, sliding into
Paz's Civic or Pol's Corona with her crusted underwear crumpled into
her jacket pocket; thought about the questions they would think but not
ask, thought about sitting in the passenger seat, hearing those silent questions and not answering. Instead she left Peter sleeping naked, put her
own clothes back on, went to the small galley kitchen in the apartment,
and paged Jaime 4379. HELP.

Hero understood that the code was perhaps slightly too dramatic for
the situation and sent another page that said 015. OK.

The emotional jerkaround must have been too much for Jaime, because
when he called back a few minutes later, sounding like he'd dragged himself out of bed, his first words were: If you've been ax-murdered and this is
a ghost, I lose ten dollars to Janelle, so do me a solid and still be alive.

Once Hero made it clear that she was fine, Jaime said he'd pick her up
at the Fremont BART station. I don't know where that is, Hero said. Ask
your man, Jaime countered. I'll figure it out myself, Hero said just to
hear Jaime laugh.

It was her first time on the BART, her first time really seeing the cities of the Bay, from north to south. There were several stations after Glen
Park, which had been the station closest to Peter's apartment. Only when
they reached Civic Center did Hero realize they were going through the
city itself.

After the train left Embarcadero station, the view outside the windows went pitch-black, and then they were going faster, faster, like
they'd been gripped by a giant hand and were being dragged through a
tunnel, the noise of the train screeching, reaching a volume that didn't
just deafen Hero but deadbolted her, trapped her in the cupped palm of
its sound so she couldn't get out and she knew she just had to wait there
for the lifetime it would take to end, her eyes closed, grappling at any

thought to hang from and praying her grip would catch, thinking of, of, of. Thinking of Teresa taking her to the gakit festival in Agandan, where the Gaddang people, who often used the gakit rafts to cross the Cagayan River, would build a ceremonial bamboo raft in an elaborate yearly ritual, and Hero, then a first-year cadre, confused about the meaning of the ritual, confused about how to impress Teresa, not yet aware that trying to impress her was the surest way of ensuring she would never be impressed, watched in dumb silence until Teresa held up her own arm, next to Hero's, and used her free hand to clasp them both together, blood-warm and firm, locked at the wrists, strong enough to carry a man on, a life on, and said: That's why people need a raft, donya.

It was only when the train surfaced again at West Oakland, the walls of the tunnel coming into sight, then disappearing as they climbed above them, that Hero realized, trying to catch and catch at breath that wouldn't come, that they'd been underground—that they'd been underwater—that they'd just crossed the bay.

A young man in one of the seats across from Hero's aisle took notice of her heavy breathing and said, Are you okay? It took Hero a few more minutes of trying to gasp at air before she could look up, eyes watery, and nod. He hesitated there, waiting, but when he saw that she wasn't lying, he turned around and became, thankfully, a stranger again.

Hero turned her head toward the window. Her heart was still racing as she watched the resolutely unpretty cities of the Bay roll along in front of her like a film, bright and gray, sun-bleached, warehouses, gas stations, power lines that stretched for ages, parking lots half full of cars and with each car a missing soul to drive it. Nothing she saw looked like home. She started to feel better.

Jaime was waiting outside the BART station in his brown Supra, idling illegally at the curb, an Oakland A's cap on his head, smoking a cigarette that he flicked out of the driver's side window at the sight of her. As Hero approached, she had a split-second moment of panic, thinking Rosalyn might also be in the car with him. But when she approached, she saw it was just him, leaning over and pushing the front passenger door open, blasting Janet Jackson's Miss You Much at a deafening volume.

It's nine in the morning, she said.

Jaime cupped a hand around his ear. Sorry, that didn't sound like Happy New Year?

Happy New Year, she said, and he smiled.

Okay, now you can get in the car.

She closed the door, and he shook his head. Nah, it's not closed all the way. You gotta really slam it. She opened the door again, then yanked it closed with the full strength of her shoulder, making the entire car shake. There you go, he said.

Inside, the car was practically immaculate, a set of cassette tapes arranged in what used to be the cupholder and which was now a minor library, the carpet in the footwell spotless, possibly recently or regularly vacuumed, a eucalyptus air freshener hanging from the rearview mirror, along with a rosary made of blue plastic beads and a scapular on a brown satin string, its laminated picture of the Virgin peering down at them.

Your car's so clean.

Jaime snorted. Compared to Rosalyn's toxic waste zone. He put the car in gear, started driving his way out of the station, singing along with the song under his breath.

Hero leaned her head against the window, just happy enough to be in the car of someone she knew, back in the Bay, close to home. Her jeans felt itchy, sticky; she'd taken her underwear off but the rough denim was chafing against her bare pussy. She needed to take a shower, take another piss. They hadn't used any lubricant; she thought she'd been wet enough, but maybe not; she'd probably end up with a UTI if she didn't drink some water soon. They had K-Y jelly back at home, in the drawer in the kitchen where Paz kept extra medical supplies. She'd take some with her from now on—then she jolted, stiff, at her own train of thought, how swiftly and economically her mind had gone on, making decisions for her, settling on plans.

Jaime put his cigarette out in the built-in ashtray, stuffed with cigarette butts, the only dirty part of the car. You got a little something, he said, and pointed first to his left eye, and then to the corner of his mouth, keeping one hand on the steering wheel.

Hero blinked at him, then flipped down the passenger seat visor to look at the mirror, and saw remnants of brown shadow smudged beneath her left eye. The right eye was still pristine. Most of the brown lipstick had faded, but it had been applied so evenly, the pigment pressed uniformly into the lips, that a perfectly even, winy-brown flush was left. Still, some of it had been smeared into her chin and upper lip.

Hero hadn't realized she was still wearing the makeup. She wiped at it roughly with the back of her wrist, then knocked the visor back onto the roof with more force than was necessary.

Yeah, you're good now, Jaime said.

Instead of taking her straight home, Jaime said that he hadn't eaten breakfast yet, he was hungry as shit, then asked if she was hungry—and when she said yes, ended up driving not down to Milpitas from Fremont, but back up north, to Union City.

El Rincón Michoacano was a Mexican restaurant in a strip mall, not that different from the one where Rosalyn's family's restaurant was located, though much smaller—its only neighbors a hardware store, a Mexican bakery, and a dry cleaner's. Jaime parked the car and said, They're prolly gonna ask if you're my girlfriend. Don't sweat it.

Inside, the restaurant was mostly empty. There was an older man in his forties, sitting behind the counter talking to a woman who was leaning on the wall at the threshold between the kitchen and the restaurant. It reminded Hero so much of Boy and Adela that she thought she was dreaming, one of those odd dreams, like knowing that the person in front of you was your father, even if they had the face of someone completely different, a celebrity or a stranger. But it wasn't a dream. It was just another restaurant.

The man lifted his hand up to Jaime, said, Que onda, güey, but his eyes were drifting toward Hero, appraising.

She's not my girlfriend, Jaime said, unprompted.

I thought we had something special, Hero said.

Carlos tilted his head. What, what?

She's just fucking with you, Jaime said. He took his cap off, went to the woman, who was holding her arms out toward him, entered her hug. You get skinnier every time I see you, she was saying.

Turning to Hero, the woman's arm still slung around his neck, Jaime said, hands directing his words to where they should go: Martha, Carlos. Geronima. Geronima. Martha, Carlos.

Hi, Martha said. Geronima. Good name. Usual? This was directed to Jaime.

Two, he said.

The bowls that were put before them not long after they sat down were steaming hot and full to the brim. Thick reddish-brown soup, chunks of meat and herbs, shards of tortilla half submerged. Martha put down two metal spoons on paper napkins, said, Coffee's coming.

Could I have a glass of water, too, please? Hero asked. Martha smiled, relaxing for some reason at the sound of Hero's voice. Of course.

Good for hangovers, Jaime said, digging in.

Hero picked up a spoon and took the first bite—it was pipian, like they made it in Vigan, like she'd eaten growing up, recognizing the taste of pasotes the minute it touched her tongue.

What is this, Hero said. Is this Filipino?

Jaime looked at her like she was a particularly slow child. It's just, like, soup.

There's pasotes in this, Hero said.

Epazote? Martha overheard. Yes. It's an herb.

No, I— Then Hero looked down. Her stomach growled, still queasy.

It'll get cold, Jaime warned. Hero picked her spoon up again.

After several minutes of silent eating had passed between them, Hero finally said: I'm not hungover.

Who said I was talking about you, Jaime replied, his mouth full.

She looked up at him, seeing his face for the first time without the cap shadowing it. His eyes were bloodshot, the circles beneath them dark and veiny, pale face sallow, lips chapped. Martha came back over with a tray, put two cups of coffee and a tall glass of ice water in front of them. Thanks, Jaime said, wiping at the corner of his mouth.

Martha smiled at Hero, encouraging, but Hero didn't really have anything to say, besides, It's very good, which was true. She drank the water quickly, even though the cold shocked her molars. She finished it so quickly that Martha filled her glass up again—Hero half-emptied it again.

When he'd consumed nearly half of his bowl, Jaime let out a breath. Color had come back into his face, the muscles there relaxing with newly rushing blood. He pulled out a cigarette, then leaned backward to pluck a terra-cotta ashtray from another table. He lit the cigarette, taking a long drag, rubbing at the back of his neck.

So you get any, he prompted, not a question.

Hero choked. Some.

You do that kind of thing a lot?

What, Hero said, trying to get some meat on her spoon. Fuck around? Yeah.

Not for a while, Hero answered. But. Yes.

Jaime took that in, saying nothing, smoking in silence. Then he switched his cigarette to his left hand, took in a spoonful of just soup, then a bit of meat. Hero waited for a tendril of smoke that was blocking his eyes to pass, and then asked, her jaw tight in defense. Anything else?

Jaime coughed, a wet, ugly, smoker's cough. Uh. They got AIDS in the Philippines, right? You need me to tell you to use a rubber?

No, Hero said. Martha came over, then, to refill the water in Hero's glass. Hero thanked her, and took another long chug from it, trying not to get any ice in her mouth. After she swallowed, she asked: What about you?

Jaime shrugged. There was a girl at the party I fuck around with sometimes, she lives up in the city. I went to her place, then went over to my sister's to crash. Rosalyn took the minivan, drove everyone home. I just got back when I got your page, I was about to fall asleep.

Hero didn't want to ask if Rosalyn was the one who'd picked him up from the BART station, the way he'd just picked her up, she didn't want to ask if Rosalyn had said anything about her leaving, just fucking off without telling anyone, if Rosalyn had been worried, or angry, or if she thought of Hero differently, now that she knew—well, what did she know, really. Hero ate some more corn. Silence came over them.

Then Jaime sipped at his coffee, slurping the surface to temper the heat of it. Yeah, so. I go up to the city a lot.

With Rosalyn? and. Rochelle and them, Hero added, too late.

Nah, Jaime said. She hates it up there. Well, not hates. She's just not that into going up to the city all the time. She's not a big bar person or even, I don't know. Party person, really. She used to be more into that stuff. But she's kinda over it, I don't know. I'm not that heavy into it, either. But if I do go out, when I come back down, I usually stop off at Union City. Sometimes I'll even park my car here, you know, and take the BART up the night before, so it's there the next morning. Come here for breakfast. Then go back home.

Hero didn't have to ask why he didn't go to Boy's for breakfast, those mornings-after. She knew about separating parts of her life out, too; about being one person in one place, and another person in another place. Hero wondered if Jaime knew yet—maybe he was still too young to know—that those people usually ended up meeting, in the end. She wasn't going to be the one to tell him. Jaime asked if she was going to drink her coffee; Hero gestured for him to take it. I could come up to the city with you sometimes, Hero said without looking at him. Jaime's mouth was hidden by the coffee cup, but she heard him say, Yeah, sure, okay.

When they were finished, and Jaime had paid for the food, waving off Hero's offer to pay for her half, he told her, as they both slid back into the car: Next time, we'll get the nopalitos con huevo. They're good here.

Nothing changed after New Year's Eve, at least not back at home with Roni and Paz and Pol. Way back in Vigan, back in Manila, Hero had always waited for the apocalypse of sexual maturity to come down on her, the promise of retribution sewn deep into her bones: she was a ho, that was how Janelle put it, and she knew what happened to hos. But slowly she was learning that the fear was just something she'd been taught, like a bedtime story about a mumu that would get her in the end, the skeleton in the De Vera granary that would bear witness to her evil and exact its punishment. Now she was finding out the mumu wasn't real. The skeleton was nothing but bones—just the remnants of some person, full of junk and sorrow, like anyone else.

Pol had put in a request to have his days off switched to Thursdays and Fridays. Fridays and Saturdays were impossible, Saturdays and Sundays even more so, but at least with Thursdays and Fridays, he reasoned, he could be at home and Hero could go out with her friends if she wanted to.

Paz said he didn't have to do that, Hero could just drop Roni off at Gloria's apartment on San Petra Court like before. When Roni got wind of that, she had a complete meltdown, giving up on the world—until Pol said, ending it: I'm making this decision. I'll be the one to stay home with her.

Afterward, curious, Hero asked Roni about it, You don't like Auntie Gloria?

Roni was still in her mood. It's not Auntie Gloria.

Then what. You don't like her place?

It's not her place. It's our old place. Mom still pays half of their rent. And it's where Auntie Carmen used to live with us, too.

Hero tried to understand; couldn't. So what. You don't like that they live in your old place? You miss Auntie Carmen?

NO—Roni said, her voice rising. LEAVE ME ALONE— And then Hero had to drop it, quick, before Roni started scratching her face off again.

Thursdays and Fridays became Hero's going-out days, bringing Roni home after her meeting with Adela on Thursdays and then sometimes heading straight back to the restaurant, or even Rosalyn's garage, to drink and watch movies or play pusoy dos. On Fridays, sometimes it was the same thing; though increasingly, Jaime would ask if she wanted to drive up to the city. The minute Jaime's car exited off 237 and got onto

101 North, Hero felt like she'd been unfastened from something; like she'd been treading water, and now she could go deep.

They never talked about looking for ass when Rosalyn was around; they never talked about sex at all in front of most of the group. Hero had already figured out that most of the girls, Janelle and Lea especially, but Rosalyn to some extent as well, had grown up as devout Catholics: girls determined to wait for marriage, who only spoke about sex when it happened between people who'd been dating for years and were about to get married. If anyone but Jaime or Hero ever had casual sex, they never talked about it; Janelle and Lea tended to make the loudest jokes whenever they passed by another of those new advertisements encouraging people to use condoms. Once, Rosalyn relayed some story that her mother had told her, about seeing more and more women, including Filipinas, coming into the hospital and testing HIV positive despite claiming to be in monogamous marriages. A look of disgust came over Janelle's face, and she briefly held herself away from Rosalyn as though she'd contaminated them all just by telling the story.

Sometimes the search for sex was just a pretense. Hero realized, incredulous, that Jaime—liked her. He liked being around her, he liked her deadpan jokes, he liked noticing her silences and smiling wryly at them, instead of poking and prodding at them the way Rosalyn might have. But neither of them were the type of people to say, I like you, let's hang out, so they had to use the joint project of getting ass as an excuse to hang out with each other. After making equally weak efforts at flirting with the same bartender, some morena in a bomber jacket, Jaime and Hero would just drift back together and end up talking, which was— strange, since Hero didn't altogether like talking, especially about herself, and she'd thought Jaime was the same way, that they had that in common, a kind of reserve that was enabled and protected by the larger, livelier personalities they'd surrounded themselves with.

But Hero realized that she didn't mind talking about things with Jaime, that when he pushed a second beer across the table to her and said something like, What, so you were like a rich kid, she didn't feel awkward or anxious about saying yes. There was pleasure in talking, in saying things like, I guess the stereotype about Ilocanos is that they're kind of—stingy? or The soup I was telling you about, the one that's like sopa tarasca, my yaya used to make it for me when I was sick.

That was also how Hero found out that Jaime had worked in one of the bars they went to, just out of college; that he'd lived in San Francisco with his sister for two years but they drove each other crazy and anyway he'd been going through some things so he ended up moving back in with their mom in Milpitas. Now he was working as a security guard over at Kaiser in Sunnyvale, where his mom was a nurse. Hero got the feeling Jaime and his mother were close. He mentioned things here or there about some real dumb bullshit he'd gotten into when he was in college and afterward, mentioned some dudes he used to graffiti with over in Hayward and how it'd landed him a brief stint over at Elmwood, the jail on the other side of Milpitas.

He explained how he knew Martha and Carlos from El Rincón Michoacano, explained that his parents had moved to Union City from Alviso, to the west of Milpitas. Like many of their friends they'd been turfed out of Alviso in '68 when San Jose finally annexed the city: the homes bulldozed, the families displaced, and the area zoned for industry. His father had some Mexican friends who said the East Bay was okay, and his mom was pregnant, so they moved. Jaime was born in Hayward and lived in Union City until his dad left, when he was six. His mom moved them down to Milpitas, where she had some family; a younger sister, a couple of nieces and nephews Jaime hardly ever saw.

Martha and Carlos had been friends of his dad's and they'd kept in touch, despite the fact that his mom had lost contact with all their old Mexican friends in Union City and Hayward after his dad left; she'd receded back into a Filipino world. Jaime's mom hadn't taught them any Spanish, hadn't made an effort to keep them connected to their father's side of anything. Her only concession was bringing them to Martha and Carlos's restaurant sometimes when they really whined about it, figuring Jaime needed some kind of father figure in his life, some dumb shit like that, Jaime added, his voice catching.

Cely hadn't cared about what she was and wasn't connected to, her roots, whatever, fuck that dude, we don't need him, even though Jaime still remembered nights when they were children, sharing the same room, and Cely mumbling things that she remembered about him in the dark. That his family was from somewhere in Michoacán, same as Martha—Carlos was a chilango, but Cely said Jaime's dad, not to mention Martha herself, had tried not to hold it against him, which obviously meant they held it against him with a humor so aggressive that there were times the friendship nearly fell apart over it. Hero had the sense that it was like an Ilocano tolerating the presence of a manileño. The rest of the things Cely remembered and relayed to Jaime, those lightless childhood nights, were little details. That he was light-skinned. That he smoked.

Jaime said that a year after they moved to Milpitas, Rosalyn moved in four houses down with her mom and grandparents, from San Francisco. A few Mondays later she showed up in his second-grade class. The rest was—and Jaime didn't have to finish his sentence, waving his cigarette with his right hand to indicate what the rest was. History.

One time, Hero and Jaime were at a bar in the Tenderloin and Hero had gone into the bathroom, not to fuck, just to piss after having drunk too many beers in too short a time. She'd ended up having to take an unexpected and difficult shit, and when she finally came out, Jaime was nowhere to be found, even though the chat he'd been having with another Mexipina—that word he'd taught Hero—looked like it'd been promising. She went outside, woozy and cheerful, just to check if they were smoking or making out, since usually Jaime didn't leave without telling her, and found him being charged into a wall by a man much shorter than him but no less discouraged for that fact.

Before she could even register what she was seeing, or shout for help, another, older man grabbed Jaime's left arm and wrenched it backward. Even if she hadn't been a doctor, she would have known the wet pop of a dislocated shoulder. She shouted, Police! and the two men looked up, breathless. By some miracle, they ran away, leaving Jaime on the ground. Hero went to Jaime, feeling herself sober up with every step. Then she said,

This is gonna hurt, and with his eyes squeezed shut Jaime breathed out a confused, Wha—and she promptly yanked his shoulder back into place before his tongue could touch his teeth and finish the word. There were things she'd forgotten; there were things she hadn't forgotten.

Fu-uck, he throated out, eyes still shut, the base of the lashes wet.

Hero saw the thank-you that was going to come out of Jaime's mouth next. In order to prevent it, she said: I'll be sure to tell everyone you cried. Jaime laughed, a choked-off sound. That was another way to make history.

Of course, there were things Jaime and Hero didn't talk about. He didn't talk about the years he and Rosalyn had spent as a couple; when he talked about Rosalyn, it was about their childhood or about their more recent adult friendship. Nothing about whether or not he still had it bad for her, the way Janelle described it, whether or not she was the reason he'd left Milpitas for San Francisco, whether or not she was the reason he'd come back.

For her part, Hero didn't talk about the NPA, didn't talk about dropping out of medical school, didn't talk about having become a field doctor, didn't mention Teresa. She wanted to know if Rosalyn had mentioned something to Jaime about what she'd said in Rosalyn's backyard, but she couldn't read any sign on his face that said he already understood why sometimes her story would trail off, why sometimes she'd backtrack and start talking about biguenyo generalities, food specialties, types of music she'd listened to when she was in college.

Often these were things she'd already told to Rosalyn, sometimes even when Jaime was around, but he never called her on repeating her stories. There was a difference between telling someone something when there were other people around, and telling someone something when it was just the two of you. There was a difference between having friends, and having a friend.

Paz's plan to throw Roni a lucky double birthday—double the luck, Hero heard her tell Pol, verging on shrill—came into fruition fast, after the holidays. She had put down a credit card deposit on the main hall in Milpitas Community Center for the twenty-third of February, the Saturday after Roni's birthday, which was technically the eighteenth. Bad luck to celebrate a birthday before the actual date itself, everyone knew that.

Rosalyn's family got the catering job. The same old banquet foods, with some extra afritada, Roni's favorite, Paz said—Hero still wasn't sure if it was really Roni's favorite—and a lechon. They didn't have to do desserts, Paz would go to Gold Ribbon for the cake.

There wasn't actually much coordinating to be done, Hero would have thought, yet Rosalyn was always coming into the restaurant while Hero was supposed to be working, sitting her down and asking if Roni liked pancit bihon, if Roni ate diniguan. And then, after work, Rosalyn would want to go with Hero to the community center to see the layout of the place, even though later Hero thought to herself that Rosalyn must have been to the community center dozens of times. Still, there Hero was, asking an older white lady at the entrance if she could possibly unlock the doors to the main hall so they could take a look at the space, just to know how to configure the tables. Paz had invited well over two hundred people. The capacity for the hall was 214.

Hero stood in the doorway while Rosalyn flicked on the massive overhead lights, illuminating the space, as big as a basketball court with a laminated dance floor in the center, just in front of the stage. Rosalyn lifted her chin to the stage, said, That's where Ruben'll set up his decks.

Rosalyn stepped onto the dance floor. Her voice echoed, When Jaime and I were kids, the church had a party to celebrate our First Communion here.

Hero thought of the picture she'd seen in Rosalyn's house, Rosalyn and Jaime as children, dancing together. She didn't say anything.

Rosalyn looked at her, then looked away. She pointed toward the outer walls of the room, some of which were lined with big windows. We usually set up the food here. There's gonna be like two hundred people at this thing, so we'll have just a long buffet line along both walls.

Rosalyn was doing a lot of that, recently. Looking at Hero, then looking away. They hadn't talked about what Hero had told Rosalyn on

Christmas, in her backyard; they hadn't talked about Hero taking off with a stranger, on New Year's. When Hero saw Rosalyn two days later, the morning of her first day back at work, Hero had waited for Rosalyn to make a comment, to throw it in her face. But Rosalyn just said,

Do you want the next chapter of *Vampire Princess Miyu*? I just got it in from Ruby.

Hero didn't really care about the next chapter of *Vampire Princess Miyu*. Sure, she'd said, the relief so thick in her throat she thought she might choke on it.

Pol accepted, more than participated in, the preparations for Roni's birthday. His attitude wasn't altogether that different from the one he took with respect to Roni's faith healing; it was something Paz needed, for her peace of mind, and it would have exhausted more energy to fight it, or even question it, than to simply let it happen. If there was anything he spoke up about, it was his mild disapproval of how much of the party was being paid for by Paz's credit card, when she was already so much in debt. Paz brushed the fears off, said that she'd worked overtime over the holidays and would have more than enough to pay the credit card off. By which she meant pay the minimum off, as always.

Sometimes Hero came home late in the evening and the preparations would still be going on, Paz and Pol at the kitchen table, Paz making up diagrams of where people would sit, scratching out names and then rewriting them. At least half of the people were distant relatives, some of whom neither Paz nor Pol had seen in over a decade. The rest of the people were friends, coworkers, friends of friends, family of friends, friends of coworkers, family of coworkers.

We don't know half these people, Pol said.

I see them at church, Paz replied. They're Belen's friends.

Belen was Charmaine's mother, and Charmaine was the girl who'd been involved with the fight that had gotten Roni suspended, the one who'd lied to their teacher about being involved and failed to recruit Roni to her ruse. Hero had seen her in the parking lot after school, talking to Roni: a much taller girl, with her hair in a precise braid. She was picked up in a BMW sedan by her mother, who was usually dressed in black slacks and a tweed jacket. Both Belen and her daughter were mestiza, either naturally, in Charmaine's case, or with the help of a foundation two shades lighter, in Belen's. Hero wouldn't have registered the makeup before, but watching Rosalyn's work had made her more attuned.

Paz sometimes brought supplies home from the hospital, syringes or insulin or stronger fluocinocide and hydrocortisone creams, and instead of putting them in the drawer where the extras usually went, she put them in a paper bag, labeled FOR BELEN. Hero was used to that kind of thing, knew that Pol, too, sometimes took things from the hospital to give to friends in need, but there was something about the ceremony of how Paz did it, the way she found a clean bag, the way she wrote the label painstakingly, the letters big, like the words and names were important.

On the guest list, Hero saw that Paz had written Belen Yaptangco Navarrete. But she was more distracted by what she saw above the name, the header of the particular stationery Paz was writing on.

It said, in slightly unevenly printed letters, APOLONIO CHUA DE VERA, M.D., PH.D. FELLOW, INTERNATIONAL COLLEGE OF SURGEONS. At the footer of the stationery page was their address in Milpitas and the house number, written as CLINIC NUMBER. Hero frowned at the page. She remembered Pol's old stationery, back in the Philippines, with the jagged surgeon's cursive script of his name written at the top. Then below his name, his adornments: Fellow of the Philippine Orthopedic Association, Fellow of the Western Pacific Orthopedic Association.

This stationery didn't mention those associations. Was he a fellow of the International College of Surgeons in the Philippines, too? Had Pol applied for and passed the board, here in California? As far as she knew, he hadn't practiced medicine since he'd left the Philippines. He certainly wasn't using the house as a home clinic.

Paz noticed Hero looking down at the paper and misinterpreted her look. She nodded to confirm a question Hero hadn't even been thinking of asking. Yes, her mother is one of *those* Yaptangcos.

The Yaptangco family she knew by reputation, if they were the ones Paz was hinting at. They'd founded one of the largest paper manufacturing businesses in the Philippines, owning and operating pulp and paper mills from Bataan to Cebu. Their name had been bandied out on Amihan's long list of oligarchic families whose chokehold on the country's resources was cannibalizing its future, before Eddie would hold up a hand and say, Does being an insufferable bore again count as cadre abuse? Why Belen was living in Milpitas if she'd come from such an illustrious family was a mystery to Hero. Although someone might say the same thing of her.

Who cares what their name is, Pol said. Paz flattened her mouth.

Pol had never been impressed by illustrious families, not in Vigan, not in Manila, not anywhere. Perhaps it was something as simple as a sense of pride; why should he be impressed by a family that was no better than the one he himself had issued from? But that wasn't it, Hero knew. He'd been detached, not just from the De Vera name itself, but from the social obligations it demanded. Hamin and Concepcion cultivated friendships with the other landowning families of Ilocos Sur and Ilocos Norte, made regular trips to Manila to visit strategic friends: businessmen who were becoming politicians, politicians who wanted to do business. Pol had never done any strategic cultivation. He'd become a man far from the society of his peers, having lived and worked for so long in Indonesia, and the fact that he was a surgeon and not a budding mayor or industrialist only further distanced him from the daily politics of being a De Vera. Not entirely, of course; in the end, strategically or not, he'd cultivated and been cultivated. Tito Melchior had been the one to introduce him to Josefina Edralin in the first place, saying: Marcos has a very pretty cousin.

When Hero first left for Isabela, she thought that would be the last she'd hear of people like the Yaptangcos, the Marcoses, the De Veras. But they were everywhere. And now they were even here, in California.

They were the mothers of Roni's classmates, they were in the restaurant asking for a rush order of lechon for an upcoming banquet.

There were things Hero had hoped to cast off forever, but it turned out there were things that she couldn't dislodge or forget, like the sound of Pol's voice on the phone when she'd called him to ask for a place to stay, the night before she officially left for the mountains with Teresa and Eddie. Weeks before, uniformed soldiers had burst into the UST dorms looking for the students who'd been suspected of corroborating with the Communists, asking questions, making threats. By that time she was already living in Cubao, at an apartment belonging to one of Teresa's journalist friends, waiting to be taken up to Isabela. She couldn't stay and risk endangering Teresa's friend for much longer, so she needed a place to sleep for the night. Eddie could drop her off somewhere quickly but not linger too long himself, just to be safe. The next morning he and Teresa would pick her up and they would leave for the mountains for good.

The only phone number of Pol's that Hero remembered wasn't his home phone number in Dagupan, but the number of Nazareth General Hospital. She had to endure ten minutes of changing her mind, then hardening her resolve, after a chirpy nurse told her that Doctor De Vera would be right with her. When he finally picked up and Hero said Hello, Pol mistook her for Soly at first. She had to say, No, Tito Pol. It's me.

Hero told him everything, then and there: that she'd dropped out of school, that she'd joined the NPA, that she was going into hiding and could she stay overnight at his house in Dagupan before she and her comrades left for the mountains. She said it all without letting him interject. Afraid he would talk her out of it, afraid she would listen.

At the time she hadn't thought of what Pol must have felt; how he must have felt, someone who'd supposedly been at Malacañang that evening on the twenty-sixth of January, just hours before the palace turned the lights off and soldiers turned Armalite rifles on students and protestors. He must have seen just how cruelly his own comrades, so to speak, would deal with hers. She never thought about the possibility of Pol one day being called in the middle of the night and being invited to some far-flung regional morgue. Being asked to identify a dredged-up body: packed tight with river and earth, gouged of its soul. Having to say, Yes, I know her. She's my family.

If Pol said no, she thought, this would likely be the last time she ever heard his voice. Before that thought could sink deeply enough into her heart to change it, Pol spoke. He asked her when.

Paz made Roni try on two different birthday dresses, one from a department store in Palo Alto near Paz's work, the other one made by the relative of a coworker. Both of them were pink. The first one, which Paz had bought really as a backup option, was simpler, the pink duskier, a better match for Roni's skin tone; it had a full skirt, capped sleeves off the shoulder, and a bodice covered in lace the same color as the rest of the dress. There was something old-fashioned about it—or, not quite old-fashioned, but mature. The second one was a loose interpretation of a terno; puffy butterfly sleeves made of iridescent taffeta, sequins all across the bodice in what looked to be rose shapes, and instead of the traditional straight skirt, multiple layers of transparent fabric, alternating between white and the kind of bright pink that made the undertones in Roni's skin look greenish.

Hero tried not to laugh at Roni's face when she came out of the downstairs bathroom in the second one, scratching at her arms, shoving the bottom of the butterfly sleeve up over her shoulder so the taffeta wouldn't irritate the oozing plaques that were climbing up her inner elbows toward her armpits.

That's—nice, Paz said unconvincingly.

No way, no *way*, Roni said, giving up on scratching and crossing her arms.

It's your first terno, Paz reasoned. Auntie Ariel's sister made that specially for you. Even your Ate Hero wore a terno when she was a kid.

Roni whipped her head around to stare at Hero, betrayed. You? You wore this?

I had a terno when I was your age. Ternos, Hero amended. She noted that Paz had used her as an example, not herself. Paz had almost certainly never owned or worn a terno.

And you liked it?

Hero didn't look over at Paz. I hated it. Mine was very itchy and tight.

In the end, they went with the department store dress. When Paz was out of earshot, saying there was another bag she'd left upstairs, Roni said to Hero, grinning slyly, that the skirt was big enough she might even wear shorts underneath.

Paz came back with another bag that said Nordstrom on it, handed it to Hero. Dread rose up in Hero's throat, just at the look of mounting glee on Roni's face.

I also bought you slacks and a blouse, Nimang. You don't have to wear it. You can borrow something of mine. A dress or something.

Paz's voice forged through, confident, dismissive, and it was only the way the fabric twitched in her hands that told Hero that she was self-conscious.

Hero looked inside the bag. It wasn't anything remotely like Roni's, to her relief and to the girl's visible disappointment. It was just a pair of loose black pants with suspenders and a white rayon blouse, soft to the touch.

Kasi you don't like dresses, 'di ba? Paz asked, her voice now rising, openly anxious, seeing the look of surprise come over Hero's face and interpreting it, not entirely mistakenly, as discomfort. That's what Pol said.

When Hero went to her room to try the clothes on, the trousers and blouse fit well, loosely, enough for her to feel comfortable. They felt like the clothes of someone more stylish, more graceful, more—more. They felt expensive, more expensive than the clothes Paz wore on her days off, more expensive than anything Hero wore. But the feeling of being in them, the feeling of being that woman, or looking like her at the very least, wasn't. It wasn't bad.

She descended the stairs in the outfit, facing Paz and Roni, her arms outstretched to show the look off for them. Paz's face lit up. Roni jumped to her feet, outraged. You look nice! No fair!

A few days later, she saw Pol leaving the house on his day off. He was dressed in a tan linen suit and polished tan leather shoes, a cream shirt, a wide bronze and gold tie, Windsor knot thick and tight at his throat, the kind of clothes Hero was used to seeing him wear in the Philippines, and which she had never seen him wear in the States. His security guard uniform consisted of a black polyester blazer, gray polyester slacks, a white oxford shirt, and a navy blue sweater that had the company's name, Exar, embroidered onto the left side of his chest, just over the heart. To the uniform he usually added one of his many ties, the only item of clothing he regularly wore that Hero recognized from the Philippines. To the tie, he'd add a gold tiepin; to the shirt, he'd add gold cufflinks. Hero knew they'd been heirlooms from his father; in her childhood she'd seen Hamin with similar ones.

Perhaps he had bought a suit for Roni's birthday, and was testing it out? Hero thought about it for the three hours it took for Pol to return to the house. When he did, he smiled sunnily at Roni doing her homework at the kitchen table, then at Hero.

Nag-guapo ka, Hero said in Ilocano.

Pol didn't even look down at his clothes in modesty, but his smile broadened. Agyamanak unay.

What's the occasion? Hero asked.

Just taking some pictures, Pol said. He approached Roni and leaned over her shoulder, peering at her homework and pressing his cheek to her cheek. The lapel of his blazer brushed against the back of her neck, and she swatted at it. It's scratchy, she said, but kept her cheek pressed against Pol's nevertheless, nuzzling.

Upon entering the community center the afternoon of the party, Hero realized that she had grossly underestimated the labor that had been going on behind the scenes to make the event happen. There were a handful of women Hero didn't know hanging up streamers across the windows, blowing up balloons and attaching them to the backs of chairs, folding napkins into shapes, arranging fresh pink roses into what looked like glass vases, but turned out to be thick plastic.

When Paz arrived in the banquet hall, an eruption of Pangasinan began amongst the women. Then, seeing Hero shrink and go quiet, they switched to Tagalog and took on a gossipy tone ostensibly to make Hero feel more comfortable, involved, but which only made her feel more exposed. She didn't even know who anyone was talking about, at least not enough for idle chatter. At one table, a group of men were sitting, starting in on a cooler of beer; the women's husbands and boyfriends, Hero supposed. Dodo! Lerma yelled. Hero didn't understand the rest of the command, but one man stood and started helping Lerma hang streamers from the highest point of the windows, too high for her to reach even standing on a chair.

Roni idolizes you, confided one of the women, either Gina or Diana, the wife of Paz's brother, Boyet. Roni had been taken by Paz and Gloria to the bathroom to get changed into her dress.

I don't know about that, Hero said, though her face grew warm with pleasure. She helped Gina or Diana unfurl another large white tablecloth over one of the thirty or so tables, skimmed her hand down the fabric to smooth out any wrinkles. Gina or Diana's gaze passed over Hero's hand.

What happened to your hand?

Nobody had ever looked at Hero's hands and then immediately asked about them. Even Rosalyn had let weeks pass over in silence before bringing the subject up.

I—I broke them badly a few years ago, Hero explained, the warmth draining from her face.

Did you get surgery for that? Did they put a plate in?

Wrong-footed, Hero explained that yes, but by then it was too late—

Gina or Diana pressed on. And range of motion? How is it? You can drive?

Ah—fine, Hero replied, trying not to stutter. It's not bad. It looks worse than it is. I drive.

It looks pretty bad, Gina or Diana agreed easily. Have you done PT for it?

Some, back in the Philippines. Sorry, Hero said, her brow wrinkling. Are you a PT, or—

Gina or Diana laughed, hands up, backing off.

Just nosy! I'm an RN now, but I wanted to be a PT. You should ask Pacita to recommend you a good one, she knows people. You might have good range of motion now but if you push it, you'll put yourself at risk for early arthritis. You're still so young!

Hero was still holding an unfolded tablecloth. O-kay. Thank you. I'll ask.

Same thing happened to my boyfriend, Gina or Diana added, gesturing for the tablecloth. Boxer. It's serious, but pretty common. Rolando fracture, 'di ba?

Hero felt the cloth stretch away from her, and together they spread it over the next table. She was starting to smile; the shrinking feeling of discomfort had ebbed away. She hadn't appreciated how much she missed being around people who talked medical like it was everyday conversation, as ordinary as talking about the weather. Pol used to be like that, in Vigan, used to name all the bones in the hand, used to walk Hero through the points of transfemoral amputation. There was comfort in talking about injury with people who dealt with injury all the time; the deep, practical reassurance of it. Diana had seen injuries like this before. Serious, but pretty common—those were her words. To Hero, they were tantamount to words of love. Yeah. Rolando, Hero said.

Rosalyn showed up with nearly the entire crew of people who usually populated the restaurant on Thursday and Friday nights: Jaime and JR carrying stacks and stacks of trays, nodding at Hero, Boy, and Adela doing the same, Ruben and Isagani wheeling in their equipment, Rochelle coming up to give Hero a joyous and somewhat unexpected hug. Janelle, Lea, and Maricris followed behind, along with Dante and a couple of other men Hero had only had passing conversations with, whose names she could't remember.

There wasn't all that much serving to be done, Hero knew; all they had to do was put down the trays and set up the portable heaters beneath them to make sure the food stayed warm. Rosalyn met Hero's eye and stopped for a moment, then lifted her hand in a rigid wave. She seemed apprehensive, for some reason, and started transferring all of that nervous energy onto her brother: nagging him about where he should put the food down, why he'd forgotten the plates, did he remember to turn the stove off, was he finished with his homework for the week.

Just from listening to their conversation, Hero figured out that her brother was in high school, probably his last year of it, that he was quiet and withdrawn in a way that was different from the way Hero, or even Jaime, could be quiet and withdrawn; that his quiet wasn't a form of reserve, concealing a self-possessed and observant humor, the quiet of someone who just needed to be teased out by the right person. His was the quiet of fear, ungainly and overgrown. He gave off an air of not being sure what to do with his own body, mottled beard already on his chin, but still kid-soft and fatty in his shoulders and stomach, like he'd grown into something he still couldn't quite believe was himself, his limbs full of barely restrained power, so that it always seemed like he might drop everything he was carrying, or accidentally crush the barbecue sticks as he tried to arrange them in neater rows from where they'd been jostled by the car ride. He was taller than Boy, taller than Adela, taller than Rosalyn and Hero, taller than most of the men at the party. He'd already developed a hunch. When Hero spoke to him, just to ask him if there was another tray of pancit she should put down next to the one she'd just put in place, he talked in a stuttery mumble, not meeting her eyes, until Adela came in and saved him, bearing the missing tray.

Rosalyn stopped in front of Hero and didn't say anything for a moment. Then blurted out:

You look like the Purple Rose.

Hero blinked at her. Rosalyn shrugged with one shoulder and went on, You know. From *The Glass Mask*. At the blank look on Hero's face, she muttered, What, you forgot about it already—

You're wearing a skirt, Hero said in lieu of admitting that she had.

Rosalyn kept her gaze level with Hero's, steady or pretending to be. Yeah.

It looks nice.

Rosalyn didn't break her gaze but let out a breath through her nose, low, so that Hero might have been imagining it, how measured and shaky it sounded. Then Rosalyn turned her head, acting as if someone was calling her, even though Hero hadn't heard anybody. They still need my help with the serving, Rosalyn demonstrably bullshitted, still not looking at Hero. I'm, uh. gonna go.

The adults started arguing about when to bring out Roni's birthday cake so that she could blow out the candles, before or after everybody had already gotten their food from the buffet. Hero backed away from the debate, mostly between Paz and her sisters, and saw Pol doing the same.

As Hero hung around the back of the hall, leaning against a wall next to the laid-out food and coolers full of ice, she saw Rochelle approaching with a hand raised, smiling. Could you get me a beer?

Hero picked the first beer out of the cooler, the cold momentarily making her hand lock up so that she almost dropped the bottle; Rochelle jerked forward to grab it by the base, still smiling. Shit, how many have you had already, we're like twenty minutes in! Hero forced herself to laugh, but found that she didn't have to force herself.

Rochelle leaned against the wall next to Hero. So I meant to ask, what happened on New Year's?

She said it plainly, smiling, like it wasn't the first time anyone except Jaime had spoken to Hero about it.

Hero coughed and played it off like a burp. Uh. Did Jaime say something?

Not really, Rochelle said, gazing at the stage where Isagani was making exaggerated movements to the opening strains of I Wanna Dance with Somebody. After you left, he just said you were talking with some dude in the house.

Who bet him that I was gonna get ax-murdered?

Rochelle started laughing. He told you that? Janelle. Don't worry about her. She thinks everyone's gonna get ax-murdered if they look at someone sideways. Her dad used to be a cop. She looked at Hero out of the corner of her eyes. Was it any good?

Hero shrugged, leaning against the wall, one foot propped against it.

Rochelle laughed again, turning her body to fully face Hero now, reaching out to drag a chair over from the nearest table so she could sit on it backward, loosely hugging the backrest.

You're gonna have to give me more than that—last time I saw a dick that wasn't Gani's, it was a sixty-year-old dude and I was giving him a sponge bath.

Does Gani know you like older men? Hero tried to smile, knew her heart wasn't in it. She didn't want to talk about New Year's.

Rochelle gazed at her, arms still folded across the top of the backrest. Rosalyn said you used to be a doctor, she remarked. Are you gonna try to get a job here in the Bay?

Hero shook her head.

Rochelle made a sympathetic sound. Bullshit with the degree? I know tons of nurses who just came over who used to be like pediatricians and radiologists and shit and couldn't get those jobs here. Had to start all over with a nursing degree or something totally different.

Something like that, Hero said. I'm fine doing what I'm doing now.

Okay, Rochelle said, shrugging. Well, if you do ever decide to do nursing, let me know, we're always understaffed at the retirement home. The folks are okay. I mean, there's some wild shit sometimes with the old Vietnam vets if you look Asian or whatever, but. The pay's good. I mean, my rent gets paid on time, let's put it that way.

Hero knew that Rochelle, unlike most of the friends in Rosalyn's gang, didn't live with her parents, but in her own apartment in Berryessa, near the flea market. Jaime had mentioned once that Gani still officially lived with his family in Milpitas, but spent most of his time at Rochelle's apartment; they were practically engaged, but there was something in his pride that kept him from making it official. Jaime said he thought it was because Rochelle obviously made more money than Gani, who was still trying to mostly DJ full time, still dreaming about winning the DMC World DJ Championships.

I don't think I'd be a very good nurse, Hero said. It always seemed much harder than being a doctor.

Pretty much, Rochelle boasted toothily. Then she shrugged. I don't know. Even if you don't think you'd be good now, you'd probably learn on the job. If I just did stuff I was naturally at, I'd still be a B-girl right now. With hella neck problems and bad carpal tunnel. Look at Gani. Lugging all that equipment around.

Following your dreams.

Rochelle snorted. Yeah, right. Nobody tells you that your dreams might be dumb as hell.

Hero could feel her smile widening. You think having dreams is dumb?

Nah, it's not like that, but—I mean, it's fine, whatever, but—like, I believe in bills paid and people fed. That's my dream. Rochelle shrugged. Maybe I'm cold. That's what Gani says.

Then she cocked her head to the side, eyes half closed, mouth crooked, her gaze not on Hero, not on anyone in the room.

I was pretty good at suicides, though, Rochelle said. But all those moves are way easier to do when you're younger.

After the cake, after the singing, after the offering of presents that would only be opened at home, they kept with tradition for the first dance: Roni and Pol took the floor. The live band was made up of four Filipino men, all bakla, all dressed in barong tagalogs. They were jokingly calling themselves the Mabuhok Singers, after the Mabuhay Singers. The song they started playing was one Hero recognized from some of the karaoke nights at the restaurant, Jose Mari Chan's Beautiful Girl.

Coooooorrrny, Rosalyn heckled, seated across from Hero at a table near the back, but the smile on her face was real.

It'd been so long since her seventh birthday; Hero couldn't remember if she, like Roni, had danced with her father alone on some dance floor, or one of the inner courtyards of the De Vera house, to some terrible love song, popular at the time, forgettable forever if not for having been chosen for this moment. Pol had one hand on Roni's shoulder, one hand tucking stray hairs behind her ear, even though earlier in the evening Janelle and Rochelle had made a point of shellacking her ponytail with hairspray, Rochelle covering her eyes to shield her from the mist.

Hero watched Roni throw her arms around her father's waist, settling her face snug against his belly, blissful, not even bothering to do anything more than hug him and sway. She had a thought, then, sudden as a knife between the ribs: for all she knew, Teresa, Eddie, and Amihan were dead, while she was still alive. Sitting in a community center hall in Milpitas, watching her cousin turn eight years old. That this could be the actual condition of the world—a world in which there was still corny music, lechon kawali, heavy but passing rain, televised sports, yearly holidays, caring families, requited love—seemed to Hero a joke of such surreal proportions the only conclusion she could make of it in the end was that it wasn't a joke at all; and if it wasn't a joke, and it wasn't a dream, that meant it was just. Real life. Ordinary life.

There was a feeling in Hero's chest she'd felt vaguely before, but had never thought to poke at, knowing instinctively that to let it lie would be better. Now she knew the feeling was—hate. Just a tiny, tiny hate, humble and missable, heavy as lead, nothing in comparison to the true affection she knew she felt for the girl, the everyday devotion she'd been consecrating to her since the moment they met. Just a tiny, tiny hate, circulating through her blood, occasionally reaching the heart, then passing out again. It was that tiny hate that spoke in her when Hero thought to herself what a formidable thing it was, what a terror, really— a girl who was loved from the very beginning.

Then she heard it back, the sound of her own thought, like someone was replaying it through a loudspeaker, lingering on each word, making the playback count. Disgust surged up within her so fast she felt herself dry-heaving, her hand closed in a limp fist on her lap, and when a voice in her head spoke up to admonish her, the voice wasn't her own. Jealous of a kid, donya, really?

The lead singer was crooning, I just knew that I'd love again after a long, long while—

There were things Hero had hoped to cast off forever, and then there were things that wouldn't dislodge, no matter how hard she tried, no matter how deep in the mountain she went. And then there were things she thought she'd never lose, dailinesses she hadn't only taken for granted but taken for eternal—things that had vanished in an instant, forever, like the minute she'd left for Ilagan City, her turn to make the usual supply run, not even saying good-bye to Teresa or Eddie, thinking she'd be back in time to assist the midwives with a young cadre who looked ready to go into labor.

Instead she was pulled over on the highway in broad daylight, just outside of Tuguegarao, dragged out by her hair so she felt a chunk of it near her neck tear off at the root, choked out at first and then when that was taking too long, knocked fully unconscious with the butt of a rifle, someone from behind she couldn't see, never saw.

When she woke up she was in what looked like a maid's room, and probably was; a military safe house, an ordinary domicile from the outside, nothing to draw the eye of a passerby. It took her two weeks to be able to talk at all, but she pretended that they'd done permanent damage to her vocal cords and kept up the silent act for another week. If she couldn't talk, they reasoned, then we'll give her a pen. Though they didn't literally give her a pen; they gave her a Crayola crayon, used. She pretended she couldn't write, scribbled shapes when they asked her to give up names, which was when they put the first cigarette out on her belly. And how they figured out that she could, in fact, make sounds.

They didn't break her thumbs until more than a year later; they gave her that long, to give something or someone up. After the year, they moved her, put a hood over her head and shoved her in the back of a van, where she felt, heard, smelled, the presence of at least two other people, another woman, from the sound of it, much older, crying and pissing herself. The ride was long, long enough to go all the way to Manila, which was where Hero correctly assumed they were going, and the whole time she tried to think of something to say to the woman. When she opened her mouth she realized she couldn't talk. She was crying, too.

She was kept in a private quarter that looked more like a stripped-down locker room than a cell, never once saw any other prisoners in the camp—already then she was fairly sure the second location was a camp, not a safe house—though she. Heard. There was a regular rotation of guards, men in T-shirts, flip-flops, and machine guns, who gave her thin rice gruel that occasionally stank of fetid water and once, when she'd been especially uncommunicative, of semen. One of them had an Ilocano accent when he ordered her to eat, so a few days later she wrote down with the paper and Crayola stub they'd left her with: Awan libég a di aglitnáw. A proverb. There's no such thing as cloudy water that cannot become clear again. He read the words, looked at her, and hit her across the face with the back of his hand, fist closed.

By that time, she knew they had taken her because they thought she was Teresa. They thought Geronima was another of Teresa's code names. A year and a half in, starving, her thumbs useless, she was still insisting that she was just a countryside doctor. Her persistence, and the fact that she spoke Ilocano, was what got them worrying. From the beginning there had been rumors about who she was; those rumors were, undoubtedly, what had prevented them from raping her, never mind killing her altogether. They'd had reports of a cadre doctor, Ilocana, who might be the missing Geronima De Vera, former medical student at UST, daughter of Benjamin De Vera, niece of Melchior and Apolonio De Vera, friends of Marcos.

In the meantime, her thumbs started to heal, badly, though she'd tried to splint them by tearing off strips of her shirt with her teeth to create small slings for the appendages. If she'd still had the Crayola, she could have used that. She was ashamed, in a professional capacity, of her poor work.

She turned thirty in the camp, just before her release. It was Soly who told her, that first month in between lives, that Ninoy had been assassinated, Marcos had been deposed, Cory was president—not that Hero believed it made any material difference when it came to the military and the NPA. It was Soly who told her about what had happened at EDSA, the streets full of protestors. Epifanio de los Santos. Perhaps that was why the guards had been scarce, toward the end; she couldn't know.

Were Teresa and the rest of them still alive? Hero didn't know how to find out. The whole point was for their location to be difficult to find, but she'd never expected to be on the other side of that wall. And if she did make it to their hideout, if by chance they were still staying there, or if someone told her where they'd moved to, she didn't know what she would encounter once she arrived. If Teresa, Eddie, and Amihan would still be there, or if just—just—one or two would be missing. Or if everyone, everything would be gone. She'd lived ten years of her life on that mountain face and now she had to admit that she didn't know her way back. The only way to find out anything for sure would have been to get in a car and drive from Soly's, back up to Isabela province, try to remember where to begin the three-day hike, where to turn left, find the village they'd last stayed at and ask the locals if they had any idea at all where the cadres might have gone next. The first time she thought about it, she'd barely been able to bathe herself, let alone drive.

She tried it finally, just once, shortly before leaving for America. Got into Soly's car, put the key in the ignition. She didn't even make it out of Caloocan, her hands freezing on the wheel so that she was stuck in the middle of the road, surrounded by honking, until some young man on a scooter pulled up next to her, and instead of shooting her clean in the head as she'd expected, knocked on the window and called, Hoy, ate! Okay ka ba?

The next time she drove was when Pol and Paz asked her to drop off Roni at school. Then, she hadn't time to be afraid of whether or not she could do it. She'd been asked to be useful, there was no way of refusing. Her hands worked. She wasn't afraid.

At the front of the buffet line was a woman Hero recognized, even though she was absolutely certain she'd never met her. It was only upon seeing Paz approach her, saw the two of them embrace, that she knew it had to be Carmen, Paz's older sister.

Carmen rarely came to the house in Milpitas. Occasionally she would drop off some of Gloria's food while Gloria herself was at work, and on those rare evenings, Roni would be holed up in her parents' bedroom, electing to watch television in bed, refusing to come down. Hero assumed that Roni simply didn't like Carmen. From Paz, Hero knew that Carmen was also undocumented, but unlike Hero she'd been living in the States before 1986 and was thus eligible for amnesty, which was the reason Paz was currently paying for an immigration lawyer.

It was plain to see that Carmen had been a stupefying beauty in her girlhood, and now, in her late thirties or early forties, she was still staggering. She wasn't mestiza, which added to the marvel; all it took was to be a little mestiza to be considered halfway pretty, at least. If anything, she was quite a bit darker than Paz, just a bit darker than both Hero and Rosalyn. More than that, she was tall, taller than all of the women at the party and most of the men. Carmen's mouth was heart-shaped, even without lipstick. She looked a lot, in fact, like her possible namesake, Carmen Rosales. There was the high hairline and high cheekbones, the laughing, upturned eyes, the narrow nose. Carmen Rosales would have had to have plastic surgery for that kind of nose, but this Carmen had been born with it, like a royal but illegitimate foundling left at a church door. When she smiled back at someone who was greeting her, a single large gold tooth on the right side of her mouth glinted back.

Hero couldn't imagine the effect such a smile might have had on someone when Carmen was younger; the smile appeared to be designed specifically to bring people to their knees. Carmen didn't have any of Paz's clenched, straining beauty, the way Paz's beauty was an argument, requiring daily proof to secure renewal. Carmen had the calm, easy demeanor of someone who didn't know she'd been born poor, someone who had been protected from knowing it; she'd been the favored daughter, raised like a rich girl.

The closer Hero got to Carmen and Paz, the more she saw of Carmen's face, especially when Carmen finally turned slightly so that she was no longer just in profile. It was only then that Hero registered that the entire left side of Carmen's face was paralyzed. Carmen's left eye and the left side of her mouth drooped downward, the hungry pink of her inner lip gleaming with wetness. Abruptly, Hero remembered that one afternoon, when she and Roni had come home to Pol putting artificial tears into Paz's red, unmoving eye.

When Paz saw Hero staring at the two of them from across the room, she lifted a hand to wave her over. Hero, flustered, hurried toward them.

As she approached, she saw that two young men, handsome, younger even than Jaime and Rosalyn, were standing behind Carmen, both of them in jeans and T-shirts; one shorter, skinny moreno with a patchy beard, the other taller, with a build similar to JR's, not quite mestizo or chinito but still notably lighter, baby-faced. When Hero reached them, Paz was saying in English, with an almost brutal hospitality,

What, you're not hungry? There's plenty of food! Go eat! Jejo, Freddie, you're not hungry? There's everything! May lechon, may pancit, may lumpiang shanghai, may—!

Then Paz stopped, remembering. That's right. Roni hasn't eaten pancit yet.

Carmen's eyes fell on Hero, greeting her first. You're Pol's niece, right? Nimang? I've heard about you. From Vigan, 'di ba?

Ah—yes. From Vigan. Nice to meet you, po, Hero said, wondering why she felt so nervous. It was just the quality of Carmen's stare. Carmen was staring at her so openly that Hero felt as though she couldn't move.

Paz blinked, seemed to remember that she'd been the one to beckon Hero over in the first place. Oh—Nimang, this is my sister, Carmen. Carmen, this is Nimang.

We introduced ourselves, Carmen laughed. She turned back to Hero. And how do you like California?

She gestured to one of the windows in the hall, where rivulets of rainwater streamed down the glass in a curtain. It's not as hot as you imagine, right?

Oh, uh. No, Hero admitted. I thought it'd be, ah, sunnier.

Carmen remembered the two men behind her. Oh—you haven't met my brothers. Our brothers, she said, glancing briefly at Paz. This is Jejomar, Jejo, she said, pointing to the taller one with the baby face. And this is Freddie, she finished, pointing to the shorter one with the beard.

Nice to meet you, Hero said to them. The taller one gave her a meek smile, the oil on his face gleaming in the hall lights. Hero saw another tight, falsely calm look pass over Paz's face.

Sorry, you couldn't meet our mom, ha? Carmen said. She wasn't feeling that well tonight, so she couldn't make it. Sayang naman, to miss her granddaughter's birthday.

Paz spoke up again, this time in Pangasinan. It sounded like she was still telling them to go eat, because not long after she finished, the two men started making their way to the buffet table.

Carmen squeezed Hero on the shoulder just before she left and smiled, the same smile as Jejo's, only made slightly crooked from the palsy. Good to meet you, ha?

Good to meet you, Hero said, and watched her walk away. When she turned to look at Paz, Paz was watching Carmen walk away, too. Pol was approaching, holding a plastic cup of what looked like Coke.

Have you seen Roni? Paz asked him, refusing the cup when he offered it to her.

He shook his head. Then he put his cup down on a nearby table and extended his arm out in a flourish and took Paz's hand, pointing his chin to the dance floor, where Ruben was starting to play a Sharon Cuneta song Hero didn't recognize.

Paz frowned and tugged her hand out of Pol's grasp. I'll just go ask Belen.

Naglalaro sila, Pol said, reaching for her hand again. Let the kids play.

Just for some pancit, Paz said. She pulled away again and stalked across the dance floor, dodging bodies.

Pol sighed, met Hero's gaze, and lifted the side of his mouth in a not-quite-smile. Hero felt embarrassed for him, embarrassed that she'd witnessed him being rebuffed. To change the subject, she said, I didn't know Paz had two younger brothers.

Pol leaned in, as if he hadn't heard correctly. She doesn't, he said.

I just met them. Jejo and. Freddie, I think.

Pol took a sip from the cup. He looked to be debating something to himself. They're Carmen's sons, he said finally. From when she was in college. Grandma Sisang adopted them as her sons, but alam sila ngayon that their mother is Carmen. They didn't know growing up, but they know now.

Hero's face must have been the picture of confusion, because Pol took pity and continued,

Carmen used to live with Paz, when Roni was still a baby and I was still in the Philippines. She left when the police came looking for her, so then of course, tago ng tago siya. She went back to San Francisco for a while. She's in Burlingame now with her boyfriend, the puti. Amerikano. But Jejo and Freddie are legal. They're registered as Grandpa Vicente's sons, so they're sons of a U.S. citizen.

They were the ones who used to babysit Roni, when Paz and I were working. Along with Auntie Carmen and Auntie Gloria and Uncle Boyet.

Pol smiled at Hero, the smile she'd known and loved since she was a child.

That was before you came along, he added. He made the words sound final and full of solace, like the last lines of a fairy tale. Happily ever after, the end.

It'd been so long since Hero had been to any party of this scale, let alone a Filipino party, and she was exhausted. There was a reason she'd run away from the De Vera parties, hid in her room or in the library, only opened the door when she heard Lulay's distinctive knock, bringing her a plate of food and a disapproving glare. In the hall, guests more than twice her age were still on the dance floor, shouting out requests; even Boy and Adela were amidst the dancers, holding each other close.

Ruben and Isagani looked increasingly harried. They'd just had to play a full album of Anastacio Mamaril's cha-chas, each identical-sounding cha-cha met with unflagging enthusiasm from the crowd, from Maharlika Cha-Cha to Barkada Cha-Cha. Now they'd been browbeaten into playing Amormio Cillan Jr.'s Besame Mucho on a loop for what felt like half an hour, until Isagani visibly couldn't take it anymore and put on Rhythm Nation, which sent the adults to get more food.

Roni was still nowhere to be seen, and nobody seemed to miss her, which was no surprise—the celebrant was little more than an excuse, a starting point. She couldn't see Paz or Pol in the crowd, either; they were probably looking for Roni.

Man, they pushed the boat out on this, Jaime said, looking around at the hall. Ten thousand, easy.

It's tradition, Hero said, but she thought of Paz, working three shifts in a row for months, the credit card bills she left unopened. How she would come home in the afternoon when Hero and Roni were back from the restaurant and stare at them with a glassy, vacant look, like she'd worked for so long she didn't recognize the people she'd come home to. The expensive clothes Hero herself was currently wearing, the silkiness of the new fabric on her skin.

She turned to Jaime. Is your mom here?

Nah, he said. She doesn't really come out to these things. She has a different group of friends. She, uh. She and Rosalyn's mom used to be friends, but. He made a vague motion with his head, tilting it back and forth. He had some frosting on the corner of his mouth. They kinda don't talk anymore.

Why, Hero said, but knew the answer.

Uhhhhh, Jaime said.

Because you guys broke up?

Jaime stared at her. Who told you about that?

Hero shrugged, casual. It seems like everyone knows about that, she said. Janelle was talking about it at the New Year's party.

Okay, Jaime said slowly. So you know, what. That we used to go out.

For a long time, Hero said, surprised at how easy it was to say.

Jaime paused. For a long time, he repeated. Yeah. You—and they told you why we broke up?

Hero shrugged again, shook her head. She didn't know why she'd been putting off talking about it for so long. Talking about it made it real, made it immutable.

Janelle and them think you guys should get back together, Hero added, playing with the tablecloth and then stopping herself.

Jaime didn't respond, but kept chewing on his cake, one cheek puffed up like a chipmunk so Hero couldn't tell if the shape on his mouth was a smile or not.

Rosalyn came back from the dance floor, hair matted to her head with sweat, eye makeup creasing across her lids. Jaime accepted with equanimity the sloppy kiss and punch she gave to his cheek and upper arm.

Lowme, you got shit all over your face, Rosalyn was saying. She smeared at his mouth with her thumb, deforming his lips with the strength of her gesture, obviously in the throes of a massive sugar high.

A jerky beat of silence passed, then Jaime said, Drink some water before you have a heart attack, while wiping at his mouth with a napkin.

Some of the older adults who had taken a break to eat and drink were now clustered at the edges of the dance floor again, clamoring for another dance number, something new to cha-cha to, and then somebody yelled out, I—play mo Boystown Gang!

Hero saw both Jaime and Rosalyn tense at the same time; even JR, who'd been silently playing his Game Boy all night, looked up at the shout.

When the Boystown Gang cover of Can't Take My Eyes Off of You began, the crowd of hecklers cheered, rushing the floor. Isagani clambered back up onto the stage to get away from all the bodies, leaving Rochelle to stumble to safety, looking annoyed but laughing through it.

Hero knew the song itself, but like many of the songs they'd played during the party, this was a different, disco version of it, one she'd never heard before, the perfect rhythm to cha-cha to. Jaime and Rosalyn were looking at each other.

What passed between them would have been plain to anyone who saw it, and Hero—saw it. She saw it as if she'd been there, as if she'd grown up with them, as if she'd been there to witness them send cassette tapes of the song to each other, dedicate it to each other on the radio, run to find each other whenever it came on at a house party. Rosalyn was staring at the dance floor, but Hero knew her gaze was really on Jaime, felt the trajectory of that internal gaze like the windtrail of a bullet not meant for her.

Jaime sighed. Got up, jerked his head to the floor.

Rosalyn covered her eyes with her hands, then slid the hands down and looked up at him, her nose and mouth covered.

Jaime didn't say anything, but started doing the cha-cha steps in place, just in front of Rosalyn's chair.

Rosalyn snorted, then stood up. Without looking back, Jaime turned and started making his way toward the crowd, movements already in beat with the song. Rosalyn followed for two steps, then turned back to Hero.

You coming?

I'm gonna find Roni, Hero said.

Rosalyn looked at her. Hero watched her considering, and then discarding, things to say.

Okay, go get her. The song's like nine years long anyway—

Hero watched as Rosalyn ran off then, shaking something off, then crashing purposely into Jaime, who was already fully in step with a group of aunties. He turned to Rosalyn easily, like he knew by heart the shape of her next to him, knew just how far back to step so they could slip into the dance.

The spotlights circled the floor in a dizzying figure eight, shining green and orange light onto the dancers, so Jaime and Rosalyn's faces looked gauzy and sheer, like veils dappled in human features. Jaime's face was tilted down at the floor, and the breadth of the hand he held up was angled and open, so she could gently dip into its space, then dip out.

Rosalyn shoved at his shoulder when they did the turn and she was facing his back, then kept her hand there, steadying herself. They were performing, exaggerated, but there was too much well-worn ease in the
movements for the performance to come off as just performance. Hero
thought to herself: You don't ever really stop having a song. It's easier to
stop having a person, than to stop having a song.

Hero stood up. It had been a lie, but she might as well make good on
her word. She went to look for Roni.

Hero surveyed the tables for Roni's face among the guests and strangers,
but she was nowhere to be found. She lifted some of the tablecloths,
peeking underneath the tables, calling her name in a shout, which still
barely registered against the deafening backdrop of music. She passed
Charmaine and her parents, seated at one of the tables, Charmaine's father looking at his watch. Charmaine was tugging simultaneously at her
mother's sleeve and the itchy neckline of her dress, her voice high and
anguished: I wanna go *home,* pagod na *ako*—

After she'd searched the entire hall, she saw some of the guests leave
through the entrance, men who looked like they were going for a smoke;
Hero remembered that there was also a kind of lobby, just outside the
hall. Maybe Roni had gone out there to play with her friends, escaping
the raucous noise of adults having fun at their children's expense. She
pushed through the doors, searching. There were several kids who looked
about Roni's age playing with each other, but no Roni.

Hero made her way through the empty back halls of the community
center, winding her way past what looked like a series of smaller conference rooms; this felt like the wrong direction, Roni wouldn't have gone
this far. She backtracked, made her way back toward the lobby, then
down another corridor, which took her through the supply closets and
then, farther down, into what looked like an industrial kitchen, all of the
lights off, just the light from the hallway bouncing off the stainless steel
countertops and fixtures. From that direction, she heard noises. She
quickened her pace.

As she approached, she recognized male voices. Huh, why not? You don't even come to the house anymore. Don't you miss playing—

Another male voice. Come over, we'll sing karaoke again.

Roni saying, laughing but with no joy in it, Just stop—

The first voice, a genuine laugh, So ticklish!

Hero reached the doorway to the kitchen, grabbing at the threshold to steady herself, to catch her breath—she didn't even know why, until she understood that she had run. Roni was sitting on one of the stainless steel counters, which was too high for her to climb up onto by herself. Jejo and Freddie were standing in front of her, posture loose. Jejo was playing with the sleeve of her dress, his thumb in her armpit, dragging pained giggling out of Roni, who hadn't noticed Hero yet. Freddie stood, his body blocking the path out of the kitchen.

Roni, Hero said.

Roni whipped her head around. She probably would have jumped down, but Hero was striding toward her, fast, her arms outstretched, wanting to be there when or if she jumped, ready to yank her down if necessary, pushing past Freddie, their shoulders jostling. Her hand touched Jejo's for a stomach-upturning moment when she hooked her arms around Roni, lifted her off the counter with all her strength, cradled her heaviness, and bolted from the kitchen.

Hoy, hoy, hoy—one of them was calling, but Hero didn't, couldn't, stop moving, was still carrying Roni when she made her way down the corridor, almost running, toward the lobby, Jaime, her throat thick with words that wouldn't come or even form, wanting to say something to Roni but not knowing what to say, knowing only to keep moving, to hold on.

They were halfway through the hall, Ruben and Isagani playing VST & Company's Awitin Mo, Isasayaw Ko. There was a sensation, warm breath over Hero's ears, a dull sound. She ignored it, but then there came a thump on her shoulder blade. She leaned back; Roni was telling her something, her face scrunched up. The tendons in Roni's throat were strained; she was shouting.

What, Hero shouted back, practically into her face, unable to control the volume of her own voice.

You can put me down now! Roni yelled.

Hero stared back at her, registering the words but not their meaning. Her arms were frozen and unyielding around Roni's body, like they would stop working if she tried to unlock their grip. The glitter on Roni's shoulders had been sweated, or wiped, off. Hero tightened her hold.

Roni!

Hero turned around, saw Paz and Pol approaching. Despite the heat in the room, Pol was still wearing his jacket and blazer, his tie unloosened, pin in place. Paz had started the evening in a jacket with strong shoulders; now the jacket was off, and her strong shoulders had come off with it. She looked small next to Pol, furious. She was holding a plate of pancit.

Where were you? Paz cried. Hero felt Roni shrink in her arms. We've been looking everywhere for you!

Playing hide and seek, Roni said. Ate Hero found me.

You have to eat pancit. It's almost midnight, you have to eat it right now!

Roni looked up at her father. I'm not hungry.

Just one bite is fine! For long life!

Hero felt Roni tug away from her; obeying the silent request, she finally put the girl down, was surprised to find she could. Roni approached her parents. Paz was forking up a spoonful of pancit far too large for Roni's mouth.

Pol tsk-ed and said, Ang dami naman. That's too much, she'll choke.

Paz let a few noodles slip back onto the plate. Roni opened her mouth obediently. Paz fed the bite into her mouth, watched her daughter's lips close around the noodles, watched their length and promise disappear as she chewed, her cheeks puffed out with the volume of food contained by them. Pol tsk-ed again, but on Paz's face came a look of relief so acute it discomfited Hero to witness it.

Okay, Paz said, low, anchored. Okay, good.

She stood back up, then looked down at the still full plate of pancit in her hands, unsure of what to do with it. Nimang, gutom ka? You can have this if you want—

I'm full, Hero said. She gestured to Pol, but Paz shook her head on his behalf before Pol could even react.

Ayaw siya, she said. He doesn't like pancit.

Hero looked at Pol, and remembered: Pol in the De Vera house, the-atrically sliding his portion of pancit onto Hamin's plate while he wasn't looking, then gesturing, fake-frantically, for a ten-year-old Hero to do the same. Hero didn't like pancit, either.

Pol turned to Paz.

Magsigarilyo lang muna ako, ha, mahal.

It's cold outside, Paz warned.

Pol tugged on the lapel of his jacket. Just for one cigarette.

Can I come? Roni asked.

Pol shook his head. No. It's too cold. Stay inside, there's still cake.

Roni glanced up at Paz, then at Hero. But the other kids are still play-ing hide and seek—

Stay in this room, Hero nearly bellowed. Stay where we can see you.

Roni flinched, then looked up at Paz, who looked just as surprised as her daughter. Stay in this room, Paz confirmed.

Hero turned, to tell her what she'd seen, with Roni and Jejomar and Freddie, what it—but she saw Paz's face, sunken and lost, lit up in a pink and blue halo of moving spotlights. She couldn't yell it into her ear now, fighting to be heard over Menage's disco version of Memory.

Gutom ka, Nimang, Paz was saying, slightly too low to be heard, but too tired to speak up louder. Hero shook her head.

Paz straightened the jacket thrown over her arm. Maybe I'll eat some-thing.

She took a step, then turned back to face Hero. Salamat, ha, Nimang? For finding her. I was looking everywhere.

It's nothing, Hero said. Paz shook her head minutely, dismissing He-ro's words. Then she made her way over to the buffet table, where most of the food had been ravaged through. There was no one there, and Paz made a lonely shadow with her plate of pancit, adding it to a miscellany of leathery lechon-skin scraps and lumpia ends.

The hell?

Hero turned. There was a film of sweat on Rosalyn's face, her ponytail loose from dancing. We just saw you fuckin' haul Roni in like you stole her. What happened?

Hero opened her mouth, trying to focus in on Rosalyn's face, but found she couldn't say anything other than:

Paz was looking for her. I found her.

O-kay, Rosalyn said slowly. Come dance then. She took Hero by the arm, dragging her just by force of will for several steps, almost making it there, before she felt Hero's weight suddenly give resistance.

Don't gimme some bullshit like you don't dance or whatever—

No, I. Hero stopped, leaning one hand against a tabletop, bunching the tablecloth there.

Rosalyn stopped. Stepped closer, which didn't help.

Hey. You good?

Hero turned her head, just to make sure Roni was still in the room. She was there, at the table, distributing cards in what looked like a game of B.S., a boy leaning over her shoulder to watch.

Whoa, whoa, whoa, and Rosalyn was ducking into Hero's space, thrusting a shoulder underneath Hero's arm as she felt her hand lose strength, felt her lower body give way beneath her.

Rosalyn lowered her into the nearest chair. Whoa. You okay? You need air? Water? Want me to go get you some water?

I'm fine, Hero said.

Stay here, I'm gonna get you some water, it's hot as balls in here—

I'm fine, she repeated rigidly. Thank you.

It had been a long night, it was too noisy, she'd eaten too little, there were too many people, she was tired, she'd—she was tired. I'll go get you some ice water, wait here, she heard Rosalyn saying.

She didn't look up at Rosalyn when she returned, yanking a chair around to position it directly in front of Hero. A plastic cup was put to Hero's lips; she didn't even have the energy to keep up her pride and say that she could hold it herself. She sipped at the water, cringing as the ice touched her sensitive teeth.

Thank you. I'm fine now. Just tired.

Rosalyn didn't respond, but brought the cup back up. Hero sipped at it again, longer this time. She glanced over at the dance floor, where Jaime was dancing with Janelle and Lea at the same time.

Out of the corner of her eye, she saw Paz walk toward the table where Roni was sitting with a couple of friends. But instead of sitting down with them, Paz sat down at a table just behind them, so she could watch from a distance, picking at a piece of what looked like kutsinta.

I told Gani to look for Hate by Talk Talk so he could play it tonight, Rosalyn said without looking at Hero. He couldn't find it, though.

Hero lifted her head, reached for the cup herself and shook an ice cube into her mouth, crunching down onto it. Let out a breath without taking her eyes off the dance floor. Hero saw Rosalyn watching the way Hero picked up the cup, by the base using mostly her palms instead of her fingers; the instinctive way she'd adapted, to avoid putting stress on her fingers when she was tired. Hero was too tired to pretend to hold the cup normally. It looked like Rosalyn wanted to say something, but she kept her mouth closed.

I'm fine now, Hero said again. You can get back on the dance floor for the last few songs.

The muscles in Rosalyn's jaw worked. Then she picked up the cup to drink from it herself, finishing it in a few gulps, leaving just the ice clinking dully against the plastic.

I'll just get you some more water, she said.

Unthinking, Hero put a hand out to stop her from leaving, instinctively grabbing onto the first thing she could touch, which happened to be Rosalyn's hand, the meat of her palm. Rosalyn froze. Hero thought about letting go, but letting go took too much effort; even thinking about letting go was exhausting. She put her head down on the table, the white cloth cool and sticky against her face. Actually could you just stay here for a minute, she said, still holding Rosalyn's hand, the sweaty, bony, mortal warmth of it. Sure, Rosalyn said, her voice cracking.

Flores de Mayo

HERO WAS IN HER FIRST AND ONLY YEAR OF MEDI-
cal school when she saw the White Lady in her dorm at UST. It felt like
everybody in the dorms but Hero knew about her, about the genre of
woman from which she issued. White Lady ghosts were the ghosts that
started appearing, supposedly, when Spanish friars moved into the Philippines, and they remained when those friars were replaced by American
soldiers. According to most of the stories, the White Lady ghost was a
murdered woman: some abandoned daughter, some betrayed nobya.
Sometimes she had a Spanish friar or American soldier father who denied paternity, some bruto who pushed the girl off a building just to get
rid of her, some bilyano in blue jeans who promised to marry her and
never did.

The most famous White Lady was the White Lady of Balete Drive in
Quezon City, of course. Even Hero, who'd come to Manila ignorant of
the city's mythologies, knew about that one. She was killed in a car accident, they said, so it was often late-night taxi drivers who saw her, picking
up some girl wandering around the streets late at night, only noticing the
smell of old blood once they'd dropped her off at a far-flung and abandoned outpost. Other people said that the White Lady was a girl who'd
been raped by a taxi driver; that was why she often visited them, seeking
vengeance.

Hero's own sighting happened late at night. She was alone, taking a
shower in the communal bathrooms. After a while, she grasped that she
wasn't alone—in one of the stalls on the opposite side of the room was
another person taking a shower. Hero could hear the jagged sound of
running water cascading along the planes of a human body, and so she
did something wholly uncharacteristic of herself and yet familiar to anyone living in a dormitory: she started chatting aloud mindlessly, to dis-
sipate that always eerie feeling of being in an institutional building late
at night.

But the woman didn't answer. When Hero got out of the stall, it turned out that the woman had already finished her shower. She could only see the woman from the back, putting on her white clothes. Hero observed that the woman had long, long black hair, entirely covering her ass. She still hadn't said a word. Hero shook herself out of staring at her and dressed hurriedly, having given up on small talk, now only thinking of drying off and getting to her bed.

The woman left the shower rooms just before Hero, so that once Hero was fully dressed and back out in the corridor, the woman was nearly twenty feet ahead of her down the hall. Hero could barely hear the steps she made, so soft was her footfall. She caught herself in a stare again, openly admiring: the long elegant line of the woman's back, obscured and then revealed by the sway of her hair; her slender ankles; her regal silence, heavy and safe, like a velvet curtain. Hero gave her a wide berth.

Finally, to Hero's relief, or to her disappointment—she couldn't quite tell anymore—their paths diverged, and the woman made a turn. The minute she was gone from view, the world jolted back into place. The woman was gone; Hero was sober again, ordinary again.

It was only later that night, in bed, that Hero remembered that the area the woman had turned into had been under construction at the time—there would have been no floor to walk upon, there where she was walking. Hero fell asleep, turning this over and over in her head, trying to figure it out.

The next morning, Hero told some of her older classmates about the woman she saw. Long hair, down to here? one of them asked Hero, gesturing at her own ass. Hero nodded.

They looked at each other again. Finally, they told Hero that the woman had been a medical student, who, years ago, had fallen out of the bunk of her dorm room bed and hit her head on the way down. Hero's classmate said that new medical students were the ones she showed herself to most often.

Hero was still waiting for the secret bruto to enter the story. But no matter whom she asked, the story stayed the same: the girl was a medical student, and she fell out of her dorm bed. She died quickly, and without pain. There wasn't even a hint of a bruto in the character list.

Hero felt strangely disappointed—and then, strange for feeling disappointed. The accident was an accident. The White Lady she'd heard so much about and finally seen, the ghost she'd been so awestruck by, was a student, just like Hero. She wasn't killed by or didn't kill herself over some asshole. Tragedy could be unsensational.

One evening not long after the party, she and Paz passed each other in the hallway between the bedrooms. No time like the present, Hero thought to herself, and held up her hand to stop Paz in her tracks. It was just then that she realized she had no idea how to tell Paz about what she'd seen in the community center kitchen with Roni and Jejomar and Freddie. She didn't know what she'd seen. She was about to tell Paz that she'd seen her brothers—nephews—doing what, exactly.

Jejo and Freddie, Hero began, waiting to see if just the names alone would spark some buried knowledge in Paz's eyes, but Paz just looked at her, blank. They were with Roni when I found her. They—they were tickling her.

Paz furrowed her brow. Tickling?

Hero felt sweat spring up on her palms. Oo, tickling, and—

Was she making too big a deal out of what she'd seen? All she could go on was instinct, the blood-draining certainty she'd felt when she'd seen Roni on that counter, but—it was possible she was wrong, of course it was possible she was wrong. Tickling her. They were holding her and tickling her.

Tickling, Paz was repeating again, the purple-gray bags underneath her eyes emphasized by the squint of disbelief she was offering up.

Hero pressed her lips together. They shouldn't be so rough with her, she said finally.

Paz looked at her, and then nodded, brisk, a task in hand. Okay. I'll talk to them. She turned around and disappeared into her bedroom. Hero went to her own bed, and didn't sleep for hours.

Ruben and Isagani were invited to DJ a party in San Jose with three other dudes they'd started to loosely form a crew with, tentatively named Knuckles of the South Star, which Hero mildly said made her think of someone getting fisted. Not long after, Ruben and Gani said they were going to change the name to Vinyl Phantomz.

At the party they all congregated in the living room, watching a group of four young men practicing a choreographed dance to a mix Isagani had made himself, a hysterical-sounding remix of Michael Jackson's Smooth Criminal. The men's movements were convulsive and robotic, but somehow still eerily affecting, like watching reanimated bodies of beloved people. Hero had never been a big fan of dance, but she found she, like the others, couldn't tear her eyes away, clapped when they were finished.

That put everyone in a good mood, the pleasure of bearing witness to other people successfully pulling off something that they'd labored at, and by the time Ruben and Isagani's mix started playing an oddly soulful remix of Baby Come Back, the original of which she hadn't heard since riding around in Teresa's jeep, Hero was leaning against a wall, talking to a girl, loose in her body, biding her time. The girl, Vanessa, was saying something about the upkeep of her undercut in response to something complimentary Hero had said about it that she now couldn't remember, eyes fixed to the place where Vanessa was bending her head forward to reveal the long line of her nape, the black fur where the shave had grown in.

It was as Vanessa was saying, It's so coarse, feel it, that Hero heard a chorus of voices, the soprano among them Rosalyn, going, Ohhhhh!

When she turned her head, she saw Jaime, Rosalyn, Rochelle, and Janelle surrounding a taller woman who was laughing, ruffling Jaime's hair and accepting Rosalyn's hug with one free arm.

As Hero stared, Rosalyn craned her neck around, then finding Hero, stopped when she found her. After a beat, she beckoned with her hand, mouthed, Come here, come here.

Vanessa's head was still bent down, waiting for Hero's hand. Hero pulled back and said, Sorry, I'll be back in a minute.

This is Cely, Rosalyn said when Hero arrived, facing the woman who was being bounced against on both sides by Janelle and Rochelle. Jaime's sister. Cely, Hero. Hero, Cely.

What's up, Cely said, waving the hand that was caught in Janelle's fist, then tsk-ed good-naturedly. You guys are acting like I just came back from the war.

You left us for the city, it's the same thing. How come you didn't even tell us you were back in the South Bay tonight? Rosalyn turned to Jaime. How come *you* didn't tell us?

She paged me like half an hour ago to say she and a friend were on their way down, I'm supposed to be psychic?

Cely—Araceli—was several years older than Jaime, maybe only a couple years younger than Hero, and looked completely different from him, morenang morena. Rosalyn left Hero's side to resume a hug that had only just been paused, Cely acting long-suffering when it was more than obvious she relished her return to the younger women's worshipful parish. Rosalyn was showing Cely her hair, saying it'd gotten so long since they'd last seen each other, what did Cely think of the grown-out bangs. Hero turned away from Cely ruffling the face-framing layers, saying it looked cute.

Janelle said, So how's your master's going, are you finished? Cely said, Ugh, I'm never gonna finish.

Hero politely asked what she was studying. Cely replied, Adult Education at SF State, with the tempered pride of someone who'd worked too hard for everything she had to be modest about it.

Around the corner of Cely's eyes was a halo of blackened-bronze eyeliner, the style of it unmistakable, even half-rubbed away from the day. Her lashes weren't curled. She sat watchfully and spoke precisely, sensitive to minute changes in people's expressions, making fun of her brother and Rosalyn with a dry, fond humor. It hadn't occurred to Hero that Rosalyn might have a type.

Jaime took one look at Rosalyn, then at Hero, then stood up, saying he'd get everyone another drink.

Later, when Jaime and Cely had gone back out to the driveway to

take a look at something that was apparently wrong with Cely's car—
Why don't you just change your oil once in a while, Jaime muttered—
Hero found herself alone with Rosalyn.

I'm glad you guys finally met, Rosalyn sighed. It sucks she moved all
the way up to Frisco.

Maybe she was tired of Milpitas, Hero said irritably.

Rosalyn blinked, then scoffed. What, you saying you are? After what,
not even a year?

Is that not allowed?

When Jaime and Cely returned, Hero and Rosalyn were still stuck in
awkward silence. Rosalyn brightened and dove back into her chatter.
Hero didn't realize she'd barely spoken or moved until Cely turned her
gaze to Hero and said,

You're pretty quiet.

Hero tried to smile back and it didn't work. Sorry, I'm just going to
the bathroom.

She made her way back into the party, back amongst the blessedly
unfamiliar faces. As she was opening a door that turned out to lead to a
closet, a hand brushed against her shoulder.

You disappeared, Vanessa said. Are you guys leaving or something?

Hero looked at her. I'm not leaving.

Vanessa smiled, eyes crinkling. What, like ever?

Fifteen minutes later Hero was following Vanessa out of the party,
moments after Vanessa said, looking her in the eye: I live just a few streets
away from here.

On her way out she saw Jaime, alone with Cely. Seeing her—the
sharp edge of her jawline when she laughed, the easy way her shoulder
pressed onto her brother's—it was tempting to slot Cely into all the
scenes Jaime had described in their conversations: the cool sister who'd
driven Jaime and Rosalyn to their first comic book store, their first high
school dance, their first house party, maybe the first person who'd introduced Rosalyn to makeup, maybe the first person Rosalyn had ever
crushed on, maybe the first person Rosalyn had ever kissed. Hero tried

to rein in the impulse, tried not to piece the stories around Rosalyn just because she wanted to—what, exactly. Know more. That was it.

Hero was ready to leave without saying good-bye to anyone, but it was too late, Jaime had spotted her. He asked, You about to take off? when she approached. She nodded.

Cely smiled at her. It was good to meet you, Jaime's told me a lot about you. Next time you guys come up to the city, hit me up.

Hero glanced at Jaime and saw clearly that he knew they would never hit Cely up, not together. She said, Sure, and punched Jaime on the arm in farewell, their usual send-off, but there was no real heart in it. Hero didn't see Rosalyn until she—saw her, hanging back, holding a plastic cup, talking to Rochelle but staring at Hero.

Vanessa's undercut went all the way up to above her ears, which were sensitive to kisses, and she moaned so sweetly when she came that Hero wondered if it was for show—then, when she was sure it wasn't, felt more smug than was appropriate. Vanessa offered to get a strap-on or a vibrator if Hero wanted it, but Hero didn't want it, didn't know how to say that she wouldn't be able to hold a vibrator in her hands, that the one time she'd held an electric razor back in Soly's house, intending to shave her hair off in what she knew now would have been an overly dramatic gesture she would have regretted later, she'd dropped the instrument before she'd even properly closed her fingers around it, the vibration making the nerves in her hand feel crazed, miswired. While Hero was thinking all of this, she'd apparently been looking at Vanessa's mouth so intensely that Vanessa chuckled. I can take a hint.

The next morning, they ate defrosted waffles, still cold, the oven and microwave both broken. You live around here? Vanessa asked.

In Milpitas.

Vanessa was leaning on her knee, having brought her right leg up on the chair, a gesture Hero had hitherto thought was only Filipino. She'd thought Vanessa was Filipina at first, but Vanessa had said at the party that she was American, and only after they fucked did she say that her parents were lawyers from Vietnam who now worked as technicians on the manufacturing floor of a medical device company all the way up in Santa Rosa, in the North Bay—the wine country, Vanessa explained, like Hero might know what that meant.

They work with a buncha Filipinos, Cambodians, Laotians, Vanessa added, the end of her sentence lifted up like an open palm, waiting for Hero to make any note of comprehension, and when she didn't, a silence of misplaced intimacy came between them. Still, when Vanessa stood and brushed past her, ostensibly to get another waffle from the kitchen, but deliberately swinging her underwear-clad ass in Hero's face, Hero stopped her, spread her legs so Vanessa could climb onto her lap.

Afterward, Vanessa said it was fun, but pointedly didn't ask for Hero's number, or if they could see each other again. There was a pair of shoes Hero saw by the door, slightly bigger than Vanessa's feet, and Hero nodded, relieved. She asked if she could use the phone before she left.

Hero paged Jaime to pick her up, self-aware enough to realize she'd been taciturn and even rude to his sister. Her first page said 5012124. Sorry.

The page came back quick, easy: 80085. BOOBS. It was his signature; they were fine. He picked her up in less than an hour and they went to El Rincón Michoacano, had the nopalitos.

Things were only subtly different after that. People who didn't already know, or had some idea, looked at her differently: Janelle and Lea often found a reason not to sit next to her; Ruben and Isagani took on an awkward, uncomfortably jokey air with her, like she was one of them, which she wasn't. Only Rochelle and Jaime acted the same.

One Tuesday toward the end of April, Rosalyn cornered her during a lull in the workday, fists at her side, and instead of shoving a new manga into Hero's face like usual, said, while holding her gaze so hard it looked like she wasn't even letting herself blink: Can I talk to you before you leave today.

The tone of her voice sounded almost angry, so Hero's first thought was that Rosalyn was still offended about how Hero had behaved when they'd met Cely. Her hackles went up, reflexively, but she calmed herself, decided she would apologize without hesitation or protest.

Hero was rooted on her feet and ready with her apology when they were outside in the parking lot, standing in front of Pol's Corona, the restaurant empty, Boy and Adela starting to wipe the tables down. When she opened her mouth to say sorry, Rosalyn blurted out:

So you're okay with girls.

Hero went still. Girls?

I mean. You're okay with. Rosalyn was wringing at the fabric of her shirt, a faded and oversized FILA T-shirt that looked like it might have belonged to Jaime or Boy. I mean, you go home with girls. You sleep with girls. Women.

Not exclusively.

Sure, not exclusively, Rosalyn repeated, her voice too high. But, I mean. Women. Also. Are okay.

Yes, Hero said, the first time in her life she'd ever said something like that to anyone.

So then what about me, Rosalyn asked, all the words said in the same breath, the same flat tone, like if she put any emotion into the words they would slip out of her grasp.

Look, Hero said.

Uh-oh, here we go, Rosalyn said, finally relaxing, like the uncompromising tone in Hero's voice had done the opposite of what Hero had intended. Rosalyn always looked relieved when Hero stopped being polite; it was unnerving.

Look, Hero repeated. If you want to experiment, there are plenty of women out there. Your own age.

What are you, like, six, seven years older than me, just chill with that, Rosalyn muttered. I'm turning twenty-seven next month, anyway.

If you want to experiment, Hero repeated. There are plenty of other people to do that with. People who aren't— She found she didn't like that approach, changed direction abruptly.

Does anyone else even know? About you?

Rosalyn crossed her arms. Just say no if you're gonna say no.

Hero sat down on the hood of the car, heavy, slipping until she could balance herself with one foot on the curb. You might have noticed, she said finally, but I don't say no that much.

Rosalyn, sharply: Okay, so, what, you can never say no? Or it doesn't matter?

It's just not a good idea, Hero said after a pause just as long as the first. Because you don't want to.

It's just not a good idea.

Once again Hero saw Rosalyn think up and then discard two or three different responses. That's not really a no, she ventured finally, quiet.

Hero opened her mouth, and the first word that came out was, Why.

Rosalyn scratched at her jaw. You're asking why?

Hero nodded. Rosalyn looked down, smiling wryly at the curb.

I didn't think I was being all that subtle about it.

Hero opened her mouth again, but Rosalyn jerked forward, lifting her head and holding up her hand.

Wait. Stop. Don't answer yet. Just—think about it. That's all. That's all I'm asking for. Just think about it. I'm not. I'm not asking you out, or anything, like. Dating. I just mean—we could also. You know. But, no pressure.

It's getting late, Hero said. I have to get the car home before Pol's shift.

Will you just. Think about it? Rosalyn asked, mindful not to step too close to Hero. Hero, who was already thinking about it, no need for future tense; she was there, in the future. Thinking about it. I will, she said, wincing at what it sounded like, which was a promise.

The older Hero got, the less she got along with romantics: people who liked courtship and courtly love, people who had big ideas about how men and women should behave in their relationships with each other— since typically these people thought only of men and women when they thought of romance. She found, oddly, that those people were often the least suited to sexual or romantic relationships, were staggeringly selfish and borderline abusive both in bed and in life, and treated their partners and friends more like protagonists and side characters, props in the love story they were constructing, in which they played the starring role, full of grand gestures and pronouncements.

She'd befriended and slept with a few romantics in college, finding herself eventually doing their homework, their laundry, personally interpreting the minutest detail of their daily lives while rarely getting a word in edgewise to share anything of her own—in those days, it wasn't like she'd wanted to share things about herself anyway. But it rankled that she was being conveniently employed to shine the spotlight on some narcissist who'd never even bothered to remember that Hero was from Ilocos Sur, not Iloilo. Hero had no truck with people for whom the heart was a dreamt-up thing, held together by divine saliva, a place where gods of love still made their beds. A heart was something you could buy on the street, six to a skewer or piled on a square of foil, served with garlicky rice and atsuete oil. In high school, when they'd had to operate on piglet fetuses, only Hero and two other boys were able to successfully remove the heart without puncturing it.

What—worried—Hero was that Rosalyn was obviously a romantic. She hadn't made any effort to hide it: the parts she squealed at in movies, the way her mouth dropped open in an unconscious pant as she read the last chapter in the manga, as her chosen couple finally came together.

After that night in late April, Hero went into the restaurant half hoping that nothing would have changed between them, that Rosalyn would pretend that their conversation had never happened.

But when Rosalyn came in on her regular break, Hero knew there wasn't any hope. Rosalyn hadn't forgotten; she wasn't going to let Hero forget. She snaked around Hero to get a calamansi juice out of the drinks refrigerator, brushing against the back of Hero's calf as she knelt down, then standing slowly, deliberate. You want some, Rosalyn said, holding out the box, plastic straw poked through the foil hole.

Sensing she had to be the adult in the room, Hero glared back. No pressure?

Rosalyn fumbled the juice in her hand, terrible spell broken, laughing. Okay, okay, okay. She scurried out from behind the counter, made her way to the kitchen saying she had a question to ask Adela, which almost sounded genuine.

In the weeks after Roni's birthday, Hero spotted Pol taking folders with him to work, manila envelopes full of papers. She'd noticed that he was receiving more mail from the Philippines; when she first saw the Tagalog letters on the envelopes, she felt her entire throat close up in terror, sweat springing up in her armpits at words like REPUBLIKA NG PILIPINAS, or TANGGAPAN SA PAMAMAHALA NG MGA KASULATAN AT SINUPAN. Records Management and Archive Office. It took several minutes for her vision to shimmer back into focus, for the terror-stricken goose bumps to settle back into skin, for her brain to realize that the name on the envelope was not her own, but APOLONIO C. DE VERA.

Hero didn't have the courage to ask Pol what the papers were about, but she got a glimpse at what was happening when she was bringing Roni home from school, and instead of being asleep, as Pol usually was on the days when he had to work that evening, Pol was already awake, with papers spread over the kitchen table, where Roni was used to doing her homework.

He looked up at Roni and Hero, blinking, harried, unrecognizing and unrecognizable. He looked like someone who'd come in off the street to break into this house, like someone who didn't know Hero or Roni, wasn't connected to them or part of them in any way. Then his face relaxed, and one hand floated down to rest over the papers in front of him. Hi, anak, he greeted Roni. Did you have a good day at school?

Uh-huh, Roni said, backpack slipping down to hang from the crooks in her elbows, approaching Pol and glaring down at the papers covering the table. How come you're awake?

I'm just finishing up some things I can't do at work anymore, Pol said. Do your homework on the living room couch today.

Then can I watch TV while I'm finishing it?

No.

Glum, Roni made her way to the living room, the backpack now slumped nearly all the way to her ankles.

Pol smiled at Hero. Gloria brought some fresh lumpiang sariwa, you should eat some. Take it into the living room, give some to Roni.

As Hero was bringing everything over to Roni, she caught sight of some of the papers spread out on the desk, many of them salmon-colored. DEPARTMENT OF CONSUMER AFFAIRS.

Later, when Hero and Roni had finished their snack and Roni was deep in her subtractions, Hero heard Pol get up from the kitchen table and walk. She stood, collecting the used plate and cutlery, taking them to the kitchen and leaving them in the sink to soak. On her way back to Roni, Hero hovered at the edge of the table to take a closer look at what Pol was working on. BOARD OF MEDICAL QUALITY ASSUR-ANCE. APPLICATION FOR A WRITTEN EXAMINATION OR FOR AN ORAL AND CLINICAL EXAMINATION. FOR GRAD-UATES OF FOREIGN MEDICAL SCHOOLS APPLYING UNDER SECTIONS 2101 AND 2102 OF THE CALIFORNIA BUSINESS AND PROFESSIONS CODE.

Next to the application were several copies of the same black-and-white picture of Pol, wearing the tan linen suit she had seen him wear that one day, just before Roni's birthday party. In the black-and-white photo, the subtle colors of the outfit didn't come out, so what had been a lushly woven cream oxford shirt was now the color of dishwater, the suit a muddier gray. The bronze tie looked gaudy, and its discreet pattern of tiny diamonds now looked like polka dots in the overexposed image.

Since arriving in California, Hero had been distantly aware that Pol was applying for American citizenship. Paz had hers, and she'd given all her workbooks and reference texts to Pol. Pol took the books with him to work, and Hero supposed that was where he did all of his studying, just to pass the time in the middle of the night when no one was around and all he had to do was check the computer screens, make sure nothing was happening to the computer chips, or whatever it was he did at his job.

If he was applying for citizenship, he might apply for an American medical license. She thought of Pol, tried to remember his age. Sixty-one, sixty-two. She thought of Vanessa's parents, the lawyers who'd become technicians. Pol, an American doctor. Hero couldn't fathom it.

In Milpitas, they rarely talked about Hero's citizenship situation. But she knew that it was likely she would have to stand at the receiving end of Paz's self-shattering charity, if she wanted one day to have papers in this country. They couldn't afford to think about that yet, which was a relief to Hero, who wasn't quite prepared to be more indebted than she already was.

Seeing Carmen had brought home to Hero a realization she'd been suppressing; she, too, might become a tago ng tago if someone reported her, if she got pulled over without a license, if—there were a million ifs, a million ways to go. But—it would be fine. She had to think it would be fine. She didn't dwell on the stories Paz told, about friends she'd known and nurses she worked with who'd been deported, sometimes reported on by their own friends and coworkers.

When Hero first arrived in California, she hadn't thought much of it. She'd known there was nothing she could do, and worrying wouldn't help. Soly had said there was a place for her with Tito Pol. She hadn't thought twice.

Rosalyn's birthday was on the thirty-first of May, which fell on a Friday. She'd been telling people for weeks that she didn't want to do anything big, that they'd just have the usual party at the house that night. She said she didn't want any presents—If you have to get me something, she said with a grin, how about money?—which earned a resounding groan from everyone within earshot. I'll draw you a picture of money, Gani promised.

Hero was grateful to think about Rosalyn in a way that was—safe, fine, which was why she didn't expect it when Rosalyn called her at the house, the Saturday before her birthday, and asked if she was doing anything the next day.

Tomorrow? Sunday?

That's usually the day that follows Saturday, Rosalyn said. In the afternoon. Just after lunch. Are you free?

I guess. I'm just watching Roni, Hero said. Can I bring her?

She heard Rosalyn hesitate on the phone. You could bring her to the restaurant and my grandma could watch her, Rosalyn said finally.

Hero frowned. I have to ask Pol or Paz if that's okay. You could've told me sooner, she could've gone to play at her friends' house.

Rosalyn was silent for a long time. I didn't wanna give you too much time to think about it and turn me down, she said. Hero didn't say anything back.

Okay! Rosalyn punctuated, hard and cheerful. Well. Uh. I'll pick you up tomorrow. At, like, two. If you can't come out, then just, you know. Call or page me. But. Try to come. Okay?

Okay, Hero said, but Rosalyn had already put the phone down.

When Hero called Paz at work, Paz at first said it was fine for Roni to stay at the restaurant with Adela, but then she interrupted her own approval to say—Or! She could go play with Charmaine. Let me call Belen and ask what Charmaine's doing on Sunday. They live in Milpitas, too, you know. By Hillview Drive.

Hero had never yet driven that way, but she agreed to wait while Paz gave Belen a call. That evening, when Pol was awake and readying for his night shift, Paz called the house from work and told Hero that she'd gotten a hold of Belen and Roni was more than welcome to come play with Charmaine, that they were holding a Couples for Christ/Kids for Christ meeting at the house and Roni would meet all sorts of other kids there that she could play with, it would be fun. Paz would give Hero a bag of things to drop off with Belen, just medicines and things like that for Belen's mother's diabetes, nothing too big.

Charmaine's house was just on the other side of Jacklin Road, and yet it felt like a completely different town. The houses were only slightly larger than the ones in Roni's neighborhood, that wasn't the issue; it was that they were older, more imposing, the driveways were longer, the houses farther apart from each other. The hedges in front of each house looked carefully trimmed, the flora meticulously chosen to express something about the people inside. The cars were of a different make than the ones Hero saw driving home; than the one Hero was driving to get there.

Roni was quiet that morning, but Hero was pleased to see that her eczema had gotten significantly better in the months since they'd first met; the patches around her eyes and mouth were mostly gone, or slowly healing into the brownish-pink, marbly flesh of fresh scar tissue. The plaques on her neck and arms and legs were still fairly vicious, and now that it was spring again, Roni was running around in loose tank tops and shorts, all her wounds on display. Paz had said multiple times that the fact that Roni hadn't been hospitalized once that winter, that fact alone, meant that all the time she was spending at the restaurant with Adela was worth it, and working.

Hero rang the doorbell and a tinny melody that might have been Mozart could be heard, dully, even through the door. She looked down at Roni, who had involuntarily stuck her tongue out at the sound; she was struck with the urge to reach out and touch her hair. She did, resting her hand on the top of the girl's head lightly.

Roni looked up, eyebrows cut together; grumpy, but not at the touch, which she was leaning her cold nose into like a dog.

Are you gonna be okay? Hero asked. Roni frowned. I don't know the other kids, she mumbled.

Hero wasn't used to Roni being timid; she didn't know what to do with it. Roni didn't seem to know what to do with it, either. You'll be fine, Hero said awkwardly.

Charmaine opened the door, followed by a skinny, wizened woman in a tweed jacket and black slacks, the spitting image of Belen but aged, who looked at Hero, and then at Roni, as if they'd brought in garbage from off the street.

Hi, Ron-Ron, Charmaine greeted. She was wearing a dress too fancy for playtime; she must have just come from church. Her grandmother reached over to fix a lopsided ribbon in her hair.

Hi, Roni said, but before she could finish, Charmaine grabbed her by the arm and dragged her into the entranceway. Come on, come on—

Unsure of what to do, Hero stepped into the house, too. It was less a house than a mausoleum decorated in what looked like Louis XIV style. In the living room, there were three baroque chaises, none of which looked like a human body had ever sat upon them, a tapestry depicting a scene of frolicking white angels playing guitar to a nymph, and upon a nearby side table, porcelain figurines of besotted noblemen chasing after milkmaids. Next to the chaises was a towering grandfather clock, and next to it a series of gleaming veneered mahogany cabinets inlaid with what looked like abalone or tortoiseshell, adorned with candlestands and unlit candles, their wicks still white. On the mantelpiece there was a picture of the family posing with someone Hero recognized as a former secretary of finance for the Philippines.

The entire living room was cordoned off, and the carpet looked pristine. Everything was arranged in a kind of ongoing still life; even in that short moment Hero sensed that the scene in front of her, despite the impression of eternal and divine wealth it was meant to convey, was frail, frozen so long that a warm sigh would shatter it. It was too late to reach out for Roni and snatch her back, put her in the car, speed back home. Hero saw her at the end of a corridor, being surrounded by a group of children her age, looks of appraisal on their faces, all of them still dressed for church.

Belen approached Hero, smiling, greeting her in a mix of English and Tagalog, saying it was so nice to see her again. When Hero handed the bag of medicine over, she casually rifled through it like she didn't want to be too blatant about checking that everything she'd asked for was there. She lifted her head, apparently satisfied, and smiled brightly. Her eyeliner looked as though it might have been a tattoo.

Salamat, ha? She said that Hero could pick Roni up at six. Hero agreed, and was about to leave, but couldn't help it; she stopped, called out, Roni!

Roni turned. Hero didn't have anything to say, but raised her hand, throat tight. I'm leaving now. Roni's face was expressionless, but she nodded, and waved, and then was taken by some new friend out of view.

Hero was still staring after her when Belen opened the door, ushering her out but talking cheerily to smooth over the process. And! Please give my regards to Doctor De Vera, she ended, smiling encouragingly. She didn't say anything about Paz.

Rosalyn was waiting in the driveway of the house when Hero got back. She pulled up next to her, parking the car. When she got out, Rosalyn had already opened her car door, one leg out, her hand up in greeting.

You're early, Hero said.

Early bird gets the worm, Rosalyn said, shoving her other hand in her pocket. Where's Roni?

I just dropped her off at a friend's house, Hero said.

Oh, cool. Rosalyn went quiet, then jerked her head up. So do you—wanna go?

I thought you said it started at two. It's only one.

No, it's. It's an ongoing thing. It's whatever. We could go now. Unless you're hungry. But they'll have food there—

I'm not hungry, Hero said. Let's go.

In the car, Rosalyn was quiet for a few minutes and they sat in silence; she wasn't even playing music on her stereo, which was a first. Finally Rosalyn said, You don't eat enough. Probably.

I eat plenty. I'm always eating at your place.

Nah, you're a fake eater, Rosalyn said, signaling to turn left. I know a fake eater, I used to be one. I mean. Just for a couple of years, in college. It was a dumb phase.

Hero tried to hide her surprise; she couldn't imagine Rosalyn not eating. But you're fine now, Hero said, half a question.

I'm fine now, Rosalyn confirmed. It wasn't like I ever got real thin anyway, that wasn't gonna happen. And it wasn't the point, but whatever. Anyway. I can tell when other people are doing that kinda thing.

I'm not, Hero said. I'm eating fine. I've never had a big appetite.

They went quiet. Rosalyn was driving them down a street Hero had never seen before. Sorry if I'm bugging you, she said suddenly.

You're not.

Rosalyn shook her head. Nah, I am.

It never stopped you before, Hero said, but with her face turned fully toward Rosalyn so the small smile on it would be unmissable. Rosalyn bit the inside of her cheek, so Hero saw a pinch of skin fold inward at the pressure.

She drove them to the large parking lot of what looked like another strip mall, not all dissimilar from the one where the restaurant was located. The largest sign there was for a Filipino restaurant, by the looks of the palm trees that bookended the name of the place, Pearl of the Orient. The rest of the stores were dry cleaners and Vietnamese sandwich shops, an LBC Express.

The parking lot was filled with cars, and people sitting on top of their hoods, ready to watch what Hero saw was gradually shaping up to be a procession—she saw the banners, the children in costumes, the wreaths of flowers, the candles, and then she remembered what time of the month it was.

It's the Santacruzan, she said, soft.

Rosalyn was putting the car in park, turning the engine off, opening her door and getting out before Hero could meet her eye. My birthday falls at the end of the Flores de Mayo, she said. So sometimes I watch the pageant.

Hero followed her out of the car. Rosalyn tested the hood with her hand, said it was still too hot to sit on, so they leaned against the front bumper. Hero felt the heat from Rosalyn's arm as she pointed out people, children milling around dressed up in costumes to play characters that Hero hadn't seen since she was a child, when a mix of children and Vigan's most eligible beauties did the Santacruzan procession down Calle Crisologo. Here in Milpitas, they only had the parking lot.

The hood had cooled down, so Rosalyn slid backward onto it, held out a hand to Hero to help her up, then let it go before Hero could think about the touch.

I hate them, Rosalyn grumbled. When Hero gave her a questioning look, Rosalyn pointed at the restaurant sign. Pearl of the Orient. They're dicks. And they're so competitive with us, which is dumb because they know their place is, like, banquet-level stuff, it's not even the same customers we're catering to.

She made another face. I mean, Pearl of the Orient? Ugh.

The procession was starting. Rosalyn went on pointing out people. The Reyna Mora, the Reyna ng Saba, girls about Roni's age dressed like the Queen of Sheba, carrying jewelry boxes, faces painted. Matusalem, a boy with a paper beard strung on his face, secured behind the ears, faking a hump. Rosalyn shook her head, said, Look, they still put blackface on the kids who're playing the Aetas. Some fucked-up shit.

They watched for a while in silence, laughing and aww-ing when one of the younger queens started crying in the middle of the procession, self-conscious and frightened in front of all the people. The small rondalla, only two guitarists and a ukulele player, not the full bands Hero remembered seeing in the Philippines, followed the procession, singing Dios Te Salve. Next to her, Rosalyn was humming, half singing, Y bandito es el fruto, Y bandito es el fruto.

Who did you play? Hero asked, bringing her knees up so she could rest her chin on them.

Rosalyn shrugged, toying with her shoelace. Nah, I was never part of it. I was too young when we were in Manila, and shit was still too crazy when we were in San Francisco, and then when we got to Milpitas, I remembered it, and wanted to do it, but, you know, it's organized by like, some rich Filipinos. People like the Couples for Christ gang, so. It was all those kids who were part of the big Santacruzan. It wasn't like in Manila, where every barrio did their thing, whatever. I mean, you can see, this is just the one for this neighborhood, like. And they only started doing it a few years ago. The really big one, the main one, they hold it at Milpitas Town Center. Kids and adults are in it, they do a big pabitin, they have a beauty pagent and everything. The mayor shows up. That one's fancier.

Who did you want to be? Hero asked. When you wanted to be in the procession.

Oh. Well, it was—you know, in Manila, or well, in my barrio, we did it at night, so like. The atmosphere that I remember was really different. Like people would have candles and stuff, it was. I just thought it was magic. So I wanted to be Reyna Candelária, you know the one who carries the long candle. But really—uh!

But then she scrunched up her face, embarrassed, and didn't go on.

But really, Hero prompted.

Rosalyn's eyes were still closed, and for good measure, she covered them with her hands. I—okay, the one I really wanted to be? But. Don't make fun of me.

Hero waited. Rosalyn was laughing somewhat hysterically to herself.

Okay. I wanted to be Reyna Elena.

Hero started smiling. Reyna Elena. The last one. The—

Yeah, yeah, yeah, the most beautiful girl in the whole pageant, okay, you said you wouldn't make fun of me!

I never said that.

Rosalyn threw her weight to the side, shoving Hero with her shoulder. She straightened, touching her own cheeks and forehead with the back of her hand like she was feeling the temperature of a feverish child. That was the point at which Hero knew she shouldn't have said yes, when Rosalyn had asked her to come out.

Did you have the Santacruzan in Vigan? Rosalyn asked.

Yes.

Were you ever in the pageant?

Yes.

Rosalyn perked up, eyes gleaming. So who were you?

Hero closed her eyes for a moment, then opened them. Reyna Judít, usually. They made the head of Holofernes out of papier-mâché and I played it so many times they let me just keep it in my house and reuse it every year.

Cackling, Rosalyn hugged herself. Reyna Judít, shit. That's so you. Some dude's head in one hand and a sword in the other.

When I got older, and people knew I wanted to be a doctor, I got to be Reyna Doktora.

Reyna Doktora, Rosalyn said, no other comment, just rolling the name around in her mouth like she liked the taste of it.

They watched as Reyna Elena, a lipsticked girl of about thirteen with large breasts displayed above the low neckline of a wrinkled satin gown, appeared at the rear of the procession, bringing the pageant to a close. The parents started to cheer, the flashes of cameras reaching a frenzy though people had been taking photos and videos from the beginning. The whole thing had gone by fast, faster than Hero remembered the procession going when she was a child.

When she turned her head back to look at Rosalyn, she saw that Rosalyn had been studying her for longer than she'd been aware, arms around her knees, the gaze alert and considering. She looked at Hero like she'd looked at her this way a million times before and would do so a million times more; like she was looking at something she was used to but not tired of, something she could trace on paper with her eyes closed.

I wish I coulda seen you back then, Rosalyn murmured, her voice just loud enough to pass in the space between them, and no farther.

It would have been easy then, for Hero to just lean in, tilt her chin down, sip the breath off Rosalyn's mouth, in a parking lot full of people they didn't know, who weren't even looking at them. It took more effort not to do it than to do it, they were that close. It took more effort, but Hero put the effort in. She turned back to watch the people gradually disappearing into the Pearl of the Orient, where the celebratory pabitin for the children would be taking place, in the restaurant's enthusiastically advertised BIG BACK GARDEN, GREAT FOR EVENTS! The people left in the parking lot were leaving, so Rosalyn cleared her throat, mumbled, Yeah, okay, let's go.

In the seconds that it took for Hero to clamber awkwardly off the hood and walk toward the passenger door, she had a calm, demented moment of feeling completely content, consoled even. Thinking, of course it was better that they didn't, reminding herself that it was a bad idea, and she hadn't wanted to, anyway. Hero knew well the feeling of spinning a lie to herself to keep going; she'd done that for two years, telling herself she hoped no one she loved would endanger their lives and come looking for her. No one came looking for her, and now she was here, sliding into Rosalyn's dirty passenger seat, kicking aside an empty soda can and a cracked cassette tape.

It would have been easy on the hood of the car; that was the moment to do it, and the moment had passed, it was over. Hero moved to put her seat belt on, and had it halfway across her body when she caught sight of Rosalyn clicking hers in place, face carefully blank, avoiding Hero's eyes—and instead of just letting it go and doing the same, Hero leaned forward, straining over the armrest and the cupholder filled with balled-up napkins. She brought Rosalyn's face back up, and kissed her.

Hero heard a brisk click that she realized was Rosalyn fumbling with one hand to pop her seat belt off in a frenzy, throwing herself forward, backing Hero up against the passenger seat even though that meant the armrest was jabbing her in the stomach, one hand anchored in Hero's hair behind her ear, the other on the headrest but twitching so much Hero could see it even out of the corner of her half-closed eyes, like Rosalyn wanted to slide the hand down and cup Hero's face but was too nervous to go through with it, unsure if what was happening was really happening. Hero felt a shudder that didn't start in her body but ended there, deep down her throat and in a fizzing line to her groin like a quick-burning fuse.

Hero grasped Rosalyn's unsure hand and yanked it down by the wrist, even though she didn't know what to do with it now that she'd caught it. She ended up holding it, tangling their fingers, in a way that only further numbed out her numbing-out hands, delirious, roving, full of ideas. Sounds were coming out of Rosalyn's mouth that were muffled against Hero's mouth, then against her jaw, the long tendon in her neck, sloppy and hot, all over the place, like someone who hadn't been kissed all that much and hadn't learned to contain her excitement when it happened. Only when she and Rosalyn were mouth to mouth again did Hero understand—with what at first she thought was pure horror but which then revealed itself to be a white-hot lick of scalp-to-toe arousal—that the sound she was hearing in the background was Rosalyn begging, beside herself, distraught with need, voice lower than a whisper like she wasn't really talking to Hero at all, like she didn't even know what she was saying and would be mortified later when she remembered it: Please—please—*please.*

It took them a while to leave the parking lot. It'd been years since Hero had just made out with someone, and that was all she thought was going to happen, until Rosalyn buried her face in the steering wheel and then said into the space where the air bag was stored: Nobody's home right now.

Hero leaned back, mouth puffy. She put her seat belt on, and gestured with her head. Rosalyn squeezed the steering wheel, hard, like if she let go she'd wake up.

What Hero had only speculated on before turned out, in practice, to be true: Rosalyn hadn't slept with that many people and in all likelihood hadn't ever slept with a woman. She had enthusiasm in spades, but enthusiasm alone, historically, wasn't generally what got Hero to come. She'd never pretended to be someone who could come with penetration; her enjoyment of penetration had always been separate from, though related to, her need to come. More often than not she found herself annoyed and distracted when a well-meaning partner tried to thumb at her clit while inside her, smug and charitable; combining the two sensations dulled both of them and took her out of the moment. She liked the pressure, being filled up, being taken someplace and never getting there; there was a world of pleasure in that. But after the world was over, she needed to come.

That was what she thought, and thought, and thought, and thought, her mood souring, as she lay in Rosalyn's childhood bedroom and felt Rosalyn sucking ineffectively at her labia for the nth time since they'd started. She should have gone down on Rosalyn first, but by the time they'd stumbled into the bedroom, Hero already sore between the legs with wet, clutching desire, Rosalyn had barely been capable of coherent speech, shaky and wild-eyed, so turned-on Hero almost told her to calm down and breathe, refraining only because she knew how condescending it would sound. She wasn't all that calm herself, but seeing Rosalyn go to pieces before her put Hero in a responsible frame of mind.

She'd let herself get pushed onto the bed, let Rosalyn take her pants off, let Rosalyn push her shirt off, then closed her eyes and waited. Let Rosalyn go at her own pace. Jumped, when Rosalyn touched the four-year-old pockmarks on her belly and didn't let on whether or not she could tell that they were cigarette burns. Jumped again when Rosalyn kissed them, and moved down.

It—well. Hero was a patient person, generally, but this was testing her patience, and worse than that, the longer it took her to come, the longer it took Rosalyn to figure out how to make her come. It wasn't that Rosalyn was ignorant, she manifestly knew where the clitoris was, only she kept adorning her movements with unnecessary flourishes rather than just staying in one place like a decent human being. Which unfortunately gave Hero time to start thinking, which was usually how things fell apart.

She let herself lie there for another few minutes, calm with the knowledge that she'd tried it, they'd tried it, but it hadn't worked out, the, the, the chemistry wasn't there, if that was the way to put it, and better to find that kind of thing out at the beginning. She put her hand on Rosalyn's shoulder to tell her to stop, only to feel her entire chest cavity jolt with sudden and total refusal. Then, instead, she heard herself say: Could you. use your hand.

After getting out of the camp, Hero had masturbated extremely infrequently; even when her hands were healed, she lacked the dexterity to keep going the way she needed to, and she hated the feeling of just rutting desperately against her own palm or wrist, settling for any friction. There were girls she knew back in college who said they could come just from sitting cross-legged in the jeepney, rumbling down España Boulevard and trying not to let it show, but she'd never been one of them. She liked precise movements, and she couldn't give herself precise movements, so she went up to the city with Jaime for the closest thing—which wasn't that close at all, but it was better than nothing. It was mostly better than nothing.

Hero's entire body remembered those tiny facts when Rosalyn's middle finger touched down, sure, and sent a flare of pleasure through her body so severe she screamed. Starving, stripped-bare and keening for it now, unfastening everywhere but where she was gripping at the sheets, ignoring the pain it sent all the way up to her elbows. The pain helped to ground her, as it always did, but then it turned out that the feeling of being grounded only ramped her up more, teeth rattling, and worst of all, Rosalyn was suddenly being uncommonly and infuriatingly sanguine about the whole thing, her words and movements now unrushed and confident, like she knew what she was doing—but that was the problem. She did know. It turned out she did know.

Hero had been told before, not always in a complimentary way, that she was loud when she came—near-silent panting all the way through, and then deafening, devouring cries when it happened. Since arriving in California she'd toned it down, couldn't let herself go, thought she'd changed; she was a medical professional, she knew well enough that all sorts of physiological changes happened when you got older. But when she finally came, slick-lipped, lifting her hips to grind her clit shamelessly against Rosalyn's finger so that every point of skin contact between them was live-wire, galvanic, endless, she felt Rosalyn physically startle at the volume of her cry, fingerhold briefly slipping, before she rallied and rubbed Hero through it. When Hero's cries petered out to a whine, Rosalyn slowed down to a bare flutter, just for few seconds, only to gently wind Hero back up again, circling, no mercy, so it didn't take long for Hero to give it up a second time, growling, annoyed—at how good it was, at how much she'd missed it, at how much more she wanted. Shit.

She tipped her pelvis away slightly, a sign that Rosalyn could stop moving if her hand was tired. Rosalyn stopped, but didn't take her hand away, said only,

More? And Hero turned her face into the sheets with a grimace, found out. Silently she tipped back up.

After that, Hero didn't remember how many times she asked for it, how many times Rosalyn gave it to her, how many times she tried not to be greedy, how many times she told herself she'd had enough, how many times Rosalyn wordlessly told her otherwise.

When she woke up, Rosalyn was awake, leaning on her propped-up hand and looking down at her, smiling benevolently.

Hero jolted upward, an apology in her mouth before she'd even fully opened her eyes: she'd passed out, she hadn't even gotten Rosalyn off.

Ears ringing, she heard herself saying, in a voice hoarse from use Sorry, I'm, I'm sorry, but Rosalyn looked exceptionally pleased with herself, in a way that Hero knew she wasn't going to be able to live down anytime soon.

Am I—a genius? Rosalyn began, leaning back so that Hero could take a better look at her breasts. I mean, I made you come so hard you passed out, so I think I—might be a genius. Like, this is why I flunked out of every class in high school and college. I coulda been valedictorian if I'd just majored in handjobs.

Hero leaned over, kissed at the seam of Rosalyn's mouth. Murmured, Let me eat you out, and Rosalyn shut up, face ashen. I—okay.

When she touched the flat of her tongue to Rosalyn's clit, penitent, Rosalyn nearly strangled her with the force of her thighs, convulsing, so Hero put a steady palm down on one of them, keeping her spread and still, to which Rosalyn responded with a fervent Shit, shit, shit, shit, shit, oh *shit*.

She came just once, taking a long time, longer than anyone Hero had ever gone down on before, her entire body locked up like she'd been petrified that way, like she was afraid of what was happening to her and had to put it off as much as possible, one hand clenched in a fist at her hip and the other hand reaching for Hero's head then pulling back to cover her own face instead, Oh fuck fuck fuck fuck-fuck God—and then, after a small forever, going bucking and silent, an atoll of relief.

Afterward she slapped at the bed like a wrestler tapping out, closing her thighs, tendons sore from being stretched open and taut for so long, hand still tight over her eyes. When Hero dipped her head low, chin wet, ready to go again, Rosalyn whimpered and let her try, before laughing like it was being clawed out of her throat, Wait-wait-wait-stop, too much, too much, too much, fuck.

Hero decided not to push her on it. Everyone came differently, who was she to judge. And then it was six o'clock, and she had to go pick up Roni from Charmaine's house.

Hero dressed slowly, feeling the tension between them thicken with every article of clothing she put back on. Rosalyn was still in bed, though she'd put on just a pair of sweatpants, and was sitting there, cross-legged, breasts bare, watching Hero warily, the way one would watch a horse that might spook.

So we're good, Rosalyn said. This is—we're doing this? I guess?

I, Hero began.

Hastily, Rosalyn added, You know. Uh. What I said before still stands. We don't have to be. Exclusive. There's no pressure.

Without waiting for an answer, Rosalyn put her shirt on, baliktad, and picked her keys up off the floor. I'll drive you home.

She passed Hero, went to open the door. Hero reached out to tug at her shirt. Rosalyn let herself be pulled like she'd been waiting for it, anything, her face cracked open. Hero felt bad; she hadn't meant to tease her. She yanked gently at the tag on the back of Rosalyn's neck. This is inside out.

True Love Comes
for Mine Fujiko

THE FIRST TIME YOU ATE A GIRL OUT WAS IN 1985,
somewhere south of Echo Park, your first time out of the Bay since you'd
arrived from Manila when you were five. You and Jaime had more or
less broken up by then, and in three years or so, you guys were going to
go back to what you'd been at the beginning, which was: friends who'd
lie down in traffic for each other—beyond family, beyond lovers, more
like warriors in arms, medieval in your loyalty. By the time of the
breakup, you'd known you were going to have to drop out of school; it'd
never been your thing, not really, even though you'd gone into it opti-
mistically, some dumbass dream of becoming the American Nora Aunor
still hanging around in your heart, deathless. But you soon figured out
that just because you majored in theater and always memorized your
lines didn't mean anyone was going to give you any parts, at least not
any good ones, and definitely not the leads. At best you kept getting cast,
again and again as: the evil witch, or as some white girl's friend with one
or two kinda funny lines, or more typically, as the port whore picked off
right at the beginning of the play. That last one was even written by
another Pinoy at San Jose State, some aspiring screenwriter who told
you that you looked a little like Lea Salonga, only not as light. His play
was knockoff *Miss Saigon,* but at least you got really good at primal
screaming—now you knew the technique of how to do it so that your
vocal chords wouldn't be ripped to shreds the next day. That was the last
thing you ever learned about acting.

You moved backstage, where, it turned out, all the Pinay and Vietnamese kids had been hiding the whole time. That was how the makeup
thing started, and to your surprise, you liked it even more than acting.
You started doing it on the side, for neighborhood girls—debuts and
cotillions and graduations and weddings, shit like that. Your theater
hookups meant you knew where to find the professional makeup stores

dotted around the Bay that sold stuff like Ben Nye, Kryolan, mixing mediums, and you came up with workarounds, like how to add yellow pigment—sometimes food coloring, when you were desperate—to some pink-as-hell foundation a girl came to you bearing like a grail, convinced it was her shade. Ading, they don't make *people* in that shade, you replied.

You liked it, liked the feeling of being the one to put a girl's first armor on, even though sometimes, admittedly, you didn't always like the kinds of armor you were routinely asked to provide: how to shade and lift a flat Pinoy nose, how to buff shadow around an eye to make it look bigger, how to make a heavily talc-based pink blush not look like chalk on a morena's cheeks. You pushed back on some of it, got a reputation for being stubborn, but at the end of the day, you served your community: when a client wanted a white nose, you gave her a white nose. Soon enough word got around, from Milpitas to Frisco: Rosalyn Cabugao makes you look bomb.

By the time you knew you were going to drop out, you were bored of the house parties, the break dancing, hovering around while some shaved-head moreno who used to put his hand down the front of your skirt in kindergarten DJ-ed to an audience of worshipful acolytes, using equipment mostly paid for by his nurse mother. When you went to L.A. for the first time with some theater buddies, you ended up fucking a white girl who touched your hair too much but not in a sexy way, and kept saying, I wish I had Asian hair, it's so silky. It was your first orgasm with a girl; you faked it. Then you couldn't find your underwear on the floor so you'd had to go home without it, denim chafing your ass the whole car ride from Los Angeles to Milpitas, where your theater buddies—the friends you'd been so desperate to make at San Jose State just to be able to gossip with people whose mothers didn't work with yours—spent most of the ride smirking at each other without looking at you. None of them lived in Milpitas. They dropped you off at home with promises to call and get together soon. You told Jaime; you dropped out of school; the buddies never called.

But you never thought of packing it all in and moving up to Frisco, you never had any suburban angst; you liked the smallness of your world. The only negative was that if there were any girls who were maybe interested in putting their faces in between your legs, you never met them. Or there was an alarmingly high possibility the girls knew your family—had eaten barbecue or sung karaoke in your grandparents' restaurant, had worked at the hospital with your mom, had their house exorcised by your grandma. The gift of the small world was that it was small. The curse of the small world was that it was small.

Back in the Philippines, you'd been an easily possessible kid. That was the only way of putting it. It wasn't rare for children around you to be occupied every now and then by some minor engkanto—early demon possession was more common than pneumonia—but your case was probably the worst in the barrio. If you'd grown up in another type of family, richer, college educated, then maybe you would've been put in a hospital, or sent to church, or forbidden from going outside. If you hadn't been born on stilts above Manila Bay, the homes demolished within a year of your birth and everyone relocated to places like Santa Mesa, a concrete block along the San Juan River where Quezon City's raw sewage drifted along on its way to the Pasig, then maybe the possession thing would've become a real problem. But you were, and so it wasn't: your family and neighbors accepted with clinical detachment the existence of dwende, hexes, the possibility of being fucked up from head to toe by something you couldn't see, only feel. Everyone knew what the symptoms looked like when a lowly, lonely demon with abandonment issues had a crush on you.

Your grandma, the preeminent bruha of the barrio, knew most of all. She knew when the voice coming out of your throat wasn't your own; when you moaned, I feel heavy, I feel heavy, she knew how to take that foreign but familiar weight from you. She was your first doctor. The first person to tell you that you weren't special, and mean it as a promise;

the first person to put a cold hand on your sweating face and laugh-reply to the question you mumbled into her sleeve: Of course you're going to live, stupid.

Your mom didn't want anything to do with your grandma's work, refused her inheritance of herbs and demonry, and instead dove headfirst into her destiny, the other word for which was modernity: modern women didn't rub coconut pulp and Efficascent onto their neighbors and friends; modern women didn't negotiate child custody rights with engkantos; modern women kept studying at home even when they'd gotten pregnant just out of high school, modern women were the only kid in the barrio smart enough to get a scholarship so they could take night classes at a nearby nursing school, modern women let their childhood friend turned shotgun husband drink half a bottle of Ginebra then beat them blue almost every day until their own mother had to take them aside, look them in the eye, and declare: If you don't leave him, I'll take Rosalyn and go to the States myself, with or without Boy's green card or your visa. And bahala ka na sa buhay mo.

When you were a kid, Lolo Boy used to tell you the stories that his father and uncles had told him: about the signs they'd seen in Sunnyvale and Mountain View that said GET RID OF ALL FILIPINOS OR WE'LL BURN THIS TOWN DOWN; about the Filipino men attacked with clubs and slingshots in Exeter for bringing white girls to a local carnival; about the hundred-strong mobs of white men who raided ranches that employed Filipino workers, like the one in San Joaquin Valley where Lolo Boy's father had thinned lettuce for years.

Lolo Boy was sixteen when he came to live with his father and uncle in California, picking and handwashing asparagus, peaches, melons. For most of his young life, Lolo Boy had known himself to be a United States national, free to leave his tiny fishing village in Abucay, where the Dutch once massacred nearly three hundred Pampangans in an attempt to take over the region from its Spanish rulers; free to come to America and look for a job; free to have rocks thrown at him by white men who didn't even want those jobs. That was how he knew he belonged to America. But in 1934, he became free; an alien. In the end, Lolo Boy, his father, and his uncles took their prematurely arthritic limbs back to the Philippines, knowing that if they chose to remain, as many did, Boy would likely never see his mother or older sisters again.

The only work Boy found upon his return was on the U.S. naval base in Cavite, first as a dishwasher, then as a cook. His father drank the rest of his years away; his uncles, much the same. By the time Lolo Boy got his green card, his father was long dead of a heart attack and Boy was in love with a sharp, stalwart girl who cleaned the rambling Santa Mesa house of a navy accountant. A twenty-year-old named Adela with a six-year-old daughter, a fading Ilocano accent she never explained, two gold teeth, and a stare Boy couldn't shake.

Lolo Boy stopped talking to you about all of that by the time you entered high school. In fact, Lolo Boy became quieter and quieter as he got older; new people just assumed he didn't speak English. They were always surprised at how American he sounded when he finally did open his mouth. Sometimes you got the feeling that he spoke Tagalog with people in the restaurant just to keep his hand in, out of obligation more than any real sense of ease in the language.

You don't know why he told you all of that in the first place, since you never heard him and Lola Adela talking about it between themselves. It was like he thought laying his heart bare to a kid was the same thing as laying your heart bare to a pet, or a priest. It didn't really count. Of course, half the things Lolo Boy told you were things he'd heard from his father and uncles—back when he, too, used to be a kid-pet, a kid-priest. If there's one thing you've learned, it's that everything counts when you're a kid.

You, your mom, Lola Adela, and Lolo Boy all lived in San Francisco at first, in that tiny studio apartment on Eddy Street, before moving to Milpitas on the advice of one of Boy's friends who said there was a Filipino restaurant looking for a cook. It took almost another ten years before the owners of that restaurant finally sold it to Lolo Boy and Lola Adela. It was the first place anyone in the family ever owned in America.

The restaurant would forever be your real home: the place you went when your mom yelled at you over your report card, the place you went after you and Jaime had sex for the first time, the place you went to watch your grandma divine the maladies of strangers, making your own seem manageable for once.

When you became Bay-famous for your makeup skills, you were offered not a small number of higher-paying jobs at fancier salons: in Sunnyvale, in Mountain View, in Stockton, in Modesto. You might have even afforded rent out there. You didn't even blink. You stayed at Mai's. You never told anyone about the job offers.

It was because of your grandma that you eventually got into manga. She'd been into komiks growing up and gave you a bunch of her old ones from the Philippines, things like *Reyna Bandida, Darna, Pobresita,* old issues of *Hiwaga* and *Espesyal,* so old and weathered the color had stripped off the covers. You'd read them religiously in Manila, kept reading them in California until you were about ten or so. You only stopped because you had to focus on your studies, scrub your accent away and conjugate English verbs. But you never lost the love of them, and when a comic book shop opened in Milpitas, you and Jaime checked it out together, begged Cely to drive you even though she only had a learner's permit and was technically only supposed to drive with an adult in the car. You never went back to that comic book shop after the first couple of times, put off by the cool reception of the white men who ran the store, the only white people you ever came across in Milpitas.

Ruby was the one who introduced you to Japanese manga and renewed your love for komiks, which now you called comics. You and Ruby used to be inseparable when you were kids, growing up together as the daughters of the same strip mall; she, so delighted to meet someone who would appreciate her meticulous translations, and you, so delighted to hang out with someone who didn't already know everything about your family. Sometime around high school you drifted apart, though; felt like her parents didn't want her hanging out with a Pinay with an undercut and a tattoo and no path to Stanford or anywhere like it, didn't want their daughter going to the restaurant, to parties with people like Jaime or Ruben, with their spoilered cars blasting music from one end of the parking lot to the other. Your relationship became a transactional one, with only the translations to bind it, and you and Ruby never again shared the complicity you'd had as children. Though sometimes you caught a look on her face, the sheepish knee-jerk smile of someone running into an ex.

In high school, you tried to go back to your grandma's komiks, just out of curiosity, but page after page swam in front of you, senseless, until your vision blurred and you had to shove the magazines away. Tagalog, the first language you'd ever spoken, and now you could barely read a sentence. It wasn't just reading; for years you'd replied in English when your grandma talked to you, stopped understanding the teleseryes and movies that your mom picked up at Magat along with pastillas and sampalok. Now you couldn't even read fucking komiks. Not for the first time, your own mind terrified you: the careless black-hole greediness of it, that you could leave things there thinking they were safe, and then turn around and find that they'd been eaten away, gnawed on without mercy or honor so that not even the bones were left, destroyed nonchalantly by something mightier in you, something mightier than you, some big-time fucking asshole, whose name was, what, even? Forgetting. You could forget an entire world, the person you'd been there. It scared the shit out of you.

It scared the shit out of you—but not enough to go back and try to learn it all again. Most of the time, when you had the shit scared out of you, you ran. And so you ran from it, the eaten-up place where your first language had been. Ran like hell, left it for dead.

You clocked Hero's hands the second time you met. Once you looked at them, really looked at them, it was pretty obvious something was fucked up there, had been fucked up for a while, probably. You'd never broken a bone in your body—but. You were pretty sure that what you were looking at was old. Both thumbs, gnarled-up and knobbly, not just double-jointed. Fucked, like. Not like an accident. Like someone else had broken them, maybe. That didn't have to be it; Hero might've just had a bad fall sometime in the past couple of years. But twenty years on, you still remembered the telltale signs of getting beat on, what that looked like on a woman, so when you saw Hero's hands, you thought the worst. What you thought at the time was the worst. Though later, as always, you'd realize that what you knew about the worst of the world, the knowledge about life you'd stored up, tart and proud because of where you'd been born, what you'd run from, what'd made you, all amounted to—mostly nothing, like anyone else's stupid history. It didn't make you any wiser or stronger, the way you hoped, the way you usually played it. It just made you you.

You saw Hero's hands, and then after that, you started noticing little things, like the way Hero opened a door more with her wrist than with her hands, or if she had to grip the knob, then she'd use the four other fingers, trying not to tax the thumbs; the way she held a cup at the base, and never at the handle, sometimes with two hands, steadying it; the way she drove with her palms, mostly, the touch light—kinda hella scary, to be real; the way Hero flattened the manga you lent her, breaking the spine so she could read the books splayed out on the table without having to really lift and perch them in her fingers; the way Hero's teeth were always a little yellow, her tongue a little white, probably because she couldn't brush her teeth for very long; the way you never once saw her hold a pen or pencil, or even write anything down.

In daily life she used her hands—if you weren't looking for it, you probably wouldn't look twice. And plus the injury, or its effects, didn't seem consistent, anyway: there were some movements that Hero did that you would've thought would hurt like hell if you'd broken your thumbs as badly as Hero looked like she had, like maneuvering a stick shift, or picking up Roni's backpack by the strap even when the kid said she could carry it herself.

The other thing that bugged you out from the beginning was how Hero didn't even look like she minded being called Hero. It was a fucking ridiculous name, ridiculous even for Pinoy nicknaming standards, so ridiculous you skipped all the way past the safety of mockery into full-blown tenderness like a sucker. You should've known then that that was the beginning, should've recognized what was in your gut, roaring up in your organs, something terminal and excruciating, like the bad ending of the whore you'd been so good at playing on stage when you were eighteen. But you'd always been a dumbass, so.

You didn't even realize what you were feeling until right after Hero and Roni left after that first meeting, and by that time, as usual, you'd already made a fool of yourself by being yourself—the way you always were with new people, hella dramatic and flirtatious but with no real roots in it, no firm ground underneath it, the way you were with everyone. Only like a minute after Hero left the salon did you figure out that you didn't want to be the way you were with everyone, with Hero.

When you offered Hero a job at the restaurant, you'd done it mostly out of solidarity, had figured out quick that Hero didn't have any papers. What you hadn't counted on was how good Hero would be at it. She had a natural knack for serving people at the restaurant, had a way of being invisible at the right times and then silently appearing to provide an extra fork when it was needed. Hero was detached, but her boundaries were nothing like the ones you'd thrown up in phalanxes when you were a kid, new in California, snarling at anyone who looked at you sideways because of how you pronounced the letter *f.* Hero was like one of those upper-class Filipino homes in the Bay that your fam catered at sometimes, the Couples for Christ houses, the ones with polite owners who paid on time, called Lolo Boy kuya, took the trays off your hands. It was only after you'd been in the house a couple of times that you'd wise up to the fact that you'd never really gone past the entrance.

It didn't take long for you to start giving Hero stacks and stacks of manga. You didn't realize afterward that Hero must have figured out quick that your tastes generally ran toward romance, that everything you recommended to her was mainly about girls feeling out their independence, falling in love with boys, who were generally either stable and responsible from beginning to end, or rude as shit at first but then juicy-soft the minute the heroine ever got into some real wildness. The stories all ended the same way—thank god for that. You knew that Hero didn't think much of your reading habits, that she found the stories sentimental and full of clichés, was possibly even offended by some of them, although she was polite about it, thanking you for the latest book even if it had been patently obvious that she'd thought it was a pile of steaming tae not good enough to spit on.

Hero knew the kinds of stories you liked, which meant Hero thought she knew something about you: what you wanted out of love, what you wanted out of life, the things you dreamt about, the things you touched yourself to, the things that dragged you without protest into the undertow of dreamless, fearless sleep. She likes dumbass romance between boys and girls, so that's what she really wants—that was how Hero's thinking probably went. It felt like Hero was just waiting for the moment to come when you would just shake yourself awake from some heavy-ass dream, blink a few times at Hero like you didn't recognize her, and the feelings you'd been feeding and feeding off of would just vanish, like a hunger that went away the more you starved it. Like she was just waiting for you to wise up and get with some dude. Jaime, probably. The manga-perfect kiss, framed with flowers. Dumbass romance. Boys and girls.

Better to give up and get the fuck out now, crowed the biggest and smartest part of you, the part whose job it was to acutely detect when you were out of your depth, or when your dumbassness was approaching life-ruining levels. The part of you that said *Enough* after the last onstage primal scream. The part of you that visited Jaime in jail, stared at him through the glass partition, picked up the phone and uttered the first words you'd spoken to each other in three years: You look like shit, Lowme.

Okay, so you were out of your depth. The life-ruin meter was wailing. That was all true. But it was too late—too late to have your mind changed by something as minor as the truth. You didn't want a way out. You wanted a way in. Any way in would do.

Hero knew what she was doing when it came to fucking. You saw for yourself the way Hero would go home with almost anyone who asked, those first few months when you were just friends and you had to grin and turn your head, stand around at parties up in the Excelsior and wait until someone whispered in Hero's ear. But you saw Hero leave with a girl once at a party in San Jose, which meant it was on the table, at least. Hero went home with almost anyone who asked—so you asked. It wasn't that deep. Or that was what you needed Hero to think.

Less than a year later she was letting you nose around her pussy like a teenager at prom, licking overextravagantly at folds that you usually ignored on yourself, or poking, shallow, into Hero's hole, hoping for a reaction, not really getting one. Then Hero asked you to use your hand.

I got this, you said when you finally got your shit together, meaning, wanting to mean, wanting it to be true so much there was no way you could ever fucking say it aloud: I got you. You pressed your middle finger down on Hero's clit—slick, saliva-warm, too wet if that was even possible, fuck, you'd been sloppy as hell, no wonder—enough. No time to lose it. Time to work. You pressed your middle finger down onto Hero's clit, gentle at first, the way you liked it, and started in on the familiar slow circle, not trying anything fancy, aiming straight for the heart.

Hero had known for a long time about your crush; that was pretty clear. It was also pretty clear that Hero was dead set on telling herself that it was just a crush: nothing to get worked up over, easy enough to work around. Hero was probably gonna keep on fucking around with other people; you'd never asked her not to, and even if you'd wanted to, you had the feeling your skills in bed were, to say the least, nothing that suddenly would get Hero hyped about monogamy.

That was fine. You were patient, or could be. What you didn't want was for Hero to take one look at you, and know. Just know. And then—run like hell. Leave you for dead.

Bíba, Babaero

THE PROBLEM WITH HAVING SOMEWHAT GOOD SEX
with someone reasonably available—well, reasonably; immoderately
and extravagantly available, more like—was that, once had, it was difficult not to want it all the time. It was difficult for Hero to remember
that she'd spent months and months filling up her days with something
that wasn't fucking around with Rosalyn, that in fact she'd gone most of
her life doing things that weren't fucking around with Rosalyn, that she
had an entire lifetime's worth of evidence showing that it was possible to
think about things that weren't fucking around with Rosalyn—and yet.
Hero found herself ignoring all the evidence in favor of spending her
days thrumming, like a machine that had been left turned on and then
forgotten about, leaking electricity, draining itself dry, until Rosalyn
got within hand's reach again.

It didn't help that Rosalyn kept finding absurd reasons to call Hero
into the kitchen and then to shove her against the sink and crane up for
Hero's mouth, needy, hip to hip, acting like she'd gone deaf to any attempts at reason, while Boy and Adela were out in the restaurant talking
to customers about what everyone had been talking about that week,
which was the impending eruption in Pinatubo.

Hero heard about the tens of thousands of American soldiers who'd
been airlifted out of Clark Air Base, had been trying to keep up on the
news while she was in the car, but found she was too exhausted from
work to watch the evening news, as Pol did before he left for work. Most
of the people in the restaurant were concerned, but not particularly
scared; volcanic eruptions happened all the time, like with Mount Taal.
Pinatubo was bigger, of course, but still.

Rosalyn put her thigh between Hero's, giving Hero something to rub
up against, and then, in her haste, Hero knocked over a container of barbecue sauce, the entire day's worth.

Hero broke away like she'd been shot, looked down at the mess she'd made. Rosalyn started laughing, her hand over her mouth. Punyeta, Hero hissed, then grabbed for paper towels, her hand smarting from moving too quickly. She waved at Rosalyn without looking at her. Just—stop laughing—

Rosalyn's shoulders were still shaking with laughter when Adela came back into the restaurant and demanded, Anong ginagawa ninyo dito? What the hell are you guys doing in here?

Butterfingers over here spilled all the sauce, Rosalyn said. Adela tsk-ed. Get the extra in the fridge. I'll make more.

Hero tried to get up, her hands sticky and red, barbecue sauce on her jeans, her shoes, the bottom of her shirt. I'm sorry—it was my fault. I'll clean it up.

Adela shook her head, waved Hero to the sink. Just wash your hands. Do you need to change your clothes? Rosalyn can lend you some, just go back to the house—

No, Hero interrupted, much too fast and much too loud, refusing to acknowledge the look of what she could tell was wolfish excitement rising on Rosalyn's face. No. It's fine. I'll just wash my hands.

Despite the fact that they were all over each other the minute they were alone, Hero was surprised at how little Rosalyn let on when she was around her friends and family. Hero had always assumed that no one, barring perhaps Lola Adela, knew about Rosalyn's preferences, and so she'd already known that she and Rosalyn would have to hide whatever they got up to. But she hadn't expected Rosalyn to be so good at it. They could have been fucking in her bed half an hour before going to one of Maricris's rehearsals, but once Rosalyn was in the presence of other people, she would look at Hero the way she'd looked at her when they first met, interested but separate, even as Hero would stare at Rosalyn's fingers and know that if she lifted them to her face, she'd smell herself there, find herself under the fingernails.

It discomfited Hero, at first, how good Rosalyn was at hiding—at lying, really—but then Hero took her coolheadedness for a good sign: Rosalyn, having now slept with the object of her attention, was probably now in the swan song of her crush, faced now with the real face of the fantasy she'd nursed her minor infatuation on; dimmer, rucked-up and used, human-sized. It was a good sign, Hero told herself, and told herself, until she half believed it.

All in all, it was a problem. It was a problem how much she liked it, it was a problem how little she was thinking of other people, it was a problem. Which was why, less than two weeks after Lola Adela had found them in the kitchen, Hero asked Jaime if he wanted to go up to the city.

They hadn't gone up together in a while, not since the Calaveras Hills were still green and not straw-beige and dried out like they had been over the summer. Instead of going up to the city, Jaime invited her to a house party in Hayward, a going-away party for one of his old friends from his time in Elmwood. Jaime mourned in the car on the way.

Fucking everybody's moving away, man. Down south, or to Vegas. The Bay's getting too steep.

They separated not long after arriving, and later she glimpsed Jaime being kissed into a couch by a girl much shorter than him, dressed in tiny shorts and what looked like a cropped Warriors jersey. It was hot that night; Hero was wearing a tank top, too, and so was Jaime, the tattoo high on his arm that she'd seen through his T-shirt the first day they'd met finally visible again. It was too far away to be sure, but it looked like Baybayin characters. Hero didn't know how to read Baybayin, but there was a poster in Rosalyn's bedroom that looked like it had been hung there for years, and the letters in that poster matched the letters on Jaime's arm. Hero turned away from Jaime, and let her gaze lock on to the lanky moreno who'd been eyeing her since she'd walked in, who didn't have tattoos, didn't resemble anything like Rosalyn's bedroom.

When she got home, her mouth chalky-dry and bleachy with traces of semen, Paz and Pol were both in the kitchen. Paz was on the phone, shouting in rapid-fire Pangasinan, and Pol was watching her, occasionally interjecting in Tagalog or English when he understood something Paz or her sister Rufina had said.

If the highway between Manila and Pangasinan is full of ash, of course they shouldn't travel, he said.

Paz, confused by Pol's Tagalog, started speaking in a broken Tagalog to her own sister, jumbling it up with her Pangasinan, then sometimes breaking into English, so Hero could eventually make out that Paz was ordering Rufina not to breathe the ash in, to cover her face with a panyo, to stay inside, that they didn't know if the volcano would erupt again, why didn't she stock up on water like Paz had told her to weeks ago, how much food did they have. The tone of her voice was stuck on a peevish, high-pitched yawp, like she was angry that she even had to be saying what she was saying, like she had to be angry, because the anger was her last fortification against the fear.

Quietly, Pol said, You're shouting, and Paz turned to him, hand over the receiver, and shouted back in English, I'm not shouting! This is just how I talk!

On the phone, Rufina was saying, switching to Tagalog once she understood that Pol was also listening, that there wasn't much ash to breathe in, the typhoon was hardening most of the ash into mud.

Pol saw Hero standing there. While Paz spoke to her sister, he and Hero stared at each other. The wall of Pangasinan cut them off, gave them a shroud of privacy. When he finally spoke, he spoke in Ilocano, confirming what Hero had understood, but giving her the brutal mercy of receiving the news in her own language. Bimtak ti Pinatubo.

At the restaurant all through the week and into the weekend, when the worst of the eruptions and evacuations took place, people watched the news in silence, tapes of anime movies forgotten to the side of the VCR. Hero came to the restaurant on the weekend just to have something to do, was surprised to see that so many people did the same. Hero knew Paz was doing the same thing at work, with the rest of the nurses. Pol, likely with the other security guards. Paz came alive in scenes of emergency, relieved to push aside superfluous detail and make do with basic commands. She would call Rufina regularly, briskly gathering information, trying to find out who else needed money, if anyone's home had been destroyed, trying to remember if she knew people who could give them a place to stay, if she knew coworkers who had family in the area and might have a free bed or five. Pol's expression was grave, but composed. It was the expression of someone who knew without having to find out for himself that all of his family members were safe.

Hero asked him, just once, if he'd called anyone, if he'd talked to Soly. She didn't mention her father's name. He shook his head. Paz, who was in the room when Hero had asked, interrupted to say she'd called one of Soly's children. Everyone was fine.

Hero knew from Amihan's lectures that it was mostly Aetas living near Pinatubo, just as in Isabela many of the people they met and lived among were Aeta. Back then, Hero was still sometimes calling them negritos, a holdover from her parents, and the berating from Amihan was. Thorough. Beyond that, Hero knew only that Philippine National Oil had been working on a geothermal exploration program in Pinatubo for years. The building of the Magat Dam in neighboring Cagayan had made everyone in Isabela aware of the patterns that led to land theft. They joined up with NPA Cagayan and with Aetas from Cagayan to protest against the drilling, often risking retaliation from the soldiers who protected the building sites. By the time Hero got out of the camp in '88, drilling had begun. The news in California didn't mention the Aetas.

Rosalyn sensed that the eruption had left Hero more withdrawn than usual. Did you, uh, know anybody—she started, tentatively. Hero shook her head, curt; annoyed that she didn't know if she knew anybody, annoyed at her own safety, annoyed that after ten years in Isabela, she could still react to disaster like—a donya from Vigan, safe in her interior courtyard, paved with damili tile.

Rosalyn reached out to touch her, but Hero's limbs locked up in defense. Rosalyn pulled her hand away. Sorry, she said.

After that, she gave Hero space, anxious and hangdog, waiting for the slightest hint of invitation. The shock of the disaster hadn't endured in her, not really; for her, the horror of it all felt too far away, Hero could see that. Something that happened thankfully to someone else, somewhere else, a place that Rosalyn was now only distantly related to; not home, not anymore. That was true for Jaime and the rest of Rosalyn's friends. It was truer for Hero than she cared to admit.

Paz said both Clark and Subic Bay bases had been destroyed by Pinatubo. That would please Amihan, Hero thought. If Tarlac was within the radius of the eruption, Amihan in all likelihood knew people who were affected. Would the ash have fallen all the way to Cagayan, all the way to Isabela? Would Teresa have gathered the cadres in a rescue mission, evacuating villagers, meting out tarpaulin for makeshift shelters, accepting aid from white missionaries with her eyes smiling and her mouth flat? The clinic would be full of the injured: people who'd slipped and broken an ankle on a mountain incline that the typhoon had made as soupy as monggo, people who'd protected someone else's body with their own when a part of a roof had caved in under the weight of the ash and rain, people who'd desperately need treating and Hero—wouldn't be the one to treat them. There were other cadres with medical experience in Isabela; Hero had reluctantly trained most of them after failing to convince Teresa that the idea of her teaching anybody anything was absurd. They would be the ones to step up, the ones to bark out orders to the men with strong upper bodies, tell them who to carry and where, the ones to ration out the rubbing alcohol and then, when the rubbing alcohol ran out, to ration out the Ginebra, the ones to stay up until morning watching over the sleeping wounded, silently chewing betel quid to keep themselves awake. It was failing to remember the taste of betel nut in her mouth that made Hero get up from her stool behind the register, turn around, walk to the kitchen, and throw up quietly into the sink.

Boy was at the stove, frying atsuete seeds in oil to store for the week. Hero didn't look at him. If he said anything, she didn't hear it, ears ringing.

When she was done, she rinsed the vomit away, sprayed the sink with the disinfectant that Boy and Adela usually used for the countertops, splashed water on her face, and dried it with the front of her shirt. Then she went back out again into the restaurant, where a customer was waiting.

Hero knew that lust was one of the time-honored antidotes to sorrow, but that had never been her relationship to sex. Whatever sorrows lived in her heart were either too superficial to need such soothing, or too burrowed-in and settled to be eased out by something as mundane as coming for the fourth or fifth time against Rosalyn's fingers in the kitchen late at night when the restaurant was long closed; Rosalyn multitasking by leaving eggs and longanisa frying in an oily pan while grinding into Hero's lap, hand down her unzipped jeans, until Hero unclenched her teeth from Rosalyn's ear and said, Something's, uh, burning, and Rosalyn cursed and hopped off.

Hero waited for her body to just get bored with it already, the chasmal gorge of her desire, many-chambered and spacious, a sunken caldera so deep she kept feeling and feeling for the floor of it—but every day she still came up wet, groundless. Rosalyn would get bored with it, then. She just had to wait.

While she waited, Hero learned small, stupid things, like the wounded sounds Rosalyn made when she was about to come, or when she was moved by the death of a cartoon character. Like the fact that while Hero had a habit of falling into a sleep like the dead after sex, Rosalyn turned even chattier, energetic and restless, usually leading them on a hunt for snacks like Yan Yan or shrimp chips. She learned that Rosalyn hid things under her bed: old school notebooks with things like fLiP prYde and aZn LoVe scribbled onto the covers, or videotapes and manga she didn't show anybody, which Hero found when she was on her knees in front of Rosalyn and saw them sticking out from underneath the mattress. Drawings of half-naked men wrapped up in each other, sometimes chained up, sometimes wreathed in flowers. *Zetsuai Bronze, Ai no Kusabi,* Hero read, climbing up from the bed, her knees cracking. Rosalyn made a dying-dog sound of embarrassment and covered her face, to which Hero said, Is this—is this pornography? And Rosalyn said SHUT UP SHUT UP SHUT UP.

Hero learned that in spite of the naked men in chains and flowers, Rosalyn could be prudish and uneasy about her own body and especially its odor, diligently shaving her underarms and mustache every other day, catching Hero's bemused eye in the bathroom mirror as she smoothed a men's razor across her upper lip. That Nair stuff burns my skin off, so. Hero said: You said you liked my mustache. Rosalyn huffed out: Yeah. Yours.

And despite the fact that Rosalyn had gotten into the inconvenient habit of leaving hickeys all across Hero's inner thighs and breasts, which were the first hickeys Hero had received since she'd been in high school— she thought once of teasing Rosalyn with that fact, only to pull back when she remembered that Rosalyn genuinely hadn't fucked that many people since high school and thus had probably never unlearned that age's overeager fantasies of what ardor looked like, hadn't had enough lovers to tell her that suck marks and bruises were, were, annoying or, or, but Hero couldn't finish the thought, thumbing unthinking at the marks through- out the day, the twisted-up pulse in her pussy a damning rebuttal—Ros- alyn was also sometimes prudish about sex. If Hero went to eat her out and Rosalyn hadn't showered or was on her period or felt in any way that she stank, she'd cover her crotch with a hand, and no amount of teasing or tickling or assurance would get her to move that hand away. It's not dirty, Hero would say, to which Rosalyn would reply, I didn't even kaw- kaw this morning. Once afterward, Rosalyn asked hesitantly, What, what does it smell like, and Hero replied, You know those shrimp chips you get at Magat, and Rosalyn slammed a pillow into her face so hard Hero nearly choked on her own saliva, laughing.

She learned that Rosalyn sometimes, haltingly, spoke of Jaime, about the person he was, and more rarely about the people they'd been to- gether. She talked about Jaime's beauty, the fact that he'd been that beau- tiful even as a kid, all lashes and lips, and people, boys, never stopped giving him shit about it—This dude in the eighth grade called them cocksucker's lips, I got suspended for throwing a Coke bottle at his head—and that even though Rosalyn had been the new kid in school, she was the one who first swept him up into her care, bossed him around, made sure older boys left him alone. She and Cely, that was what they did, she said: looked out for Jaime. One afternoon in Rosalyn's bed, Hero asked about the tattoo on Jaime's arm.

Rosalyn's face went blank. Oh—you saw that?

It's Baybayin, right? Hero asked. Rosalyn nodded. I don't understand Baybayin, Hero said.

Who does, Rosalyn mumbled, flopping back on the bed, hiding her eyes from sunlight that wasn't in her eyes. It's just some dumb thing we did in college. Like every other Pinoy couple in the Bay.

So what does it say, Hero prompted.

Rosalyn took her hand away. It's my name, she said. She pointed at the poster Hero had remembered that night at the party, and had slept with someone to forget.

Hero was quiet, and Rosalyn went on like she didn't notice, hasty: Well, not technically. It's like, Dosalin. There's no R in Baybayin, whatever.

She stopped, closed her eyes. I have one, too, she added. Ha-me. I wanted to get Lo-me but he stopped me. Then she laughed skittishly.

Hero stared at her; she'd seen Rosalyn completely and thoroughly naked, and had never seen a tattoo, not even a hint of one. Where?

Rosalyn lifted the hair from the back of her neck. Hero still didn't see anything. This used to be shaved, Rosalyn said. I had like—look, when I was in college, I tried a bunch of different looks, okay? So I had, like, kind of a mohawk. Mine is under the hair there. If you part it you can see it.

Hero parted the hair, saw it; just the small curves and swirls of black ink.

Jaime wanted it on his arm, though. You remember, Song of Solomon? Place me like a seal over your heart, like a seal on your arm?

For love is as strong as death. Hero remembered. Her parents had always disliked the Song of Solomon.

That was his whole thing. I mean, we were both kinda more Catholic then. Like everybody else. Anyway, my mom almost killed me, Rosalyn laughed, with that laugh that wasn't really a laugh. Shaved head *and* a tattoo. And I was drinking a lot then, to top it off. The only reason she didn't was 'cause she thought me and Jaime were gonna get married—She stopped talking, abruptly, and Hero knew they'd reached the end of the conversation.

Rosalyn, for her part, was learning small, stupid things, too; learning when was most effective to come close, when was most effective to give Hero a finger's width or a town's width of space. Learning that even though Hero liked to come easily and a lot, what she liked even more was to be edged: brought close to the precipice then gently pulled back from it, pushed a bit closer, then pulled further back, again and again and again, until Hero was practically hectic with want, dissolving, until Rosalyn saw fit to end her agony. Perhaps the most significant thing Rosalyn learned was that Hero wanted her, really wanted her; that it wasn't humoring or pity or even a one-time thing. It definitely wasn't a one-time thing.

They fought, sometimes. Hero had never thought of herself as an argumentative or even confrontational person before, and yet she occasionally threw sparks on tinder, like the time Rosalyn mentioned the first time they'd had sex and how bad she'd been at it at first, and Hero said something offhand and blunt about how yes, really, it was odd, Rosalyn should have been able to get a lot more practice in, and Rosalyn had asked what she meant by that, and Hero had shrugged and pushed, said something about Rosalyn not being a teenager anymore and it wasn't their parents' generation, people didn't really have to stand around and wait for Prince Charming to come along, she could've gone to any club or party and found the one girl drinking alone, could've found some dyke bar in the city and worked her way through pussy from the top of the Bay all the way back down.

I would've, at least, Hero concluded, and Rosalyn blew up, spittle flying:

Not everyone's fucking like you, okay!

Like what, Hero said, baiting, and finished the sentence before Rosalyn could stop or apologize: A puta, a kontrabida—and Rosalyn lost it.

That's fuckin' easy for someone to say who, who—do you live here? Do you have to deal with seeing people who knew you when you were fucking ten years old coming into your place of work on a daily basis? Into your home? The fuck you know about it? You're new here, no one knows your business, if you get up to some bullshit no one thinks any different of you, but things are different for me, they're different for my mom, you—you were rich or whatever, maybe you could hide the shit you got up to, but I have to be more careful. You think it's fucking easy to do what you and Jaime do all the time, you think anyone but the two of you could fucking live that down? Fucking look at Lea. She fucked

Dante for a month then left him for Arnel and no one'll let her forget it, Ruben is still fucking giving her shit about it like his sister's ass belongs to him, you think I could just—what—put myself on the buffet line and, and still live here? And don't fucking tell me to just move.

Rosalyn was nearly hyperventilating by the end of it, her eyes red but dry. Are you finished, Hero asked.

No, Rosalyn snapped, then, low: yeah.

This, Hero said, the corner of her mouth lifting, gesturing between the two of them, is you being careful?

Rosalyn flopped under the covers, grumpy but within forgiving range. Then she resurfaced, face somber.

I was being serious, she said. It's not like I didn't want to—do things. It's just.

I get it, Hero said, reaching for her. I'm sorry.

Rosalyn was learning things that Hero didn't even tell her, like the time Hero fell asleep again in Rosalyn's bed, then when she woke up, still cum-dumb and groggy, Rosalyn was staring at her, face expressionless.

Who's Teresa?

Hero shot up in the seat. What?

You were talking in your sleep.

It's late, Hero said, sobered. Take me home.

Rosalyn tightened her jaw. Considered and discarded one or two responses. Then put the car in drive.

The ride was tense and silent all the way to the house, but in the driveway, when Hero kissed Rosalyn good night, she felt Rosalyn's mouth, stiff and unyielding at first, eventually melt, sucking in Hero's bottom lip with a soft groan. Afterward, she silently handed Hero the container of homemade peanut butter that Adela had labeled FOR RONI, when Roni had mentioned the week before that the kare-kare at the restaurant was better than her Auntie Gloria's, a rare compliment. Adela had said the secret was making the peanut butter from scratch, and gave Roni part of the next day's batch. Rosalyn paused for a moment, and Hero waited patiently, letting Rosalyn gather whatever thoughts she wanted to gather, until she realized that Rosalyn wasn't trying to think of something to say; she was giving Hero the chance to say something.

See you tomorrow, Hero said.

Rosalyn froze, then shuddered, then took that for the bone it was. See you tomorrow, she said back.

No—whatever sorrows lived in Hero's heart were too burrowed-in and settled to be eased out by something as mundane as Rosalyn's face—Rosalyn's face when she asked who Teresa was; or her face when Hero wouldn't tell her; or her face again, when she gave up on the thing she needed and settled for the thing she wanted. At the kitchen table alone, Hero thought about telling Rosalyn about Teresa: saying her name, coming up with language to describe her, what she'd been to Hero, what she'd done for Hero, the world she'd given her, which Hero thought would last forever, only to discover that in that world she'd only had a short-stay visa; she hadn't been a citizen, not even a permanent resident.

Hero didn't know how long she sat there, unmoving, her face and hands numb. At some point her eyes, blurry and hot, finally focused again, saw the container of peanut butter in front of her. Adela had put a wood-handled spoon inside, saying that if they used too thin a spoon to stir the peanut butter, the metal might bend with the thickness of the paste.

Hero lifted the spoon out of the oil that had congealed on the top of the peanut butter, trying not to get the grease all over her fingers so at least she could get a good grip on the handle. She tried to stir the oil back into the dry, hardened nut paste, the effort coming out of her as if from another person, another hand, stirring and stirring and stirring again, long after the oil had been evenly distributed and her hurt hand was covered in grease, and the grief finally settled, like a stone in the sea, and her swollen eyes opened, and the peanut butter looked like peanut butter again. She put the spoon in her mouth. It tasted okay.

At the end of August, after Pol accepted birthday cards from Paz, Roni, and Hero, he smiled at Hero and said, And what do you want for your birthday, Nimang?

It was nearly eleven o'clock in the evening, and they'd all been sitting at the dinner table, three-quarters of a mocha roll cake in front of them. Paz had gotten back from work in time to see Pol cutting the cake with Roni, and was now on the phone with Rufina. Rufina sounded almost amused by Paz's panic. She confirmed that the streets were still full of sludge but easy enough to drive the tricycle through; people were already getting on with their lives, as always. Paz seemed confused and unsatisfied by these facts.

Roni turned to Hero with eyes as big as dinner plates.

What? It's your birthday? When? How old are you turning? What do you want to do? What do you want as a present?

Thirty-five, Hero said, and watched Roni's eyes glaze over at the enormity of the number.

She went on: And I don't want to do anything. I don't want a present. It's not that big a deal.

Roni slumped, looked lost. But I didn't even make you a card—

Hero wasn't planning to say anything about it to anyone at the restaurant, but of course Roni remained upset about it for days, and when Rosalyn asked her on Thursday what was wrong, Roni told her. Which was how Hero managed to have two people furious with her that week.

Who the hell doesn't tell people when their birthday is? Rosalyn demanded. What, you have some dumb complex about your age?

It's just not that big a deal.

Did you even eat pancit?

Hero didn't dignify that with an answer, went over to see if Roni was hungry or if just the halo-halo was enough for now. Roni lipped morosely at a cube of bright green nata de coco and said nothing.

Rosalyn called Jaime while he was still at work, which meant when he arrived at the restaurant after his shift, he had a plastic bag in hand, containing three stick candles and one candle in the shape of a five. They were out of threes, he explained. The stick candles were covered in flaking sparkles, and Minnie Mouse hid daintily behind the number 5. Roni and Rosalyn tried to balance the candles in a single puto, then, seeing that it was too crowded and would likely fall over from the weight and burn the entire place down—We don't have that kinda insurance, Rosa-lyn warned—they tried four separate puto, a candle in each one, which looked. Hideous. Boy and Adela got the rest of the restaurant to join in on the singing, which compounded the horror. Make a wish! Roni said, holding her puto closest to Hero's face, so that Hero had to lean back to avoid being singed. And not, like, for everybody responsible for this to get food poisoning, Rosalyn said.

Hero didn't want to make a wish, but a wish had formed in her chest; it calcified and stuck to her ribs before she could stop it. Too late. She leaned forward, blew the candles out one by one, and made herself smile.

Later it was Jaime, not Rosalyn, who crouched and leaned his arms over the driver's side window as Hero was about to take Roni back home. She'd tentatively agreed to being picked up by Rosalyn later, something Rosalyn had muttered out of the corner of her mouth while Hero was helping look for any leftover pancit that she could eat, just for tradition's sake.

Jaime turned his head away so he wouldn't blow smoke into the win-dow, then said, You guys were saving up for a car, right?

Hero nodded. Jaime continued, My friend up in the city said he's sell-ing his Accord. You remember him, the bartender over off Minna? The one with the earring? Hero remembered.

It's old, but still runs okay. I could have Roy at the garage around the corner check it out. You interested?

Hero was sure that what she had saved wasn't enough, even for a used car, even with whatever deal Jaime could work out. She'd have to ask Paz and Pol, who'd made no secret of having been saving to get Hero a car anyway, despite the fact that Hero had already told both of them that she would pay for the car herself. Pol and Paz hadn't allowed Hero to contribute financially to the house expenses at all, insisting that her ser-vices as Roni's babysitter and chaperone were repayment enough. Hero knew now that Paz liked people being indebted to her: she liked loaning people money, liked being the financial benefactor of her various rela-tives, regardless of whether or not she actually had enough money to spare. She liked people turning to her in supplication, liked being on the other side of that transaction; at last not the needy, but the needed.

Think about it, okay? Jaime told Hero. Hero nodded.

Rosalyn showed up earlier than Hero was expecting, saying they could catch the last showing of *Terminator 2* over at Serra Theater. Roni was still awake and wanted to go, but Pol overheard the conversation and said she had to go to sleep, she had school the next day, and besides, they'd already seen the film. But I want to see it *again* and it's Ate Hero's birthday, Roni reasoned, to no avail.

Pol greeted Rosalyn warmly when she lingered anxiously at the edge of the garage door, and said he still remembered how wonderful the food was at Rosalyn's party, and how kind Rosalyn and her grandparents had been to come through so well, how much everyone had loved everything, and that the barbecue had been especially delicious. Rosalyn went flustered at the compliments, which Hero teased her about all the way down Jacklin Road as it turned into Abel Street, all the way into the parking lot, and straight through to the movie theater, where Rosalyn stuffed popcorn into her mouth and grumbled.

Hero had never seen the first *Terminator,* so she asked Rosalyn what it was about. But Rosalyn was still in her mood, and told Hero to just watch the fuckin' movie and find out.

What Hero could tell before she could tell anything else was that the movie took place in California, even if supposedly it took place in the future; she recognized California, the quality of sunlight on the people's faces, the way its particular weight flattened and loosened people's expressions. Knew it, most of all, because Arnold Schwarzenegger was conspicuously not Californian, not even American, and the fact that he was playing a robot was entirely incidental to his foreignness, which wasn't a question of being or not being human, but being or not being from around there. Naked in a biker bar, knowing nobody, asking for clothes, money, a motorcycle.

Hero hadn't appreciated how absorbed she was in the film until she realized Rosalyn's hand was high up on her thigh and had probably been there, waiting, for half an hour. Instead of guiding the hand to its intended destination, Hero picked it up and laced their fingers together, eyes still glued to the screen.

John was teaching the Terminator the ways of the world: how to speak, how not to kill people, how to tell people to chill out, how to insult people; how to tell someone good-bye, how to tell someone you'd see them again, how to say you'd be back. How to know the difference. How to give a thumbs-up right before sinking into a vat of molten steel; how to be an optimist in America, right before you died.

When the credits were rolling, Rosalyn made to stand up, but Hero didn't move, was still holding Rosalyn's hand, so hard the base of her fingers was sore. Rosalyn peered into Hero's face. Said, Are you.

Hero made a noise and covered her wet face with the hand that wasn't holding Rosalyn's.

Jesus, Rosalyn said, bringing her knuckles up to Hero's face, wiping at the tears there. And you make fun of me for the movies and shit I like?!

Hero didn't say anything. Rosalyn hesitated, then when the theater was empty and the lights came on, said: It's bad luck to cry on your birthday.

That's New Year's, Hero said in something that resembled a blubber, choky and peeled-open. And it's not even my birthday.

Rosalyn brushed again at Hero's cheeks, half laughing, and half—not. Oh, okay, never mind then, she said.

By the time Halloween came and went, Hero was driving a decade-old forest-green Accord sedan whose headrests were stuck in place but which had a sound system more tricked out than she could make sense of, and which she left alone until Jaime, seeing her drive up to the restaurant silently more times than he could apparently bear, said, Okay, I'm gonna show you how it works.

In the end, Paz and Pol had helped her to cover what her savings couldn't stretch far enough to pay, and refused when she said she'd pay them back. Roni loved the car because it was new, or new to her at least; she tried out every seat, wanting to see what the view was like, the feel was like, before giving up and hopping back into the front where she knew she belonged, chewing on a licorice whip and only settling when Hero said, No shoes on the seats.

Everyone had mostly stopped talking about Pinatubo although Hero still saw Filipino newspapers—or, newspapers about Philippine news but published in California by California-based Filipinos—folded over and crumpled on the passenger seat of Paz's car: pictures of churches and houses with their roofs caved in under the weight of the lahar, people piled into the back of a truck, still covered in ash, leaving for places unclear.

Hero hadn't fucked anyone but Rosalyn since Pinatubo. For some time, she'd started to have the sense that Paz and Pol knew about what she was doing outside of the home—once, she'd driven Roni to school completely sober, and yet Roni turned to her just before getting out and said, You stink. After that, Hero started taking a shower when she got home, no matter the hour.

Once Paz met her in the kitchen, Paz on her way home from work and Hero on her way out to either Rosalyn's house or a bar with Jaime. Abruptly, Paz said, Teka muna. Nimang. I have something for you.

And then she reached into the drawer in the kitchen, where she kept the extra medical supplies and drugs, ruffled through them to find something she'd apparently stuffed at the bottom, hidden by packets of A&D ointment—two boxes of condoms.

Hero squirmed. Okay lang, Tita, I—buy my own, she said, thinking of the small drugstore across from Roni's school, close to Magat, and on the other side of town from the strip mall where the restaurant was located.

Paz, already in the middle of the transaction, pushed them into Hero's hands. You have to be careful. You don't know what anyone—be careful. And. If anything happens, don't hide it. Don't take care of it on your own. We'll help. Okay?

Hero stared back at her and once again felt that upsurge of affection for the grim practicality of a nurse. Okay, she said.

Around Christmastime, Roni got the chicken pox, which worried Paz and Pol, since apparently she'd had it before and should have been immune. Hero'd had it when she was around Roni's age, and she remembered the mind-cracking torment of the itch, Lulay slapping at her hands every time

Hero tried to scratch. It came just when Roni's skin was the best it'd ever been, with eczema flare-ups only when she ate the things Adela had asked her to avoid, or when she had a particularly stressful day at school, or when she saw Gloria's car pull up to the driveway, bearing food.

Hero herself felt an itch under her skin rise when she saw the car, staring at it to make sure Gloria was the only person inside, feeling icy terror close up her throat when she saw a male figure in the passenger seat, helping carry in a tray. Hero hurried up the stairs, and stood outside Paz and Pol's bedroom door, where she knew Roni was barricading herself. She didn't try the knob, didn't care if it was locked or not. She stood outside, leaning against it, and nearly fell backward half an hour later, when Roni opened the door, having heard the car drive away through the open window. Ow, Roni said. You're on my foot.

Hero spent Christmas at home with Roni, watching anime movies in the living room and occasionally telling her not to scratch. Roni's chicken pox meant that Paz and Pol had, extraordinarily, both taken their Christmas holidays instead of working for the extra overtime, and were trying to put together a small plastic Christmas tree that one of Pol's coworkers had sold him—a small business he had on the side— saying it was much easier and less messy than real Christmas trees, and you could reuse it year after year. They only had the standard ornaments that came with every tree, a couple dozen small, vinyl-shiny red apples.

Rosalyn called to wish them a Merry Christmas, then asked Hero to pass the phone to Roni so she and Jaime and everyone could wish her a Merry Christmas, too. Hero eavesdropped on the conversation, and heard Rosalyn tell Roni she was sorry she was so sick, chicken pox was the worst but it would get better soon, and everyone at Rosalyn's house for the Christmas party this year missed her. Did she want Rosalyn and Jaime to come over later with food? Roni said they had plenty of food, and they were all watching *Ranma ½* and it was really good, and they even had a tree for the first time, and the decorations were pretty. Then Hero watched her give more or less the same report to Jaime.

When Roni gave Hero the phone back, no one was on the line, Jaime in the middle of passing the phone back to Rosalyn.

Uh, hi, hold on, um. Let me go to my room. Are you alone?

No, Hero said. They didn't have a cordless phone, and the cord was stretched enough as it was, from the kitchen to the living room. Okay, Rosalyn said. She started laughing. I didn't have anything to say, really. Just. Merry Christmas.

Merry Christmas, Hero said.

We're going to the city for New Year's again, you coming?

I don't think Roni's gonna be better by then.

Okay, mom. If you wanna come, let me know though. Tell Roni I hope she feels better.

You already told her.

Tell her again, but cuter.

You're, Hero said and stopped, aware people were listening. Okay. Merry Christmas.

Merry Christmas.

They hung up, and Hero put the phone back in the kitchen. When she came back, Pol was trying to string lights onto the tree, a cigarette hanging out of his mouth. Do you need help, she asked, but Pol waved her away. Paz had given up on the project, eating bibingka on the couch with Roni, scrutinizing the television. There was a space between them, and Roni looked wooden, like she wasn't used to her mother being relaxed next to her, or being next to her at all.

The phone rang again, and Hero sighed, knowing it was probably Rosalyn again. I can get it, she said, making her way back to the phone. Hello?

There was a crackling of static. A standardized female voice was speaking, and at first Hero was confused, thinking it was a wrong number, but then the voice was saying it was a collect call from—and the recording fell away, and Hero heard a voice say, clearly and slowly, SOLEDAD DE VERA, and then the robot voice was back again, asking if Hero would accept the charges.

She froze, the words stuck in her throat. The voice asked her again.

Ye-yes, yes, I accept the charges, she said, even though later she told herself she should have asked Paz and Pol first. She called out once, in a voice too high, Tito Pol—it's—it's Tita Soly—and at the same time there was that familiar voice, raspy and deep, saying, Hello? Hello? Mang Pol? Mang Pol?

Tita Soly, Hero managed.

Another crackle of static, then, a shout, like the shout she'd given when Hero showed up at her door. Nimang—

Hero felt her knees buckle. She nearly missed the chair, hunched on the edge of it. Naragsak a Paskua, Soly was saying. I called last year but no one picked up the phone.

Hero closed her eyes. Naragsak a Pasuka, she said back, the Ilocano words feeling chunky and metallic in her mouth.

Nimang, Soly said, soft. Kumusta?

Nasayaat met. I'm. I'm fine.

Really? Soly asked.

Hero thought about it, and didn't feel like it was a total lie. Really, she said.

It's good to hear your voice.

You, too.

Soly hadn't ever been a talkative person, but that had been a gift to Hero. Soly had been the first person to bathe Hero's body, making no comment on what she saw of Hero's nakedness, the things written there, the things carved away. Now there was a sweet bashfulness between them, which, in that moment, Hero wouldn't have traded for anything.

Nimang, Soly said. Are you really doing okay? How is California?

I'm okay. It's okay.

How are your hands?

Hero went quiet, then cursed herself; she was probably worrying Soly. They're fine. The same.

You have to do the exercises regularly.

I do, Hero lied. It's fine. I also help take care of Roni.

How old is she now?

Eight.

Soly was silent except for a long exhale through her nostrils, rippling against Hero's ear. Listen, Nimang. I still try and talk to Mang Hamin, but.

Hero interrupted her. It's fine.

I'll tell them you're doing well. I'll keep trying—

It's fine, Hero interrupted again. She didn't know if she wanted to hear about her parents; if there was news, if they were sick, if they were well, if they were asking about her, if they wanted to talk to her, to see her, if nothing had changed and they never wanted to see her again, if she was still dead to them. She didn't know if she wanted to know, so she interrupted Soly before she could find out. It's fine. You don't have to tell them anything.

Nimang, Soly said, then sighed, dropping it. Can I greet Manong Pol now?

Hero turned to where she knew Pol had been standing, his back to the conversation in a show of privacy, at the border between the living room and the kitchen. When he got on the phone, he said, in the way that a person could say a name differently from anyone else in the world, simply because it was that name, in that mouth, passing between those two people, the deep-in-the-gut intimacy of siblings that Hero had never felt: Soly—

Roni still had chicken pox on New Year's; they watched the ball drop on the television to the tune of Roni slapping at the itchy spots, Hero making sure she wasn't scratching them with her nails and causing scars.

Pol was home, but he drifted between watching the television and making himself another coffee, saying what was the point of just watching a shiny ball drop. Paz had called around eleven to say she was on her way, but she arrived home half an hour after midnight, saying, Did I miss it, knowing she had.

Early the next morning, when Hero woke around dawn as usual after having slept only a couple of hours as usual, she didn't expect to hear her pager ring four times. She didn't expect to hear a doorbell shortly after, and more than all that, she didn't expect to see Jaime's mother's minivan in the driveway when she opened the front door. Jaime had rung the bell and run right back to the car, hurrying over to the passenger side, where he'd begun unbuckling the seat belt of a slumped-over Rosalyn.

When Hero walked into the driveway after him, still wearing her house slippers, she could smell the alcohol even standing three feet away. What—what the.

Okay, Jaime said without greeting Hero, hoisting Rosalyn up by the armpits, which made her furrow her brow, looking at Jaime, smiling dopily, then lifting her gaze to Hero. She started groaning. Oh no oh NO—

Happy New Year to you, too, Hero said, feeling hurt, and then ridiculous.

She's still drunk, said Jaime.

Take her home where she can sleep it off, Hero said, and Rosalyn joined in, Take me *home*—

Oh, now you wanna go home, Jaime muttered. Not like you were yelling at me to bring you here all night or anything.

Rosalyn grinned blurrily, hopelessly at Hero. Hi, she whispered, bedroom-soft, then lurched violently sideward.

Okay, okay, easy, no suka in the van, Jaime said.

Rosalyn was still listing to and fro like she was on strings, head knocking right into the side of Jaime's, skull on skull. He gritted his teeth, pushed her head back onto the headrest.

What happened?

She got into a fight with Janelle, Jaime said over his shoulder. She was making fun of two girls at the party. Saying something about lesbians. Rosalyn went off on her.

Jaime hesitated, then: She, uh. She told everyone you guys were. You know.

Hero slumped against the car door. Shit.

Yeah. Jaime scratched the back of his neck. I think Rosalyn might've hit her if me and Rochelle hadn't pulled her back. She wanted to come here all night, she was about to steal the keys to drive herself. I ended up taking her just to keep her off the wheel. I forgot Roni was sick.

Roni! Rosalyn cheered, swinging from recognized word to recognized word.

Hero almost reached out to brush the sweaty hair from her face, but her hand remained still and cold at her side. She should get home and rest, she muttered finally. I would help, but Roni's still—

I know, I know, shit, Jaime said, wincing. Sorry to blow your pager up at like five in the morning. I forgot. I'll just take her home. She'll be all right.

Then, to Rosalyn: Come on, Princess Suka. One more stop. Legs in. Seat belt on.

Hero chewed the inside of her lip. I can come if you need—

Nah, you're good, Jaime dismissed. She's just gonna throw up and pass out. It'll be like old times. You should get some sleep anyway.

Jaime slammed the passenger door closed, then went to the driver's side. Hero pushed herself off the car and followed him.

You can page me again or call the house if you need. Anything, she added, too raw, ridiculous again.

Jaime nodded and opened his door, but then paused for a minute, staring at the door handle.

What, Hero said.

Jaime sighed, rubbing at the inner corner of one of his eyes. He glanced at Rosalyn to make sure she wasn't listening. She wasn't, sleeping again, her mouth open and drool dripping gracelessly from it. Hero watched him watch her, then made herself stop. Old times.

She's a dumbass, Jaime said.

Yes.

You're a dumbass, too, he added, turning back around to study Hero's face this time.

Yes, Hero agreed; quieter.

Okay, Jaime said, after a long moment. Happy New Year. Tell Roni I hope she feels better.

Jaime stayed. Rochelle stayed, and because Rochelle stayed, Gani stayed—though that was tenuous, considering they'd only recently gone through a tough, not quite complete breakup. Maricris stayed, and Rosalyn said it was just because a rising pop star needed a makeup artist, and

Maricris replied without hesitation, Yeah, and? which put Rosalyn genuinely at ease for a rare moment. But Janelle, Lea, and Ruben stopped coming to the restaurant; when Isagani left early sometimes, everyone knew he was going to meet up with Ruben for some gig, some party, which Rosalyn and the rest of them hadn't been invited to. Rosalyn and Hero specifically, the rest of them by association.

Rosalyn was more imperious than ever, her cheerfulness a carapace, but Hero saw the grief that came into her eyes when a young college-age woman came in, acne across her cheeks, asking if Rosalyn could do the makeup for her dance troupe of fifteen girls. Rosalyn's skills were still in high demand and those skills were still the best around: stippling thicker concealer onto acne patches with a fine brush that looked like it might have been an oil painter's, flesh-colored stripes along the back of her hand, hands deft and sure. Rosalyn was a professional, so only every now and then did it look like the work was absolutely, categorically killing her.

Hero didn't know what to say, how to make it better. She'd never lost friends over something like this, had never had that many friends to lose, or had friends whose opinion she cared about when it came to things like who she fucked or how often—I *don't* fucking care, Rosalyn growled when Hero made the mistake of saying as much once.

The only time Hero saw Rosalyn falter was with Adela and Boy. Rosalyn would be in the salon all day working, not even coming by to bug Hero with comic books like she usually did. She'd stopped coming to the restaurant almost entirely, throwing herself completely into her makeup work, booking appointments practically on top of each other so that she never had time to stop, let alone think. When she came into the restaurant it was tentative, as if she were afraid Janelle or Lea might be in the restaurant, waiting for her; as if she were afraid of how much she wanted Janelle or Lea to be in the restaurant, waiting for her. Hero had never seen her hesitate before the door of the restaurant before; she'd always strolled through its doors with the confidence of a dauphin.

Hero tried to go to the salon once or twice during her own lunch break, just to see her, to take over some food, but Rosalyn would always be with a client and Hero couldn't stand the rigid, polite smile that

Rosalyn would give to her in that moment, the kind of smile Hero knew she'd given to Rosalyn every day for months when they'd first met. Hero gave up on the visits.

Adela and Boy seemed to already understand that Rosalyn needed her distance, prepared for all contingencies in the manner of grandparents who'd done most of the parenting. So every day around lunchtime, Hero would watch as Boy silently made a plate of food: barbecue, pancit, rice, some kutsinta on the side for dessert, all the things that Rosalyn usually came by the restaurant to eat during her break. He covered it with two layers of foil, took either a guava or guyabano juice out of the drinks re-frigerator, put that on top of the plate, then handed it to Adela, who just as silently took the plate and left the restaurant. She always came back quickly, empty-handed; Rosalyn wouldn't have given her any time to talk, Adela would probably have had to leave the food at the reception desk with Mai. But by the end of the night, even if Hero hadn't seen Ros-alyn all day, she would notice that Adela had brought the plate back, empty, foil crumpled in a ball, juice box drained and collapsed in on itself.

When Hero first saw the empty plate, her stomach clenched, thinking of all the times Soly had left a plate like that on the floor beside the living room couch, all the times she'd half emptied it by the next morning.

The closest Rosalyn came to talking about her friends' reaction to her sex life was when she and Hero were in the car, parked just outside of Ed Levin Park, tucked into the foothills of the Calaveras Mountains that over-looked Milpitas. They'd been going there every now and then for months, late at night when the restaurant was closed, Roni was dropped off back home, and no one would miss either of them for a couple of hours.

The first time Rosalyn took Hero up into the mountains, she didn't say where they were going, steering them up Park Victoria Drive, then turning into a bumpy hill road, passing a sign for a horse farm. Huge pink mansions whose windows glowed with golden light punctuated the very tops of the hills, as far away as satellites, so that even as Rosalyn's car climbed higher, the houses seemed to retreat still farther. Finally, they stopped in a small clearing that jutted out like a cliff edge; it was nearly midnight, and two other cars were already parked there.

The view was of a Milpitas that Hero had never seen before, the small town cratered with dim lights, and then, beyond its outer edge, something that Rosalyn called the Coyote Creek lagoon: a minor kingdom of sloughs, creeks, lagoons, and salt ponds from Alviso all the way to the Bay, the blue-gray reflection of shallow water flicker-lit by the surrounding towns, mud and salt paths snaking through them like the carved handle around a mirror.

Hero knew a makeout spot when she saw one. That first night, she'd opened her mouth to deflate the mood, to say something like, You must bring all the girls here, and then she'd stopped, knowing that Rosalyn hadn't come here with any girls. The person Rosalyn had probably come up here with, for years and years, was Jaime.

I don't want you to think that just 'cause I told people stuff when I was drunk that means I expect anything, Rosalyn was saying now, her eyes on the steering wheel, hand still poised to take the key out of the ignition.

Hero had already taken off her seat belt. She had to think for a minute to remember what Rosalyn was talking about.

Rosalyn went on. I'm not like—I wasn't like outing you officially as my girlfriend, or.

Even in the dark Hero could see the nervous twitch of her jaw. I never thought that, she said. Don't worry.

But the resulting expression on Rosalyn's face wasn't one of relief; Hero saw, before Rosalyn shuttered it away, the hiccup of disappointment.

Rosalyn leaned forward, and Hero leaned in, too, eager to move on, but was thrown when Rosalyn bypassed her mouth for a moment to switch on the radio and turn the volume up loud, as they usually did on those nights. Rosalyn still had one of Hero's old tapes in there, so all of a sudden an Aztec Camera song burst out of the speakers. The chirping buoyancy of the song was so jarring that when the keyboards started in on their fake calypso steel drum, Rosalyn and Hero turned to each other and swiftly broke into laughter. By the time they'd calmed down, there wasn't any room left between them to bring the subject up again. Rosalyn tipped her face up, mouth slack but jaw still slightly tense, ready for the kiss she'd evaded earlier, and Hero—couldn't make her wait. Gave it to her.

By the time spring emerged from the February rains, Paz had a new project, which Hero later suspected she must have been planning more or less since Roni had been suspended for fighting: she wanted to send Roni to a Catholic school on the other side of the Bay, over in Los Altos, an elementary school called St. Michael's that, Paz boasted, had been named a Blue Ribbon School.

In 1980, Pol said, looking through the brochure.

Paz had gotten the idea, unsurprisingly, from Belen, who had planned to send Charmaine to St. Michael's, only the commute was a bit too far, and Belen said she got nervous driving on the highway, especially during morning rush hour. Belen had pointed out that St. Michael's wasn't all that far from the Veterans Hospital in Menlo Park where Paz worked—couldn't Paz drop the girls off at school on her way in? Belen would arrange somehow to pick them up and bring them back to Milpitas; either herself, or she'd get her husband to do it, or a friend. It'd work itself out somehow.

Paz reported all of this with a passion and deliberation Hero rarely heard from her, and which dimmed only somewhat when Pol thundered,

The only reason she wants Roni to go to that goddamn school is so Charmaine can have you as a chauffeur! What about what Roni wants?

Silence. Then Paz said, firm: It's for her own good.

If she were in the Philippines, she would only have a few years left until high school, Pol reasoned. She would skip the seventh and eighth grade, be in college at sixteen.

Well, she's here, Paz shot back.

From the eavesdropping position on the stairs where Hero was frozen, she heard Pol sigh, or exhale cigarette smoke, she couldn't quite tell.

How much is it going to cost?

Paz made a high sound of dismissal in the back of her throat. Akong bahala.

More silence, and then Pol said: Mahal—

Paz repeated that she would take care of it. Akong bahala.

Hero didn't hear them discuss St. Michael's again until one Wednesday a month later, when Paz was in the kitchen on the phone with the school trying to find out when the entrance examinations would take place and what Roni would have to bring with her.

Pol, who'd silently left the kitchen as soon as he'd realized it was St. Michael's calling, was now standing behind the couch in the living room and watching the television, his arms crossed. He raised his voice, uncharacteristically. Shh! They acquitted the police officers.

What? Paz asked, confused, then turned back into the phone, No, pardon me, I'm still here—

Pol said again, even louder, as if he were directing the words not at Paz but at whoever was on the other end of the phone: They acquitted the police officers!

Paz murmured, Excuse me, and pulled the phone cord behind her as she slipped into the garage, still in her house slippers, the door to the garage left ajar by the stretch of the cord, curly-taut, curly-taut.

For the rest of the week, Pol watched the news every evening before leaving for work, always standing behind the couch, not sitting, his arms crossed. Maúyong, he said in Ilocano, without looking at Hero. This country. That was the only thing he said.

At the restaurant, they'd been talking about it, too. There was a fucking video, Rochelle said. What else do they need? On the restaurant television, they watched the riots in Los Angeles unfold over the rest of the week. One of the afternoon regulars, an Ilocano navy veteran who'd lived in San Diego for years before moving up to the Bay and who often made disapproving and racist comments about the music that came out of Ruben and Isagani's cars when they drove up to the restaurant, joked to Rosalyn: Tell your grandpa and grandma to barricade the doors. Rosalyn barked, That's not funny.

Maúyong. Hero didn't disagree with Pol, but there was something about the way he said it that made her feel uneasy, like someone pulling a curtain down over a screen in the middle of a film. Pol had stood there for a few more minutes, and she'd tried to think of something to say.

After a moment, Pol cleared his throat and said he was going to work. Paz was still in the garage on the phone—Pol passed her without saying good-bye.

Later, Hero would wonder what she should have said in that moment; if Pol had been looking to her, as the newer arrival, to tell him that he was wrong in his judgment about the country. But no, that wasn't it. The look on his face was the look of a surgeon. A doctor-to-doctor look, waiting for a second opinion: waiting to be told that his diagnosis was flawed, that the patient in question wasn't terminal. But Hero wasn't a doctor anymore.

Roni started spending more time with Charmaine, so that there were even days when Paz told Hero ahead of time that she didn't have to pick Roni up from school, she could work straight through at the restaurant, that Belen had offered to pick Roni up along with Charmaine so they could play and do their homework together.

During those bereft, Roni-less days, Hero was adrift in the restaurant. Rosalyn tried to take advantage of the extra time, find some excuse for the two of them to buy groceries or pick up something at the house, but without Roni, Hero's moods were duller, her mind elsewhere, and eventually Rosalyn gave up, said Hero could leave early and pick up Roni from Charmaine's house.

One week in early April, Hero was helping Rosalyn bring food to some Couples for Christ event at the community center, not in the large banquet hall where Roni had celebrated her birthday, but in one of the smaller conference rooms. It made Hero oddly uneasy to be back at the community center, seeing the doorway to the large hall, seeing the corridor that led to the kitchen. Rosalyn noticed her discomfort, said, You okay? Hero shook it off, nodded.

Rosalyn entered the conference room first, which was full of adults and children, the former in small groups, gossiping, the latter either running around and hitting each other, or playing Game Boys.

Rosalyn put the food down on the long buffet tables set up at the edge

of the room, then looked around at the guests, vexed, and said: I don't
see the auntie who's supposed to give me the check. Wait here, I'm gonna
go look if she's in the bathroom or something.

Hero nodded, and hovered awkwardly at the door. An older woman
wearing a string of pearls approached her with an inviting smile on her
face, said, Are you a member, my dear?

Hero shook her head, said, I'm with the catering.

The woman's face shuttered, warmth drained from it. Oh, okay, she
said, still upbeat, then conveniently found someone else to speak to.

Hero heard a Pssssst come from outside the conference room; hers
wasn't the only head who turned toward it. She saw half of Rosalyn's
head, as she beckoned Hero out of the room.

Suppressing an eye roll at Rosalyn's customary theatrics, Hero followed, then stopped short. Behind Rosalyn was Roni, looking sheepish,
her hand closed in a fist.

Hero startled. What are you doing here?

Roni tilted her head. I was supposed to play at Charmaine's house but
they said they had a thing so they brought me here.

And what if I had come pick you up and nobody was there? Hero
said, the pulse in her throat jumping. Nobody called me at the house or
at the restaurant, did anybody even tell Tita Paz or Tito Pol—

Okay, okay, chill, Rosalyn said, putting a hand between Hero and
Roni, who looked like she'd been slapped.

I just went with them 'cause they said I had to.

The blood in Hero's temples was pulsing. And if they told you to
jump off a bridge, wou—

Just *chill*. Rosalyn placed her hand on Hero's chest and pushed her
back slightly. Roni, we're busting you out. Is that okay with you?

Yeah!

Run in there and tell Charmaine that you're leaving with your cousin.
Tell her to tell her mom.

When Roni returned, Rosalyn silently opened up her bomber jacket
so that Roni could duck her head inside, and then the two of them, looking far more conspicuous than if they'd just walked at a normal pace

next to each other, hurried out of the community center, into the parking lot, and toward Rosalyn's car—which, as was customary, she'd forgotten to lock.

All part of the plan, Rosalyn said as Roni climbed giggling into the front seat, which Hero allowed without negotiation, just this once. All part of the smooth getaway.

From the back of the car, Hero saw that Roni's fist, just the one, was still clenched tightly. What's wrong with your hand, she said.

Roni looked down, then opened her fist. There was a large wad of chewed-up gum in it.

Rosalyn let out a loud, theatrical ewwww sound. Man, Roni, that's hella gross, just throw your gum away in the trash like a civilized person—

It's not my gum.

Rosalyn turned her left signal on. The hell? Whose gum is it then?

It's Charmaine's grandma's.

Why the hell are you holding Charmaine's grandma's gum?

Roni shrugged. She told me to open my hand and then she took it out of her mouth and put it there.

Both Rosalyn and Hero fell silent, stumped. Then Rosalyn plucked and peeled the gum out of Roni's hand and threw it out of her open window, flicking several times to get it off.

That's littering, Roni said solemnly. There's a fine. Our teacher said.

They ended up driving to Serra Theater and watching the only thing that was on that early in the afternoon on a Sunday, which was *White Men Can't Jump*; the person selling tickets gave Roni a skeptical look, but handed them three tickets without comment. Rosalyn told Roni she could sit in between her and Hero, but Roni refused, said she wanted to sit in the aisle.

Roni laughed all through the movie, a sound Hero nearly blushed to hear. Rosalyn threw popcorn at Roni when she laughed too loudly and conversed openly at the characters in the movie, saying, SOME of us are trying to enjoy the film, in exactly the same loud tone as Roni's. They were the only people in the theater, so nobody was around to complain except for Hero.

Afterward, instead of going back home, still in the bubble of their stolen day, they took their merry caravan to the restaurant, where Rochelle and Jaime were already in the parking lot, the hood of Rochelle's car popped open and Jaime leaning into it, shaking his head.

Where you guys been, playing hooky? Rochelle asked from the curb where she was sitting, shielding her eyes from the late afternoon sun.

How'd you know? Rosalyn asked.

Who played hooky with you in college? I know that look.

Where's Maricris?

Went to Vallco to pick up a new outfit for the show.

Lowme, when you're done with Rochelle's car, come fix my radio, one of the speakers is all fucked up again.

What about my hourly rate, Jaime said, but he was already slamming the hood shut and coming over to the Civic. Roni ran after him, saying, We watched a movie today—!

Rochelle clambered off the curb, pulling a Twix out of her pocket. She held it out to Hero. Wanna share?

Hero had never eaten a Twix before. Sure.

They found themselves sitting on the trunk of Hero's Accord, watching Jaime, Rosalyn, and Roni toggling with the controls of Rosalyn's speaker, Roni obviously getting in the way but Rosalyn calling her Jaime's trusted assistant.

Gani's been calling me, Rochelle confided, chewing.

Hero turned to her, whipfast. Okay? And?

Rochelle lifted a shoulder, eyes on the ground. I don't know.

Hero thought of all the recent nights Rosalyn had spent excoriating Isagani's character in Rochelle's defense, before thinly admitting that she missed his dumb fucking face, Do you want to get back together with him?

I miss him, Rochelle said, biting down on her Twix, cupping a hand to catch the biscuit crumbs that fell, a string of caramel swooping onto her bottom lip before she licked it up. I don't know what that means. He says he's been acting like an idiot. He—he says he's ready to have kids.

The chocolate was melting between Hero fingers. She could hear Rosalyn whining, Wait does it work now? Check if it works now—no, don't play that, play Soul Flower, play Soul Flower—and Jaime, exasperated, saying, What does it matter what I play if we're just testing it?!

I haven't told them yet, Rochelle said. You're the only one who knows so far.

Me?

You don't know him that well, so I figure you won't judge him as hard as they do, Rochelle said, gazing at Rosalyn and Jaime. Hero could hear in Rochelle's voice that the word *him* also meant *me*.

Do you love him?

Rochelle nodded. She finished her Twix, licked her fingers, then groaned into her hands. Then she looked up and nodded again.

Hero exhaled, heavy. Do you trust him? Does he make you feel safe?

Rochelle frowned. Is it bad if I say no to the first question but yes to the second one?

Hero stared at her. Well—

I know! Rochelle dug the heel of one hand into her eye. But what am I gonna do? When I think about getting old, when I think about—I don't know, the person I want to see at my deathbed, I can't imagine anyone but Gani. He's my first love. But that's probably dumb. People aren't supposed to stay with their first loves. I fucking *know* that.

That's not necessarily true.

Rochelle crumpled the Twix wrapper in her hands. What happened with your first love?

Hero watched Jaime smack the back of Rosalyn's head, lightly, as she turned the volume up so loud that Roni scrambled out of the car, hands over her ears.

Nothing happened between us, Hero answered.

When was that?

A while ago. A long time ago.

Do you regret it?

Hero thought about it. Sometimes, she said.

Rochelle bit at her thumbnail. Do you think I'm gonna regret it? If I don't give him another chance.

Hero finished the rest of her Twix. You'll find out either way, she said.

They were quiet for a while, and then Hero felt the weight of a gaze on her. Rochelle was watching her watch Rosalyn, Pharcyde's Soul Flower (Remix) echoing from the parking lot all the way to North Milpitas Boulevard, a song so blooming and joyous Hero felt as though she could practically hear the weather in it: sun-hot cars in driveways, sweaty beer bottles, the feeling of pulling the damp collar of a shirt away from a body. It was almost evening but the song made it feel like it was daylight all day, sunshine blaring down on them, warming everything it touched, thawing Hero all the way through the skin, into the bones, down deep into the marrow. I mean, you got it pretty bad yourself, Rochelle teased, trying to sound upbeat and not quite getting there. Hero didn't even try to pretend like she wasn't watching Rosalyn; didn't even try to pretend like she wanted to look away.

When Hero and Roni finally came home, Hero waited for Paz or Pol to bring up the fact that she'd more or less absconded with the girl for the entire day; that Belen had noticed the girl was missing and had been reliably informed of her whereabouts. Instead she only heard Paz ask Roni if she'd had a good time at Charmaine's house; only heard Roni reply, Yeah, it was fun.

Hero showed up to work and found the restaurant empty, blinds drawn, CLOSED sign hanging unmoved on the door, all the lights still off. The restaurant was always open at seven, at least an hour before Hero ever showed up after dropping Roni off at school.

She walked over to the salon, eyes scanning the parking lot. Neither Rosalyn's Civic nor Boy's truck were anywhere to be seen. Mai greeted her when she opened the door and the bells rang, used to her by now. Not long after she'd started working at the restaurant, Hero had taken up Rosalyn's suggestion to get her hair cut at Mai's salon every now and then; nothing fancy, just a simple trim to keep the length of her hair mid-back. Rosalyn sometimes jokingly volunteered herself for the job, but when Hero said she was fine with that, lacking the vanity to be wary of Rosalyn's limited skills, Rosalyn chickened out.

Has Rosalyn come in?

Mai shook her head. No, but she doesn't start until noon today.

Do you know why the restaurant's closed?

No, is it? Adela's not there?

Hero shook her head. Mai's brow rose. I don't know. You want to call somebody?

Could I?

Mai waved her toward the phone at the counter near the door, where Rosalyn sometimes sat and wrote people in for their appointments. Hero knew Rosalyn's number by heart, knew she wasn't dialing it wrong, but still she dialed it again and again. No one picked up. She paged Rosalyn twice, then paged Jaime three times, knowing that Jaime was more reliable at answering his pages, both times leaving the number at the salon. She waited there for a while, eyes on the parking lot, waiting to see if the Civic or the truck would show up.

The phone at the salon rang again, and she leapt for it, not even thinking that it might be a client. Hello—uh, hello Mai's Hair and Beauty, Hero amended.

Hero?

Hero felt herself slacken with relief. Jaime? Do—

We're at Kaiser, Jaime said.

Adela had woken up in the middle of the night to pee, only to notice Boy unresponsive next to her. She'd called 911, and the ambulance had sped the two of them to Kaiser, Rosalyn and JR tailgating in the Civic behind them, Rosalyn wearing her sweatpants and Hero's Baguio T-shirt, an old pair of oversized tsinelas not safe enough to drive in. Boy had a heart attack overnight, and then another one in the early hours of the morning. They called his death at 7:29 a.m.

Hero broke the speed limit to follow the directions Jaime gave her to Kaiser, and by the time she parked in the visitor's area, her hands were stiff and burning-sore, on top of the customary cold-weather ache in the joints that started in November and lasted until March. At the front desk, she gave Boy's name, then remembered that of course Boy wasn't his real name, but she didn't know his real name. She was aware that she'd started alternately babbling and freezing, claiming that she was there for the grandfather of Rosalyn Cabugao, the husband of Adela Cabugao, was there a Cabugao that had been admitted the night before— and then Jaime and Isagani appeared next to her, both of them in security guard uniforms. She's with us, Jaime said to the receptionist.

You work at Kaiser? was the first thing she said, addressed crazily to Gani, thinking to herself that she hadn't even known, Rochelle hadn't said anything about it when they'd last talked, had that been part of why they'd gotten back together, was he giving up DJ-ing full time, or.

I just started last month, Gani said gently. Jaime hooked me up.

Come on, Jaime said.

Rosalyn, Adela, Rhea, and JR were in the hospital room with Boy, eyes closed on the bed. Later, Hero found out that their insurance only gave them access to a shared room, but a Filipina nurse who knew Rhea had given them a private room that was going unused. Adela was holding Boy's hand, murmuring prayers, stroking his face. Both Rhea and Rosalyn were sitting in chairs next to the bed, blank with shock. JR was the only one crying, his face stern, wiping angrily at the tears slipping down his cheeks.

Rosalyn, Jaime said. Rosalyn didn't look up. He went over to her, knelt down and put his hand on her knee. Rosalyn. Hero's here.

Rosalyn looked up at Jaime, the misery on her face childlike, their noses an inch apart.

Hey, Jaime said quietly. I said, Hero's here.

It's okay, Hero said from the other side of the room. Lola Adela, I'm so sorry.

Adela didn't look up from her prayers, but nodded slightly in Hero's direction, her eyes fixed on her husband, prayers unfinished. Rosalyn joined her grandmother at Boy's side, hands creeping up to clutch at the blankets around Boy's feet, feeling around his toes and heels, salvaging for some last living part of him, somewhere, anywhere.

Rosalyn, Rhea said, eyes on her daughter, coming to life, her voice strained and hard. Rosalyn, don't cry on him. Rosalyn. Don't let your tears fall on—

Rosalyn shouted, I KNOW!

JR was still crying, far enough away from the body so as to not incur the wrath of Rhea's superstition. Hero knew the rule, too. No tears from the living on the bodies of the dead, or the person crying would soon follow. Rhea, usually so hostile to superstition, to anything that smacked of her mother's work, was now observing the tradition like a hawk. But Hero couldn't blame Rhea for wanting Rosalyn and JR to be safe; Hero would have said the same.

Jaime put an arm around Rosalyn's stomach, holding her back or holding her up. Let's get some water. Come on.

I'm not leaving.

Hero wants some water. Let's go.

Hero came up next to Rosalyn, didn't know whether she should touch her. There's a vending machine outside, she told Jaime over Rosalyn's head. Jaime's teeth looked like they were clenched, trying to pull at Rosalyn's body without being rough with her. Rosalyn. Come on.

Rosalyn let herself be walked out of the room. At the vending machines, Jaime bought a Pepsi, then a Dr Pepper. He handed the Dr Pepper to Hero, cracked open the Pepsi and held it up to Rosalyn, who hadn't moved. Drink something, Jaime said.

Rosalyn's head snapped up to Hero. How'd you get here? Did Jaime pick you up?

I drove here, Hero said.

Rosalyn pushed at Hero so hard the unopened Dr Pepper fell out of her hands.

Are you fucking out of your mind? What if you— Then Rosalyn's voice lowered to a whisper, with no less venom in it. What if you'd been pulled over? What if some CHP cop saw that you didn't have a license and looked you up?! You could've been—

You should drink something, Hero said, nodding at Jaime, who was now holding both cans.

Go home now, Rosalyn ordered. Jaime, you drive her.

My car's already here, what am I going to do with it? Hero asked, exasperated. We drive to the city all the time. Don't—

I don't care. Leave me your keys, I'll get JR to drive my car home.

I want to be here if you need me.

I don't, Rosalyn said. She turned to Jaime. Get her keys. Drive her home. Now.

Rosalyn, Jaime said.

If I see either of you still here in a half an hour, I'll never talk to you again. I don't care.

Rosalyn stalked down the corridor, back the way they'd come. Then she turned her head and called to Jaime without looking at them: When you drop her off, go back to work. Your break's been over for two hours.

Hero glanced at Jaime, who stood there staring after her in his uniform, hair gelled, baton in a holster at his side, lanyard with ID hanging from his neck. A photo of him, much younger, unsmiling. JAIME CABRAL.

I'll stay in the waiting room out by the entrance, Hero said. They have to talk to the doctor and sign some papers, I'll keep an eye out for when they get out.

Hero sat in the waiting room and read the latest magazines without really understanding any of them, the bland, pitiless confidence of the English blurring into one unintelligible article; *Vogue* and *U.S. News and World Report* and *Newsweek* and *Time* and *National Geographic*. Jaime stood at his post by the entrance, sentinel-stiff, only occasionally talking to Gani when he made his rounds every hour and passed by Gani's station on the other side of the hospital.

Not more than an hour later, Jaime poked his head in and said, You eat breakfast yet? Gani got us some food on his break.

They ate McDonald's on the hood of Jaime's car, a Filet-O-Fish for Jaime—I'm trying to be healthy, he explained—and a cheeseburger for Hero, chicken nuggets to share, and a large order of fries. Neither of them looked expressly at the entrance to the hospital, but both of their bodies were aligned on the hood in such a way that they'd immediately see anyone who left.

As they were eating, Hero finally saw Rosalyn and JR passing through the front glass doors. Rosalyn spotted them immediately. She mumbled something to JR, who made his way over to the Civic while Rosalyn approached.

What did I fucking say.

We're having lunch, Jaime said, wiping his hands with a napkin.

Jaime—Rosalyn folded a hand over her eyes. Her shoulders slumped. Mom and Grandma are going with him to the mortuary. Then they'll bring him home. The burial's next Thursday at Redwood Memorial. In Fremont.

I know where it is, Jaime said. Gani said Rochelle's calling people.

Okay, Rosalyn said. We're going home to get the house ready.

Hero looked through the rear window, into the car, where JR was in the passenger seat of the Civic, bent over, face buried between his knees. Can you drive?

Rosalyn lifted her chin in a dismissive nod. You're gonna go pick Roni up?

Hero nodded. You want us to help you at the house—

Rosalyn shook her head. Just. Come get some books and stuff out of my car. I was supposed to lend them to Roni today. She—we're not going to open the restaurant for a while. Not until after the novena. Tell Roni—I don't know. Tell her something.

I'll tell her the truth.

Rosalyn's face started to crumple, but she shook it away. Let me get you the stuff.

Rosalyn popped open the trunk and started rummaging through the mess, cursing, pushing aside a lime-green sleeping bag that looked like it hadn't been used for years and a stack of paper napkins.

I know I put them in here. I promised Roni I'd lend these to her, I promised—

Hero put her hand on the back of Rosalyn's neck, thumb aching as it stroked behind her ear. Rosalyn shuddered and went still, hunching into

Hero's touch, then away from it, stiffly shrugging it off. Hero opened her mouth to say something but Rosalyn was already talking.

Lechon kawali, man—they say it's a killer. Hero didn't say anything. She reached out again. Rosalyn let the hand remain this time. Hero put a hand on the back of Rosalyn's neck and stroked the curling baby hairs. Rosalyn still made no move to lean farther into the touch, her body taut, strangerlike, but Hero could feel the irrepressible flutter under her skin as she swallowed.

I gotta go get the house ready, Rosalyn said finally, pulling away, voice hoarse. You—drive safe.

They brought Boy's body back to the house in a white coffin, the lacquer flaking off of it, and kept him in the living room, shoving the couch out of the way. His face in repose was calm, heavily made up; there was a visible layer of mismatched foundation and powder along his nose and cheeks. Rosalyn looked ill when she saw it, but didn't say anything.

Hero brought Roni to the house in the evening, after making sure she finished her homework. She knew she wouldn't be able to keep the girl out long, it was a weeknight, even if in a few days she'd be on summer vacation anyway. Some older relatives of Rhea met Roni and remarked on how mature she looked. Ang dalaga na siya, one woman marveled, which Hero disagreed with entirely, something under her skin prickling. Roni wasn't dalaga. She wasn't anything close to dalaga. It was only that the eczema on her face was mostly gone, that the scarring around her eyes and lips had disappeared enough to reveal that she had very dark lashes and a small, full mouth. That didn't mean Roni was dalaga. But Hero wasn't going to argue with a near-stranger at Boy's wake.

After dropping Roni off at home on the first night of the wake, Hero drove back to Rosalyn's house, intending to sleep over. Many of the relatives and well-wishers had left, having been fed to bursting by Rosalyn and JR, who had begun cooking together the minute they'd arrived home. As per usual, no one who left the house was escorted out, nobody swept the floor, nobody let their tears fall on Boy's body, and if anybody sneezed they were pinched by at least three or four people within arm's reach. Boy's feet faced the door.

Jaime and Hero brought Rosalyn to her room. Despite her protests—she wanted to sleep on the floor in the living room with Adela and Boy, she said—in the end she went easier than expected. She'd been up since three in the morning, and had barely eaten anything all day; Hero knew the adrenaline would crash any minute. Jaime shoved her into the bed and told her to cover herself up with the blanket, she complained, and complained, and then fell asleep, mouth open, forehead wrinkled.

I'll leave in the morning to bring Roni to school, Hero said to Jaime. You?

I'm gonna go check on JR.

You're staying, too?

He lifted his chin in a nod. You want some coffee?

I'm gonna try to sleep. Hero looked down at Rosalyn.

Jaime followed her gaze, then nodded. Okay.

When he left, Hero turned off the lights then felt her way back to the bed. She pulled back the covers, then thought better of it, climbing on top of them instead and turning her body toward Rosalyn. Rosalyn made a snuffling sound and rolled away, curling up into a ball of herself. For a long time, Hero stared at the knuckle-like bone in the middle of Rosalyn's back, poking out slightly through her thin T-shirt.

In the middle of the night, Hero woke up to an empty bed, only the radiant trace of warmth next to her any indication that someone had been there.

All the lights in the house were off except for a small one in the living room. She tiptoed out. Jaime was asleep in an armchair, his neck bent at a painful angle, the abuloy box next to him on the pushed-aside coffee table. Adela was asleep on the couch, curled onto herself, face looking even younger than usual. Boy's casket was still open and he, too, looked like he was sleeping. Rhea was sitting in a kitchen chair next to the casket, her arms crossed, eyes open and gaze fixed on Boy's face. She made an abortive move with her head, sensing Hero's presence, but Hero backed out of the living room before their gazes could meet.

Hero went to the kitchen, but all the lights were off, Rosalyn wasn't there. She went to the window, saw that the Civic was still in the drive-way. She hadn't left. Then she saw that the blinds to the sliding doors leading out to the garden had been pulled open. When she approached, she saw that the sliding door had been closed, but was left unlocked.

She stepped onto the patio, arms going up instinctively around her-self at the chill in the air. It was too dark, and the patio light came on immediately, the new motion sensor that Boy had installed for the house last summer. Hero slid her feet into slippers that probably belonged to JR, like boats around her feet. She stared out into the garden, saw noth-ing but rows and rows of plants, until, far out, next to the fence that separated the garden from their neighbor's, under one of the old persim-mon trees, she saw the lump. A figure in a lime-green sleeping bag.

Hero made her way toward Rosalyn in the dark, seeing her own breath making white clouds in the air in front of her, stuffing her hands underneath her shirt, warming them against the furnace of her belly.

Hero unzipped the sleeping bag, and only at the sound of it, the feel of cold air rushing in, did Rosalyn stir. The fit was too tight, Hero couldn't zip up the sleeping bag again once she'd crawled inside. Rosalyn stopped her from trying. She reached out blindly and warmed Hero's hands, putting them around her own waist, then opened her eyes; warm, wretched, awake, alive.

He was old, Rosalyn said finally, hoarse from exertion. Hero's gut clenched at the swelling around her nose and eyes.

She went on: It wasn't like—it was probably his time.

He's not. He's not our biological grandpa, did you know that? Hero remained quiet, except for a small noise to let Rosalyn know it was okay to keep talking. I don't really know the whole story. I don't know who our actual grandpa is. I mean, grandma's sixty-six, and my mom's fifty-two. So. Do the math.

He wasn't our biological grandpa, Rosalyn corrected herself. She started crumbling. He *wasn't*. Shit. I keep messing up.

No—

I keep messing up, Rosalyn went on, like she hadn't heard Hero.

Everybody's being so strong and I'm—I yelled at my mom in the car over fucking nothing, over where to park at the grocery store—and she and Grandma are even getting along, just, like, getting shit done. She and Grandma and even JR, they're just cooking all the food, collecting all the donations and sorting through the money, calling people to tell them—Rosalyn started crying again, folding her face into Hero's neck.

After a while, she brought her face up, streaked with tears and snot. Did you ever know anyone who died?

Hero looked at Rosalyn's eyebrows, not her eyes. Yes.

Rosalyn's voice cracked. Does it get better?

Hero smiled weakly, brushing the wet strands away from her face, and Rosalyn half groaned, half sobbed. Oh, GREAT—

I'm just trying to be honest with you, Hero said. You fucking picked your moment, Rosalyn sobbed into Hero's chest, but she wrapped her arms around Hero's waist, her breath humid on Hero's breasts. Hero kept her back to the cold and tightened her own grasp around Rosalyn, didn't let herself fall asleep until she was sure Rosalyn had gone first.

Hero woke up just as the sun was rising. Rosalyn's body was warm, but her face was cold, exposed to the air, her neck bent at a weird angle from resting on Hero's arm, her torso curled inward like a pako, the tree ferns that Hamin used to love eating in a salad with salted egg—and at the sudden unbidden thought of her father, the face he'd had in her childhood, the twice-lightning rareness of the look he wore when he wasn't entirely displeased with her, everything in Hero choked to a halt. But then the face vanished again, as quickly as it had appeared. A pillow, Hero decided, when her heart rate slowed back down. She climbed out of the sleeping bag. Rosalyn stirred, a moan of protest escaping, then she curled up into the warm space Hero had left, greedy for it.

Hero made her way back to the sliding doors, tried to open them quietly, remembering that Jaime and Adela were asleep nearby. She wasn't expecting to see Rhea, seated at the kitchen table, longanisa

frying on the stove behind her. The bags under her eyes were prominent; in the end, she'd been the only one to stay up all night to watch
over Boy.

Hero thought of simply sneaking past her, into Rosalyn's room to get
the pillow she'd been aiming for, but there was no way of getting to the
bedroom without crossing the kitchen. She swallowed, stepped forward.
Rhea looked up. Oil in the pan spat.

Is Rosalyn in the garden? Rhea asked.

Hero nodded. She's still sleeping. I'm going to get her a pillow.

Were you out there all night, too?

Hero didn't say anything, didn't know if she should nod. Rhea's face
tightened, then she stood and walked over to the stove without saying a
word, turning over the longanisa. Hero left to get the pillow.

When she came back, Rhea was still at the stove, her stiff back still
turned, a wall. Hero hurried back into the garden, where the sun was
starting to cast light upon all the living things that Boy and Adela had
planted together.

Hero put the pillow under Rosalyn's head, positioning it so Rosalyn's
neck was supported. She didn't try to get back into the sleeping bag. She
crouched next to her on the ground, leaned against the trunk of the persimmon tree, and waited for Rosalyn to wake up, too.

Seven days later, they buried Boy at Redwood Memorial Park in Fremont. The men who'd spent the past few nights playing pusoy dos and
drinking in the garage to keep Boy's body company until burial were the
ones to carry his body out of the house, head first: Jaime, Gani, Ruben,
Arnel, Edwin, Dante. Tradition stated that no immediate relatives were
permitted to carry the body, so JR had to watch. Nobody looked back.
Afterward, everyone went to the restaurant, knowing they couldn't go
straight home or the dead would follow them. But they all knew Boy
would follow them home anyway.

The song they played on repeat at the restaurant was the same song
they'd played on repeat during the wake, Palaging Masaya by Tres Rosas.

It had been his and Adela's song, Rosalyn explained. It was an upbeat, sixties type of song that reminded Hero of the Beach Boys, bright and sunny, with a vein of minor-chord melancholy running through it. She tried to imagine a younger Boy, an even younger Adela, falling in love to the song. Adela's face had been a study of stately composure for days, but at the first strains of the song, Hero saw Adela abruptly spin around and disappear into the kitchen, away from the people noisily eating food, asking each other for more Mang Tomas, more napkins, to pass the sawsawan. Both Rosalyn and Rhea stood. Rhea motioned for Rosalyn to sit down, then followed her mother into the kitchen.

At the restaurant, a woman Hero had seen at the house during the wake but hadn't recognized sat down next to Jaime, her body turned toward Rhea's retreating one. She looked almost exactly like Cely, which was how Hero figured out that she was Jaime's mother. Later, she saw the woman again—Auntie Loreta, Rosalyn informed Hero, sounding wistful—talking to Rhea outside the restaurant, standing by Boy's truck. Loreta was holding Rhea's hand.

Rosalyn led the prayers for novena. Hero was there for all nine of the days, sometimes with Roni, sometimes alone. On the ninth day, Rosalyn recited, face translucent with grief, her voice splintering:

Our brother Boy was faithful and believed in resurrection. Give to him the joys and the blessings of the life to come.

The weekend after the last novena, Hero went to Rosalyn's house, when she knew she would be home alone, the same time they usually had sex. Rosalyn was listless and dull when she answered the door. A look of open surprise came over her face at the sight of Hero, which then turned awkward and remorseful—she was trying to figure out a way to say that she wasn't in the mood to fuck, Hero realized.

Hero pushed past her into the house, making her way toward the kitchen, bag heavy on her shoulder. From behind her, Rosalyn called, What's—

Sit down here, Hero said. At the table.

Rosalyn obeyed. Her face was gaunt; she'd lost a lot of weight in such a short amount of time, Hero observed. She'd deal with that later.

Hero poured Tanduay rum into the plastic tabo she'd brought, then put a few quarters in it. It was supposed to be basi, of course, and the coins were supposed to be Filipino. Even some of their neighbors in Vigan thought it was quaint that the De Veras performed this ritual; not all Ilocano families did, certainly not the wealthy ones. One more proof of the indissoluble indio blood in the De Vera family tree. Hero didn't know why they did it, only that they did.

She'd never before done this for another person, hadn't done it herself since she was a child, and even then, it'd been in a group of people, never alone, never just with one other person. She'd never been the one to preside over the ceremony; she'd always been the bystander, not the priest.

Hero took out a washcloth that she'd also brought in the plastic bag. She dipped the cloth in the rum, wrung out of some excess, not too much; it had to be just wet enough. Then she turned to Rosalyn.

Close your eyes, she said, but Rosalyn's eyes were already closed.

Hero rubbed the damp towel over Rosalyn's face: across her forehead, over her eyelids, down over her cheeks, across the upper lip where her fine moustache had grown in because she hadn't had the time to shave the past couple of weeks. Along her chin, down her neck, over her décolletage, into the dip of her collarbone. She took Rosalyn's left arm and ran the cloth down from the cup of her shoulder, down to the elbow, rubbing gently, avoiding a new patch of eczema on the inner elbow that had shown up the first day of the novena, then down her wrist, into her hands. She took Rosalyn's right arm and repeated the gesture.

Hero put the cloth down and said: We should have done this right after the funeral. The next day you're supposed to wash your hair in the river.

Rosalyn opened her eyes, bleary. We have a shower.

Hero nodded, stood up. Rosalyn didn't move, reaching out to hold Hero's hand, which was sore from the exertion. She didn't say anything. Take your time, Hero replied.

Amihan hadn't wanted to bury Jon-Jon. He'd told her back in Tarlac that in the event of his death, his wishes were to be cremated and scattered over the rice and cornfields in Isabela. He'd seen the way his older brother had died, unrecognizable except to those who'd loved every part of him and would have known those parts anywhere. He hadn't wanted to go that way, and so they'd made a pact that if either of them died, the survivor would arrange the pyre.

Jon-Jon had gotten caught in what they later learned was a skirmish with two men suspected of being AFP officers in civilian dress. At that point they'd been deep into planning the attack on the sawmill, and Jon-Jon had been one of the key strategists. When he first came to Isabela, he'd been defined by Amihan, his mentor and leader: like her he was taciturn and suspicious, quick to suggest liquidation at the faintest sign of treason, the first to volunteer on assassination missions or dangerous supply raids. But as the years passed, he'd come into his own as a conceptual thinker. More than any of them, he'd had a way of digesting and explaining larger ideas with a speed and an ease that far surpassed Amihan, even Teresa. The day he died, he'd just been in a nearby village, collecting what they'd come to call revolutionary taxes, the small fees paid by locals in exchange for protection and—liberation, Amihan said, eyes flinty, whenever someone wondered aloud what the difference was between the logging middlemen who took bribes, and the cadres.

He'd been shot in the thigh, the belly, and the upper arm; his face was bruised, but the swelling on his fists said he'd fought back. Whoever attacked him had left him for dead, easy enough to pass off as a robbery gone bad. Nestor, an Agta tree cutter, found Jon-Jon on the side of the road, and recognized him as the young man who'd taken over some of the early Marxist lectures, made them bearable. Nestor laid Jon-Jon out in the back of his truck and brought him to the foot of the hill where they'd made their camp. By the time Nestor got up the hill and Teresa and Amihan had gone back down, Jon-Jon was unconscious, bleeding out. On Hero's table, he woke up to Amihan gripping his hand. He said something to Amihan that Hero couldn't hear, then called out for his mother. Ima. Hero still heard that call in the middle of the night, still saw Amihan standing at the edge of the pyre, closest to the flames, her face a wet red mask. She and Hero hadn't slept together for over two years, but when the other cadres tried to get Amihan to release her hold on Jon-Jon, she refused to move—not until Hero put a bloody hand on her forearm, saying nothing.

Later, Teresa came to Hero's clinic-room, where Hero was still cleaning the table, sterilizing and rearranging her supplies. There had been long arguments among the cadres about Jon-Jon's death; someone must have tipped the army off about the impending sawmill attack, why else would they have targeted someone so important to the operation?

You don't have to be strong, Teresa said, quiet. Okay lang umiyak.

Hero tightened her hands around the cloth. You want me to cry so people know I'm weak, or so people don't think I might be a spy?

Teresa leaned against the doorway. I don't want you to not cry because you think you're not allowed.

Hero went back to wiping the table. She hadn't been a twenty-year-old in front of Teresa for a long time—the last to leave the conversation, the first to say yes to an order. She tightened her jaw, said nothing. Focused on a thin wisp of Jon-Jon's blood that was there, until it wasn't.

Donya, Teresa said. Nandito ako. Kung kailangan mo ako.

It had been the truth, and Hero hadn't cherished it enough at the time. I'm here. If you need me. A year later, the world had ended. She wouldn't make that same mistake again.

Roni had passed some exam for St. Michael's, and she was officially enrolled to begin the following school year, along with Charmaine. Paz told her the news thinking Hero would be glad, glad to no longer have to drop Roni off at school and pick her up. Hero tried to be glad about it, Roni would spend more time with her mother, every morning in the car. She tried to be glad about it, and thus had to avoid the maw of grief in her chest, yawning open indifferently whenever she let her guard down.

It was difficult to get any idea of what Roni thought about the change; she was strangely detached from the whole thing, as if she didn't quite realize what a new school would entail, that she'd have to be with an entirely different class, go to school in an entirely different city. She talked about her old classmates, or Rosalyn and Jaime and Adela, like she'd be able to see them every week. Hero didn't have the heart to tell her that things would be different.

At the beginning of July, Pol's citizenship was finalized. Hero found out because she came home from Rosalyn's one evening to find him alone in the kitchen, pouring from a bottle of Beefeaters. He looked up at her, unseeing.

Amerikano-ak, Nimang, he said, holding up a piece of paper.

Hero took the paper and looked down. *I certify that the description given is true, and that the photograph affixed hereto is a likeness of me. Be it known that, pursuant to an application filed with the Attorney General at:* SAN JOSE, CALIFORNIA, *the Attorney General having found that* APOLONIO CHUA DE VERA *then residing in the United States, intends to reside in the United States when so required by the Naturalization Laws of the United States and had in all other respects complied with the applicable provisions of such natural- ization laws and was entitled to be admitted to citizenship, such person having taken the oath of allegiance in a ceremony conducted by the* UNITED STATES DISTRICT COURT FOR NORTHERN CALIFORNIA *at* SAN JOSE, CALIFORNIA *on* MARCH 17, 1993 *that such person is admitted as a citizen of the United States of America.*

Hero had known Pol's signature since she was a child. He had even taught her to forge it on the days when she needed a guardian's signature on something and her parents were too busy with their political or social manipulation to sign a field trip release form. Pol's signature had been a distinctive surgeon's scribble, hasty yet precise, as a doctor writing so many prescriptions per day needed his signature to be, but it had a par- ticular orthographic secret in it. After his name, he wrote M.D., as in A. De Vera M.D. Hero had incorporated that tic into her own signature, whenever she practiced for her future role. G. De Vera M.D. But in the end, she'd never used it.

The signature on Pol's certificate of naturalization, however, was a signature Hero had never seen before, in a handwriting she recognized as Pol's but only through the shape of the letters. It said only: Apolonio De Vera.

As far as she knew, it wasn't a signature he'd started using in California; Hero had seen him sign checks, sign Roni's attendance folders and report cards for school. His signature hadn't changed. This wasn't it. But on the certificate was written the unmistakable direction: *Complete and true signature of holder.*

Pol held his glass up toward Hero. Mabuhay, he said, and emptied it.

A week after his citizenship came in, Pol said he wanted to take Roni to visit the Philippines. She'd never been before, and it was time for her to see where her parents were from. Paz, still wary and accommodating from her recent victory with Roni's school transfer, agreed.

We can plan for it next year, she said. Christmastime, maybe.

Pol said he wanted to go in August.

In August! Paz cried. In a month? You know how expensive that'll be? I can't take off work! It'll be rainy season!

Pol said he'd been saving up—all that cash he'd kept in the closet, Hero thought. He said he'd talked to Roni about it and she'd given her enthusiastic approval: she was starting a new school, a new chapter in her life, and it would be a symbolic trip to mark that passage into the next phase of her growing up. Pol pulled out the best flowered of all his platitudes, as if he were talking to one of Roni's white teachers on the phone, and not his wife, in their kitchen.

Paz said yes, knowing that if Pol had enough money to pay for both his ticket and Roni's ticket, there wasn't much she could do to argue. She reminded him that Roni's new school began in September. September 14, she repeated every few days.

Roni was excited, pestering Hero for information about the cities she was going to see, Manila and Vigan in particular. Saying things like And is it big, and is it pretty, and are there a lot of people, and do they look like me, and can I speak English, and what kinda food do they have, and do they have *Sailor Moon*?

Do you want any souvenirs? Roni asked Hero at the airport, her hands clutching at a backpack, bought new, ostensibly for the new school year but she'd been too excited about it and wanted to break it in on her trip.

Mm, Hero thought about it. Can't think of anything. Surprise me.

Cool, Roni replied.

Pol was kissing Paz's temple, brushing hair behind her ear, murmuring something Hero couldn't hear. Then he turned to Hero. Take care of yourself, Nimang, Pol said, somber.

She nodded, uncertain at the formality. I will.

Pol and Roni were the only Filipinos traveling with just a backpack and one checked suitcase. All the other passengers on the Philippine Airlines flight had brought balikbayan boxes, throwing their hands up in frustration when the airport scale said a box was overweight, getting into conversations that were part argument, part groveling with the airport employees, explaining that they had a scale at home and they'd weighed all of the boxes beforehand, and Please, weigh it again, sir, thank you so much, then once the employee was out of earshot, Anak ng puta.

Hero caught Pol's gaze before he and Roni were about to leave for their gate. She stepped into the hug he half-held out for her, the smell of English Leather filling her nose. Take care of yourself, ha, Nimang? he said into her hairline. Take care of your Tita Paz.

Hero nodded uncertainly at the formality, then was reminded, abruptly, of another formality, a lifetime ago. She touched his upper arm and before she knew what she was doing, said: Apo Dios ti kumoyog kenka.

For a moment Pol looked stricken—then he burst out laughing, the fondness on his face so plain Hero felt her face warm at the sight of it. His hand came over hers on his arm, and he patted it. Agyamanak, he thanked her.

As they left, Hero watched Roni's ponytail sway and waited for her to turn around. She did, once. Hero waved. Roni waved back, beaming. Pol turned as an afterthought, and waved hastily. Next to Hero, Paz's face was frozen, her eyes filled with tears. When she became aware of

Hero looking at her, she wiped hastily at her face and spun around, car keys jangling.

The trip was for the whole month of August. During their stay, Hero talked to Roni on the phone just once, the line crackling, Roni sounding remote and exuberant, telling Hero about the people selling handkerchiefs, biscocho, and Juicy Fruit chewing gum on EDSA, like it was something new to Hero.

Roni said they would go visit Vigan next. That's where you're from! Roni chirped.

Later, she heard Paz briefly speaking to Pol, asking how things were, reminding him of the dates of their return flight.

Taking out the trash shortly after Roni and Pol had left, Hero saw a sheaf of salmon-colored papers, half-crumpled and stuffed deep into the plastic bag. She pulled some of them out, shaking the pages free of sauce and dried granules of rice. It was the application she'd seen Pol filling out, months ago. BOARD OF MEDICAL QUALITY ASSURANCE, 1430 Howe Avenue, Sacramento, California, 95825. Papers that listed Pol's fourth-year clinical rotations, beginning in 1953. Certifications of clinical training, signed and stamped by University of Santo Tomas's Dean of Medicine and Surgery. Pol must have been compiling the information for months.

On the last page, a note: APPLICATION MUST SIGN THIS STATEMENT. I HEREBY CERTIFY (OR DECLARE) UNDER PENALTY OF PERJURY UNDER THE LAWS OF THE STATE OF CALIFORNIA, THAT THE FOREGOING INFORMATION CONTAINED IN THIS APPLICATION AND ANY ATTACHMENTS IS TRUE AND CORRECT. Here, Pol had put down his true signature.

There was nothing wrong with the application, as far as she could see; perhaps it was just an extra copy that he hadn't needed anymore. Maybe when he returned from the Philippines, he would start an internship at a local hospital. Just beneath the application papers in the trash can was a copy of the photo he'd taken that day, also crumpled and stained. She saw again the photo of Pol with his diamond-print tie. He looked more like Hamin in that photo than she had ever seen him look before. She turned it face-side down.

Hero skimmed through the wrinkled pages, the facts she already knew. University of Santo Tomás for his medical degree. V. Luna General Hospital and National Orthopedic Hospital for his internships. She turned a page then let in an abrupt breath. A single page, not salmon-colored. A photocopy of an old, old document.

Be it known that Apolonio Chua De Vera, having passed the examination given by the Board of Medical Examiners and having complied with all other requirements of the law regulating the practice of Medicine and Surgery in the Philippines, is hereby admitted to practice as a PHYSICIAN, is registered as such and empowered to assume such title by and under the authority of the Republic of the Philippines.

It was Pol's certificate confirming that he'd passed the board; that he'd become a surgeon. He must have needed to show it, to apply for a medical license in California. That must have been one of the official documents that he'd been receiving from the Philippines, all those months ago.

In the upper right-hand corner was a grainy picture of Pol. Not only had Hero never seen the picture before, but she had never seen this face before: young, thick-lipped and thick-eyebrowed, shiny cheeks, in a bow tie, smiling vaguely, gaze turned slightly rightward, reticent. The gothic letters, spelling out the words *Granted in accordance with the provisions of Republic Act No. 546, under the seal of this board at Manila, Philippines, this 30th of January, Anno Domini nineteen hundred and fifty-six,* with the *fifty-six* handwritten.

In this older photo, Pol looked—Hero knew it with a bolt of clarity so fierce she thought her chest would crack from it—just like her. She felt that reticent smile on her own face, the light bouncing off the high apples of her cheeks, her own thick De Vera lips, her own thick De Vera eyebrows with the same centuries-old cowlick. A kid in his first lifetime. The photograph was signed; here, again, the signature was the one Hero had always known. Suddenly, she was sure that this was the first time Pol had ever officially used it.

Hero glanced from the photo of young Pol to older Pol. She put both back into the trash.

Then, before she'd even pulled her hands back, before she'd even really let the photos go, she took everything out again. She took her time wiping the pages clean with a paper towel. She brought everything back up to her room, where she stored the papers with the old clothes, the unused bottle of Tabac cologne, the thumb exercises.

Toward the beginning of September, Paz went to the airport to pick Pol and Roni up, as scheduled.

Hero was still at work at the restaurant, thinking, unusually, about two things: her birthday and the thumb exercises. The year after a death, you weren't supposed to give or receive gifts; you weren't supposed to celebrate birthdays or anniversaries at all. But Rosalyn had mentioned wanting to do something for Hero's birthday, just to get her mind off of Boy, and Hero was considering whether or not she should let her. They hadn't done anything for Rosalyn's birthday that year, as Boy had been buried only a couple of weeks earlier, and Rosalyn had seemed angry, almost, at the prospect of her own birthday.

On the subject of the thumb exercises, it was just the sight of them when she was putting away Pol's documents that had planted the seed in her mind. She hadn't thought about them for months, but now the reminder of them, underneath her bed, pecked at her.

When she got back home, she was still thinking about it, was ready to go back upstairs and retrieve the exercises, maybe even do some that night. But Paz was in the kitchen, alone, her shoes still on.

Where's—Hero said. At the look on Paz's face, she stopped. Pol and Roni hadn't come back. They didn't come back that month. Or the next. Or the next.

America Isn't the Heart

BY OCTOBER, HERO KNEW ENOUGH NOT TO ASK THE question. Paz worked sixteen-hour days, sometimes twenty-four-hour days, and she never took time off anymore. Sometimes Hero would hear the garage door open at midnight and then take a long time to close, knowing that Paz was still sitting in her car, the engine still running, as if only her body had come back from work; the rest of her still limping its way down 237, grasping for flesh.

Where's Roni. Hero had asked it, the day Roni and Pol were supposed to come back. A week later, she'd still been brave enough to ask it again, when she ran into Paz in the kitchen, looking at a stack of papers, registration for Roni's new school, a list of school supplies. Paz was making checks and notes along the list; things she had, things she could get, where she could get them.

Is she coming back—that was how Hero had put it, the second time.

Oo naman, Paz said, still staring at the papers, brows low and voice high. Of course. If not now, then. Pol will bring her back to visit for Christmas. This year, maybe. Or next. Or I can go and see her.

Hero stared at the figure Paz made, hands dry from overwashing, not a tremor in them. Bring her back for Christmas? To visit? Is she—what about school? What about—

Then she stopped, trying to gather herself, searching for the right words, finding all the right words gone, having to make do with what she had.

She lives here, Hero said at last.

Paz put the papers down. Pol wants to practice again.

Can't he practice here? What happened to his application for a medical license in California?

Paz whipped her head around to face Hero. You knew about that?

I saw the forms. I saw he was receiving documents from the Philippines.

Paz's shoulders lowered. Sixty-two na siya, she said quietly. He would have to be a first-year intern, do everything all over again. Akala niya, his credentials would make him different from other immigrants. I told him that's not how it works here. Siguro he never submitted the forms. He wants to go back home. Practice there.

He'll still be a sixty-two-year-old doctor in the Philippines, too. He hasn't practiced for ten years. Who would hire him?

The director of Lorma Medical Center in La Union has been offering him a post there since before Roni was born.

At the mention of Roni's name, Paz's face twisted. She looked back down at the list of school supplies in front of her. Then she said,

He'll bring her back sometimes. He wouldn't—Paz stopped, seeming to realize she didn't have a firm enough handle on what Pol would or wouldn't do.

He'll bring her back sometimes, she said finally. And I can visit, too, when I'm off.

Sometimes, Hero repeated.

Paz's small hand quavered, then clenched.

Hero said, You can't let him do this.

Paz was still looking down at the list. She underlined SET OF 24 CRAYONS (CRAYOLA OR SIMILAR) and put a question mark next to it, then wrote the words *Longs Drugs or Walgreens?*

You have rights. You're her mother.

Paz lifted her gaze, meeting Hero's. Hero saw that her cheek was twitching slightly, not from laughter or suppressed tears. It was a nerve twitch; the start of the palsy.

I know your family, Nimang, Paz said calmly. Do you?

Hero had never even felt ambivalence toward Pol, never in her life. She'd only ever known what it felt like to love him, to keep the minor altar of admiration for him in her heart well cleaned, its flowers rotless and blooming. What she hadn't known was that her love was a room, cavernous, and hate could enter there, too; curl up in the same bed, blanketed and sleep-warm. She looked into Paz's face and saw in it not defeat, not anger, not even the hate Hero could feel buzzing in her hands, scraping at her chest—but acceptance. Acceptance and something worse: confirmation. Paz hadn't been blindsided. *I know your family, Nimang.* Paz had never expected to keep Roni forever.

Do you? Paz repeated.

Yes, Hero answered, no strength in the word.

Then huwag kang makipag-usap sa akin tungkol sa mga rights. Don't talk to me about rights. You know the minute they stepped off the plane in Manila, nawala ang rights ko. My rights were gone.

Hero didn't speak. At Hero's silence, Paz scoffed and turned back to the list of school supplies and picked her pen up again. She underlined the words NUMBER 2 PENCILS.

The first couple of months after Boy's death, Adela hadn't asked for any help, had done all the cooking and the gardening, but one night not long after Roni had been taken, Rosalyn had found Adela falling asleep, still standing, about to collapse into a boiling pot of sinigang.

After that, Adela was only allowed to work from morning to evening at the restaurant four days out of the week, not six. JR and Rosalyn took over the cooking in the evening, and the cooking for the next morning; they alternated who took over the garden. Rosalyn was still doing makeup on the side, but she'd quit working at the salon to help out at the restaurant. Mai said she could come back at any time, but both of them knew Rosalyn wouldn't be coming soon.

The atmosphere in the restaurant had changed, with Rosalyn at its helm; Hero would have thought that Rosalyn would be a natural successor to her grandparents' legacy, vivacious and welcoming, but the pressure of being the matron in the room seemed to make Rosalyn crumble, and her vivacity came off as overbearing and forced. Hero hadn't realized how much of the soothing pleasure of being in the restaurant simply came down to Adela and Boy's particular brand of calm, nonjudgmental openness, or how difficult that was to re-create with one of the biggest pieces of the puzzle missing. Adela took a break from her faith healing, though people still came to the restaurant looking for her.

JR elected not to go to college, and started working as a security guard along with Jaime. Rosalyn and JR were the ones who now took care of all the catering jobs that were left to fulfill. Jaime sometimes showed up when Hero was leaving for the day, to help wash dishes or sweep up the floor with JR.

At first, Hero didn't notice that she wasn't being asked to help on the catering jobs. It was only toward the beginning of one workday, when Rosalyn and JR were just about to leave to drop food off at a big Couples for Christ fund-raiser, that Hero got the sense that something was off. Rosalyn and JR were in the kitchen, stacking trays of food that Adela had made the night before, and preparing to load them into the van. There weren't any customers in the restaurant yet.

I'll help you carry those, Hero said as Rosalyn was on her way out with a stack of three trays of pancit.

No, it's fine, Rosalyn said without looking at her, continuing out the door, passing JR, who was coming back for his second trip.

I can help, Hero said to him.

JR frowned. Uh, Ate Rosalyn said that you shouldn't—

What?

Rosalyn came back into the restaurant empty-handed. JR, where's the doorstop, the door keeps banging—

I can help, Hero said to Rosalyn. Without waiting for an answer, she went to the kitchen, where the rest of the trays of food were waiting. She heard Rosalyn mutter something and chase after her.

We're fine, we're good—

You'll be here all morning and the fund-raiser starts at nine.

Rosalyn stood next to her in the kitchen and surveyed the remaining trays, over a dozen. She stacked three trays flat on top of each other and set them aside. She picked up one tray of puto, then turned to Hero.

Hold out your arms, Rosalyn said, indicating how she wanted Hero to do it, forearms flat. Hero did, and Rosalyn put the tray down, then turned to pick up the three she'd put aside. Go on ahead of me, she said, her back still facing Hero.

I can take more than one tray, Hero said flatly.

Rosalyn didn't say anything, but after a moment she took another tray and put it down gingerly on Hero's forearms. Then she stacked a fourth tray onto her own three, and shouldered past Hero to make her way to the van outside.

Out in the parking lot, Rosalyn put her trays down in the open backseat, and turned around immediately to take the two trays out of Hero's arms. Hero pulled back from her and instead placed each tray down on the floor of the van herself, slowly.

I can take more than two trays, she said again, not quite getting angry, not yet.

Rosalyn shrank. Look—

Put me to work. I'm not a child.

Hero had to choose her words precisely, coldly, beyond anger, or she was going to get something worse than sympathy, which she didn't want and had never needed; something even worse than pity, which she was perfectly fine with in principle, at least when it was wholehearted, the grip of it unforgiving and final, the way Lulay's lifelong pity and scorn had given her no quarter, held her like a vow.

Rosalyn attempted, I'm just thinking about your hands, you don't have to—

If you don't need my help then don't accept it when I offer, Hero said, holding Rosalyn's gaze. But don't treat me like I'm useless.

The lines between Rosalyn's brows were so deep they formed a number eleven. Hero opened her mouth to say it again, but Rosalyn closed her eyes and bit out an, Okay. Fine. Okay.

Okay, Hero clipped out, walking away fast before Rosalyn could change her mind or ruin it with an apology she obviously didn't want to give and Hero didn't want to receive. Rosalyn hurried to catch up, and when they reached the kitchen, she got to the remaining trays first, reaching out and grabbing hold of their edges faster than Hero could. There were only five more trays, anyway. Hero held her arms out, and Rosalyn put two trays down. When Hero still didn't move, not even remotely fucking around, Rosalyn put down a third.

Later, when Rosalyn and JR came back from the fund-raiser with armloads of steel chafing dishes and trays that needed to be washed, the restaurant wasn't even half full. Hero followed Rosalyn back into the kitchen and wordlessly put on Adela's rubber gloves, picked up one of the trays, and started squirting dish soap into it.

Fucking quit that, Rosalyn said.

It won't take long.

Rosalyn growled to herself, marched up to the sink, then took the hose suspended above it. She turned it on, then aimed it at the back of Hero's neck.

Hero jumped, away from the tray, sticky gloved hand going up to the back of her neck instinctively. What—

I get it, you're a tough cookie! Rosalyn shouted, anger deforming her face like fire curling a page. Don't do this hardass robot shit with me just because I'm fucking worried about you! Carrying every tray in the restaurant isn't gonna bring Roni back!

Hero stood there, water dripping from her nape. Rosalyn closed her eyes, the hand holding the hose dropping to her side.

You think I don't know that, Hero said slowly.

Rosalyn rubbed at the bridge of her nose. Maybe you just need to take a break. Go home—

Go home where, Hero said, thinking of the kitchen table where Roni's chair had been left empty for months; the garage door that creaked opened at midnight to let Paz in, and then at five in the morning again to let her out; Vigan where her parents had been telling people that she'd been dead for years; their new house in Bantay that she'd never seen, where she was sure her parents never spoke of her at all; or Isabela, No Permanent Address, where she didn't know if all the people she'd loved were still there, still alive, if she'd ever again see the lighthouse look of irrevocable and unwreckable love that Teresa wore when a cadre who might not have come back from a mission—came back. Hero was roaring from her chest by the second time: Go home where?

Rosalyn stared at Hero, mouth soft and open. To shove that stare off of her, Hero turned away brusquely and started to remove the dishwashing gloves, trying not to wince at the pressure and, judging from the look on Rosalyn's face, failing. She held them for a moment, about to put them back near the sink where they belonged, but found herself unwilling to cross the invisible ravine of pity between herself and Rosalyn, or show Rosalyn that her hands were trembling, all the way up into her armpits. She left them on one of the counters near a stack of dirty chafing trays, soap suds sliding down the fingers and dripping onto the floor.

In the parking lot, it took Hero a while to find her keys, and even when she found them, she fumbled them. She stood at the car's driver's side, praying she wouldn't drop them, at least. Behind her, she heard Rosalyn in the restaurant yell something to JR—*could you, for a minute*—and the door opened again.

Rosalyn stalked toward the passenger side, wrenched the door handle outward, and when the door didn't open, stared down at it, waiting. Hero hadn't even gotten in the car yet herself.

She unlocked her door, opened it gingerly, and sat behind the wheel. She leaned across the armrest to unlock the passenger side door. Rosalyn slipped inside, silent. Hero left her own door open.

Rosalyn reached across their laps and took hold of one of Hero's hands, holding it in both of hers. Without looking up at Hero, Rosalyn began lightly kneading along the meaty part of Hero's hand just beneath the thumbs, where she had probably glimpsed Hero sometimes massaging herself.

It's fine, Hero said finally. I'm sorry for yelling.

Rosalyn didn't move, kept kneading. Hero moved to pull her hand away.

The things you told me at Christmas that one time, Rosalyn said, still not looking at her.

Hero went still.

I don't wanna force you to talk about stuff you don't wanna talk about. I told myself a while ago I wouldn't. But. I'm not gonna lie. I wanna know.

Hero didn't say anything, even though Rosalyn gave her a long time to answer.

Rosalyn finally added: Sometimes I think you wanna talk about it, too.

Hero leaned to the left without pulling her hand from Rosalyn's, although the movement made Rosalyn tighten her grasp by instinct. Hero closed her door, shutting out the ambient sounds of the parking lot, the nearby streets, so she could more clearly hear Rosalyn's breath quicken, could hear the twitchy scratch of her sleeve against Hero's palm.

Am I wrong? Rosalyn asked.

Hero tugged again, so Rosalyn loosened her grasp, reluctantly letting go at last, but that wasn't what Hero was after. She brought Rosalyn's hand over to her own lap so that it was in her line of sight when she said,

You're not wrong.

Then Hero was quiet for long enough that Rosalyn nodded to herself, seemingly content to leave it there for now, and pulled the car keys out of Hero's hands. I'll drive you home, Rosalyn said, opening the passenger door again and getting out.

At first, Hero thought Rosalyn was going to drive them to Ed Levin Park, which was usually what happened when Rosalyn said she would drive Hero home, and was surprised when Rosalyn, true to her word, drove them back to Paz and Pol's. She turned the engine off in the driveway, bringing the keys out of the ignition and gripping them in a fist on her knee. Hero wondered dumbly for a minute if Roni was still awake, then remembered. It was past midnight, but it didn't look like Paz was home yet; probably she was working a night shift again, another twenty-four-hour day, which had become more and more frequent. The house looked big, parked there in front of the driveway, and Hero had to remind herself again, as she always did, that it was just average-sized for one of the newer-built homes here in the South Bay.

Teresa was the kumander of our group, Hero said.

Is, she corrected herself, then didn't know if that was right, either.

Rosalyn turned, so she was facing both Hero and the direction of the streetlamp, her shocked face glowing amber. The pad of Rosalyn's middle finger was stained red with pigment, the way it usually got from dabbing color onto a client's lips. Hero forced herself to focus on that rosy middle finger as she took a breath and said,

I joined around March 1976. I was twenty, going on twenty-one.

She came with her second-in-command, Eddie. They were recruiting college students, people who were participating in the demonstrations. I'd been studying to be a doctor at the University of Santo Tomas. I'd just finished my first year. I said I could help with field medicine.

To be honest, I wasn't all that good at first. I had very little practical knowledge. I had to learn a lot as I went. I don't know if I was a good doctor, really.

Hero stopped. Do you even know what the NPA is?

Rosalyn nodded minutely, like she was afraid if she made any sudden movements, Hero would stop talking.

I heard about it on the news and people talked about them sometimes, Rosalyn said. I thought they were.

Terrorists? Hero finished. Rosalyn shrugged.

I didn't kill anybody, if that's what you're wondering. But Teresa did. Eddie did. Many people did. The only reason I didn't was because I didn't usually accompany them on the raids to stock up on supplies or weapons, or the assassination missions, things that targeted local government officials, landlords, military personnel. I stayed in the village and waited for everybody to come back. I patched people up. I treated people in the village. It worked well. To gain people's trust. We weren't just asking them to hide us, or join us. We were offering our services, too. Trying to improve conditions. That was the foundation. Safer, freer lives. That was what Teresa always said.

Rosalyn asked, How old was she?

Older than me. By twenty years or so.

So, what, was she like a mom figure to you?

No, Hero said, too fast, too low.

Rosalyn blanched. Were. Were you in love with her?

No, Hero said again, still too fast, but louder.

Rosalyn leaned her head against the headrest, twisting her leg up so it was tucked under her. Her voice was painstakingly even when she murmured, Are you sure?

Don't reduce it to that.

It's not that small a thing.

It wasn't anything you're thinking.

Hero stared at the dashboard, gathering herself. They were my family, she managed. But it wasn't family. It wasn't—it wasn't anything you're thinking.

She turned her head to look at Rosalyn, saw that was a bad idea, and turned her head back to the dashboard.

I spent ten years of my life there, Hero said, throat tight. It was my home.

Rosalyn rested her chin on her raised knee, chewed on the inside of her lip, then looked over at Hero.

Do you miss it?

What, Hero said, even though she knew what Rosalyn meant.

Living there. Teresa. Your friend Eddie. That life. Them.

Hero didn't meet Rosalyn's eyes. Nodded once, jerky.

Do you hate it here? Rosalyn whispered.

Hero still didn't meet her eyes, but this time she shook her head. Okay, Rosalyn said softly.

Hero didn't tell Rosalyn everything that night, or even a week later, or even a month later, or even years later. It was only that a small, small door inside of her had been left ajar, not thrown open, and things started to emerge, sluggish and night-blind. Rosalyn started to ask things; in bed in the afternoon or up in the foothills, gazing down at Milpitas. Never big things, but things like, How tall was Teresa, and How long were you and Amihan fucking. Sometimes they didn't talk at all, but there was a newfound resonance to their silence.

A week or so after their conversation, Hero bought a phone card at Ruby's. Now that Roni wasn't around, Hero's purchases had simplified; no more renting anime movies, no more after-school snacks. Hero bought a single five-dollar phone card, good for Southeast Asia, Hong Kong, and Taiwan. The austere purchase seemed to inspire respect in Ruby; there was a hush of duty when she rang it up, the way she insisted: Scratch it here and try it out on the phone, make sure it works.

Sometimes they don't work. If it doesn't work, come back, we'll get you a refund.

But the card worked. What didn't work, often, were the numbers she called. Hero tried Soly's at first, but she'd gotten the time difference wrong. She thought the Philippines was sixteen hours behind California, but it was the opposite; the Philippines was sixteen hours ahead. It was with an inchoate shame that she realized she thought the Philippines was behind California because she—well, because she thought that California must be in the future, ahead, and the Philippines in the past, behind.

When she finally figured it out, she called at midnight in California, alone in the house. Four o'clock in the afternoon in Manila; Soly would just be waking up from her siesta. Maybe her kids would be home from school, maybe she'd be busy—but there wasn't time for another maybe, because Soly picked up the phone.

Hello?

Tita Soly, Hero started, trying to stick to the script she'd written in her head.

Hel—Nimang?

Siak datoy, Hero said softly. It's me.

Nimang!

Hero thought she'd never in her life tire of the sound of that, Soly's cry of recognition. It wasn't the same tenor as that first day after so many years, in Caloocan, but. It was a worldly sound. The sound of being called into the world. Hero closed her eyes to it.

It's good to hear your voice. Soly's own voice was small as she said it. You should call more often.

Hero pressed her face into the phone, her eyes still closed. She saw it, Soly's kitchen, the chairs covered in plastic, the washed blankets on the sofa waiting for one of her sons to bring them upstairs to the cupboards. The smell of Johnson and Johnson baby cologne and Arpège, the sheen of eggplants on the table, Soly's favorite food, despite the fact that a doctor had told her it was aggravating her arthritis. Hero was going to back out; she wasn't ready to do this. Then Soly said,

You're calling about Manong Pol.

Hero's throat ached. Did he come to see you?

Soly didn't say anything for a while.

Then at last: She looks so much like you when you were younger. Singkit. Chinese eyes. Like nanang. She's a papa's girl, Soly went on. Just like you were with Manong Pol.

A thin needle of horror knit its way beneath Hero's skin. For years she thought she'd never reach the limits of Soly's charity, but just at the sound of Soly's voice, she knew: Soly wasn't going to betray her brother for Hero. Soly wasn't going to help her.

She's happy here, Nimang, Soly continued, her voice rising. She's happy to live with her father. He showed her a school in San Fernando—

San Fernando, so they were in San Fernando, Hero told herself, manic, fraying.

—next to Lorma Medical Center, and she liked it. She's young. She'll learn the language. He'll take care of her. You know that. You don't have to worry about her.

I'm not worrying about her, Hero said.

Oh, Soly said. That's good.

I just want her to come back home.

Soly went silent.

She's not at home there, Hero said, her own voice growing louder, encouraged by the silence. If you met her, then you know. Tito Pol knows. Her home is here. Her mom is here. She has friends here. I'm,

Hero started, then had to swallow. I'm here.

Soly ventured, You could come back—

I'm not coming back, Hero said, the first time she'd ever admitted it to anyone, let alone herself.

Soly didn't say anything, but scratchy, muffled sounds traveled across the line. She was crying. Hero swallowed again, the skin around her fingers tight and itchy where she'd been holding the phone, sweat making her grasp slippery.

Nimang, I know what you're trying to say, but Manong Pol can give her a good life here. Try not to think badly of him—

I do think badly of him.

Hero could hear Soly on the other line, exhaling heavily. He's not happy there in California, Nimang.

So fucking what, Hero said, knowing she sounded like Rosalyn and clinging to that knowledge, drawing strength from it like a well. He can join the goddamn club.

Nimang—

Roni's family is waiting for her. Tell him to bring her back before then.

Nimang, Soly tried again. Her family is here, too.

It might have been true, in a purely biological sense, but Hero wasn't interested in truth, in the pure or biological sense. For the first time since leaving the camp, she felt like the person she'd been in Isabela for all those years, the person she'd become beneath the aegis of Teresa's care and tutelage, the person she'd become sucking at the hair of a mango seed next to Eddie, the person even someone like Amihan had been grudgingly intimidated by and infatuated with—the person she thought she'd lost, not even in the camp, not even in the years of recovery, not even in California, but that very first afternoon, in the pulled-over jeep, her hair in the only unloving fist she'd known for ten years. Now clipped, coiled, feet on the ground, pouring alcohol over a gaping wound with a steady hand. That person was still there. I know her family, Hero barked, like asking Jon-Jon for her knife. Her family is here.

Soly didn't reply.

If he doesn't bring her back, Hero said coldly, then tell him he's no different from his brothers.

Nimang, Soly breathed out. I'm sorry.

You don't have to be sorry, Hero said. Just tell him to bring her back. Then she pressed her finger down on the hook, ended the call.

There was only one family eating beef kaldereta in the restaurant on Thursday afternoon. Adela was sitting at her customary table in the back, having already done all the cooking for that day, and Hero expected her to leave early, as usual; go home with a plate of pinakbet and rice that she would put in front of the framed picture of Boy that Rosalyn and Rhea had set up on the altar in their house's entrance hall, red Virgin Mary candles burning on either side. Every time Hero had come to the house since Boy's death, a full plate of food was in front of the picture, always fresh.

But instead of getting up to make that plate and then leave, Adela called from her seat:

Hero. Halika dito.

Hero clambered off of her stool and approached Adela's table. Po?

Adela gestured for Hero to sit down. She'd been eating tamarind candy again, and there were several yellow cellophane wrappers lying in front of her, next to a bottle of Efficascent oil. From what Hero remembered, Adela never used Efficascent oil on Roni during their sessions; Hero had thought, privately, that the fact that Adela hadn't been using the oil meant that she was the real deal, not a quack like all the rest.

Adela opened the bottle and rubbed some into her palms, the cool hit of the camphor and menthol briefly clearing Hero's sinuses. Then she gestured with her chin. Give me your hand.

Hero gave it to her, saying, You don't have to—

Adela lifted Hero's hand, poured some of the grass-green oil into the center of her palm, and started rubbing, smoothing the thin grease all the way up to Hero's inner elbow. Hero winced instinctively, though the pressure was mild at best. Then Adela took one of the cellophane wrappers and started rubbing the yellow plastic over Hero's palm, her fingers, her wrist, up her forearm, into the crook of her elbow. She did the same to Hero's other hand.

Hero only vaguely knew what Adela was doing, had never seen her perform this procedure on Roni, though she could guess what the cellophane was supposed to find. Sites of sala, sites of malady. The places where the cellophane stuck were the places where a faith healer had to place the most attention. The cellophane stuck to the meaty part of Hero's hands, just beneath her thumb. Adela began to massage there.

You don't have to do this.

Adela didn't look up at her, kept massaging. You know what I was treating Roni for, when she was here? Hero's fingers flexed, making to close into a fist, but Adela kept them outstretched.

May tinik sa puso. You know what that means? Like she has a fish-bone in the heart. She's angry about something. Galit sa puso niya, she's angry in her heart.

About what? Hero asked, trying to keep her voice level.

She doesn't know why. Maybe it's allergies, maybe it's what she eats, but with skin disorders ganyan, a lot of the times it's psychological. Some kids are just like that. Rosalyn was like that, too, when she was a kid. Sometimes you grow out of it. Sometimes not.

Hero was subdued for a moment, just at the mention of Rosalyn's name. So what did you do to fix it?

Adela looked up at last. You know, your thinking is wrong.

Hero was stung. That's why I'm not the healer.

Adela laughed, then leaned back, finally letting go of Hero's hand. You were a doctor, 'di ba? Na sa Pilipinas.

Hero's hand felt loose, warm, unfamiliar. She closed her fingers into a fist so the dull ache would rush back into the flesh, and become her hand again. It didn't.

Did Rosalyn tell you that?

I can just tell. You have a harder time with albularyos and faith heal-ers. Doctors do. More than nurses, so I can tell you weren't a nurse.

Hero frowned. Roni was coming to you for months. I just wanted her to get better. I didn't want to see her in pain.

Yan, Adela said, voice clear as a bell. That's it.

She paused, then said: If she never got better, then what? If I couldn't fix her. Tapos? Ano?

It doesn't matter what I think, Hero said, instead of saying, It doesn't matter anymore.

What did I say to you? Adela asked, indignant. Your thinking is wrong. According to you, healing is a relationship between doctor and patient. 'Di ba? Pero you're wrong. Alam mo, healing? Ay mundo yan. It's a world. So what you think about it matters. You're involved.

Hero went silent, then finally said: I don't understand what you mean.

Yeah, alam ko, you don't understand, Adela said, her stare fixed. So then tell me. If Roni came to you now and said, Ate Hero, ako ang sira? Am I sira? Then? Anong sasabihin mo sa kanya? What would you say to her?

Sira was too big a word, there wasn't even really an equivalent for it in Ilocano, or at least Hero couldn't remember what it might be. Sira was—broken, damaged, defective, once good but left in warmth to rot, now covered in fine mold. A car's engine could be sira, a week-old adobo could be sira, a torn shirt could be sira, a future could be sira, a village after a typhoon could be sira, a young girl with pus-leaking eczema and a penchant for throwing punches could be sira.

Was Roni sira? Roni in tank tops and flip-flops and covered in scars, Roni eating microwave pizza, Roni still with a gap in her teeth from that early fight, a tiny chip of adulthood just starting to jut out from her gum. Roni the warmth at Hero's hip, Roni the lingering smell in the living room, on the couch, in Hero's car—the smell hadn't gone away.

Roni growing up a playboy surgeon's daughter in Vigan. Roni, spoiled and imperious, treating her yayas badly. Roni using bleaching creams and kojic acid soap. Roni going on vacations in Cebu. Roni going to the University of Santo Tomas. Roni in the Philippines; Roni in the Philippines, forever.

Hero buried her face in her hands. The thin layer of Efficascent left on the palms made her cheeks burn icy-cool, then sting and flush with heat where the tears spilled freely over them. She hunched into the table and sobbed.

After a moment, Adela's hands came up to touch the crown of her head, the place where she'd once been soft when she was a baby, like everybody else.

Then she said the words that Hero had heard her say to Roni, that first day in the restaurant. Only now, Hero didn't have to strain to hear them. This time, the words were for her.

Huwag kang matakot. Ligtas ka dito, Adela murmured. Don't be afraid. You're safe here.

Teresa never said anything like, Don't be afraid. Never said anything like, You're safe here. At the time, Hero had admired and cherished the restraint—the fact that Teresa refused to make grand promises when it came to the lives in her hands. For reassurance Hero had to rely on her senses, on what she saw and lived, from one full stomach to the next. She'd had to know without being told that the way Amihan drove slightly less maniacally when Hero was in the car was a kind of rampart; that the way Eddie would tease her from morning until evening but then still make sure she had enough on her plate even when their rations were low, having wised up to Hero's habit of giving away two-thirds of her plate to anyone who looked hungry, was also a kind of rampart.

In her ten years in Isabela, nobody had ever told Hero she would be safe. Hero thought she didn't need those kinds of words, but then, most needs were inconstant things, mutable, malformed and full of shit. Or so she was beginning to figure out. It had been an easy, even welcome thing when she was hard and twenty, shearing her needs down to the bone, making herself into a bulwark, but. Needs weren't hungers, or longings, or lives; they had nothing to do with the fatty bit of the crab that Teresa sometimes talked about, a Kapampangan dish she'd loved growing up, taba ng talangka, the paste of fat and roe that she used to eat by the spoonful before her father told her she'd have a heart attack at ten if she kept on like that. Teresa was famous among the cadres for her high blood pressure.

Hero couldn't imagine Teresa at eight or nine, gorging herself on tiny oily crablets, but the fact that Hero couldn't imagine it said less about Teresa and more about Hero. Teresa had been that girl, too, in another life. No—not in another life. The same one. Hero was starting to figure that out, too.

Hero got back to the house earlier than usual, accustomed to sneaking into the house long after midnight. She was long used to coming home to an empty house, so she couldn't stop herself from yelping at the shadowy figure sitting at the kitchen table in the dark.

The shadow said, I was just eating, and Hero turned the light on and it was Paz.

Hero knew her eyes were still swollen, her face blotchy and used. She rubbed at her face, embarrassed; it would be obvious to anyone looking that she'd been crying. Paz wasn't looking. She was sitting at the table, hands in her lap.

Hero glimpsed something in Paz's hands; Paz felt her gaze and stiffened. When Paz brought her hands up to her mouth Hero realized she was holding a pair of dentures, the metal wiring glinting around the ivory teeth and viscera-pink base. Hero had never known until that moment that Paz wore dentures. Just before Paz hurried to refit the teeth back into her mouth, Hero saw for the first time what she looked like without them: the denuded rosy gums and the loose curl of her upper lip, collapsing slightly inward and shining with saliva.

When Paz was done, she still didn't look at Hero. At last, she said: There's pancit in the ref if you're hungry.

Hero swallowed, nodded, and went to the refrigerator. She let the cool air settle on her face for a moment while she gathered herself. There was pancit from Gloria next to a plate of old longanisa, the sausages dried up and affixed in their own grease. She opened the freezer and saw the stack of Roni's microwave pizzas, which Paz had kept buying, even though neither Hero nor Paz ever touched them.

Hero closed the freezer. She took out the pancit and longanisa and microwaved them both. When she put the plates in front of Paz, Paz didn't move. Hero had to push the plate farther toward her for Paz to jolt awake, blinking. She picked a sausage up with a limp hand and started eating it. Hero followed suit, chewing slowly with a mouth that felt stuffed with gauze. Her eyes itched.

Were you at Adela's, Paz filled the silence, rather than asked.

Hero looked up at Paz and nodded—and as she nodded, she realized that Paz was sitting in Roni's customary seat, not her own. The feeling of nodding in that direction gripped Hero with a vivid sense memory of staring at Roni over microwave pizza, startled at a child's kindness and trying not to cry from it, long before Roni had been anything to her, before she'd been anything to Roni.

Hero wanted to talk about her so badly that her throat felt clogged with it, only she couldn't manage to shape her tongue to form Roni's name. So instead she said,

She's good at what she does. Adela.

Paz formed a mound of longanisa-greased rice with her fingers and nodded warily.

Hero swallowed and continued: The healing, I mean. I think. It was good that. that Roni went to her for so long. I think Adela helped.

Maybe, Paz said, after not saying anything for too long.

It got better, Hero said, trying to fill a silence that was making dread form in her stomach. The eczema got better.

Yes, Paz said, looking down. Hero saw hesitation pass over her face, saw her shake it away and nod. Yes. It got better.

What, Hero said.

Paz shook her head, didn't say anything, but the glimmer of something that Hero had seen was still rippling there, just beneath the surface of her silence.

What, Hero said again, the worn, lived-in fear in her bones making her bold. What did—what?

Paz kept staring at the table, then finally sighed and looked at Hero, hard.

I started giving her Decadron around her birthday. Before that she only took it every now and then, but she started taking it regularly. I thought you knew.

Decadron, Hero repeated.

Dexamethasone, Paz translated.

Hero knew of it. She'd learned about it in an early pharmacology class that she hadn't done particularly well in; too many things to memorize, too many long tests. Still, she remembered the name. A gluticosteroid, usually given to cancer patients to manage their symptoms, most commonly as an anti-inflammatory, meant to treat things like edema in the extremities, most common in patients with cancerous tumors, especially in the brain and the spine. It prevented infection-fighting white blood cells from congregating in areas of inflammation, often shutting down signs of inflammation altogether by shutting down the body's natural immune response. It reduced swelling and soothed autoimmune skin disorders, but patients often became more susceptible to infection with long-term use.

Hero thought about Roni's bout with the chicken pox over Christmas. Had she been on Decadron by then? Yes, according to Paz. She thought about Roni's face, the burgeoning beauty of it, emerging from the receding scar tissue. Dexamethasone. Hero knew it made some patients irritable, sometimes insatiably hungry. Taken for years it would likely weaken Roni's immune system, thin her spine. But the eczema would begin to disappear, at least as long as she took it. Hero didn't know how Paz administered the drug, pills, or injections; she was certain Roni wouldn't have had a prescription for it. Was she still taking it in the Philippines, had Pol known about it—Hero didn't know. Couldn't know.

Oh, she said.

Whatever Paz heard in that *oh* made her lips flatten, her face harden. She didn't have to answer to Hero, and clearly didn't care for being made to feel like she did, which hadn't been Hero's intention at all; she just didn't know what to say. What would Hero know, really, about being a mother. She barely even knew anything about being a daughter.

Hero thought they were going to end the conversation there and go up to their separate rooms in silence, as usual. She was already pushing the plate of half-eaten longanisa away from her and readying herself to stand up when Paz suddenly spoke again, her voice faintly desperate—Hero realized with a pang that she must not have wanted to be alone yet, either.

The longanisa in Vigan is different.

Hero startled at the abrupt change of subject. Y—es. It's different. Smaller.

You use vinegar. Sukang Ilocos. It makes it sour. It's not sweet like the ones you get here.

Hero pulled her plate back toward herself and picked up one of the sausages. No. It's sour.

Roni will like the longanisa in Vigan, Paz said tonelessly. Hero's chest lurched. In the same blank voice, Paz went on: She likes things that are asim.

Hero's teeth tore through the longanisa that she wasn't tasting anymore. She swallowed before chewing it properly, choked quietly, and took another tasteless bite. Then she said, her voice raising with every word,

You can't do this. You can't let him do this.

Tama na, Paz said, low. Enough.

Roni can't grow up there. She doesn't belong there. Her life is here, her home is here. Her family is here.

Pol is her family.

Hero almost started laughing, unraveling. And you're what, nothing?

Both of us want what's best for Roni, Paz said. She seemed to realize she was still holding a longanisa and put it down, wiping her fingers on the rice.

Pol thinks he can give Roni a better life in the Philippines. Away from—here, from, people like.

Wala akong pakialam, I don't fucking care! Hero yelled. He took her for his own reasons, he wants to practice medicine again, you said that yourself, what the hell does he care what's best for Roni? What the hell would he know about what's best for anybody? Like every other De Vera all he cares about is himself, maybe that's all he ever cared about—

And who do you think paid for your surgery, Paz replied evenly.

Hero went still.

You think your parents paid? Your mother and father wouldn't even pick up your Tita Soly's calls when you showed up at the house. Soly had to ask Pol for the money. Even though he barely had any left, he'd been paying off all of your Tito Melchior's gambling debts after he died. Pol was the one who told Soly to tell you it was your parents.

It was sunny, the day Hero was released from the camp. She could feel the sun on her face, warming her neck, even under the hood they'd thrown over her head, making sweat spring up behind her ears and in

her armpits. Someone took her by the arm, not that roughly, and guided her into the backseat of what felt like a minivan. It was probably the Ilocano guard, she thought she recognized the shape of his hand, the large ring he wore on his pinky, which once scratched her face from earlobe to chin. She'd thought that scratch would leave a scar, but after a month there was no trace of it. They untied the rope from around her wrists and shoved her out of the car, the last hard touch. There weren't any final words, no good-byes. She was sure she was being taken to a field, or perhaps just along the side of a not-so-busy road, to be shot and dumped into the nearest ditch. She'd long accepted that inevitable outcome. When death seemed to be running late, she took the hood off herself. Pushed it off, more. She still couldn't use her thumbs. When she looked around, she didn't recognize where she was—a disused lot, with just one Dumpster filled with old wooden planks rotten from humidity. In the distance, the shape of what looked like a mall she didn't recognize, newly built. She didn't know Manila that well at all.

She'd stumbled toward the shape of the building, down the shoulder of a wide street, the occasional tricycle zooming past her contemptuously. The air around her was heavy and opaque, the damp heat settling on her neck like a shawl. She didn't know how long it took her to walk. It'd been easier to move in the camp, where she couldn't move much at all. Now she had to remember how to get from point A to point B again, how to lift her hand when a car came by and look like the kind of hitchhiker a good Samaritan might want to pick up. She'd been holding her numb hand up intermittently the whole way but nobody came for at least an hour, until she drew closer to the mall and the street became busy enough to merit a sidewalk. Just when she felt she would have to sit down to avoid collapsing entirely, a small van half-full of Franciscan nuns in gray habits pulled up to the curb and slid open the door. A man was driving. He was dressed casually; the driver, not a priest. One of the nuns, round with a large mole on her left cheek, said: Saan ka pupunta, hija? Hero, without even thinking about it, answered: Caloocan.

She didn't remember much of the car ride, only that when someone tried to feed her something that tasted like a sandwich of white bread spread with condensed milk, she gagged and threw up bitter bile, into her own lap. The nun who gave it to her—older, thin-lipped, almost noble in her bearing—asked one of the younger sisters for a towel. Hero tried to apologize, but passed out instead.

When she woke up, they were idling in a gas station in Caloocan, and someone had put a lukewarm wet towel on her forehead. The rounder nun was waiting with a nylon lunch bag open on her lap. There were three boiled eggs and two more of those condensed milk sandwiches, probably the nun's lunch for that day, and Hero used her palms to devour everything, boorish, licking sticky milk off her wrist when it dripped, gnawing the tasteless bread down to the crusts. She would have eaten the eggshells if the eggs hadn't been peeled. The older nun reached out to help her, but jumped back when Hero snarled, involuntary. They let her eat alone, the car filling with the farty smell of the eggs.

Afterward, the driver and the nuns said they wanted to bring her to a hospital. The driver's voice was kindly, accommodating. The kind of person who opened a car door to a gaunt stranger, half collapsed on a Manila street. But Hero shook her head to the kindness. Told them Soly's address. She still knew it by heart, from writing it down in the dorm registration book, under the title MOTHER'S INFORMATION.

When Soly later escorted her—practically carried her—into a hospital somewhere in Quezon City, a place Hero wouldn't be able to find again or recognize even if given a map and directions, she'd spun a long, rambling yarn about how Hamin and Concepcion had paid for the surgery, but were still angry with her and wouldn't talk to her. Paying for the surgery had to mean that their hearts were still open to her, Soly reasoned, and Hero shouldn't worry, Soly would work on them, they would come around eventually, and the important thing now was to focus on getting better. Hero hadn't had the presence of mind to say anything back then, and they never returned to the conversation.

Soly had always been angry at Hero's parents. She'd never been able to hide it. Back then, Hero thought Soly was angry at Hamin and Concepcion because all they'd done was pay for the surgery; no phone calls, no visits, only that. Now Hero understood that Soly had wanted her to believe that her parents had done at least that. She'd wanted to let Hero keep the universe in which her parents had done something.

Hero was grateful that she had already cried earlier in the day with Adela; there was nothing left inside to heave up and crest out of her. There was just a fist of emotion in her chest, but it was too tightly closed to tell just what emotion it was; she figured it was grief, or even just shock, but she knew it wasn't that, not really. It was close to the feeling of someone finally turning out a light in a room that had long ago been emptied—shelves dustless, floor bare. Every time Pol had asked her if she wanted him to call her parents, Hero had only said things like, They won't talk to me. When Soly had insisted that she was still trying to get through to them, she'd only said, It's fine. But she had never told Pol or Soly to stop trying. She had never been able to bring herself to utter that last daughterly lie: I've given up on them.

Hero looked up to face Paz, whose mouth was downturned in regret. There were mercies, and there were mercies. The fist loosened.

You were his favorite, you know.

Hero didn't reply. Paz got up to go to the cupboards and retrieve two glasses, which she filled with water from the sink faucet. She pushed one glass in front of Hero, who stared at it blankly for a long moment before finally picking it up with both hands.

He thought of you like his daughter. That's why he named Roni after you.

We're both named after Lola Geronima.

Paz smiled faintly. He always wanted to name a child after his mother, that's true. When Manong Hamin beat him to it, he was mad, but I think he gave up on the idea. When he was married to Marcos's cousin, he said Josefina never liked the name Geronima, anyway. And he loved you so much, anyway, how could he be mad for long?

When Pol found out I was pregnant, he said, *I want to name her Geronima, after Nimang. We'll call her Roni.* Paz met Hero's eyes. At that time, he was sure you were already dead.

At first, I didn't want to name my first daughter after a woman who died the way Pol thought you died. I thought it was bad luck. But I did always like the name, it sounded. Classy.

And then the way he talked about you—there was never any other option. When she came out we knew it was her name.

Roni wasn't even in kindergarten yet when Pol found out about you. It was Manang Soly who called and told him—

And here Paz spoke to Hero for the first time in Ilocano since they'd met at the curb outside the Philippine Airlines arrival area of SFO, Paz behind the steering wheel and saying in English, *I'm your Tita Paz,* then switching seats with Pol so he could be the one to drive them home.

Sibibiag ni Nimang. *Nimang is alive.*

They were quiet together again for a long time, rinsed of any remaining will to speak.

Wait here, was the first thing Hero said when the breath returned to her chest.

What, Paz said, but Hero was standing from the table, walking out of the kitchen, and up to her bedroom. When she found what she was looking for, she took them downstairs, sat back in her chair, which was still warm. She put the stained but no longer sticky papers in front of Paz.

I found them in the trash and kept them, Hero said. You should have them.

Paz looked down at the application for Pol's medical license. She took hold of the edge of the pages gingerly. Her grip became more confident when she turned the pages, saw the newer photo he'd taken.

I never saw this.

He took it before Roni's birthday.

Ah, Paz said, still frowning down at the picture. Hero reached over to point at the paper underneath the application, the photocopy of Pol's certificate for passing the board. Paz's eyes widened.

I never saw this one, myself, Hero said.

Paz stared down at the photo of a Pol neither of them had ever met.

The Pol in that photo probably wasn't too much older than the age Paz had been, when she'd first fallen in love with him.

Then Paz began laughing, covering her face and shaking her head, her shoulders alive with tremors. The dry crinkle around her eyes let Hero know that Paz was indeed laughing, not crying, but still Hero was afraid that her gesture had somehow torn apart the frail gauze of sympathy they'd wrapped around each other. But when Paz finally raised her head, she only looked at Hero and said, the words bubbling out helplessly:

Nimang. Birthday ko ngayon.

Hero heard herself shout: Anía?!

I'm forty. Forty and two minutes.

She met Hero's gaze then started laughing again, her hands curling around the photocopy of Pol's certificate, her fingers crumpling his face so the features were unrecognizable; more unrecognizable than they already were.

You're—Hero stopped, squeezed her eyes shut, then opened them again.

When she opened them, Paz had stopped laughing, but she was still smiling; a hopeless, Salvador del Mundo smile.

She said, We have Beefeaters in the cupboard. She pointed, but Hero was already standing up.

Hero dragged her chair with her, brought it to the cupboard, stood on the seat and opened a cupboard door to find the bottles of Beefeaters and Tanduay stuffed in the back. Pol hadn't finished everything on the night of receiving his citizenship, and sure enough there was a half-empty bottle of gin behind a large sack of gray-green mung beans.

She pulled the bottle out, cradling it in her arms. Paz was already pulling out two fresh glasses from the dishwasher and Hero filled each one with enough gin that it was difficult to tell the difference between the glasses of gin and the glasses of water.

You know I never drank Beefeaters before, Paz said. When I was a kid I thought it was fancy.

She took a surprisingly large swig from her glass, and at the look of shock on Hero's face, laughed. I'll have to call in sick tomorrow, she said unconvincingly.

You have to eat pancit also, Hero said when they'd downed the third glass, realizing Paz hadn't touched the other plate full of it. No, I'm, Paz held a hand up but Hero pushed the plate in front of her, put the fork in her hand, wouldn't take her eyes off of her until Paz took one small bite, then another larger one, slurping the glassy noodles into her mouth before holding her hand up, indicating she couldn't take any more.

Hero made herself a plate and started eating the pancit, too, and just the sight of her eating seemed to push Paz to take a few more bites on her own, each of them chasing every few bites with another big sip from the Beefeaters, which Hero made sure to refill whenever the glasses seemed less than half full. When they were both finished eating, they sat there, palpably embarrassed, too shy to put down their utensils.

Naksel, Paz said to herself, inexplicably. Somehow she seemed far more sober than Hero, despite having drunk much more, despite being much shorter. Hero would never have thought of her as someone with a high alcohol tolerance.

When Hero looked at her in dull, unfocused confusion, Paz said, patting her belly: That's what busog means in Pangasinan. Full. Naksel.

Oh, Hero said. Naksel. Yes. I remember. She reflected for a moment, her thoughts syrup-slow. I also know the word *morhon*.

Paz nodded. That's what we call embutido. You can also say morcon. And gali-la.

Tayo na. Let's go.

Ambetel.

Cold, Paz nodded. Malamig. She rubbed at the sides of her arms, feigning. *Ambetel* was the word Roni sometimes used when they would leave the warmth of the restaurant and have to brace against the crisp air, Roni's small trembling body coming up to nestle into Hero's warmth. Hero had quietly let her do that for months, before finally asking her what the word meant. As usual, Roni had looked at her like she was a complete idiot, then told her.

Now Hero nodded at Paz, chest constricted, and feigned like she was shivering, too. Ambetel.

The same shy, pinkish silence came over them. Paz started to smooth out Pol's picture with her thumb and instead of watching her, Hero picked up the bottle of Beefeaters and spilled it, more than poured it, into their glasses again. The next morning, Paz left for work at seven o'clock, just half an hour later than usual. Hero slept until noon, arrived at the restaurant with her head splitting open, straight into the arms of Rosalyn's squawking.

At the beginning of December, Hero went with Rosalyn, Jaime, Rochelle, and Gani to see Maricris's group perform at the Santa Clara County Christmas Fair, over in the fairgrounds in San Jose. Hero approached the event with a mild feeling of dread, only to discover that not five minutes after stepping foot onto the grounds, she was enjoying herself—she liked the rides, the carousel, the Ferris wheel, the kids running around with their faces painted clutching at cotton candy, the smell of animal shit, the long stretches of patchy, dried-out grass where families had splayed out their picnic blankets, people shivering in puffy jackets while manning grills small and large, lazily intrepid and foolhardy in the way that Hero knew enough now to recognize as Californian. Rosalyn took exaggerated delight in Hero's unexpected but undisguised pleasure, offering to get her cotton candy, to win a big stuffed animal for her at the shooting gallery. What about like a big tiger. As big as me, Rosalyn said. I already have one of those, Hero replied.

Maricris's group was set to perform sometime around three o'clock in the afternoon, which meant Rosalyn had to regroup with them at one, to start doing their makeup. They'd changed their original name from 5ive Senses to Just Harmony, after one of the five girls left the group, having caved under her parents' pressure to go to nursing school. They weren't the headliners; that was a white rock musician Hero had never heard of, and in whom the others showed no interest. The plan was to go back to either Maricris's house or Rosalyn's after the performance.

It was the first time Hero had ever seen Maricris perform—Rosalyn had invited her to their performances enough times, but somehow she'd always found her way out of it. She didn't know what she thought about the music, either saccharine ballads or upbeat tracks with a tinny drumbeat; she felt embarrassed and protective, seeing Maricris on stage in tight Lycra pants and Rosalyn's makeup. She thought of Rosalyn's old, put-away desire to be an actress, which she only talked about in bed, and then, rarely, even less than she talked about her relationship with Jaime. Would she have been able to be onstage—well, not quite like this, Hero supposed. Not as a singer. But still, Hero imagined it: sitting in a theater, watching Rosalyn lit up from all sides, being someone else for a couple of hours. The thought unsettled her, but she didn't hate the unsettling.

Next to her, Jaime and Rochelle were cheesing at her and exaggeratedly tapping their right feet on the ground—mimicking her, Hero realized, when she looked down at her own foot and saw it tapping on its own.

Rosalyn leaned in and shouted into Hero's ear, I really wanna kiss you right now. Then she pulled back, one corner of her mouth lifted in an almost-smile. Said more quietly: I won't, though, don't worry.

Hero looked at her, then tilted her chin downward in wordless invitation. Rosalyn stared, didn't move. Hero rolled her eyes, leaned over, and ate the twist of disbelief off Rosalyn's mouth, ate up the little gasp that followed, and didn't pull back when she heard, distantly, a few men starting to cheer. There was a solid, immovable weight in Hero's chest, something that resembled a burden, but that wasn't what it was.

She was having fun. She was having fun, there in the crowd; she was having fun, there in the line for corn dogs and funnel cake; she was having fun, in the backseat of Jaime's van and listening to Rosalyn and Rochelle debate the finer points of whether or not Just Harmony's lead singer was good enough to front the group and wouldn't Maricris be a better choice, if she just came out of her shell a bit more onstage. She was having fun, hours later sitting at a folding table in Rosalyn's garage and dealing out the cards for pusoy dos; she was having fun, lifting her hand to accept the beer that Jaime was putting in it. She was having fun. Soon enough, they would see each other again. Maybe for two weeks at a time. Paz hadn't confirmed anything, but maybe Pol would bring her back to visit this Christmas and Hero would once again cart her over to Rosalyn's for Noche Buena and they would play cards like they had before, Hero drunk and confident on a folding chair, a small flame of life just behind her.

Hero. Hero. Hero, someone was saying.

Hero looked up. Rosalyn was staring at her.

Can you help me with some food inside. Hero put the cards down, stood on numb legs, and followed Rosalyn.

What do you need help with, Hero said, looking around, and Rosalyn pushed Hero down into one of the kitchen chairs.

You keep spacing out.

Hero took a breath through her nose. I'm fine.

Let's call her.

Hero said, Who. Rosalyn gave her a look.

Wait here, she said, leaving for the direction of her bedroom.

Hero stared down at the phone, then at the international phone card that Rosalyn tossed down on top of it when she returned. It was the same brand that Hero had been buying.

Hero looked back up at Rosalyn, who tilted her head. You think Ruby and I don't talk?

Not now, Hero said. Let's do it later.

I don't wanna do it later. I don't wanna have to look at your face like this for the rest of the night, I've been looking at it for weeks already. Just call her like you've been doing.

I haven't been calling her, Hero said. I've been calling my aunt in Caloocan.

Hero squeezed the card in her hands, trying to draw some pain into her palms, but the hands had been better for weeks, either Adela's doing or the thumb exercises, so she had to soldier on, unmoored.

I don't know how to reach them. Pol. I don't know where they are. My aunt won't tell me. She's protecting—it's complicated.

Oh, it's complicated? Okay, never mind, then, Rosalyn said sourly.

It's three o'clock in the afternoon over there right now, my aunt won't be back from work.

Then leave a damn message!

Hero looked down at the phone. Rosalyn picked the receiver up and put it into Hero's hands.

I probably won't even get through, Hero said, one last protest. Focus, Rosalyn ordered.

A man picked up—Soly's boyfriend, or one of her sons, maybe he'd already gone through puberty and his voice had dropped since Hero had been away.

You're looking for Soly?

Hero answered in the affirmative, and waited for him to tell her she wasn't home yet and she should call back later, but instead he said: She's right here, hold on.

Hello?

Tita Soly, Hero said, stuttering at her own surprise, and at Rosalyn in front of her, back straightening with interest.

Nimang, Soly said, sounding exhausted.

I want to know where Roni is.

Nimang, I told you—

I'll keep calling until you tell me how I can talk to her.

I don't know either, Nimang.

I don't believe you, Hero said, then watched Rosalyn turn her attention to someone in the doorway to the garage, shushing them, then getting up from out of her chair to bring what they apparently had come into the kitchen for, a tray of barbecue.

Soly was saying, You don't have to believe me. It's true.

Then you at least know someone who does know where they are. In Manila? Or in Vigan? With Tito Mel's kids? Tita Orang's? Tita Ticay's?

Soly went quiet. Hero parsed the silence, and felt the fist in her ribs.

Hero asked, Are they staying with my parents?

Basang, Soly said.

Nobody but Soly called Hero basang, not even her parents, not even Pol. She wanted to say, I'm not your girl. Instead she said,

Give me the number in Bantay.

Manong Pol might not even be there anymore, Soly rushed to say. They were only staying there until Pol heard back from Lorma Medical—

Give me the number, Hero said. Please.

Nimang, they won't tell you anything. If they hear your voice they'll put the phone down. It was probably the most honest thing Soly had ever told Hero about her parents.

Rosalyn came back down to sit in the chair in front of her, mouthed, Everything good? Hero nodded once, curt, and returned her attention to the phone.

Tita Soly, she said. At least let me call to thank him for paying for the surgery.

Soly didn't say anything for so long Hero thought she might have hung up the phone in shock, and Hero was about to say, Hello, are you still there, when Soly started speaking again, the words pouring out in a flood, harsh and helpless,

He made me promise never to tell you, he made me promise to tell you that it was your parents, he made me swear on my life. But I wanted to tell you the truth, basang, I wanted to, pakawanendak—

She trailed off into sobs. Then they were silent on the phone, expensive seconds ticking away. Hero heard only the sound of her own breathing, as slow and dry and yearning as a death rattle. She couldn't think of anything to say. There wasn't anything to say. Except one thing. Give me the number, Hero said for the last time.

So who's that, Rosalyn asked, peering down at the number Hero had written down with the Sharpie Rosalyn had scrambled for when Hero had mouthed, Pen, pen, as Soly finally agreed to give Hero the number.

My parents, Hero said.

Rosalyn stared down at the numbers, then dragged her eyes, wide, up to Hero. When's the last time you spoke to them?

Nineteen seventy-six, Hero said, rubbing at her eyelid. And I'm not going to speak to them. I'm going to disguise my voice. They probably won't recognize me.

And if they do?

Then they'll hang up. Hero looked down at the number, picked up the phone again, then found that her fingers weren't working, she couldn't press the buttons, and the numbers were starting to swim together. She placed the phone back on the receiver, then lowered her head to the lip of the table and let out a breath.

Shit, take a minute, Rosalyn said.

That's what I'm doing, Hero said, irritable and grateful for the irritation.

Rosalyn was looking out into the garage. The music was less curated than it usually was, just the radio tuned to Wild 107.7, at the mercy of the evening DJs. Gani hadn't brought any of his equipment, and he wasn't anywhere near as performative as Ruben, who jumped at the chance to spin at anybody's party, brought his equipment with him as a rule. Gani was playing pusoy dos with Rochelle, Jaime, and Maricris's boyfriend, from the sound of it—Hero couldn't remember the boyfriend's name, until, Bernardo, she could.

Still looking out at the garage, Rosalyn said: I'll do it.

Hero wasn't going to let that inanity hang in the air any longer than it had to. No, she said. I'm doing it. She picked her head up again, reached for the phone.

Rosalyn pressed down on the hook, insinuated her head between Hero and the phone.

Listen. They don't know my voice. I'll put on an accent. I can say I'm a friend of Pol's or something. Heard he was in town, dadadadada. They'll give me the phone.

First of all, Hero said, even though she didn't have a first of all yet.

Rosalyn grinned, sly, like Hero didn't know by now what her heartbroken face and all its hiding places looked like. What, you don't wanna introduce me to your parents yet or something—

I don't ever want to introduce you to them.

Don't think by being sweet to me you're gonna change my mind.

Hero huffed, at the end of her rope, and Rosalyn leaned forward, her face hardening. Okay, enough now. Phone.

He's waiting for a job offer from a hospital in San Fernando he used to teach at, Hero said when Rosalyn had pried the phone from her weakening fingers and started dialing the number on the phone card. Lorma Medical Center. You can use that.

Rosalyn made a shushing gesture.

Hero waited, folding her hands underneath her thighs to keep from fidgeting with them, her head down, gaze aimed at the floor. Someone answered the phone, Hero could hear the voice from the receiver end of the phone against Rosalyn's ear. A man, but not Hamin. Not Lulay. Someone Hero didn't know.

Rosalyn, to Hero's shock, put an impeccable manilenya accent on her English, sounding remarkably like an upper-middle-class doktora who'd moved to La Union for work and never bothered to learn Ilocano, spoke English to her children and only allowed them to go to the ritzier resort beaches, not the local ones, then sent them abroad for college.

Aysus, Hero thought. She's fucking good.

Hello, this is Doktora Cruz, calling from Lorma Medical Center. May I please speak to Pol? Pol De Vera?

Apolonio, Hero muttered to the floor. Apolonio De Vera, Rosalyn finished smoothly, still in character.

Hero heard Rosalyn get put on hold by the servant, looking for Pol. Perhaps Hero could have made the call herself; she should have remembered that it would be rare for Hamin or Concepcion to ever pick up their own phone. She heard the servant come back on the line, ask for Rosalyn's name again.

Doktora Adela Cruz, calling from Lorma Medical Center, Rosalyn repeated, tone-perfect, somewhere between flirtatious and haughty.

Hero heard the servant's voice repeat the name to someone next to the phone, then heard the person repeat the name to himself. She hadn't heard the voice in years. It hadn't changed. She'd recognize it in her sleep, on her death bed, in the next world, as a ghost.

Hero heard her father say in Ilocano: Get Pol, he's out on the terrace smoking.

There was a long silence on the line. Rosalyn covered the mouthpiece with her hand and whispered, They're getting him.

I can hear, Hero said.

Her ear stayed alert to any other leaked-out sounds, but Hamin didn't say anything else. He'd probably walked away.

Hello? Apolonio De Vera speaking.

Rosalyn froze, said, Ah, then shoved the phone unceremoniously into Hero's forehead.

Wh—

We didn't say I was gonna talk to him! Rosalyn hissed in a stage whisper. I don't know what to say!

Hello, po?

Hero took the phone. She opened her mouth, closed it again. Then told herself, Grow up, and said,

Siak datoy, Tito Pol.

Ni—Pol cut himself off; maybe Hamin was still within hearing range. Neither of them spoke for a minute.

Agmaúyongka, Pol finally said, soft despite the words. You're crazy. What if they'd picked up the phone?

Bring Roni back home. That's all I called to say.

Nimang.

Just bring her home.

Nimang, Pol started again. His voice was low, like he was speaking discreetly into his collar.

What you're doing is wrong, Hero said. If nobody's told you that yet, then I'll tell you.

Nimang, I'm not going to talk about this with you. Roni's doing well. She likes it here. We'll see you again very soon. You have no reason to be upset.

She doesn't like it there, Hero said. Her voice wavered, so she forged her way through until it didn't. If she likes it there, then she likes it there because you like it there and she'll follow you anywhere.

Believe me, she added. I know.

Nimang, I love you like my own child.

What you're doing is wrong. You know it. And you'll regret it—

You don't have a say in how I raise my daughter, Pol cut in. Not even you.

She doesn't belong there.

She's a De Vera. This is her home.

Then Pol's voice turned gentle again, diplomatic, the voice of the person Hero ran to when everyone else's voice was all malice, gossip, indifference; a safe voice, serene and reserved, a steady hand before the first cut. How many times had she comforted herself with the knowledge that she was looked upon lovingly by that voice and its owner? Pol said,

I'm finished talking about this, Nimang. I don't want to fight, especially not with you.

That's not her home. You know that.

Hero felt a hand reach out to cup, warm and firm, around her knee. She didn't look up to meet Rosalyn's eyes.

You know that, she repeated into the phone. Her home is here. Her family is here.

This is her family, Pol argued.

Hero let out a sound that might have been a laugh, another time, another life. I know you don't believe that.

Geronima, I'm hanging up now.

Wait, Hero cried out, her hand reaching out in the air instinctively. Then:

I didn't know it was you who paid.

Over the phone, she heard Pol's breath catch.

Thank you for. Everything, Hero said. Thank you for saving me. Thank you for lying to me.

Pol let half the breath out. Ni—

Bring her home.

Pol was silent. Hamin was probably just in the next room, a room she couldn't imagine and would never see. Maybe her mother was there, too, smelling of Mitsouko, ordering a servant to fetch her an empanada. Not on another planet, not in another life. Still the same one. Hero waited for breath to turn into word.

Thank you for your call, Doktora Cruz. I'll wait to hear more, Pol said quietly, then put the phone down.

See how easy that was, Rosalyn said, one hand on Hero's knee, one hand slipping underneath her shirt through the back, by her neck, rubbing at the top of her bare shoulder blades. Hero kept her head bowed. Easy, easy, Rosalyn said as Hero tipped over into Rosalyn's lap and stayed there.

Rosalyn drove Hero home, parked in the driveway of the empty house, leaned her head against the headrest and said, So I might have to move out of the house.

Hero turned to look at her. What?

Rosalyn closed her eyes. Sorry. I didn't mean to tell you today. I don't even know why I said that.

What do you mean, move out of the house? Your house?

Yeah, my house, what other house, Rosalyn said. Her eyes were still squeezed shut.

My mom was asking about you. You and me. She's been asking about you since that time you slept with me out in the garden. You know. After. You know.

I remember.

She hasn't said she's gonna kick me out, Rosalyn said. But.

But she's going to kick you out.

Rosalyn lifted one shoulder, opening her eyes. Not in the first year after Grandpa's funeral, she reasoned. She wouldn't do that. So I have 'til winter to find a new place.

You can't talk to her?

What a great idea, why didn't I think of that, Rosalyn intoned dryly.

Look, she's been suspicious about me for years. She's gonna take a while to. Be okay with it. If she's ever gonna be okay with it. I don't know. We've never—Rosalyn flinched. Anyway. Grandma knows, obviously. I didn't even have to tell her and she knew. She knew about you and me before we even—like, before anything even happened, did you know that?

Because you made her call me that first time trying to get me to come to karaoke, Hero said. Right after we met.

Rosalyn shot up in her chair, only the seat belt preventing her from going any farther. What—you knew about that?

Hero shrugged. Rosalyn slumped back in her seat and clicked her tongue. Damn.

It was cute, Hero said. I thought it was cute. When I figured it out.

Rosalyn brightened. Oh, well—

Don't get carried away.

Ugh, Rosalyn grumbled. Anyway—what was I saying. Yeah. Grandma would usually back me up on this kind of stuff, but she's been so tired, and. I don't wanna pin more shit on her. Things have been good between her and my mom lately. They've gotten closer. I think that's good for her. For both of them. Whatever.

Just not so good for you.

Rosalyn threw both palms up in the air, all *What can you do?* I just don't wanna drive a wedge between them. Not when they're finally starting to get along. I have some money saved. From when I thought, and here Rosalyn frowned. When I thought JR was still gonna go to college. I'd been saving up, but.

She faltered but pushed past it. And working with Maricris is paying okay, since her gigs are getting bigger. If I went on tour with them next summer I could make even more money. Or I could get a job at the MAC counter at Valley Fair mall, maybe. It's not that far. Think of all the discounts and free shit I could get. Or maybe in that new mall they're gonna build in Milpitas. They said it's supposed to be the biggest mall in Northern California. They'll probably have a MAC counter in there. With that plus the restaurant plus my savings I could rent like a room. Maybe even a studio.

In Milpitas.

Obviously in Milpitas.

Why don't you live with Jaime?

Please, and have him on my nutsack all the time for how messy I am? Rosalyn shook her head in disgust. And what would that do, if I lived like two feet away from my mom? It'd just make things weirder. Plus she and Auntie Loreta are starting to talk again, too, and that's been good—

Rosalyn leaned forward and put her elbows on the steering wheel, propped her chin on top of her wrists. Anyway. I'll start looking for places pretty soon. Probably in those Sunnyhills apartments, right behind the restaurant. That'd be convenient.

Okay, Hero said. Let me know if you need help.

Rosalyn turned just her head to face Hero, cheek now resting on the heels of her palms. You're staying though, right? In Milpitas.

Wryly, Hero replied: With no papers, it's not like I can just live anywhere.

Yeah, okay, but you don't have to stay in Milpitas, Rosalyn said, face serious all of a sudden. Are you? Are you staying?

Even if Roni doesn't come back seemed to be how Rosalyn really wanted to finish that sentence. Yes, Hero answered.

Roni's first semester at St. Michael's would have ended the second week in December. She'd long ago lost her place in the school, and there were letters sent to the house, addressed to Paz and Pol, asking if Roni wanted to retake the test to begin the school year in the spring semester. St. Michael's had already taken and cashed their nonrefundable deposit from Paz's credit card, absentee student or not. Paz worked through all of the Christmas holidays, sixteen hours a day, double overtime paid out, while Hero stayed in the restaurant with Rosalyn and Jaime and debated the finer points of living closer to the restaurant, or maybe on the other side of Milpitas, closer to where the new mall was being built.

On one of the lull days between Christmas and New Year's, Hero was about to leave for work at the restaurant when the garage door opened. Hero peeked out to see Paz's car slowly pulling back up into the driveway, approaching the empty space in the garage it had just left that morning.

Maybe she'd forgotten something on her way to work, Hero thought to herself. Then she saw Pol in the front passenger seat.

When the car was parked, Roni was the first one to hop out.

We're back, she announced, standing in the narrow passage between Paz's Civic and Pol's long-unused Corona. Her tone was of someone who'd just gone out to buy groceries.

Hero stared down at her. Roni went up to her, head tilted expectantly.

This is when you say Welcome home, Roni prompted.

In the kitchen, Paz and Pol didn't say anything to each other, busying their hands making coffee, then busying their hands drinking it, and then busying their hands washing the cups in the sink, not side by side, but one after the other, rigid in their courtesy. Hero stared at them. She didn't know what was harder to believe, that Pol and Roni were standing right in front of her, or that Paz had taken the day off.

When did you—

We got here this morning! Roni said. She was wide awake and manic, which probably meant that soon she would fall asleep for about twenty hours. Hero resisted the urge to squeeze her upper arms and pinch her ears, make sure she was real.

We called mom from the airplane phone! Did you know they have phones on airplanes? Plus I threw up in the plane! Twice!

There had been a phone on the Philippine Airlines flight she'd been on, too, Hero remembered, though it had been prohibitively expensive to use. She'd heard other people around her using it, though, delighted at the novelty of being able to call loved ones on the ground while they themselves were in the air. The line, she seemed to remember, was famously terrible, worse than long-distance collect calls. She tried to imagine Pol calling Paz at work with one of those phones. Telling her they were on the plane. Telling her, through the shattering line, that they were on the way home.

Paz was staring at Roni fixedly. She can still enroll in the spring semester, she said to Pol without looking at him. She has to retake the test
but I can put in another deposit.

I'll pay, Pol said.

Paz still didn't tear her eyes away from Roni. I've bought all her
school supplies already, she said.

Hero was late for work, though when she looked down at Roni in the
chair next to her, she'd already half moved toward the phone to call the
restaurant and take the day off. But Adela couldn't afford for her not to
come in, not on a Saturday, she knew that—and she couldn't bring Roni
with her, not with Paz looking like she'd savage the next person who
came between them.

I get off work at four, Hero said to the room in general, mostly to
Roni. I'll be home right after. Okay? Okay? She looked at Roni. Okay?

Uh, okay, Roni said. Wait, can I give you my souvenir? I got you a
turtle thingy.

A what, Hero said, and then watched as Roni rummaged around in
her backpack to pull out a turtle-shaped keychain, its lustrous shell
carved from abalone or something made to look like abalone, bought at
a tourist shop at the Hundred Islands National Park in Alaminos, as the
handwritten scribble on the turtle's underbelly declared.

It's a keychain, Roni explained.

Yes, Hero said quickly.

Well, it looked like you didn't know! Roni said, defensive, mistaking
Hero's hasty reply for dismissal. Isn't it pretty?

Hero didn't even look at it. It's pretty.

When it came time for Hero to get into her car, Roni stood at the
edge of the doorway to the garage and waved, the same ritual she did
when Paz or Pol left for work, calling out the same words Hero thought
she'd never hear again. Drive safely, love you, drive safely, love you—

When Hero walked through the door of the restaurant, Rosalyn was
the one manning the counter, suffering through a lecture from a woman
around her mother's age, asking why she wore such baggy T-shirts when
her figure wasn't bad at all. Once freed from the haranguing, Rosalyn

laid her eyes on Hero. She put her hands on her hips, having likely pre-pared a long, labored list of insults and scolding, laced with sexual in-nuendo. But she stopped short, at the look on Hero's face.

She's back, Hero said, finding that she hadn't believed it until that moment, saying it to somebody, hearing it out of her own mouth. Some part of her still didn't believe it, knew that if she went back to the house, it would be empty as always, as it had been for weeks, months, and the entire morning would have just been another lonely dream she'd come up with, waking up inside a world she wanted to be in, and then waking up for real. But when she looked down at her hands, clasped around her car keys, the turtle looked up at her. The turtle was there, its fake abalone was there. She was awake. She didn't have to wake up a sec-ond time, to wake up for real.

Paz filed for Chapter 7 bankruptcy the week that Roni began at her new school. It was the only way she had of preventing the IRS from placing a lien on the house: she paid off her debt with credit cards, then declared bankruptcy. Rich people file for bankruptcy all the time, Paz brushed off, once she was sure that they weren't going to lose the house. It's nor-mal. Your credit score's only bad for seven years. Paz had paid off the first year of Roni's new school with the credit card before filing; they'd worry about next year, next year.

Between Paz and Pol, Hero had expected fights, screaming, or at least pained tension, poisonous silences. But Paz didn't seem inclined to reach for any of those options. Hero didn't see Paz speak to or even really look at Pol at all that first month, except for one evening when she came home late from Rosalyn's house and ran into the two of them in the kitchen, Pol's hand stretching out toward Paz across the table, and Paz stock-still, staring at him. Pol didn't turn to face her, but Paz caught Hero's eye, blanched, then looked away, tucking her hands under her armpits.

Sorry, Hero mumbled, and hurried out of the kitchen and upstairs to her room. Whatever they said after that, they whispered.

Hero tried to forget the expression Paz had been wearing. Of all the things she'd expected to see on Paz's face, she hadn't expected what had been there. It wasn't anger—or at least it wasn't anger alone. Instead, muddying the clarity of that expected fury was a look of lovestruck relief and agony, stringing Paz's entire body so tight that her back was glued against the chair, every atom of her resisting the clamorous desire to give in, to close the distance between them at last. When Paz realized Hero had seen her, she looked. Caught.

There was a difference, then, between loving someone and being in love with him. Hero felt that she would be able to resist leaning toward Pol for a long, long time.

Hero didn't have to drive Roni to school or pick her up anymore. Paz and Belen had worked out a system between themselves, which quickly became the only thing Paz allowed herself to rant about, when it came to Belen's family: the fact that Charmaine was chronically late to be ready in the mornings when Paz and Roni drove to her house to pick her up, uncaring that Paz was driving them to school on her way to work and couldn't afford to be an hour late for her shift—a fact to which Belen, who didn't work, was oblivious.

Equally, Roni often arrived at home late, either because Belen had decided to do some errand—*errand* made it sound like work, when more often than not it consisted of visiting a friend, some fellow mayaman housewife in a Chanel jacket—in between picking the girls up from school and dropping Roni off at home.

Roni returned tired and sullen. She didn't like Belen's friends, who'd picked up on the fact that Charmaine's little morena playmate wasn't anything special or issued from anyone special; the fact of Roni's father having once been bigatin or at least from a bigatin family had little bearing on the girl herself, who was still as quick to fight as ever, and conspicuously darkened by her time away in the Philippines. And she didn't like many of her new schoolmates, judging from the time after school she asked Hero,

Are Filipinos not real Asians?

Hero did a double take. What? Who told you that?

Alison Teng. She said she goes to Shanghai every summer. I said I've been to Asia once, too, and she said Filipinos aren't real Asians so the Philippines doesn't count.

Hero didn't know how to respond to that, and Roni kept going. She said we're more like Mexicans. And the only girl I like in school *is* Mexican. Alicia Galvez. She lives in San Jose and I'm invited to her house whenever. Does that mean we're not Asian?

It took a few weeks for Hero to ask Roni the question that she really wanted to ask. When she and Roni were sitting on the couch watching television while both Paz and Pol were at work, Hero began, afraid to know the answer: Did you like it over there?

Over where, Roni said absently.

The Philippines.

It was okay. It was weird. Everybody was so.

And then Roni made a gesture with her body, an imitation of someone buttoned-up and prim, hands folded, face angelic, proper.

Nobody even knew how to roller-skate! I had to teach my nephews. Did you know I have nephews who are older than me?

Hero smiled. We're cousins and I'm a lot older than you.

You're not that much older.

A lot older, Hero said. Like ancient.

Not even, Roni giggled. Then her face suddenly went solemn.

Do you think Mom and Papa are gonna make up, she asked.

Hero startled. I don't know. What do you mean?

They're fighting. Because I went away.

They're fighting because Tito Pol took you away.

Roni shrugged. But I didn't really mind. I liked it over there. He showed me the house, and the school. I kinda thought it was okay. It's just when I started to think about living there—

She stopped, thinking of the right words. Hero stared at her, tried to moderate the force of her stare and couldn't.

Then Roni said, I don't know. It's like when I didn't really think about it, it was okay. But then when I thought about it some more, I couldn't.

Did you tell him that?

Roni nodded. Toward the end. But he was already saying we had to go back. He said it wasn't right to stay. And I was like, Duh. But it's like. I guess I didn't get that if I stayed *there,* it meant that I couldn't come back *here.*

Did you want to stay there? Hero asked, ashen. She hadn't thought about what she would do if she'd managed to bring Roni back, only to find out that Roni had preferred living over there. She hadn't even considered the possibility.

Mmm. Probably not? Roni said.

Then it's good you came back, Hero said, nearly cutting her off in relief.

Roni's body curled inward, coy. Did you miss me?

Yes.

Did you think about me lots?

Lots, Hero said, her voice thankfully even. A lot.

I missed you, too, Roni said, smiling so hard the apples of her cheeks shone. Lots!

Hero had to tear her eyes away from Roni. Okay, she managed, ready to end the conversation and get back to watching television, but then Roni said, Oh and I met your parents.

Ah.

Roni didn't say anything else. Sensing that silence would turn Roni confused and unhappy, alone in her thoughts, Hero prompted: Were they nice to you?

Mm. Yeah? They gave us a big room. They had orange trees inside their house! There was a garden but it was inside the house! Is that where you grew up?

No, Hero said. They moved into that house after I left already.

Then she asked again, just to make sure: My parents were really nice to you?

Roni scrunched her face up. Yeeaaahh—mm. Kinda. They remind me of Charmaine's grandma.

Hero fought the urge to snort, then realized she didn't have any reason to fight it. She snorted. Did my mother put gum in your hand?

No, Roni giggled. Then, somber: They were kinda quiet. Kinda like you, I guess. I asked them if they had any pictures of you when you were a baby but they said no.

Hero looked down at her own lap, the dry, folded hands in them. She started pulling gently at a hangnail. You wanted to look at pictures of me?

Yeah. It's only fair, Roni complained. You got to meet me when I was a kid. I wanted to see you as a kid.

You're still a kid.

I mean a kid, kid.

You're still a kid kid, Hero said. Roni blew hair up into her bangs, vexed. Who had cut those bangs, in the Philippines, Hero wondered. Next week she would take Roni to Mai's and get them trimmed.

Did you see the retrato? Of Lola Geronima?

Yeah, Roni said. She shuddered. It was scary. She looks like a ghost. It's like her eyes follow you around the room.

Hero started laughing. I thought that, too. When I was a kid.

She's really white. Like really really white.

She had Chinese ancestors. The Chua side of the family—your Papa's mom, our grandma—comes from mostly Chinese merchants. Years and years ago.

Papa says I look like her. I don't think so.

Tito Pol probably wants to see you in her. She died when he was very young.

Roni made a considering noise. Yeah, I heard. Then she let her arms fall to her sides again.

Are Mom and Papa gonna make up? she asked again suddenly.

Hero glanced at her face to judge the expression there; she looked like she'd been thinking it for a long time. It couldn't have escaped her that if she'd stayed in the Philippines, she wouldn't have been living with her mother; that her parents would have effectively separated. I don't know, Hero told her. Your mom's trying to forgive him.

Roni threw her legs over Hero's lap on the couch, then leaned up to rest her elbows on her knees, boxing Hero in, her eyes large and searching.

How long does it take to forgive somebody? she asked.

Hero rested a hand on the short calves in her lap. Roni was definitely not going to grow up to be that tall; she might even be shorter than Paz. She looked at Roni and shrugged, trying to find the right words, settling for words.

One way to find out, she said.

She turned back to the television. Next to her, she felt Roni chewing on that answer, eyebrows stitched together, a line between them. She was getting older, one day at a time.

It feels like there're a lot of ways, Roni said finally.

So I found an apartment, Rosalyn said, sucking guyabano juice out of a straw and leaning against the countertop in front of Hero. At Sunnyhills. Right around the corner. Rent's okay.

That's great, Hero said, meaning it. Rosalyn smiled around her straw.

Then she pulled back, frowning. Yeah—did you even know about the Sunnyhills neighborhood? I didn't even know anything about it, it was just the manager of the apartments who told me, he gave me a flyer. Some white dude.

She put the juice down. Did you know that when Ben Gross was mayor of Milpitas that he was the first Black mayor of a major city in America?

How would I know that, Hero asked, bemused. I haven't lived here for that long.

Well, I've lived here for like twenty years and I didn't know that shit! Nobody tells you! I didn't even know Milpitas counted as a major city! The dude at the apartment building was saying that in the sixties Santa Clara County used to be like nearly all white, and then Ford—I think it was Ford, maybe it was something else—moved their plant from Richmond to Milpitas, or opened up a new one or something, and then they had to find housing for the workers, who were pretty much all Black. 'Cause housing was segregated back then or something, right? And the guy who became mayor, Ben Gross, worked with a bunch of people, developers, church people, law people to create housing. And then

Sunnyhills was the first—hold on, I have the flyer in my pocket. Yeah. Okay. *The first planned integrated housing development in California.*

Rosalyn started to speak louder and louder, the more she heard her own words, flapping the paper around. It says he even showed around some Russian politicians coming over to visit Milpitas! To see what an integrated neighborhood looked like! Do you know even who Nikita Khrushchev is?

She didn't wait for Hero's answer. I fucking don't! How come they don't tell you that in schools here? How come they don't even tell you about your own city? I lived here for twenty years and I didn't know that. Grandma didn't know, my mom didn't know, Jaime didn't know.

Rosalyn frowned. What's even weirder is to think that Milpitas was an all-white town before. That's what the dude was saying. Milpitas used to be all white people. But, like. I don't see any white people anywhere. Do you?

No.

And, like. Okay, I get that. They all moved to Los Altos or whatever. But I barely see any Black people here, either. So, like. What happened? If all that housing stuff happened in the sixties?

Maybe you happened, Hero said. Us.

Rosalyn looked startled. Us, she repeated.

There are reasons people live in places, Hero said, not realizing she was quoting Teresa until she was doing it. There are consequences, too.

We turfed out other people, you mean.

I don't know. But did you think it could only happen the other way around? Hero asked.

Rosalyn didn't say anything. She looked down at the paper in her hands, crumpled from hard handling.

Hero thought about telling Rosalyn that in the time since she'd arrived in California, she'd observed that Rosalyn's Milpitas consisted of the street where she lived, the streets where her friends lived, a two-mile wide boundary around the restaurant, and the Asian strip malls around town where the Filipino grocery stores and bakeries were located. Now, extraordinarily, it included the street where Hero and Roni lived. Hero didn't know how many other Milpitases there were; one for every person living there, she imagined. It seemed likely that somebody else might share Rosalyn's ferocious possessiveness over the town, without ever having even stepped foot in Boy's BBQ and Grill.

Hero asked, Have you seen that that barbecue place on Main Street, just by the overpass?

She'd glimpsed it every now and then, whenever she was driving Roni from her old school and they took the Main Street route that passed by Gold Ribbon, picking up pan de leche and chicharon when they were both hungry for a snack and couldn't wait until they arrived at home or the restaurant.

Rosalyn thought about it.

Yeah? I think so? Joe's or something? Jimmy's?

Have you ever gone in?

No, Rosalyn said, then a look came over her face. Hero recognized that look, remembered what it had felt like to tell other students at UST about Vigan only to discover from the look of terror on their faces that her perspective on the world had been so much narrower than she'd imagined, a knife's width.

It can't be the first time you've been wrong about everything, Hero said after a moment.

Rosalyn looked up at that; stirred, unconsoled. No, she agreed.

A few days later, Rosalyn drove Hero over to the complex, just to show her the outside of the buildings. She didn't officially have a rental contract yet, and she hadn't booked another viewing, so she couldn't show Hero the inside of the actual apartment. She said she wouldn't be able to finalize the whole thing until she was sure she got the job at Valley Fair.

But she pointed up to the window of her supposed future apartment and described it, her hands gesturing to indicate a studio apartment: the living area, where she could fit a sofa with a foldout bed; the bathroom, toward the back of the building, no window but the landlord had just put a new fan in; the curtained window from the small galley kitchen that looked down onto the parking lot where they were standing.

So if I'm cooking or doing something in there, I'll be able to see when your car pulls up, Rosalyn said.

Afterward, Rosalyn drove Hero back to the parking lot of the restaurant, empty and darkened except for the street lamps, all the stores and restaurants closed. Hero's car looked small and spare, the neon lights from BOY'S BBQ & GRILL reflected on the surface of the windshield.

Rosalyn pulled up alongside the car. Hero kissed her, then climbed out of the front passenger seat.

You got your keys? Rosalyn called.

Hero pulled the turtle out of her jacket pocket and shook it. She'd quickly grown to like the weight of it in her hands, the sight of its opalescent shell winking up at her from behind the steering wheel.

Okay, Rosalyn said, as Hero leaned down into the driver's side window to give her another kiss. Tell Roni I said hi.

I will.

Tell her to come by already. 'Cause she owes me like twenty of my books. And I think she stole a movie.

I'll ask her about it.

'Kay, Rosalyn said, putting her key in the ignition, and motioning with her head for Hero to get out of the way. Drive safe.

Drive safely, love you, Hero said, then stopped.

Rosalyn's key slipped out of the ignition. That was the only movement she made, for a moment that seemed to Hero to last an eternity—until finally Rosalyn turned just her head, eyes as big as dinner plates. It was a look she'd been shooting at Hero for months now, for what felt like forever, and to that look Hero had been wanting to retort, for months now, forever, *What the hell do you want from me,* which she knew wasn't something she could have said out loud, was barely something she could have even thought, because she didn't want to hear the answer pinging back in her head. It was a truth that Hero could have set her bones by: what Rosalyn wanted, she didn't have to give. Not to her, not to anyone, not ever, not anymore. Hero had known for years what it was like to want something that nobody in the living world could ever give you, and she wouldn't have wished that feeling on anyone—especially not on the woman in front of her now, face shucked bare, luminous, and so crushingly lovely that Hero's whole body ached to be far from her, starting deep in her chest and radiating out into her arms, circuiting through all the long ago shorted-out nerves and the staggery veins, lighting up the thin webbing between her fingers, sinking into all the hurt-hard places where for years only pain had come to settle, and gather, and home. Hero ached to be far from her, knowing that nearness would present a yet more grievous and enduring ache. She stepped forward.

Rosalyn's whole body shuddered in recoil.

Hero stopped moving, didn't say anything, and waited.

You get one takeback, Rosalyn whispered at last.

She lifted her index finger. It shook.

Hero squared her shoulders and looked Rosalyn in the eye. Said, I'm good.

Rosalyn's chest rose and fell as she searched Hero's face, fraught—searching, searching, searching; finding. Wait, are we still going home separately tonight?

No, Hero said, already opening her arms, already finding Rosalyn there.

By the time Jaime's birthday came around, Rosalyn had figured out a way to work *So by the way she loves me* into nearly any sentence that crossed her lips, much to the despair of all those around her, not least of all Hero herself.

Jaime wanted to celebrate his birthday at home, which Rosalyn protested against for at least a week. It's your thirtieth, Lowme, we gotta do something big, she said.

But Jaime shook his head. I don't wanna do anything big.

And not because of Lolo Boy, he said, completing the sentence that was about to come to Rosalyn's just-opened mouth. I just want something low-key.

'Cause you're getting old, Rosalyn surmised.

'Cause I'm getting old, Jaime allowed.

It was an ordinary birthday; cake and barbecue and pancit. The only thing different was that they held it at Jaime's house. It was Hero's first time meeting Jaime's mother, besides seeing her at Boy's funeral. Loreta greeted her warmly at the door, before eventually receding farther and farther away from the party, the louder Gani's DJ-ing in the garage got, 93 'Til Infinity echoing all the way down the street. Loreta probably wasn't used to so many people being in the house. The next time Hero saw her, she was on the couch with Rhea, nominally watching a Filipino movie but actually talking to each other, Rhea's hands waving expressively.

In the garage, Gani had started playing a remix of the Four Tops' Still Waters Run Deep, a version that slowed, amped, and then looped the wordless crooning at the beginning of the track, so all Hero could hear was a plantive Aaahhhhh-aaaahh-aaaah-oooh-aaaaah, while Maricris's boyfriend and two of his friends showed off a dance move they'd been practicing, probably just for this very occasion, Maricris and Rochelle sitting cross-legged on the floor of the garage, along with the girls from Maricris's group, their faces lit up by the fluorescent lights overhead, heads swaying to the beat.

As people started leaving, Loreta approached Hero to insist that she take home what felt like the entirety of the leftover pancit; two large foil trays, filled to the brim.

I can't take all this, she said. Give some to the others.

Loreta shook her head. Everybody took already. Just take it.

Behind Loreta, Rhea was in the kitchen making a show sliding leftover cake into Tupperware, not meeting Hero's eye or giving any indication of having seen her all evening.

How come Roni didn't come tonight, Jaime asked as he walked Hero to her car, not sounding quite as drunk as he'd been a couple of hours earlier. The air in Milpitas smelled of shit, like it always did. Hero had long ago stopped noticing it, except for the days when the smell was particularly strong, like tonight.

She has a lot of homework for her new school. I think she's making you a gift. Don't tell her I told you.

Okay, Jaime said, pleased. Then he called over his shoulder. Rosalyn, Hero's going now—

I'm coming, I'm coming, hold up, Rosalyn said, still holding a half-empty foil tray of what looked like an assortment of puto and kutsinta. She'd been tasked with the duty of distributing leftovers to everybody, along with Loreta.

You're going? You're not too drunk? I could drive you.

I just had one beer, Hero said, climbing into the driver's seat. Careful walking home.

Ha, ha, Rosalyn said. She leaned forward through the window and gave Hero a quick kiss. Hero hadn't even thought to look to see if Rhea was around, watching. From the twitchy look on Rosalyn's face, she had thought of it, but decided to do it anyway. Rhea wasn't watching. Hero shook the thought away. She started the car and began backing out of the driveway.

Jaime followed the car to the sidewalk. Then he started waving, a big grin on his face.

Okay, drive safely, love you! he called.

Rosalyn swiveled her head at the sound, then ran up behind Jaime to punch him in the shoulder, hard. I fuckin' told you not to say anything—

Jaime doubled over, laughing and grimacing, clutching at his injury. Rosalyn put the tray of food down onto the roof of the Supra then shoved Jaime hard into the lawn, where he kept laughing, even on his side in the grass. On the lawn, Rosalyn kept him pinned with one arm. She used the other to wave at Hero, I got this. Hero waved, honked her car horn twice, and drove off.

When she got home, Pol was seated at the kitchen table helping Roni with her homework, which consisted of building a clay model of one of the California missions, Mission San Juan Bautista. The clay was cheap, whitish, and looked difficult to mold, given the misshapen forms of what was supposed to be a Spanish-style hacienda, soldiers' barracks, a church, a plaza. They'd set the model up in an old Domino's pizza box, and used the miniature tablelike plastic ornament that came with the pizzas to keep the slices together, as the centerpiece of the mission itself. It was perhaps meant to resemble a well.

They both looked up at the same time as Hero walked through the door. She was jolted at how alike they looked; the exact same expressions in their faces, the same features, the same fatigue bordering on rage.

You're still up? Hero said, directing her words at Roni. You should go to sleep. It's late.

Roni said, I'm almost done. Hero looked at the mission, the crumbling clay roofs and poorly adjoined walls. It looked like the mission, after one of those earthquakes Roni was always having to do emergency drills for. There were a few blobs Hero couldn't make sense of; people.

I don't know why they give you so much work, Pol was saying. I didn't have to do this at your age.

How was Jaime's party, Roni asked. Was he mad that I didn't come?

Hero put the pancit down on the table. He wasn't mad.

What's that, Roni said, looking at the trays with interest.

Just pancit, Hero said. You hungry? You want some?

Roni looked at the trays, then down at her model. I'm done with the model, she said. After this I have another assignment but it's not due 'til day after tomorrow.

Let me get you a plate, Hero said, but Pol stood up.

I'll get it. Roni, take the model off the table.

Roni stood, shakily balancing the pizza box on her forearms. Hero held the box from the other end, and Roni walked her backward until they could set the model down safely on the floor away from foot traffic.

Then Roni went to her backpack and pulled out a sheaf of writing paper, sat back down at the table and started writing just the title of the next assignment while she waited for her food.

Hero sat down next to Roni, leaned over to take a look. A book report?

Roni nodded. But I'm making the book up this time.

What? Why?

'Cause the last time I wrote a book report Mrs. Kelley didn't believe that I read the book and she gave me an F. She doesn't believe any of my book reports. I used the word *virago* in an essay and she made me define it in front of everybody else to prove that I knew it. So I'm gonna make up a book that sounds like something she'll believe I can read.

Something she'll believe you can read, Hero repeated in disbelief.

Roni nodded. Yep.

Nimang, you want a plate, too? Pol called.

They'd barely spoken to each other since he and Roni had returned; she'd barely looked at him. She looked down at her feet and prepared to say no, but instead said, Yes, please.

Pol came back with two plates and two forks, started piling pancit onto the first plate, when the garage door started to open. It was just past midnight. Pol sagged with relief as the sound of Paz's car engine approached. Not long after, the doorway to the garage opened.

Paz jumped at the sight of everybody at the kitchen at once. Why are you guys still awake? It's late already.

I had homework, Roni said. Now we're eating.

You want pancit, mahal? Pol asked.

Paz looked at the plate in his hands. I—okay. Sino na luto?

It's from Jaime's birthday party, Hero said. I think Lola Adela made it.

Roni brightened at the name. When can I go to her again?

Ask your mom, Hero said, not meeting Paz's eyes, staring at a smooth swath of forearm skin where Roni's eczema had once been.

When you have free time, Paz said. Ate Hero can take you if it's okay with her.

It's okay with me, Hero said.

Roni clapped so excitedly she dropped her pencil, and had to lower her leg to the ground to pick it up from the floor with her toes like a monkey. Don't do that, Paz said.

Pol put a plate of pancit in front of Roni, gesturing for her to move her papers so she wouldn't get grease on them. Hero thought Roni's plate had been grossly overfilled, until Pol slid her own plate in front of her. The plate Pol had made for her was so full of pancit she could barely see the white of the melamine, could barely see the red and blue flowers edged along its rim. The pile of noodles was nearly three inches high. This is too much, Hero said. Pol balanced a fork at the side of her plate and didn't reply.

Paz was getting her own plate and fork out of the cupboard. She came around the side of the table and before she could begin serving herself, Pol took the fork from her hands and began shoveling pancit onto her plate in big, generous piles. Hero saw Paz open her mouth, probably to echo what Hero had said, that it was too much, but she closed it again.

Paz took her seat between Roni and Pol. She picked up a wedge of lemon on her plate, squeezed it over the pancit, then began digging into the mass of noodles, crunching along bits of pork and cabbage, her right leg slowly lifting up onto the chair, her white uniform pants stretching.

Hero started eating; it was good pancit, better than usual. Jaime's mom might have made this, she said. Not Lola Adela.

It's good, Paz judged. Maasim. They put a lot of lime in it already.

Mm, Roni approved. Yeah, it's sour.

You like sour, Paz said, half a declaration, half a question, checking to make sure her knowledge was up to date.

Mm-hmm.

Pol got up suddenly and went back to the cupboard. He pulled out a fourth plate, a fourth fork, and returned to the table.

Paz eyed him, fork suspended in front of her mouth. She didn't say anything.

Pol didn't say anything, either, but piled a portion of pancit onto his plate, larger even than the one he'd given Hero, if that was possible. He squeezed a lemon all over it, then squeezed another. He went back to his seat. Bon appétit, he said, with a crooked, formal smile. Then he scooped up an impossibly large forkful of noodles, much larger than his mouth would fit comfortably, and started eating.

Paz made a sound, somewhere between an uncertain laugh and a more certain cry. Dahan-dahan, baka you'll choke.

Hero tried to remember the last time she'd seen Paz and Pol eat together. She couldn't. She couldn't even remember the last time they'd all eaten together. Pol had been in the Philippines during his birthday; maybe he had eaten pancit in Vigan, or somewhere else in the Philippines at the time of his birthday, but Hero doubted it. Since coming back, Pol looked thinner, despite not having lost any visible weight in his paunch or his face. He was thinner but heavier, as if he'd gained all the weight in his bones.

Pol's second forkful was just as large as the first, and he shoved it in before the first was finished, so his cheeks puffed up, chipmunklike, running out of storage space. Roni started giggling at him, then forked up a proportionately large bite and put it in her own mouth, imitating him like she thought they were playing a game.

Paz tsk-ed at her daughter. Careful, anak.

Compelled, Hero started eating her own pancit faster, shoveling spoonfuls in, the thin rice noodles slipping raggedly down her throat, sometimes after she'd barely chewed them. She took another greenish lemon wedge and squeezed it generously onto the remainder of pancit on her plate, so the next bites made her eyes squint and her tongue sting.

Roni finished her plate first; compared to the rest of the table, Pol had given her the most reasonable portion. Wordless, Hero reached for Roni's empty plate and passed it to Paz, who refilled the plate, then passed it back to Hero, who passed it back to Roni, still instinctively taking care to bear the weight of the heavier plate with her palms, even though her grip had improved of late. That reminded her; she still needed to ask Paz if she could still recommend anybody for the PT. After she was done eating, she thought, her mouth still bulging.

Next to Hero, Roni started forking the pancit into her mouth with renewed fervor, having sensed that she was part of something that was happening both outside of her and yet also secreted within her, sourced from some inherited hollow, nameless and hungry and theirs. Pol was working on a bite of his own, just as enormous as the previous ones, noodles hanging out of his mouth and dangling wetly over his chin, slowly, slowly being pulleyed up past his lips.

Across from Hero, even Paz was starting to stuff her mouth, faster and faster, with bigger and bigger forkfuls of the long noodles, lips trembling, eyes wet and red, jaw tight except for the determined chewing, one hand raised to her mouth to make sure her dentures didn't suddenly pop out of place. Hero turned from Paz and caught Pol's gaze. His lips were all tremors, too, and his eyes wet, too, and those lips and eyes were still the same ones on her own face, and in a jerky fit of chagrin and love Hero cut her gaze elsewhere. At Roni, who had graduated to using her fingers to pincer heaps of the noodles straight into her mouth, eyebrows high on her forehead, looking around owlishly to make sure she was still in on the joke.

For a brief, queasy moment, Hero looked down, thinking she might have to spit some of her noodles back out onto the side of her plate, or perhaps more discreetly into a paper towel. Instead she kept chewing, pushing past the feeling, and looked up again. Pol was still working on the same bite, the noodles now off his chin and in his mouth, concentrating hard, cheeks shining with the strain. Next to him, Paz was serving herself again, hand closed around the handle of her fork so tightly that Hero could see bone. Hero knew her own hand was gripping the fork just as tightly.

Then, before she was even fully done with her serving, not even halfway through the mouthful she was still chewing, Hero let go of the fork, pushed it aside. Picked her plate up again. Asked for seconds.

ACKNOWLEDGMENTS

In the spirit not of acknowledgments, but of utang na loob, or absolutely unpayable debts of the heart:

Like everything else in my life, writing this book wouldn't have been possible without other people. To my mother, without whose ferocious love and support neither this book nor its author would exist. Thank you for helping with some of the fact-checking—along with seemingly the entire Filipino nursing staff in at least two Bay Area hospitals who made their editorial opinions known through the diasporic powers of WhatsApp and Skype. To my father, great friend, and the first person to say, Read this. The world without you is that word you taught me: saray. To all sides of the clan, the ones related by blood and the ones who didn't need to be, who saw me reading and left me to it, who picked us up from school after their shifts, who made food, posted bail, wired money, grew vegetables, to everyone who shared a house, a plate, a life.

To Emma Paterson: dear friend, vital first reader, and agent extraordinaire, who believed in this book before it existed, and gave its author a safe place to land. None of this would be possible without you.

To Laura Tisdel and James Roxburgh, whose care, insight, and generosity made editing this book a joy. To their respective teams at Viking/Penguin and Atlantic, without whose tireless, passionate work books simply don't get made. At Viking/Penguin, many thanks to Amy Sun, Olivia Taussig, Theresa Gaffney, Lavina Lee, Tess Espinoza, Samuel Raim, Christina Caruccio, Jane Cavolina, Juliann Barbato, Cassandra Garruzzo, and Fabiana Van Arsdell. At Atlantic, many thanks to Kirsty Doole, Jamie Forrest, and Poppy Mostyn-Owen. Thank you to John

Freeman for publishing an excerpt of the novel, and to the whole Freeman family—Allison Malecha, John Mark Boling—for the incredible kindness and support. To the foreign rights team at Rogers, Coleridge & White for helping to give this book more homes than I could have ever dreamed: Laurence Laluyaux, Stephen Edwards, Zoë Nelson, Tristan Kendrick, Nicholas Owen, and Katharina Volckmer. Special shout-out to Elda Rotor at Penguin Classics, in deep gratitude for the early enthusiasm and solidarity; getting an Ilocano thumbs-up meant everything. Special shout-out also to Matt Varga, fellow Pinoy and all-around design gangster, who gave this book its American cover, and in doing so imparted what felt like talismanic protection, in the way of anting-anting. I'm grateful every single day for this diaspora, and am overjoyed to find us everywhere.

Thank you to the Voices of Our Nations Arts Foundation (VONA) Fiction crew of 2014—Sharline Chiang, Frank Costilla, Navdeep Singh Dhillon, Junot Díaz, Lilly Gonzalez, Dayna Mauricia, Lateef McLeod, Ruby Murray, Karen Onojaife, Melissa Sipin, and Ursula Villarreal-Moura—who saw this book's ugly baby pictures and responded with more compassion and understanding than any writer could hope for. A week with you taught me more than any degree factory ever could.

To Amaal Said, cherished friend, brilliant poet and photographer; it was a pleasure and privilege to be in front of your lens. Thank you for making me feel seen, cared for, and myself.

To my girl Rachel Long, beloved friend and heart-searing poet, teacher and organizer extraordinaire. Thank you for a million, trillion things: for the days in the park and the nights in the pub, for our respective couches, for all the last trains home, and for simply existing.

To F., forever.

In terms of utang na loob, this one's last but definitely not least:

To the Bay, and in particular the 408. This book, along with its author, owes you everything.